THE INFINITE
AND THE DIVINE

More Necrons from Black Library

INDOMITUS
Gav Thorpe

SEVERED
Nate Crowley

THE WORLD ENGINE
Ben Counter

More Warhammer 40,000 from Black Library

LEVIATHAN
Darius Hinks

• **DAWN OF FIRE** •

Book 1: AVENGING SON
Guy Haley

Book 2: THE GATE OF BONES
Andy Clark

Book 3: THE WOLFTIME
Gav Thorpe

Book 4: THRONE OF LIGHT
Guy Haley

Book 5: THE IRON KINGDOM
Nick Kyme

Book 6: THE MARTYR'S TOMB
Marc Collins

• **DARK IMPERIUM** •
Guy Haley

Book 1: DARK IMPERIUM
Book 2: PLAGUE WAR
Book 3: GODBLIGHT

ASSASSINORUM: KINGMAKER
Robert Rath

WARBOSS
Mike Brooks

THE INFINITE
AND THE DIVINE

ROBERT RATH

BLACK LIBRARY

A BLACK LIBRARY PUBLICATION

First published in 2020.
This edition published in Great Britain in 2023 by
Black Library, Games Workshop Ltd., Willow Road,
Nottingham, NG7 2WS, UK.

Represented by: Games Workshop Limited – Irish branch,
Unit 3, Lower Liffey Street, Dublin 1,
D01 K199, Ireland.

10 9 8

Produced by Games Workshop in Nottingham.
Cover illustration by Lie Setiawan.

See Black Library on the internet at

blacklibrary.com

Find out more about Games Workshop
and the worlds of Warhammer at

games-workshop.com

Printed and bound in the UK.

---

*Many thanks to Will Moss, Richard Garton, and everyone who
championed this mad adventure.*

*To old gaming friends in Honolulu, who taught me how to tell stories with
pewter soldiers.*

And most of all to Danielle, for her divine patience and infinite love.

For more than a hundred centuries the Emperor
has sat immobile on the Golden Throne of Earth.
He is the Master of Mankind. By the might of His
inexhaustible armies a million worlds stand
against the dark.

Yet, He is a rotting carcass, the Carrion Lord of the
Imperium held in life by marvels from the Dark
Age of Technology and the thousand souls sacrificed
each day so that His may continue to burn.

To be a man in such times is to be one amongst
untold billions. It is to live in the cruellest and
most bloody regime imaginable. It is to suffer an
eternity of carnage and slaughter. It is to have cries
of anguish and sorrow drowned by the thirsting
laughter of dark gods.

This is a dark and terrible era where you will find
little comfort or hope. Forget the power of technology
and science. Forget the promise of progress and
advancement. Forget any notion of common
humanity or compassion.

There is no peace amongst the stars, for in the grim
darkness of the far future, there is only war.

ACT ONE: MAIDEN WORLD

NEPHRETH: *The star gods say that when we enter the fire, we shall not know death. But do you not see the tragedy? To know death is to know life.*

HALIOS: *If the gods know not life, my phaeron, what do they know?*

NEPHRETH: *Hate, Halios. Eternal and unending.*

– *War in Heaven*, Act I, Scene V, Lines 3-5

CHAPTER ONE

Before the being called the Emperor revealed Himself, before the rise of the aeldari, before the necrontyr traded their flesh for immortal metal, the world was born in violence.

And despite everything that would happen, this violence was more terrible than any the world later witnessed. For sweeping battlefronts are nothing compared to the torture of geologic change, and no warhead – no matter how large – can equal a billion years of volcanic upheaval.

It was a nameless world, for no one yet lived there to name it.

Ice sheets tall as a battle cruiser expanded and retreated. Tectonic plates ground continents together, their collision pushing up mountain ridges like teeth in the gums of a child. In the world's great ocean, an undersea volcano spewed white-hot magma into the darkness of the oceanic floor, gradually building an island. Then another. The oceanic plate moved across the hotspot, carrying the created islands north-west as the volcanic boil continued to vent itself into the cold, black water. A long archipelago formed, like the dot-dash of an ancient code running across the jewelled blue of the sea.

The first civilisations rose around these islands, in a manner of speaking.

Microorganisms ruled the warm waters, their battle for survival as worthy as any that would come after. But their struggles, their triumphs and their cannibalisms went unremarked – even by the organisms themselves. Sentience was an unneeded complication.

Then came the great city-builders. Colonies of coral polyps that erected great funnel towers, branching architectural lattices in green and magenta, cities full of life and activity.

And like every great civilisation, they built upon the skeletons of those that had come before. Layer upon layer, each generation withering and ossifying, so the living stood unthinking upon a vast necropolis of their predecessors.

Perhaps the fish that weaved through these great reefs were the first sentient beings on the world. They had little emotion other than fear, pain and hunger, yet their arrival presaged a new era – no longer was life there a march of unfeeling organisms that existed in order to exist. They could now perceive.

When the great lizards emerged from the water, the struggle became one of legs and muscle and hearts beating blood fast through strong chambers. And though these great lizards were little more intelligent than the fish, they felt. They felt the pleasure of hot blood on their tongues, the agony of a festering wound, and maternal protectiveness. They died in great numbers, rotting corpses ground and crushed by geological processes into the diamonds and crude oil that other beings would, in time, murder each other to possess.

And a few, just a few, would enter a state of deathless preservation. Trapped in silt and unable to fully decay, the calcium of their bones replaced atom by atom with rock until they were but stone skeletons. Immortal in form, yet with nothing of their bodies remaining. A mockery of the vital living creatures they once were.

Life on the nameless world continued this way for billions of years, unheeded by the rest of the galaxy.

Then one night, a saurian scavenger sniffed the wind, sensing something had changed. Pointing her long snout towards the sky, she took in a sight that had never been encountered there before.

New stars burned in the rainbow smear of the sky. Points of light that clustered together with unnatural regularity. Lights that glowed with balefires, green as the island canopies, and moved across the sky as clouds did.

To the scavenger's rudimentary brain, strange visual information like this could only be a hallucination brought on by consuming one of the island's poisonous plants. Her body triggered a purge reflex, vomiting egg yolk and root plants before she darted for the twisted labyrinth of ground trees.

As the scavenger watched, judging the threat, the lights descended. The creatures were large, with great sickle wings swept forward and bodies so black they barely stood out against the night.

Like any who survived on the island, the scavenger knew a predator when she saw one.

Cold emerald light spilled from the creatures' bellies, and the scavenger detected the foreign scent of sand baked into glass.

Two-legged creatures stepped out of the emanation, feet shattering the plate of fused beach. Starlight glinted off their bodies like sun on the sea, and their eyes burned the same green as the lights on the flying predators.

The world would be nameless no longer.

CHAPTER TWO

Ancient stories, passed from the lips of spirit-singer to spirit-singer, held that anyone who touched the stone would burn.

Thy hand shall curl and turn black
Thy back-teeth glow white-hot
Thy bones crack like fire-logs
For I have drunk from elder suns

The songs held that the gemstone was a meteorite. Wandering, semi-sentient. Absorbing the energy of each star it passed. During the War in Heaven, it was said that warriors had used it to channel the gods themselves.

Trazyn, however, had learned long ago not to believe the absurdities of aeldari folklore. Ancient though their race was, they were still given to the follies of an organic brain.

Trazyn had travelled the galaxy for so long he'd forgotten what year he'd started. Collecting. Studying. Ordering the cultures of the cosmos.

And one thing he'd learned was that every society thought their mountain was special. That it was more sacred than the mountain worshipped by their neighbouring tribe. That it was the one true axis of the universe.

Even when informed that their sacred ridge was merely the random connection of tectonic plates, or their blessed sword a very old but relatively common alien relic – a revelation they universally did not appreciate, he found – they clung to their stories.

Which is not to say there were not gods in the firmament, of course. Trazyn knew there were, because he had helped kill them. But he'd also found that most of what societies took to be gods were inventions of their own, charmingly fanciful, imaginations.

But though he did not believe the gem channelled ancient gods, that did not mean it wasn't worth having – or worth the aeldari protecting.

Indeed, the sounds of a siege echoed through the bone halls.

Trazyn allowed a portion of his consciousness to stray, if only to monitor the situation. Part of his mind worked the problem at hand, the other looked through the oculars of his lychguard captain.

Through the being's eyes, Trazyn saw that his lychguard phalanx still held the gates of the temple. Those in the front rank had locked their dispersion shields in a wall, each raising their hyperphase sword like the hammer of a cocked pistol. Behind them, those in the second rank held their warscythes as spears, thrusting them over the shoulders of their comrades so the entire formation bristled with humming blades.

Perfectly uniform, Trazyn noticed. And perfectly still.

Exodite bodies littered the steps before them – feather-adorned mesh armour split with surgical-straight lines, limbs and heads detached. His olfactory sensors identified particles of cooked muscle in the air.

Another attack was massing. In the garden plaza before the temple, where five dirt streets converged, aeldari Exodites flitted between decorative plants and idols carved from massive bones.

In the distance, he could see the lumbering form of a great lizard, long necked and powerful, with twin prism cannons slung on its humped back. Trazyn marked it as a target for the two Doom Scythes flying a support pattern overhead.

Shuriken rounds swept in, rattling the necron shields like sleet on a windowpane. One disc sailed into the ocular cavity of a lychguard and lodged there, bisecting the grim fire of his eye. The warrior did not react. Did not break formation. With a shriek of protesting metal, the living alloy of his skull forced the monomolecular disc free and it fluttered to the steps like a falling leaf.

Trazyn looked at the pattern of it through the captain's vision. Circular, with double spiral channels. A common aeldari design, not worth acquiring.

He sensed a change in the air and looked up to see the first Doom Scythe streaking down in an attack run. At the last moment the great lizard heard it, rotating around its serpentine head to stare at the incoming comet.

A beam of white-hot energy lanced from the Doom Scythe's fuselage, tracing a line of flame through the lush undergrowth. It passed through the creature's long neck and the top third of it fell like a cut tree branch. The great body staggered, heeled, stayed upright. Then the next Doom Scythe lanced it through the midsection and set off the payload on its prism cannons. Cascading detonations tore the creature apart, the purple energy blast throwing the weapons crew hundreds of cubits away.

Pity, Trazyn thought as he watched the carcass burn. *I wanted one of those.*

But he had no time for such side projects. Conch shell horns sounded across the rainforest-girdled spires of the city, and already he could see more great lizards lumbering towards the temple. One rotated a twin-barrelled shuriken cannon towards the sky and began spitting fire at the retreating Scythes. Though they were primitive, once the Exodites marshalled their numbers his small acquisition force would be overwhelmed.

Cepharil was awakening to defend its World Spirit.

Trazyn left the lychguard captain's body, rejoined his consciousness, and focused on the task at hand.

Before him stretched a long wraithbone corridor, likely salvaged from whatever craftworld these fundamentalists had used to begin their self-imposed exile. Bas-relief carvings depicting the society's exodus, fashioned from the bones of the great lizards, decorated the walls.

Trazyn had been scrying for traps, detecting pressure plates and a huge mechanical fulcrum hidden in the masonry. Beyond that waited the cyclopean gates of the inner chamber.

He finished his calculations and saw the way through.

Trazyn picked up his empathic obliterator and strode into the corridor.

Eyeholes in the bas-reliefs coughed, sending clouds of bone darts clattering off his necrodermis. Trazyn snatched one out of the air and analysed the tip: an exotic poison derived from a local marine invertebrate, unique to this world.

He slipped it into a dimensional pocket and continued forward, sensing a stone shift and sink beneath him.

A piece of masonry, hammer-shaped and weighing six tons, swept down at him like a pendulum. Trazyn waved at it without stopping, the stasis projection from his palm emitter halting its progress mid-swing. He passed it without a glance, its surface vibrating with potential energy.

Finally, the gate. Tall as a monolith, it was decorated with exquisite carvings of aeldari gods. A vertical strip of runes laid out a poem-riddle so fiendish, it would stop even the wisest if they did not know the obscure lore of the–

'Tailliac sawein numm,' intoned Trazyn, turning sideways so he could slip through the gates as they ground open.

Normally, he would have put some effort into it. Solved it by thought, then performed a textual analysis. Trazyn enjoyed riddles. They revealed so much about the cultures that shaped them. But a noemic notice from his lychguards suggested that the Exodites were pressing harder than anticipated. No time for amusing diversions.

He hadn't paused to process the meaning of the runes, just fed them through his lexigraphic database and cross-referenced double meanings, inferences and mythological connotations. Even now, he could not have explained what the answer to the riddle was, or what it meant. It was merely a linguistic equation, a problem with an answer.

An answer that had brought him into the presence of the World Spirit.

The chamber swept up around him like a cavernous grotto, its upper reaches lost in the echoing vaults of the ceiling. His metal feet sounded off a causeway, its wraithbone marbled with veins of gold. Filigreed balustrades on either side mimicked the corals of the ocean depths, for Cepharil was a world of warm seas and lush archipelagos. On either side of the walkway, pools of liquid platinum cast watery light across the walls.

'Now,' he muttered to himself. 'Where are you, my lovely?'

Before him rose the World Spirit.

It curved ahead, inlayed into the vaulted surface of the far wall. It too was made of bone, but rather than the old, inert wraithbone of the walls and ceiling this sprouted alive from the floor, branching like a fan of tree roots that had grown up instead of down.

No, Trazyn corrected, that was not quite accurate. His oculars stripped away the outer layers of the World Spirit, refocusing on the veins of energy that ran through the psychoactive material. Arcane power pulsed to and fro in a circulatory system, racing through arteries and nerves as it travelled to the highest forks of the network and back to the floor. Not roots, then – antlers. Yes, that was it, a great set of antlers, large as a mountain, the points of its forks curving away from the wall. Here and there it sprouted buds, fuzzy with new growth.

Exquisite.

Stepping closer, Trazyn appraised the object. The substance was not wraithbone, he noted, at least not entirely. This was a hybrid, a substitute, grown from the skeletons of the great lizards and interwoven with the psycho-plastic wraithbone salvaged from their crashed ship. A gene-sequence scry failed to find where one substance began and the other ended, no points where the ancient craftsman had fused or grafted the two materials together. This was a seamless blend, nurtured and shaped over millions of years, wraithbone woven between the molecules of reactive, but lower quality, dinosaurid remains. A masterwork by one of the finest bonesingers in the galaxy, an act of artistry and devotion that was at once temple, mausoleum and metropolis. A place for the souls of his slain aeldari ancestors to be at rest, united and safeguarded from the hungry gods of the aether.

Trazyn carried towards it on tireless legs, craning his hunched neck to see where the highest forks disappeared in the darkness of the vault. Once, his own kind had been able to accomplish works such as this. But the process of biotransference, the blighted gift that had moved their consciousness to deathless metal bodies, had also burned away nearly all artistry. His kind were no longer artisans or poets. Those few that retained the knack found their powers diminished. Now they forged rather than created. A work that took this much care, this much love, was beyond them.

Such a shame he could not take the whole thing.

Given time he could extract it, perhaps even lock the entire temple in a stasis field and transplant it whole to his historical gallery on Solemnace. To have the gemstone in its original context would be a rare coup. But somehow these primitives had sensed the coming of his acquisition phalanx, and there was no time. In truth, he had broken protocol by waking even thirty of the lychguard before their time. Doing so had damaged their neural matrices, making them little more than automatons that followed tactical programs and explicit commands.

But if they could not remember this expedition, so much the better – Trazyn was not supposed to be here anyway.

He approached the base of the World Spirit – the chamber was a full league across – and beheld the true genius of its creation.

The structure sprouted from the skull of a predator lizard twice Trazyn's height, its lower jaw removed and sickle-like upper teeth buried in the wraithbone floor. A glow, like the orange light cast by wind-stoked embers, emanated from the cavities of the creature's eye sockets.

Trazyn's vision stripped away layers of bone and he saw the gemstone embedded in the predator's fist-sized brain cavity.

'A carnosaur. Astonishing.'

He brushed a metal hand over the skull's cranium, an emitter in the palm casting electromagnetic radiation through its core.

It was old. Older than he had thought possible. Indeed, perhaps Trazyn should have tempered his dismissal of the aeldari tales, for it was indeed a meteorite, and one of extreme antiquity and unknown make-up. He reviewed the spectromantic divination results manually, to confirm its findings. Given the age of the components, their degradation, and the style on the beam-cut faces of the gem, it was entirely possible that it dated from the War in Heaven.

A delicious shiver passed through Trazyn's circuitry.

'Well met, my dear,' he said, his cooing tone offset by the hollow echo of his vocal emitter. 'It is not so often that I meet a thing as old as I am.'

He was so entranced, in fact, that he did not see the dragon riders coming.

Deep focus tended to dim his circumspection protocols, and the beasts' footfalls had been masked via training and sorcery.

And for all his inputs, scryers, protocols and diviners, the movements of the empyrean were muffled in his senses. When it came to warp sorcery, he was like a deaf man at a dinner table, able to make out words through dampened sounds and lip-reading, but unable to even notice the voices behind his back.

An interstitial alert flashed in his vision and he wheeled, dialling back his chronosense to slow the world and give himself time to calculate a microsecond decision.

Scales, claws and sawtooth fangs were about to break down on him like a wave – twenty cavalry riding knee to knee in tight formation, wraithbone lances braced, tattooed swirls on arrowhead-sharp faces. Scrimshawed charms dangled from the halters of their raptor mounts, each leather harness crisscrossing a scaled snout that ended in flared nostrils and hooked teeth. The raptors – underwater slow in Trazyn's enhanced vision – swung their avian frames low, shifting weight to their bunched haunches in preparation for a final lunge.

One lance came at him so directly, its tip looked like a circle in his vision.

Minimal options, none attractive. But his proximity to the World Spirit had at least given him a moment to act as they pulled their charge, afraid of smashing into their venerated ancestral tomb.

Trazyn slid left, past the first lance tip.

Before the warrior could swing the long weapon around, Trazyn gripped the haft and tore the tattooed Aspect Warrior from his saddle. He watched the rider's face twist as he fell from the mount, long hair flying free and hands sheltering his face as he tumbled to the bone floor.

Trazyn, who is called Infinite, a voice said. It was not audible speech. Nor was it telepathy, to which he was immune. Instead, it was a wavelength of psychic pulses pushing on his auditory transducer to mimic language. One of these riders must be a farseer.

He ignored it.

The riderless raptor struck at him, jaws closing on the place where his ribcage met his hooded neck. Trazyn had overcommitted himself and could not dodge.

You will not keep what you seek.

Hooked teeth met the cold surface of his necrodermis – and shattered.

Trazyn channelled kinetic force into his fist and punched the dinosaur in the throat.

Vertebrae popped, cartilage tore. The raptor went down with the noise of a bugle player experiencing sudden and unbearable agony.

Listen to the song. This world sings for the blood of Trazyn.

And it was true – even through the syrupy haze of slowed time he could hear the keening chants of the knights. That he did not have blood was no matter, these aeldari wanted it anyway.

But their formation was not optimised to deal with a single opponent. It was jumbling, folding as the knights tried to get to him. And he had just created a gap.

As the unit tried to wheel on itself, Trazyn slipped through the hole in the line – making sure to step on the fallen warrior on his way through.

Behind him, riders collided and mixed.

'Aeldari,' he scoffed. 'So old and wise. You are children to us.'

This World Spirit is our ancestry, Trazyn. Our culture. Our dead. And it will wither without the Solar Gem.

That's when Trazyn saw the carnosaur. He'd missed it before now, his focus overwhelmed by the charging raptor riders and senses clouded by witchery. It reared above him, its well-muscled chest protected by a breastplate shaped from dinosaurid bone, twin-linked shuriken cannons emerging like tusks from its chin.

Serrated blades fashioned from the teeth of aquatic predators studded the armour plates clamped to its feet and spine. A calcium scythe capped its lashing tail.

And on its back, the farseer – her willow-thin face half-covered by the mask of an unfamiliar god, graceful frame armoured in mother-of-pearl, and pink hair gathered into a topknot.

We have long known that you desire it, but if you take it, the World Spirit will die.

'If you knew I was coming,' Trazyn said. 'You should have made a contingency plan.'

I know you will return, the farseer said. *But I will still enjoy this.*

The carnosaur bit down on him at the waist, his whole upper half trapped inside the wet darkness of its mouth. Nine-inch fangs – even now, he could not stop analysing, cataloguing – sank into the tough tubes and pelvic ambulation structures of his torso. Vital systems tore and failed. Emerald sparks erupted from the wound, lighting the interior of the carnosaur's mouth with baleful flashes. He felt his legs separate.

Trazyn channelled his diminishing reserves into a fist and reshaped it into a brutal spike. He stabbed at the carnosaur's lashing tongue, hot reptilian blood spurting over his oculars. To his annoyance, his systems autonomously ran an analysis of the genetic make-up.

He marked it to read later.

The muscular tongue flipped and rolled him to the side. He sprawled, saw a sawtooth strip of light as the jaws opened.

He regretted slowing his chronosense as he watched the row of jagged teeth close on him, puncturing his oculars, driving through his neural fibre spools and crushing his skull.

CHAPTER THREE

*The World Song moves us. Speaks to us. Touch the rocks,
young warrior, and you will feel it vibrate the very stone.
When the metal glutton comes, you will know it is time
to fight for this world.*

– Prophecies of Awlunica of Cepharil,
Tablet Seven, Inscription XII

Trazyn did not, on the whole, enjoy being dead.

Which is why – unlike the aeldari sorceress – he'd made
contingencies.

His consciousness rushed into the lychguard captain's mind,
overriding the native personality and banishing it to the depths
of the captain's engrammatic databanks. Depending on the
host, this could be a struggle. But the captain had awoken
from stasis damaged and simple, an easy takeover. It was a
state Trazyn preferred in his companions, to be honest, since
it made them less likely to speak of what they'd witnessed.

The Awakened Council knew of Trazyn's project and his galleries, but not everything he collected would meet with their approval.

And they would particularly disapprove of awakening their kin early, and getting them destroyed, for a personal venture like this.

Within a second, he reshaped the captain's malleable necrodermis, the living metal flowing and changing to take on Trazyn's familiar shape. His hood sprang up segment by segment, rising over his head as the lychguard's death mask rearranged into his own features. A cloak grew out from his shoulders, each scale popping into existence with a little *ping*.

When he gained vocal control, the first thing he said was, 'Damn.'

His newly hijacked oculars told him that things were no longer running to plan.

Four lychguard lay on the steps, sparking green, their metal flesh attempting to knit together despite horrendous wounds. The shuriken fire was a torrent now, coming from every angle. Skirmishers fired and moved in blurs so fast Trazyn could barely see their troop type. One Doom Scythe wobbled by, its exterior choked by pterosaurs that had hooked on to its superstructure, digging into its wires and its exposed cockpit. As he watched, one took the pilot's head in its beak and, with a twist of its long neck, snapped it away. The Doom Scythe lost control and tumbled into the rainforest like a tossed coin. It struck the plaza and ploughed through a bone god-column before detonating in a superheated blast of smoke and emerald lightning.

He had brought a team of only thirty lychguard, a Night Scythe for transport and two Doom Scythes for aerial cover – the sort of force that would not raise any alarms among the

Council upon its awakening. Even for the aeldari – whose speed made them dangerous – that was generally enough. A shock assault force to secure the target or create a diversion while Trazyn recovered the specimen. On a normal acquisition, they were on the ground for no longer than an hour, often half that. They usually withdrew just as the locals mounted a response.

But the counter-attack had been almost instantaneous, as if the aeldari had detected the necron air assets, or sensed the distortion of the Night Scythe's transport wormhole.

Or they foresaw me coming, Trazyn thought. *Cursed witches.*

A pterosaur, its hide painted ochre with handprints, dived into the formation and snatched up a lychguard like a bird of prey taking a rodent. It flew the struggling warrior up into the air, its rider leaning out of the saddle almost upside down to riddle the necron with dual shuriken pistols. Then, the beast dropped him three hundred cubits to the plaza flagstones.

Trazyn saw more pterosaur riders incoming, a 'V' in the sky preparing to heel over and dive.

'Fall back!' he called. 'Fall back inside the temple, defend the sanctum. Beware aerial attacks.'

The force retreated in lockstep, without a glance backward to place their feet.

He summoned his empathic obliterator, the long haft of the weapon starting in his palm and building itself one atom at a time until it stood eight feet tall from pointed base to the glowing jade wings of its head. Trazyn swept it over his formation, doubling their marching speed, and then pointed the obliterator's inbuilt resurrection orb at the fallen lychguard, watching as their shattered bodies glowed with arcane energies, spines snapping and joints popping as bent limbs straightened and dismembered pieces flew together as if magnetised.

As the tide of aeldari surged up the steps, a lychguard sprang back to its feet among them. One arm still missing, its hyper-phase sword carved bloody crescents in the Exodites. The aeldari skirmishers fell upon him and the other rising dead, piercing their metal bodies with knives.

'That should stall them,' Trazyn said, and turned back into the temple.

He passed the outer sanctum of coral statuary, tramped through the rain of poison darts in the corridor and pushed the hammer column – still locked in stasis – contemptu-ously aside.

This time, he uttered no riddle. He simply took his obliter-ator in both hands and brought it down on the join. Legend held that the weapon contained a relic from a long-vanished species, a talisman of power designed to break the minds and souls of lesser races.

That seemed, as far as Trazyn was concerned, accurate.

The great winged staff head connected with a lightning flash and the acrid smell of disintegrated stone. An energy discharge rocked the huge gates on their hinges, blowing them backward and spreading cracks for five cubits down the wraithbone floor.

Trazyn strode out on the causeway and saw what he'd expected: the knights in formation, already urging their slavering beasts on towards him, and the farseer behind, her carnosaur's footfalls shaking the chamber, roaring its defi-ance through teeth stained with its own blood and blacked by the fire of Trazyn's last death.

As much as he hated them, they were exquisite. Burnished wraithbone helms, millions of years old, shining in the watery light of the platinum pools. Lance pennants woven from void-silk, insubstantial as smoke, streaming. The terrible majesty of the mutated carnosaur and the regality of its rider, her shoulders burdened with a cloak fashioned from the plumage of native birds.

They made the causeway, bore down on him.

He, in turn, held up a cube darker than the emptiness of space. Prismatic light speared out in a beam, danced on the lead rider, then spread in an arc. Questing, analysing, measuring the dimensions of each rippling muscle and strand of perfumed hair.

A keening whine emanated from the box. It shook in Trazyn's mechanical grip. He triggered the lock.

The charge stopped. It did not falter, or pull back, it merely ceased movement. Raptors froze mid-leap. The carnosaur's bellow was cut off. All was still, save for the void-silk banners, which due to their unusual physical properties, continued to slowly ripple in a non-existent wind.

And then it was gone, all of it. Not even a scent remained.

Trazyn walked through the empty air and approached the World Spirit. He so disliked to run, but the shortness of time hastened his footsteps.

'Do not worry,' he said to the cube, which burned so cold that none but a necron would be able to hold it. 'You will not be separated from your beloved gem.'

Trazyn plunged a fist through the ancient carnosaur skull. Its brittle structure cracked and sundered under the blow. Aeldari souls rushed up from the fractured calcium like embers, drifting out of whatever wraithbone had been woven around and through it.

He closed his hand around the gem and pulled it free.

His hand did not curl and blacken. His back teeth did not go white-hot. His bones did not crack.

And he had no regrets.

Until, at least, he received the security alert: something had broken loose on Solemnace.

It was easier if he focused on small things.

The whorl of the cosmos was too vast, too chaotic. There was no order of operation. Like a neurocircuit full of tangled wires, it was impossible to know where each led until you took it between your fingers and followed it.

Knowing where to start, that was the hard part.

So he started from the beginning, when all matter lay in the same place. Orderly. Satisfying. Nothing but oneness and potential energy. The last moment when the universe was truly at peace.

He savoured it, aware that it was not real. Indeed, there was no guarantee the universe began this way at all. It was merely an engram-simulation of a theorem, a meditative aid authentic enough to trick his own mind into emptying so he could feel the flows of time and matter. During powerful rituals, whole solar cycles would pass with him in this state.

He let it happen.

An explosion. He screened out the noise and clutter, focusing on what he wanted to find. Saw it, followed it.

A single particle tumbled through the dark – then light was born, and he saw the little mote whisked away on the eddies of the void, collecting with other particles of its type. Watched ages pass as it built from a speck, to a rock, to a meteorite. Watched it, haloed by flame, enter the atmosphere and bury itself in a nameless continent. Watched as a necron extractor-wraith bored the meteorite free.

Necrodermis can be reused an infinite number of times. The particle was first imbedded in the hip joint of a warrior. Then, a monolith's hull. A piece of jewellery lost and recycled.

Then – yes, there it was. Inside a cable in a doorway neuro-circuitry panel. Ancient, faulty. Its alloy impure from the moment of creation untold ages ago, stressed from overuse. Half-life draining. Waiting for the moment it was fated to short.

He reached out with a spectral hand and helped the moment come.

Glyphs, each as tall as the intruder, lit up in two rows. Sigils of protection, threatening death to any that dare enter without the assent of Trazyn, Overlord of Solemnace.

The threat might have been more potent if the glyphs themselves were not guttering like lamp wicks in a gale, the electrical fault cascading throughout the gateway. Finally, the great slab ground backward and parted between the columns of glyphs, each massive piece separating and sliding behind the inner wall of the chamber.

Trazyn had been collecting artefacts for his gallery for aeons, now. Not even the Dead Gods themselves knew how long. And while he knew his collection better than any being alive, the sprawling complex of halls and exhibition spaces was as much a labyrinth to him as it was to the intruder. Architect-wraiths followed standing orders to build outward, meaning that the facility sprawled in every direction with chambers Trazyn himself had never commissioned or visited. Some proved perfect housing for new acquisitions, while others languished, forgotten for millennia.

This was one such forgotten gallery. Empty and sterile, sealed directly after its creation. No construction debris marred its shining blackstone floor. Not even dust settled on the empty display plinths.

But before the intruder lay a group of work-scarabs. They lay on their backs like stones collected together in a river, spindly legs pointing skyward to harvest ambient energy waves to power their dormant energy banks.

The intruder stirred his metal fingers over the mindless drones, casting an interstitial command that awakened them from their slumber. He followed by interlocking his fingers in the Hexagram of Thuul, severing them from the security network.

He knelt down to their level, leaning heavily on his staff. For a moment, he paused to admire the aquamarine plates of their carapace. Gold filigree, set in geometric circuit-patterns, inlaid in their jewelled casings.

Nihilakh Dynasty, the intruder thought, sighing. *So rich, yet so vulgar. Not even the lowest scarab escapes your garish eye.*

Then, leaning down to the awakened scarabs, he whispered where he wanted to go.

Legs skittered on the hard surface of the floor, almost in excitement, then the swarm departed as one, milling around the intruder and passing over his clawed feet in their haste to direct him to the proper corridor.

Orikan the Diviner, Master Astromancer of the Sautekh Dynasty, architect of time, and the last seer of the necrontyr followed them.

Trazyn stepped out of the wormhole and closed it behind him.

No one else would be coming back.

It had been a near-run thing. Much closer than he would've liked. With the World Spirit bleeding power, the panicking aeldari savages had overwhelmed the lychguard defending the temple's gateway and forced themselves inside.

Trazyn had fled upward, climbing lizard-rib stairways to an upper gallery and used his obliterator to blast a passageway through the wraithbone dome.

The Night Scythe had been waiting for him outside, hovering upside down to protect the captive wormhole on its belly. Its wings were scored to black metal by the shuriken volleys peppering it from below, gold and green decorative dermis flaking off like rust.

Trazyn got a glimpse of the aeldari temple complex – the rainforest canopy far below him, broken here and there by monoliths and bone arches – before he leapt onto the underside of the Scythe, strode across its pitted skin and dropped into the wormhole.

He left the Scythes with an order to return, or if too heavily damaged, expend all ammunition then ram a high-priority target. Preferably one of the cursed carnosaurs.

'Chief archaeovist, overlord, master.' Sannet the Light-Sculptor, Trazyn's chief curator, knelt. His eight-fingered hands splayed on the polished floor in obeisance. 'Solemnace rejoices at your return.'

'Does it?' Trazyn responded, looking around at the receiving party. It was just Sannet, accompanied by an archive wraith ready to receive the artefacts. Behind them, a hallway wide enough to refurbish a battle-barge stretched empty for thousands of cubits. 'I see.'

Solemnace was not rejoicing. Indeed, it would not celebrate anything, by Trazyn's calculation, for ten millennia or more. Solemnace was a dormant world, its officials, warriors and servants in the stasis-death of the Great Sleep. Only Trazyn had awakened early, and he needed a mere skeleton crew to keep the world running at the standard he preferred.

'A successful endeavour, my lord?'

Trazyn swept a hand over the stasis-caskets on the wraith's back. The jewelled boxes opened, pale wisps of blue vapour curling from their interiors. Trazyn set the gem into the larger box and closed the lid manually, ensuring it locked. He nestled the tesseract labyrinth containing the aeldari war host in the smaller box, giving its top a merry tap for good measure.

'My lord, is this for archive, or display?' Sannet conjured a stylus out of his necrodermis and held it expectantly over the phos-glyph projection tablet that hovered in his hand.

'The primitives shall be displayed in the aeldari diaspora gallery with the rest of their kin.'

'Between the craftworlders and drukhari displays, I assume.'

The stylus danced on the light of the hologram tablet as Sannet spoke. Normally a necron would not need such a thing, but like many who had arisen from the Great Sleep, Sannet's neural matrix had degraded over sixty million years. The deterioration had affected his short-term mnemonics. He could remember chains of code-hexes yet fail to recall what had just been said. The constant note-taking, obnoxious as it was, helped with that. Auditory information would not imprint on his engrams, but the tactile experience of writing the words created a workaround. Though he could no longer serve as the cryptek he'd once been, Trazyn valued him for his skill with hard-light hologram projections – the method he had chosen to display his collection.

Everyone had their damage. Of the few who'd already arisen, several of the old highborn of necrontyr emerged not knowing their names. Others were complete automatons, or even mad. In dark moments, Trazyn feared that in ten thousand years, when the dynasties began to awaken in full, he would find all of his peers had diminished.

Not he, though. Trazyn had emerged with his faculties entirely intact.

'My lord?' Sannet cocked his head, the aperture of his single cyclopic eye narrowing. 'Permission to repeat the question?'

'Hmm? You may.'

'And what shall I do with the gem?'

'The gem,' Trazyn mused. He folded his hands and tapped his index fingers together with a soft *tink, tink, tink.* 'Upon reconsideration, I will handle this specimen myself.' He opened the box and scooped up the precious stone, feeling its warmth, and stowed it amongst the collection of trinkets hanging at his hip. 'The determination will have to wait pending appraisal, of course, but this may be one of the oldest objects yet collected. Meet me in the War in Heaven gallery.'

Trazyn turned to go, summoning his Catacomb command barge with a thought, then stopped.

An interstitial message burned in the corner of his vision, the holographic phos-glyphs casting a jade glow on Trazyn's death mask. Security glyphs blinked on its message seal.

He opened the message, unfurling it downward like a scroll, absorbing the technical data like the calculation machine he was. 'What's this, Sannet?'

Sannet opened an identical alert. 'Exhibit breach, in the Dawnward Sector. Gallery MXXIII, Thoth subcontinent, coordinates 52.941472, -1.174056.'

'The hrud burrow ecosystem,' Trazyn snarled. He conjured a holographic image.

The image was dim in colour, tinged with the green corposant of the chrysoprase projection, but the visuals were crisp and comprehensible. A barrel-shaped container of earth – four thousand cubits wide, and three thousand tall – floated in suspensor fields at the centre of a vast chamber. Long-limbed creatures milled about the top, struggling from holes in its surface.

Trazyn sliced at the hologram with his fingers and it split

in two like a cutaway schematic. On the inside of the earthen plug, tunnels wormed their way between vaulted worship chambers and earthen family burrows. Hrud scrambled upward, sensing their moment to escape had come. After all, they had been imprisoned inside hard-light holograms – caught like insects in amber – for at least two millennia. Thoughts frozen at the moment of their acquisition, with only the most astute and neurologically gifted sensing that any time had passed at all. Those races steeped in the empyrean – for whom the tides of the warp were part of their very make-up – tended not to fare as well.

They tended to go mad.

Like these hrud, for instance. Tearing each other apart with their shovel-like digging claws, spattering odd, viscous flesh on the tunnel walls. Strange arms, articulated like a spine, doubled in on themselves as they struck at each other like drovers whipping at a herd.

'Seismic activity?' asked Trazyn. That was usually the cause.

'No reports of stasis field failure on the tectonic plates, lord archaeovist,' Sannet replied. 'Tesseract restart protocol and stasis containment not answering.'

'Deploy the containment phalanx,' Trazyn said. 'With swiftness.'

'And hurt the exhibits, lord?'

'They're panicking, trying to dig out,' Trazyn said, pointing at the milling creatures choking the corridors. A few had split off, and were tearing at the walls, trying to find the sunlight they so despised. Anything but the centuries of claustrophobic dark. 'I have at least ten thousand more hrud in storage, but Dead Gods know when I'll acquire another intact burrow. Act now, and we can minimise tunnel and gallery collapses and repopulate the display.'

Sannet's multijointed fingers danced over a floating glyph-panel, making Trazyn recall the waving sea anemones of the World Spirit chamber.

'Immortals, lord?'

'Indeed.'

Reality cracked and sizzled among the panicking hrud, green energy blossoms searing into being as the Immortals translated to the display's surface. Hrud dropped, arms knotting and beating the ground in spontaneous seizure.

Lesser creatures, Trazyn reflected, *so vulnerable to translation proximity.*

He made a mnemonic record of the thought, factoring it into his next acquisition venture. Wasteful to harm a specimen unnecessarily.

The Immortals swung their double-barrelled gauss blasters up as one and picked their first shot.

Each one acquired a different target. No redundancy, no wasted effort, no need to strategise. Networked combat algorithms meant every Immortal knew the others' next action. They tracked their firing solutions as they waited for the order.

'Execute,' said Trazyn, sending the impulse command even before the words left his lipless mouth.

Ropy beams of energy erupted from the gauss blasters, pulling the hrud apart from the inside out, coiled electricity melting their flesh like hot breath dissolves frost. Viridian lightning raced from the emitter chambers of tesla carbines, dancing through the crowded knots of alien bodies, lighting spot fires in their filthy robes where it lanced through them.

Before the alien screams crescendoed, before the tangled stream of hrud could reverse their flight and take shelter in the tunnels, before even the crack of the tesla carbines ended, the Immortals picked new targets and fired again.

'Tesla cannons stay above ground,' ordered Trazyn. 'Dial back gauss blasters. Enable beam limiters to affect flesh and blood *only*. Any being who so much as scorches a bas-relief in the burrow chapels gets remade into a mining scarab.'

'Will you supervise personally?' enquired Sannet.

Trazyn had planned to, of course. Stream his consciousness down into one of the Immortals. Ensure the job was done right.

And yet…

Trazyn had no palms to itch. No spine to tingle. No stomach to knot when he sensed a thing out of place. Yet he still possessed a subconscious.

It was an irony of the necron race that, despite all their technological mastery, the workings of their own minds remained mysterious. Trazyn's neural systems had been wrought by the transcendent star gods, whose ways were mysterious and vicious. Trazyn did not understand how it was possible, but there were still things locked away in his mind, buried, felt rather than known.

Like a sense of danger.

He conjured a phos-glyph panel, split it into five sections, and searched through the inscription-code, slowing his chronosense so that he could process libraries of data in seconds.

'Lord?'

'Fault protocols should've caught the tesseract failure,' he said.

'They did, lord archaeovist. But they failed.'

'Obviously,' he sneered, pointing. 'The protocol should've been instantaneous. Instead it took two microseconds. Why?'

'Ageing systems? Solemnace is…' He caught Trazyn's look and trailed off, casting his monocular downward as he searched for a euphemism that would not besmirch the overlord's beloved gallery. 'Historic?'

'And the alert systems, they were unaffected by this fault, I suppose?' He looked down on his cryptek. 'This is sabotage. And not clumsy sabotage. Show me all completed door activations and curatorial assets.'

'Lord, I… odd.'

'Save the commentary for manuscript analysis,' he snapped. 'Report.'

'I have a gate activation in the reserve gallery space. Several. Two standard solar orbits ago. Encryption key matches a swarm of maintenance scarabs that are not listed as active.'

'Headed where?'

Lights eternally burned in the War in Heaven gallery. It was the only way Trazyn could stand to come here.

He was not a superstitious being. Losing one's soul, after all, tended to dampen one's fear of the mystic. And the great necropolis-capital of ancient necrontyr – filled with a blighted, death-obsessed people – was funereal long before his species had imprisoned their minds inside bodies of deathless necrodermis. Indeed, stasis-crypts covered Solemnace, each of his billions of subjects nestled in a sarcophagus that sustained their cold, metal bodies. It was the same on tomb worlds across the galaxy.

But just because one was dead did not mean he could not be haunted, and Trazyn entered this chamber of memory with bowed head and soft steps even when he was not expecting an ambush.

He kept to the deep shadows, reshaping the necrodermis on the bottom of his feet into a spongy wire lattice that cushioned his armoured tread. He kept focus, forcing himself not to look at the rows of plinths that surrounded him in a double line like a phaeron's honour guard.

They were enemies. Here, an aeldari stood mid-leap, the tip of her wraithbone dance slipper barely kissing the black display base. Next, a hulking krork, mountainous shoulders bunched and slick with battle-sweat. A Khaineite warrior in green armour, crouched low, legs wide, weaving his chainsword forward and up as if hooking it under a lychguard's shield. A jokaero maintenance-slave.

And across from them, blank dummies wearing the resplendent armour of the ancient necrontyr. A reminder of a time when they needed armour, before their bodies were living metal. The old times, sixty-five million years gone. The Flesh Times.

Their long shadows met in the centre, mingling as if they still battled.

Trazyn remembered the war. As chief archaeovist, he had attended every clash that logistics allowed. Recording impressions, taking samples. Attending the embalming of each great phaeron that fell to the Old Ones and their twisted creations. These were old mnemonics, blurry like image-plate negatives cooked by heat. Burned away by the process of biotransference that had placed him in this eternal body.

He could not even remember what his old body had looked like. At times, his mind reconstructed an image – or what he thought was an image – for a microsecond. The curve of long fingers gripping a stylus. Dark pupils staring back from a burnished mirror. Gone, always gone, the moment his mind's eye tried to focus on it. A self-protection protocol.

What came after the flames, that was clearer. Titanic clashes. Armies of metal marching with dire purpose into the faltering lines of the reptilian Old Ones. Imotekh the Stormlord, carving through the piteous ancient ones like the necrontyr death god they'd discovered was all too real. The Dead Gods, the ones he had helped murder, mouths afire as they feasted on innumerable suns. And then these aeldari and krork, beings so adept at their own particular aspect of violence. One all rage and clamour, the other grace and silence.

These intrusive mnemonic routines ran in the background, passing in the span of a finger snap as he stalked forward, primary subroutines looking for evidence of the intruder.

Scry-filters layered over his oculars, searching for security anomalies. He could see the stasis fields surrounding each plinth, shimmering like the air above a candle flame. Protection against seismic violence in this most precious of galleries. The bulbous, ever-flowing swell of the magnetic fields pressed upon each other, ensuring that nothing save Trazyn could pass without triggering an alarm.

Then he saw the hex, and relief flooded his cold hydraulics.

Because to think about this problem meant banishing thoughts of the past.

Two magnetic fields had been parted where they met, pinned back with technomantic hexes that burned with the blue-white glow of arcing electricity. Occult glyphs, engraved on the very skin of reality.

Trazyn was no sorcerer. He had little talent for the occult arts, and less patience – besides, he was an overlord, he had crypteks to deal with that sort of thing. Delegation was one of the chief joys of power.

Yet Trazyn knew hex-work. He could appreciate the fineness of the calligraphy and radiant strength inherent in the techno-plasm. He took mnemonic image-records of it for his crypteks as he ducked through the break in the field.

Trazyn nearly missed the curse-snare just beyond it – would have, if he'd been anywhere else. Yet he knew every atom of this place, and noticed the void-black glyphs on the ebony floor just before his foot passed their hexagonal boundary.

Chronomancy, he thought. He conjured his empathic obliterator and touched its glowing tips to the border.

Begone, he willed, feeling his power course into the staff.

The hex-snare guttered and died, snuffed out of existence as if it had never been. Perhaps it had not, now. The relic imprisoned in the obliterator, able to warp reality at times, was a product of ancient and forgotten wizardry.

Wizardry that Trazyn was eager to visit upon the form of Orikan.

For only the Diviner would be so bold.

Trazyn found the astromancer where he least expected him. There were so many precious things in the War in Heaven gallery. Power plants of unknown manufacture. Command diadems worn by the phaerons of antiquity. An aeldari skimmer in the colours of a vanished clan. And above all those stasis-displays floated a great metal conqueror wyrm, seeded on planets the necron fleet bypassed to hunt their population to extinction.

This gallery, the Old Necrontyr Gallery, was naught but mournful curiosities. Scrolls from when his kin still had eyes to read. Long tar pipes, so pleasurable to those who had mouths to smoke them. A cane turned from hardwood, inlaid with ivory, its head shaped like the old, hook-beaked god of wisdom.

Trazyn knew the feel of that old god well – he'd spent much of his biological life leaning on that cane.

And in the centre of this melancholy chamber stood Orikan, weaving hexes upon the air.

* * *

Trazyn is no fool, Orikan thought.

Or at least, he was not a complete fool.

He'd been fool enough to take such a small force down to the Exodite world, for instance. A force that was so easily besieged once Orikan warned the primitives he was coming.

A delicious irony: to pillage Trazyn's cultural treasures while he was away plundering the backwater world of some feral aeldari.

But that foolishness was recent, compared to what Orikan saw around him. For it had been Trazyn's crowning folly to build this place, devoting his boundless, undying energies to a museum few of their blank-eyed kin could appreciate. Once the necrons fully awakened, after all, how many would even be sane?

Then again, the fool had proven far more resilient than Orikan's divination models had predicted. His escape from the Exodites, for instance, occurred with a speed Orikan's calculations had not considered probable.

But that was Trazyn, wasn't it? Born under fortunate stars. Always the statistical outlier, never having to work for it, the bastard.

It could be the place. Abnormal chrono-streams threw off his powers of divination. Intrusions from the immaterium snarled the calculations, and this planet, well, Solemnace was a nightmare. So many objects and beings out of place, held ageless in stasis fields and tesseract vaults. Ten thousand discrete timelines worth of chrono-noise. He could feel it even on the edge of the sector, a great cataract on the eye of the universe. A blood clot in the timestream.

Solemnace would have to fall someday, but right now it was not his main concern.

But the trash data had snarled his predictions more than once during this infiltration. Orikan had even been forced to reverse his paces and sabotage the hrud burrow to provide a distraction.

Thankfully, he had all the time in the world.

Hexes and zodiacs burned around him, floating in the aether, pinning back layers of magnetic fields and diverting sensor beams back to receivers. Masking his presence from the environment-sniffers.

All those layers of security for one inert object.

Trazyn either had some inkling of what this object did, or he was the most paranoid being in the galaxy. Or perhaps the Overlord of Solemnace believed that if something should be done, it should be overdone.

Typical Nihilakh attitude.

It had taken Orikan three necrontyr solar years just to get to this point, gingerly peeling back each layer of security.

Nearly there.

The final stasis field shimmered a gossamer blue as Orikan wove the spell. Third finger and thumb of his left hand pressed together, marking the triangular borders of the working. Right hand dancing inside like a harpist's, painting glyphs forgotten by most in the ancient days. Hexes so forbidden that in the Flesh Times, any who spoke them aloud would have his teeth pulled and tongue branded.

Perfect.

He put his fingers together, spoke the final invocation, and snapped them.

The hex flared to life, dripping purple sparks where the borders held back the field.

Orikan tentatively put a metal finger to the centre of the working and pushed it inward.

Horns blared, gongs crashed. Chamber lights snapped into the full-burn of midday.

Bastard.

Orikan's olfactory transducers picked up the hint of gauss flayers powering up.

Bastard!

The beam hit him in the head, his reinforced golden headdress stripping, the beam drilling towards his precious neural spools.

Orikan slowed his chronosense, ignoring the alarming heat in his cranial chamber, the way he could feel his mnemonic banks beginning to smoke. The beam drilled, slowed, stopped. Pain – or what pain Orikan felt out of usefulness – paused between throbs. The shower of sparks from his field-cutting hex dribbled and shut off. A frozen waterfall of electricity.

Orikan completed the mental ritual, thought the words, and ran the chants through a verbal emitter in his whickering tail to ensure the incantation was not altered by the extreme heat engulfing his skull.

The beam withdrew, his cranium rebuilding itself. Sparks flowed upward into the border of the hex. Horns and war-gongs sounded in reverse, their long reverberations building to the crescendo of the first strike or blow. Hard lights shut off.

His hands, independent of him, wove backward, unmaking the spell.

And he saw it. A *hekkat* glyph insufficiently drawn. One of the staffs branching from the upper orb was unconnected, a space of two microns separating the spear of the line from the curve of the circle.

It was what made the astromancer discipline such a difficult one. Mastery required total precision, total focus. When one used arithmancy to shape time and space, even the slightest error mattered. And with overlapping hexes this complicated, errors were easy to make.

Even musing on Trazyn, though it was but a stray thought in a tertiary subroutine, had been enough to force an error.

This, this was why he'd been living the last twenty minutes over and over again. Three years, cumulative, to get from the first plinth to the object that lay within.

Orikan took a breath. Unnecessary biologically, but critical to focus, and redrew the hex. Then he activated the working and reached inside. Felt his metal hand, cold and gentle, close around the artefact and bring it out of the field.

A perfect tetrahedral pyramid, shaped from living metal. Glyphs glistened on its surface, iridescent in the low light, veins of crystalline substance marbling through its structure.

Puzzle box. Celestial compass. Key. Depending on what you believed, it might be any of these things.

And he believed it was much, much more.

'The Astrarium Mysterios,' breathed Orikan.

'Interesting,' replied Trazyn. 'I *had* wondered what that was.'

'Archaeovist.' Orikan paired the greeting with a polite bow. It achieved the proper depth and angle for a greeting of equal colleagues, but remained just shallow enough to communicate contempt.

'Astromancer,' said Trazyn, returning the bow with a nod. The proper gesture for an overlord greeting guests on his own world, serving as both welcome and a warning. It was, consequently, identical to the duelling bow. 'Had you announced your arrival I would have arranged an honour guard. A figure of your... *reputation* should not be wandering here alone.'

'Kind and proper, my colleague. Kind and proper.' Orikan moved sideways, insectile. 'But I would not trouble you, especially since, for a planetary overlord, you are so often away from Solemnace.'

They were circling each other now, pretence dissolving. They'd long been rivals, back to the Flesh Times, and Trazyn had frequently imagined what it would be like to land a blow on the Diviner. But Orikan's movements unnerved him. The curse of biotransference had made parodies of them all, but none more extreme than he and Orikan. While Trazyn had been remade into a hunched, hooded thing – a scholar eternally at his work – Orikan's slight frame had twisted to reflect the soul within.

He was all things quick and venomous. His face and headdress recalled a hooded serpent. His curled tail, segmented back armour and spindly limbs echoed the waste-scorpions of the old capital. Divination orbs ran down his spine, swirling with cloudy energy. A single baleful ocular, mocking the foresight the crypteks claimed to possess, gleamed with haughty malice.

'Thievery is beneath you, Orikan. Hand back the trinket and perhaps we can continue your research under supervision. After all, I of all beings can understand the wish to covertly acquire–'

'Understand?' Orikan snapped. 'To understand is not in you, Trazyn. You're a bird building a nest with shiny things. A child with a rock collection. You want things simply to have them. Their true meaning, their use, is lost on you.'

'Hurtful,' chided Trazyn. He dipped his obliterator so it pointed at the device in Orikan's hand. 'Even if true, I see no reason why that allows you to steal my things.'

'You stole it first. From the Ammunos Dynasty.'

'The Ammunos Dynasty is naught but inert metal now – you can't steal from the dead, that's called *archaeology*. The point is to memorialise, learn, study what came before us. We look to the past to navigate the future.'

'I prefer to look to the future to navigate the future,' said Ori-kan. 'For instance, there were twenty-seven times I could have attacked just now, but none would have got past your guard.'

'Indeed?'

'But twenty-eight is a slaying blow.'

It came faster than Trazyn thought possible. He slowed his chronosense, but it did no good. Orikan leapt to his left and conjured his star-headed staff. In Trazyn's enhanced oculars the jagged supernova head of the weapon blurred, a chrono-field boiling around it. He was speeding himself up, his weapons up, creating a pocket of reality where time moved faster than–

The jagged sun cut right past his obliterator and sheared through his upper left arm with a shriek of parting metal and a gush of sparks. It buried itself in his upper ribcage and kept cutting. Trazyn felt it lodge in his central reactor. A flash. Battery acids and reactor fluid spouted in the air, flecks dotting Orikan's leering death mask where they sizzled like oil on an engine.

Trazyn went down on one knee.

'Thus ended Trazyn, called Infinite,' mocked Orikan, twist-ing his staff deeper. 'Lord of Solemnace, keeper of trinkets, peerless in arrogance, lord of forgotten–'

And then he stopped, because the face before him was not Trazyn, but a mere lychguard.

The obliterator swung from behind him, catching the Diviner on his segmented back plates as he twisted to evade.

It connected with a flash of searing light – a brightness so pure, it overwhelmed Trazyn's oculars, refracting and scattering in the lenses so the world disappeared for a moment then snapped back painted in prismatic rainbow hues.

The blow took Orikan off his feet and sent him crashing

into a display case, shorting out the stasis field and denting the plinth with his shoulder plate. Ceramic ritual urns atop the plinth, their cracks painstakingly hardened with period-correct resin, rocked and steadied.

Trazyn picked up the fallen puzzle box.

'I like to keep a spare body in this gallery,' he chuckled. 'So much faster to stream my consciousness into it than come by barge. Translation can destabilise the stasis fields, you know.'

Orikan tried to rise, legs twitching. Sparks crackled from his broken spine.

'So, my valued colleague,' Trazyn said. 'Let's have a short symposium, shall we? You referred to this as the Astrarium Mysterios. But surely you don't believe it's the real thing? Most likely a copy, a curiosity meant to represent the object of legend, yes?'

'You –on't know –at you ha–e.' Orikan's vocal emitters buzzed and skipped from the power overload, interrupting his crow-like voice. He pulled himself along the floor, hauling his crippled form upright so he leaned against the plinth, twitching legs trailing unnaturally to the side. '–lways a slave t– the past. Ev–n if you –new what it wa– you wouldn't po-sess the vision to –se it.'

Trazyn opened his palm and cast a stasis field, pinning the Diviner in place from the second vertebrae down.

'Slave to the past? A lack of vision? Perhaps, my dear astro-mancer. Perhaps.' Trazyn tossed the puzzle box in the air and caught it again, delighting as Orikan's monocular widened in distress. The casualness was feigned. He'd plotted the object's arc two hundred times before making the throw, and put it gingerly into his dimensional pocket. 'But you are a slave to your visions, with no sense of the past. I suppose it is our natures, yes? My lot is to preserve, yours to predict. Oh, yes,

I see you do not like that word, *predict*. No doubt you think it clumsy. Well, I have a prediction for you, dear Orikan.' He released his obliterator – it stood immobile, balanced on its pointed haft – and held a hand to his steely forehead, as if glimpsing the ethereal. 'A vision of your own future.'

The glassy floor rumbled as ancient tomb-doors grated open. Monoliths rose around the gallery, scraping against the time-worn slabs as they ground from their stasis chambers.

Inside each stood a sarcophagus niche shrouded with milky green fog. The vapour washed heavily towards the floor, lit from within like storm clouds as animation systems crackled to life. And as it sank, the fog revealed crested helms. Dispersion shields and bladed weapons stood ready in inert hands. A phalanx of lychguards, eye sockets dark.

'In my vision,' Trazyn continued, 'I see you as a permanent addition to this gallery. You are, after all, a priceless antique, are you not? Orikan the Diviner, seer of the necrontyr, maker of predictions, who warned our kind against accepting the Deceiver's horrific bargain.' He chuckled, raised the Astrarium Mysterios. 'I think I'll put you somewhere where you can gaze on this. Just out of reach. For eternity.'

'The worst th-ng about biotransference,' said Orikan, his voice recovering, 'is that in the Flesh Times you at least stopped to breathe every once in a while.'

Trazyn laughed. 'I've always envied your acid tongue.' He rapped the floor twice with his obliterator's haft. 'Perhaps I'll display it separately.'

The lychguards' eyes flared as one, popping like fuses. They lowered long warscythes, snapped shields into position, and advanced. A contracting circle of metal closed on the Diviner.

'You call me a predictor, Trazyn,' spat Orikan. 'But mere prediction is no longer of use to me. What use are visions when the powerful refuse to heed them? You marched to your doom, believing the Deceiver's promises over my auguries. Why speak truth to those that choose to be deaf to it?'

Hyperphase blades, vibrating in and out of reality, drew closer around the Diviner. Energy fields sizzled in the dry air of the hermetically sealed chamber. They were thirty steps away, then twenty.

'Since you all turned your back on me, my powers have grown,' said Orikan. 'And I have changed my focus.' Trazyn could see the astromancer's cranial coolants were running at triple capacity, beads of condensate plumping on his golden hood and running down to sizzle on his long skull. 'Why predict the future,' said Orikan, 'when I can reshape it?'

'How, exactly?' said Trazyn, then to the lychguard, 'Mind the artefacts.'

'How else do you shape the future?' Orikan said, a smile in his avian voice. He fixed Trazyn with a stare. 'By destroying the past.'

Trazyn saw the blow just as Orikan's head twitched. He threw himself forward, shouting, on an interception trajectory he knew could not succeed.

There was no way to be faster than a chronomancer.

Orikan's head slammed backward into the plinth behind him. Metal dented and cracked. Levitator arrays shorted out. The eggshell-thin ceramics, rotating like a priceless constellation, dropped.

The Diviner spoke an arcane word that burst the stasis field and scrambled out of the way, hands clawing for purchase on the floor. Half-functioning feet launched him off the plinth, slamming the ground like pistons to drive himself forward. Scrambling, then crawling.

As he moved, his body superheated, welding damaged

pieces together. Ghostly vapour twisted up from the severed vertebrae of his spine, cables seeking each other out like bloodwyrms sniffing for a mate.

Trazyn cared not. He dived for the falling relics, slowing his chronosense to try to make a decision.

It was mathematically impossible to save them all. But one – he could save one priceless example of necrontyr ceramic work. Working angles and probabilities, he chose a bright purple jar. Sautekh, Fourth Dynasty. A scene of the midsummer sky above the necrontyr home world, a starfield shining through the glaze of twilight.

It fell directly into the cup of his hands. So focused on it was he that Trazyn could see the imprint of the potter's fingerprints beneath the bright paint.

But necron hands were not meant to handle such fine pottery. It contacted his palm and crushed inward, cracks shooting through it as if a summer lightning storm had split the sky of Trazyn's half-forgotten home world. His chronosense dialled back to its slowest, every moment of the jar's destruction played out in individual tragedies.

Around him, ceramics fell like hail, scattering painted shards as they smashed against the floor.

'Barbarian!' Trazyn roared, his restoration protocols already running a damage analysis, matching potsherds by break pattern and sorting artistic styles as he shouted commands to the lychguards. 'Nihilakh, Twelfth Dynasty. Kill him. Thokt, Nineteenth Dynasty. *Kill him*. Ogdobekh, Thirtieth Dynasty. KILL HIM.'

Orikan called the fallen Staff of Tomorrow to his hand as if it were a living thing.

The first lychguard bore down on him before he could even stand. A mistake. Orikan scuttled backward like a crab, thrusting his staff at the lychguard's oculars. When the tomb guard raised his dispersion shield the Diviner scythed the staff in low, the blazing halo of its headpiece severing both legs at the ankles.

As the guard fell, Orikan sprang to his feet, slamming the pointed haft of his staff into the fallen warrior's segmented throat. He shot an electrostatic discharge through the staff and overloaded the foe's neural matrix. The warrior's oculars, awakened after sixty million years of sleep, winked out.

Orikan ducked, a warscythe passing a finger's span over his head. He kicked out backward, destabilising the opponent, and broke off, dodging behind a display of gold-inlayed smoking pipes to buy himself a moment.

The lychguard recovered and stalked towards him.

'Idiot! The ceramics!' shouted Trazyn, hastily casting a stasis field around the ruined shards. 'Watch where you step.'

Lychguards stalled, turned, went around. They stalked a wide perimeter outside the priceless debris field, their circular formation growing ragged, holes in the net developing as one group pressed in faster than the other.

Orikan circled around the pipe display, keeping it between him and the closest guards, his back momentarily shielded by the broken ceramics. 'Surrender the Mysterios, Trazyn, and this can end.'

'You have broken all covenants, astromancer. All rules of protocol. Destroyed the last examples of our world's–'

Orikan planted his foot against the display and shoved. For a sickening instant it creaked over like an axed tree, the racks of pipes held in impossible symmetry until the stasis field gave out and they crashed down at the advancing lychguards' feet.

'Stop!' Trazyn pleaded.

The ancient pipes shattered. Bowls that once held dream-tar husbanded in forgotten temple gardens scattered broken amongst the feet of the lychguard, who froze mid-step, torn between the command to advance and the one that prevented them from damaging the artefacts.

Orikan put his shoulder against a case of surgical instruments and heaved. Grabbed a disintegrating scroll and threw it across the chamber like a streamer, completing his barrier of antiquities. His own warding circle of defacement.

The lychguard halted, awaiting orders.

'If you wish to treat with me, scribe,' sneered Orikan. 'Come inside.'

Trazyn obliged, vaulting the debris. Channelling power through to his leap, his obliterator swinging down like a great hammer.

It drove down on Orikan's staff, the iron clang of their meeting echoing off the walls. For an instant, the lodestones of their weapons touched, sizzling and popping like power cables in water. Trazyn shoved the Diviner backward with the haft of his obliterator. Then the staffs swirled and clashed again, wheeling so fast that they left spectral fans of energy in their wake.

'Vandal,' Trazyn roared, thrusting his obliterator like a spear. 'You have destroyed objects made by craftsmen dead long before we breathed. Pieces of our past that can never be remade.'

Orikan parried, rolling the blow upward and leaping sideways to avoid the downward chop that followed it. 'Useless things. Fetishes of a vanished past.'

Trazyn reversed his obliterator and slapped the staff into Orikan's side, staggering the Diviner. The chronomancer back-pedalled, wisps of radioactive aurora twisting from the burn in his lower thorax.

Trazyn came on again, his fury burning. Circuits flared hot. Viscous electrofluid pumped through his system like magma.

Neither of them were warriors. For Trazyn, the dust of the archive was more familiar than that of the parade ground, and Orikan had spent aeons training his mind and neglecting his body. Had this duel occurred during the Flesh Times, it would have been comical. Two withered ancients, rangy, round-shouldered, stained with ink and smelling of incense tearing at each other with barely the strength to bruise. But biotransference had, for all its horrors, made every necron an armoured juggernaut. The two swung at each other, filling the gallery with the sounds of the forge. They locked weapons, shoved and bashed their plated skulls like horned beasts.

The lychguard looked on, impassive. They knew an aristocratic duel when they saw it, though none had seen one quite like this.

Orikan broke away, whirling. 'Give me the Mysterios, Trazyn.'

'I will tear you–'

Orikan sent the Staff of Tomorrow spinning end over end across the chamber, its head burning the air so it left the after-image of a discus as it scythed into a case of antiquities.

'No!'

Trazyn smashed the obliterator down, and the Diviner met it with the Logarithm of Sullet, conjuring a swirl of ochre void that he wielded like a buckler. Incompatible realities clashed, the solar flare of the ancient weapon meeting the lightless aether in a backfire that extinguished the tiny portal and threw the obliterator from Trazyn's grip.

Such was his fury, he cared not. Trazyn leapt upon the astromancer and beat him with bare fists. Each clashing blow left imprints on the living metal of Orikan's necrodermis.

Orikan tried to scuttle out from under the archaeovist, but Trazyn grabbed a string of ritual tiles and dragged him back so roughly that one tile sheared off in his grasp.

Alarm gongs and trumpet klaxons filled the air. Swarms of restoration scarabs crawled down the walls like curtains, their auto-instinctual protocols calling them to preserve the scene.

Trazyn saw none of it. His oculars were deep-focused on Orikan, fists slamming down over and over. Sparks showering from each blow.

The Diviner laughed. Bodies as resilient as theirs could do little damage without the aid of phase weapons and flayers.

Yet Trazyn kept hammering, beating the Diviner into the floor until he felt weak.

No, he *was* weak.

Only then did he notice the Diviner's questing tail wrapped around his throat, closing off his cable-artery, pinching off the coolant that kept his neurals from overheating.

'Barbarian,' Trazyn said, rolling to the side, his anger spent.

Orikan sprang to his feet, ready, called his staff.

'This can end, archivist,' he crowed. 'Surrender the Mysterios, and it will stop.'

Trazyn struggled to his feet, metallic dust from the pulverised floor shaking loose from his scaled cloak. 'Is it truly worth so much, Orikan?' He spread a hand at the destruction.

'What it is worth to me is immaterial,' said Orikan. 'The question is, what is it worth to you? Is it worth every object in this gallery? Because I am willing to pull this chamber in upon itself if that is what is required.'

'Our heritage. Our legacy.'

'If it is so important, sacrifice one to save all.'

Trazyn wiped his hands together, a nervous habit from a time long ago – so long ago – when they were eternally stained with ink. Calculations whirled in his matrices. If/then logic problems created and discarded.

If he orders the lychguard to advance, the artefacts become irrecoverable and Orikan destroys the gallery.

No.

If he attacks Orikan, then Orikan continues this rampage.

No.

If he gives up the Astrarium Mysterios…

Trazyn slid long fingers into his dimensional pocket and withdrew the Mysterios. Such a small thing. Insignificant, really. A curiosity. A replica of a mythical object that never existed.

At least he had assumed so. Orikan, clearly, thought different.

'A bargain,' said Trazyn. His voice had a tinge of desperation so alien that he saw two of the more sentient lychguards exchange a glance. 'You are a chronomancer. Perhaps the greatest of your kind. You can undo this destruction. It would be nothing for you.'

Orikan paused, considering. 'I can.'

'Then do it.'

'First, hand over the device.'

'I am not a simpleton, Diviner.'

Orikan spread his hands. 'You have me surrounded. Once restored, you may resume your interest in my, ah, *preservation*. Shall I give away my one point of leverage so easily?'

Trazyn hesitated. Stepped forward.

Orikan withdrew a step.

Trazyn placed the puzzle box on the ground, as carefully as if it were a newborn, and stepped back.

'Now your part,' he said.

Orikan's eye narrowed, and for a microsecond, Trazyn

thought he detected regret in that gaze. He did not step forward to take the device.

'The difficulty, Trazyn, is that undoing the damage means travelling back in the timeline, before all this occurred.' He met Trazyn's gaze. 'And if I did that, you would have no memory of this accord.'

Trazyn saw the transdimensional beamer. Knew what it meant.

Canoptek wraiths used them to banish unwanted construction debris into extra-dimensional space – a large-scale version of the pocket dimension he kept at his own hip.

Orikan's snapshot caught the Mysterios, lancing it out of existence. Sending it somewhere in the great nowhere.

Trazyn dived for Orikan as the Diviner turned the sidearm on himself.

By the time Trazyn's hands got there, nothing occupied the space but empty air.

Trazyn the Infinite, archaeovist of the Solemnace galleries, stood in the centre of his ruined past.

And howled for revenge.

CHAPTER FOUR

NEPHRETH: *Do not mourn if I am slain, instead, entomb me like the phaerons of old. Not in a high ziggurat, but in a vault below flat ground covered by sand, where no questing eye shall find my bones. Raise no stele and carve no inscription, save one: 'In this tomb rests a true son of the necrontyr, unmarked by its corruption. Open and be damned.'*

– *War in Heaven*, Act III, Scene II, Line 1

Solemnace was famous for its galleries – sweeping reconstructions of battles, titanic heroes preserved in hard-light, recreations of history's greatest moments. Even before the Great Sleep, Trazyn had entertained visitors from nearly every dynasty with his collection of wonders.

What was less known, was that it also contained one of the greatest document collections in the galaxy, a rival even to the aeldari's fabled Black Library.

Trazyn, after all, had once been a chronicler and archivist. Though artefacts were his passion, he did not neglect the written word.

It was not a project that required his close attention. He handled acquisitions, of course, for that was the most interesting part, but the rest he delegated to cryptek scribes who catalogued, cross-referenced and digitised each work. Trazyn hoped that in another ten millennia, when the necron legions were destined to awaken, all of their literature, history and discourses would be accessible, a mnemonic copy sent to the library of each tomb world. A great work, for the benefit of all.

Trazyn liked great works. Indeed, he had been awake far longer than even the handful of his early-risen kin – and had learned quickly that lofty pursuits were an essential component to immortality. A necron overlord's greatest enemy was not the savage orks, the grasping humans or the cunning aeldari. Boredom was the greatest foe, one that must be continually battled lest madness or despondency set in.

So he had his gallery, and his holographic archive, ready to gift once his kin arose.

And besides, if all the tomb worlds had their own archives, no researchers would come to muck about in his. Nobody touching his precious manuscripts or asking obnoxious questions.

Trazyn was not feeling charitable as he stalked down into the depths of Solemnace, past his restoration rooms and extensive wine cellar. He approached the carved wooden doors of the library, warm and inviting, and threw them open with a shove that stressed the hinges.

His fury, though terrible, was always brief. Trazyn did not

burn hot for long – his anger was cold and dry like the desert night. A focused, lasting anger both practical and useful.

Shelves reached to the ceiling. Rotating cradles, like the side wheels of great river barges, held arcane tomes and scrolls. Crypteks paused in their copying, stunned.

'I require assistance,' he said. 'Then solitude.'

'Of course, my lord,' said the chief librarian. 'Is this about the proposed expansion?'

'The what?'

The cryptek bowed, obsequious. 'The stacks are full, my lord. We are over capacity. I have humbly suggested that we expand the collection into the space currently occupied by the wine cellars.'

'But then where would I put my wine, librarian?'

'You… you do not drink wine, my lord.'

'Of course I don't,' Trazyn snapped. 'It's far too valuable. Request denied. Enlist excavation wraiths to dig another chamber.'

'My lord…'

'And bring me everything you have about the War in Heaven, Phaeron Nephreth, and the Astrarium Mysterios. I want the physical manuscripts.'

'Quite an eclectic subject, lord archaeovist.' He called up a phos-glyph panel and ran a text scry. 'In addition to the larger works, there are many small references in various mediums that need special handling and transport. There are sheet-gold scrolls, foundation stele, platinum slab-tablets–'

'Everything,' Trazyn said, in a tone that did not brook dissent. 'Bring it all, then go away. I will be some time.'

'Yes, sire.'

'But first, bring me the legal code. The volumes on inter-dynastic theft and trials.'

'Is there to be a trial, my lord?'

'Oh yes,' said Trazyn, fingering the ritual tile he had ripped from Orikan's frame. 'There most certainly will be.'

Mandragora, Eastern Fringe
Nine Standard Years Later

Mandragora the Golden. Mandragora of the Emerald Skies. Mandragora, dynastic seat of the mighty Sautekh.

Orikan despised it, even now. Even as he'd exited the dolmen gate, the scars of his perilous journey fresh on his necrodermis, he could not help but release his venom.

'Land of whisperers and sycophants. I should have stayed with the drukhari.'

Once the third most powerful dynasty in the Necron Empire, the crownworld of the Sautekh was a dead place. Great sand dunes drifted against its ziggurats and palaces, burying them beneath golden cascades that mocked its grand title. Windstorms scoured its monuments with the planet's abrasive silica grains, stripping the gilded sepulchres and obelisks to their living metal interior and giving the entire city – or what one could see of it – the appearance of brushed steel. A few districts retained their grandeur, sheltered in the lee of great stasis tombs and spared the caustic attentions of windblown sand. There, statues of ancient phaerons still stared imperious over the desert, faces distinct and spared the weathering of less fortunate monuments.

There, the few hundred awakened members of the Sautekh Dynasty lived a pantomime existence. Accidental custodians of the silent necropolis, awakened ten thousand years too early, busying themselves taking care of a world that was largely self-sufficient. Waiting for the distant day when the countless billions of sleepers would emerge.

Orikan stayed well away from those districts. Before the Great Sleep, he'd found Mandragora oppressive. So many beings milling, clamouring, constantly interrupting. Constant politics – petty creatures struggling for petty victories.

It had been a difficult place to focus. Even achieving a basic chrono-trance required shutting the world out with slab-thick walls in his astromantic observatory, perched on the humped mountain overlooking the city, and above its sky-erasing glow.

Yet maintaining a presence was necessary. Personal preferences aside, Mandragora was the Sautekh power centre, and Orikan could not be a court astromancer from his hermitage on Rithcairn – more's the pity.

But Mandragora had much to recommend itself, in these strange days. A stable dolmen gate to access the webway. The quiet dark of a dead, sterile metropolis. And of course, an automated defence grid that was the best in the empire – just the sort of thing you need if you've stolen from one of the most dangerous beings in the galaxy.

Using the transdimensional beamer had been a desperate risk, little better than casting lots. He'd adjusted the translocation paths to his own specifications, of course – Orikan was reckless, not dull-witted – but there had been a chance some infinitesimal variable would mar his transit. A chance that, instead of the glowing tunnels of the webway, he would have sprung back into reality in the heart of a star, or floating in deep space between dimensions. Even absent those extreme cases, there was every possibility he would come out at a random point in space-time, forced to adjust and use the beamer again and again, hoping the increasingly wild translations would bring him home, and not to realities increasingly aberrant from his own.

That would not have been ideal. But also not a tragedy. After all, Orikan had time.

But his astromantic divinations proved true enough, and his translation landed him in a disused portion of the webway. Not the exact point he'd intended, unfortunately, but close enough. Then again, it was possible it was *exactly* the spot he'd meant, but that the network had changed into something unrecognisable. With the webway destabilised, it was increasingly difficult to tell.

The aeldari's great cataclysm had rocked the network to its foundations, snapping away arcways that used to see fleets pass and flinging them into the immaterium. Un-things from that dimension of madness increasingly stalked the corridors, and every cycle the aeldari's witch seers collapsed more pathways to keep the evils out.

Orikan had wound through the coils of the labyrinth dimension, clearing passages and lurking in shadows. What remained of the old enemy's civilisation was in flight. Neo-primitives like the ones Trazyn had pillaged, migrating to new home worlds. Vicious raiders hunting their own, all societal bonds broken. Refugees, eyes hollow with fear, hurtling helter-skelter through the halls without regard for where they headed.

Orikan did not blame them. After all, what the young race birthed had shaken him so badly he'd needed a century of meditation to recover, and he'd merely glimpsed it via astral precognition.

The aeldari's time upon the stage was ending in an era of lamentation and horror.

'Fair comeuppance,' he'd said, upon witnessing his first group of refugees, 'for what your decadence has unleashed upon the galaxy.'

Slithering between the chaos, the doubling back and hiding

turned a one-month transit from Solemnace to Mandragora into a nine-year odyssey. Three cycles alone had been spent burning his way through a wending corridor infested with carnivorous fungoid blooms. His carapace bore new scars – talismans of an unfortunate encounter with drukhari incubi – and his power plant needed a refurbishment.

But mostly, he required time for meditation and study.

Now, atop his astromancer's tower, he watched the stars – sensing gravity's pull on the transit of planets, its infinite algebraic possibility influencing even the smallest events in the galaxy.

The astronomers of old, stupid and superstitious as they had been, had guessed at this connection. But their pathetic spirituality had little to do with the scientific precision Orikan now used to chart the pull of gravity and flow of particles, the bending of space-time around sucking black holes, the chain of bizarre causality that could turn a breath on one continent into a typhoon on another.

And those lines of power, light, energy and time tended to snare around certain objects.

Like the one that floated, slowly turning, at the centre of the observation deck. Jade shadows underlit it from the suspensor field beneath, and phos-glyph equations and grids – written on the very air – surrounded it in a cloud.

Lines traced from each theorem to the multisided surface of the Astrarium Mysterios. Autonomic calculators measured and remeasured each face, edge and vertex.

There were eight, twelve and six respectively. A perfect octahedron.

'Which is puzzling,' he said aloud to the Mysterios. 'Because according to my engrammatic banks, you were a pyramid when I left Solemnace.'

He'd tried to review his mnemonic data and pinpoint the exact moment of this transmutation, but it was useless. The mirrored geometry of the webway – especially since the cataclysm – fouled his recall systems into a dreamlike blur.

'You have undergone a transmutation. No surprise, as that is your function. But exactly when did you change?' he asked, rhetorically. It was sometimes easier to think aloud. Split his consciousness into a portion that stimulated questions, and a portion that searched for possible answers. 'What was the catalyst for this transmutation? What was the method?'

Spectromantic analysis indicated a device composed of solid living metal. The same substance that made up the tower, his staff, Orikan's own necrodermis.

There were also trace amounts of mercury and unknown crystal buried in its heart – strange. Not standard components in necron technology.

Little wonder Trazyn – blind to the metaphysical and lacking imagination – labelled it a forgery. Even those initiated into the cryptek mysteries, if they lacked sufficient study and insight, would have thought the same.

Orikan had possessed the Mysterios for a decade, and he still could not ken the basics of its operation. Perhaps it was time-dependent, gradually opening as the aeons ground on, ensuring that the shorter-lived races would never access its secrets.

'Conversely,' he mused, the answering part of his consciousness taking over, 'it is possible contact with the webway activated it. Or that it lay inert until it passed through a dolmen gate. Such a security measure would keep it from being activated outside the control of its makers.'

The Ammunos Dynasty, Dead Gods curse their lifeless atoms, had been renowned for their secrecy and paranoia. In moments of frustration, Orikan took pleasure in imagining the solar flare ionising the neural matrices of the sleeping dynasty, shock waves scrambling their tomb world's magnetic field and rendering all systems inert. Mass neural death, in the span of a few minutes.

Too bad they hadn't been awake to feel it.

Over the past cycle, Orikan had bombarded the Mysterios with every energy wave he considered safe, spoken to it in hex-decrypt, and even tried contacting any hidden consciousness through neural-transference.

He'd raised twelve crypteks – in body only, minds still at rest – and installed them kneeling around the observation deck. He networked their blank minds with his to increase his analytic capacity and engrammatic storage, running theorems and suppositions until two of them overheated, blue flames bursting from their ocular sockets before they translated to the resurrection forge to be rebuilt.

Nothing.

He had called scarabs to clean up the ash piles when he noticed that one did not follow the swarm. One with a jewelled red back plate.

'What?' he said, resisting the urge to crush it beneath his foot.

The little drone knelt in a servile bow, shaking slightly in his presence. Its carapace scissored open to reveal a message orbuculum.

The chrysoprase projection juddered and flickered for a moment, resolving into the one being Orikan did not want to see.

'Master Orikan, Seer of the Sautekh, the one called Diviner,' said the tall being, staring into his eyes as if she were standing in the room. 'I am Executioner Phillias of the Triarch praetorians, herald of the Awakened Council. By order of the Council you are to present yourself on Bekyra with immediate haste to face accusations brought by Trazyn, overlord of Solemnace and archaeovist of the–'

'Bastard,' Orikan muttered. 'Squealed to the council, did you?'

'–relating to alleged acts on Solemnace. This scarab is slaved to your neural signature and will alert the Council if it detects noncompliant travel. Failure to present yourself in original body – not a surrogate – will be punished by the cancellation of your resurrection protocols. Glory to the Infinite Empire.'

The image winked out, and Orikan swore.

For he was going on trial.

'Is he coming?'

The speaker, Lord Nemesor Zuberkar, rested his hyperphase sword tip down on the floor of the dais. With a hard twist, he sent it spinning like a top, the unbalanced energy blade making a sound like a faulty turbofan as it rotated in place. Each time, he caught the hilt just before it lost momentum and fell.

Fwomp. Fwomp. Fwomp. Catch.

Fwomp. Fwomp. Fwomp. Fwomp. Catch.

'A summons from the Awakened Council carries full force of law,' said Trazyn. 'Orikan will come.'

And if he does not, Trazyn thought, *you will cancel his reanimation protocol and Executioner Phillias will hunt him down with that great execution scythe of hers.* Which was clearly the result she hoped for – she had been sharpening the great half-moon blade since they had convened, running a molecular smoother over the orbit of the power field, aligning the particles along the wicked edge.

Nothing more dangerous than a bored killer.

'Do you agree?' Zuberkar asked the phaerakh to his left.

'I do,' replied Phaerakh Ossuaria, her voice icy. Furious, as usual, that a mere overlord was addressing her as an equal.

'I concur,' said High Metallurgist Quellkah, leaning forward from the platform's third throne. 'This body holds authority in these disputes. So says the law.'

Zuberkar shrugged, spun the sword.

Fwomp. Fwomp. Fwomp. Catch.

'Cease that,' snapped Ossuaria, deigning to turn her head towards the overlord, her tile diadem veil clattering. 'It's interminable.'

'You may be a phaerakh,' Zuberkar said. 'But you are a phaerakh of the Rytak. I owe you no obedience.'

The two locked oculars. Trazyn had little doubt that they were trading insults through interstitial transfer.

'Please, my comrades,' Quellkah said. 'On this dais we are equals. It is the keystone of our great peace. Our body holds the empire together. We owe allegiance not to each other, but to the oaths we have taken.'

The rivals broke eye contact and, as one, looked at the cryptek.

'Not that you need reminding,' he said, shrinking back into his chair.

Trazyn swallowed a smile. Quellkah was right, of course. Not that it would help his cause. Even before biotransference, necrontyr society had been conservative and hierarchical, and those instincts held sway even in these strange times.

After the War in Heaven, when the C'tan star gods fought the Old Ones, with the necrons as their imprisoned metal army, the necrons had seen their chance to avenge the deception of biotransference. Rising up, they slew their erstwhile gods, shattering them into pieces and sealing the shards – each still powerful enough to level cities – in huge tesseract labyrinths. Yet in destroying the Old Ones and the divine C'tan, even the implacable necrons had overtaxed themselves. It was clear the aeldari were the rising race, and would shape the galaxy's next great epoch.

But the metal dynasties knew that no era lasts forever, and they had the advantage of deathless sleep. Already Orikan had foreseen the fall of the aeldari and the rise of mankind. All of necron kind, sleeping sixty million years in stasis.

The galaxy was a wild place, though, and even the genius of the crypteks had its limit. Occasional faulty awakenings occurred, perhaps only affecting one sarcophagus, or at other times the tomb of a whole phalanx. It was entirely random, part of no plan, affecting everyone from the lowliest warriors of foot to those of phaeronic rank like Ossuaria, who had woken to find herself the only conscious being on her silent tomb world.

Without the rigid class structure holding them in check, those awakened by fault fell to chaos. Some awakened whole decurions without the aid of a cryptek, damaging the neural pathways of their fellows and turning them into automatons. Others took the opportunity to settle old scores, murdering rivals as they slumbered in their sarcophagi.

It was the Triarch praetorians, an order of cloistered warriors who had eschewed sleep to watch over the stasis tombs, who finally insisted on the council. And they had given it Phillias as their executioner and – Trazyn suspected – their spy.

The Awakened Council gave the necrons a minimalist, *ad hoc* government. They protected the sleepers under pain of death and set strict limits on the number and type of

artificial risings. With premature resurrection so often leading to damage, no necron was to be animated except under
circumstances of dire necessity.

But in a society where feuds were commonplace, its greatest
task was to settle disputes with tribunals like the one Orikan
would, in a bare moment, be late to.

Phillias tested the blade of her scythe on the edge of a
metal thumb.

Zuberkar spun the sword.

Fwomp. Fwomp. Fwomp. Catch.

'One more time–'

Reality shrieked and tore, lighting the death masks of the
council with balefire. A rough translation, the kind conducted
in a hurry.

'I would prefer we make this quick,' said Orikan, green fire
still licking at his body.

'Let me summarise,' said the Diviner. 'I am accused of stealing an object from Overlord Trazyn, and destroying old,
worthless clutter.'

'Priceless antiquities,' Trazyn corrected, holding out his
wooden cane as an exhibit. The inlaid wood was snapped in
two, its splintered ends already decomposing from its time
out of the stasis field.

'Priceless and worthless are the same thing,' Orikan spat.
'And I remember a time when you were all too eager to give
up that hobble stick. But if you must, draw up a list and we
shall discuss restitution.'

'The relative worth of these objects,' Quellkah said, curb-
ing Trazyn's response, 'is not for you to decide, Orikan. If
you admit to this theft and vandalism of a tomb world, it is
a serious offence. The law prescribes banishment or death.'

'A law created by this body,' Orikan snapped. 'A body whose authority in this matter I do not recognise.'

Trazyn smiled. Same old Orikan, hostile to any authority, no matter how powerful. He would fist fight the sun if he thought it was telling him what to do. It was why Trazyn had pursued this course – the Diviner would build his own mausoleum, block by block.

'And why is that?' enquired Ossuaria. 'We have held these tribunals, without challenge, for centuries.'

'Perhaps,' said Orikan. 'But not with me. It is not a fair process. High Metallurgist Quellkah, do you recall our dispute as young adepts?'

'A… long time ago, my colleague,' he faltered. 'The stars have wheeled quite a bit since then.'

'Ossuaria,' Orikan snapped, already ignoring the high metallurgist. 'My lovely phaerakh. I believe you still owe me a debt for divinatory services. A *substantial* uncollected debt. After all, who else could've predicted where your brother the phaeron and his seven heirs would be on that unfortunate day.'

Ossuaria stiffened.

Zuberkar leaned back, laughing and shaking his bulkhead-jawed head. 'Cunning mynix. You said they were lost in a void storm.'

'And Lord… Nemesor… Zuberkar,' Orikan continued, pausing after each title. 'We've had no dealings, but the Mephrit are old enemies of the Sautekh Dynasty. I would not put it past you to continue that kin feud.'

'I wouldn't either,' Zuberkar confessed, patting a hand on his blood-coloured chest armour. The Mephrit had never been shy about their viciousness.

'Come to your point,' Trazyn rumbled, darkly, then quieted

as Executioner Phillias turned to him and placed a finger to her lipless mouth.

'In summation,' Orikan continued. 'No judgement you hand down will be free from the perception of bias. And given the size and stature of my dynasty, are you willing to risk the phaeron's displeasure when he wakes to find an unsanctioned council has executed his chief seer?'

Silence. The three figures sat statue-still on their onyx thrones – symbols of power that felt shakier than they had a moment before.

'He would, no doubt, unleash the Stormlord.' Orikan let that hang, then turned to Quellkah. 'High metallurgist, you campaigned with Lord Imotekh on Calliope, did you not? Perhaps you could enlighten your fellow... what do you call yourselves? Ah yes, *council members* about what happens when the Stormlord goes forth in his panoply of war.'

Again, silence. All knew what had happened to the Khuvu Dynasty at Calliope. Even now, sixty million years and several celestial wars later, 'Gone like the Khuvu' was a regular idiom in necrontyr speech. Back when their kind still ate, it was what one said after clearing an entire plate.

'It would...' began Quellkah. 'Ah, it would be prudent to remove the appearance of bias.'

'Perhaps we should suspend proceedings,' said Ossuaria. 'Only until a suitable representative of the Sautekh has arisen to oversee the proceedings on behalf of the dynasty.'

'It is what they would do for us,' added Zuberkar, aware that the transcription-scarabs would record his words, but not his disbelieving tone. 'Will that serve you, Trazyn of Nihilakh?'

'It damn well won't!' Trazyn shouted, dialling back his

venom when Phillias put up a hand. 'It damn won't,' he repeated. 'Until a Sautekh representative awakens? It's not scheduled for another ten millennia. And this jackal-son… the defendant… can control the stasis-crypts on Mandragora. The phaeron will awaken when he wills it. As the accusatory, I cannot accept this.'

'Have you a solution, then?' Orikan asked. 'If this body is not willing to continue, then what else is there to do but suspend it and issue a continuance?'

Trazyn paused, reviewing the volumes of necrontyr law he'd encoded in his last decade of study. He watched Orikan smile, the Diviner clearly misinterpreting his hesitation as a loss for words. *Keep smiling, reactor leak*, he thought.

'If this tribunal cannot hear the case,' he said. 'As accusatory I assert my right to a mediator.'

'A what?' Orikan said.

'A mediator,' repeated Quellkah. 'Yes, indeed that is the proper procedure.'

'It is?' Zuberkar narrowed his oculars.

'When the council formed,' Trazyn explained, 'you all voted that the legal codes of old held sway in all instances not covered by the new codes. And I assert my ancient rights to a mediator of overlord rank or above, one that has no ties to the Sautekh or the Nihilakh dynasties.'

The council members looked at Quellkah.

'It is proper,' the cryptek said. 'It could be done.'

'But where to find a mediator?' asked Ossuaria.

'Forgive me for interjecting, phaerakh,' said Trazyn. 'This is a council world, one with dynastic representatives entombed below. And I'm sure the high metallurgist could call upon his skills to raise one in safety… provided we came to agreement on whom to select.'

Trazyn cast a glance at Orikan, scrying his demeanour.

Though the seer's death mask remained impassive, Trazyn received a glyph-message via interstitial link.

Bastard.

The selection process took two standard years of bickering, politicking, and the occasional threat of violence. It was, in other words, a standard necron court case.

It was no accident that all dispute resolutions were, by highly practical tradition, observed by an armed executioner. More than a few cases in the ancient records ended with the phrase: *Case dismissed after accusatory's dismemberment.*

But finally, the council made their selection.

'It… has been sixty million years?' said Overlord Vokksh, his orange oculars blinking with the haze of tomb-sleep. He would remember soon that he no longer needed to blink.

'Indeed, overlord,' said Quellkah, bending over the stasis sarcophagus, which was propped up at an angle, its occupant still within. 'It would be best not to move your body overmuch, my lord. We have primarily awoken your neural matrices and vocal actuators. This will assist your re-entombment procedure afterward.'

'Why?'

'We need you to adjudicate a case, my lord,' the high metallurgist explained. 'After all, you were chosen to be the Charnovokh representative here, were you not? I have encoded the particulars of the accusatory's writ. Do you see them?'

'Yesssss,' the overlord hissed, one slow hand gripping the narrow steel beard that jutted from his chin and rubbing it between two fingers. 'Proceed.'

Trazyn stood before the onyx dais, preparing his case. It was not exactly how he'd expected this to play out, but then again, trying a case a mere twelve years after an offence was almost scandalously fast by necron standards. The sort of frontier justice portrayed in the theatrical dramas, not how things happened in reality.

Trazyn activated an orbuculum, casting a projection of the Astrarium Mysterios in the centre of the chamber. It rotated in space, semi-translucent, surrounded by ocular-captures of Orikan burglarising.

'Twelve standard years ago, Orikan – called the Diviner, seer of the necrontyr – feloniously entered the tomb world of Solemnace in the attempt to steal this artefact, the Astrarium Mysterios. In his addled state, he believed it to be a prize worth destabilising the peace for. I apprehended him, and in his escape he destroyed a host of precious cultural objects recovered from home soil.'

Trazyn swept his hand left and right, scrolling through chrysoprase holograms of snapped canes, shattered vessels, a pipe with a broken stem. 'These objects...'

'How did you obtain that?' pointed Zuberkar. 'The pipe?'

'Standard acquisition procedures,' he evaded. 'All above board.'

'Go back,' said Zuberkar. 'That pipe's Mephrit made. It should be in our gallery.'

'My dear overlord,' Trazyn said, 'Solemnace holds all of these objects in trust for the good of all our kind.'

'Damn that! It has my family sigil on it.'

'If you make a formal request through the proper channels, we can certainly arrange its return,' Trazyn said. He of course made all decisions regarding the gallery, but had always found that 'we' was a magical word for deflecting blame. 'But we firmly believe that these precious relics should be in a place where experts can ensure their proper preservation and display.'

'This enquiry is not concerned with Overlord Trazyn's acquisition processes,' cut in Overlord Vokksh, his vocal actuators now calibrated to cancel out the sleep-slur. Trazyn could see why the overlord was known for his power as a magistrate – he had a fine orator's voice with an undeniable sense of authority. 'You are in the right to protest the Diviner's intrusion, as well as his vandalism. It is no small thing. But I see no reason to pursue death or banishment. Restitution can be made through the re-engramming of several thousand Sautekh warriors and their transfer to your command, or the surrender of planetary tithes. Indeed, that may be too radical considering your dubious ownership. Given that, why have you escalated this petty dispute so high?'

Trazyn reconjured the projection, settling it on the puzzle box.

'This is the Astrarium Mysterios, the object of Orikan's desire.'

'A puzzle box?' asked Vokksh.

'A mere puzzle box,' said Orikan, before a glance from Vokksh hushed him.

'A *map*,' corrected Trazyn. 'An encrypted celestial chart. In certain esoteric corners of our society, an astrarium was used to reveal the location of occult gatherings or arcane pilgrimage sites. They can be activated by a spoken key-phrase, or coordinates, opening when they're at a specific point on the galactic plane. Each one is individual, and each becomes inert after its successful use. I believed this one to have been already used or even a replica.'

'But you no longer believe that?'

'Orikan would not have been so rash if he though it inert.' Trazyn stared at his rival, but instead of hatred, Orikan's hooded eye was fixed on him with interest. 'He suspects that it leads to a fabulous treasure.'

'And do you have any idea where it leads?' Vokksh leaned slightly forward in his casket, propping himself up on an elbow. Quellkah approached him, fussing, and he waved the high metallurgist away. 'Do not make us wait.'

'According to the encoded glyphs on its surface,' Trazyn said, pausing to enhance the drama, 'the Astrarium Mysterios leads to the tomb of Nephreth the Untouched, the last natural phaeron of the Ammunos Dynasty.'

There was a pause, then a barking laugh from Zuberkar.

'Nephreth the Untouched?' he mocked. 'From that god-awful long tragedy?'

'Yes,' said Trazyn. 'Nephreth is primarily known as a character in the theatrical drama *The War in Heaven*, but he did exist.'

'Of course he existed,' Phaerakh Ossuaria sniped. 'It's a historical play. Or history-inspired, at least. But to suggest that any of it resembles what actually occurred...'

'You remember, do you?' enquired Trazyn. 'I mean truly remember. Step forward, if you recall the days before biotransference. Can anyone tell me, with certainty, that their mnemonics contain a perfect record, with no deterioration during the aeons of sleep?'

None stepped forward. The high metallurgist shifted uncomfortably. They all knew what biotransference had done to them. Mnemonics of the Flesh Times were like the memories an adult has of childhood. One knows that one was a child, that one was born and lived years only through second-hand stories. Knows that there are friends, once close companions in youth, who are nothing but fleeting ghosts in memory. Sensations disconnected from context. Things retained, but with no memory of learning them – one knows the colour blue, but cannot recall the first time one knew its name.

Indeed, it was the purpose of those mawkish stage dramas to reinforce necron history, lest they forget. It was the reason why even oafs like Zuberkar knew the characters and plots inside out despite hating their length.

(They had, to be clear, grown punishingly long. Now that actors could memorise thousands of pages via engrammatic recall, and the audience had no biological needs to interrupt the performance, the forgotten cryptek-playwrights who'd contributed to the drama had gone overboard. A full performance could take well over a decade.)

'My research has concluded that the dramas may be more accurate than previously believed,' said Trazyn. He waved towards the orbuculum, summoning bas-reliefs depicting the War in Heaven. Necrontyr warriors and star-chariots, worn free of detail by the antiquity of the carving, advanced on the Old Ones' doom engines.

'It appears that, indeed, Nephreth was called Untouched due to a genetic resistance to the radiation-induced cancers afflicting our former bodies. Further research suggests that his rebellion against the star gods – his doomed resistance to the process of biotransference – indeed occurred.'

Trazyn looked at Orikan. The Diviner stared intently at the holographic bas-relief, rubbing one of the strands of tiles that fell from his shoulders. One tile was still missing, the one Trazyn had ripped from the Diviner during the struggle on Solemnace. It hung at Trazyn's hip now, amidst the aeldari gemstone and other curios that dangled there – a reminder of his revenge.

But Trazyn had difficulty reading the Diviner's mood. Apprehension, perhaps, or merely interest? How much of this did he know?

'Here drama and history diverges,' Trazyn said. 'In the drama,

Nephreth was killed attacking the star gods, scorched to nothing by the Burning One. But my archive contains an account that Nephreth's own dynasty betrayed him, murdering their phaeron and his followers to broker peace with the star gods and gain the, ah, *gift* of biotransference.'

'Quite an anticlimax,' Vokksh muttered.

'Indeed,' said Trazyn. 'But his relatives in the Ammunos Dynasty – despite their betrayal – apparently wished to hedge their bets. After all, they possessed the only genetically uncorrupted sample of the necrontyr species, free of disease and blight.'

Trazyn swept the projection, calling up a manuscript illustration of a death-procession carrying a stasis-casket into a towering gateway.

'They hid the dead phaeron in a stasis tomb complex called Cephris, hoping to return and recreate the species if they found biotransference not to their liking.'

'So why didn't they?' asked Vokksh. 'Return, I mean?'

Trazyn shrugged. 'Unclear. But just as we cannot remember Nephreth, his followers may have forgotten how to activate the device. Over time, they forgot even what it led to – thus its name. The Mysterios. A mystery.'

'Fascinating,' said Vokksh. 'What purpose do you have for keeping this object, Trazyn?'

'I…' Trazyn stopped.

'He wants it for his gallery,' said Orikan. 'To stare at it, or rather, not to stare at it. He didn't even know what he had. It will simply collect dust, a curio serving no purpose.'

'And what purpose would it serve for you, Orikan?' asked Vokksh.

'None,' growled Trazyn. 'He doesn't believe in a return to the flesh. Orikan wants us to be…' He waved his fingers in the air.

'Energy beings. Things of light. If he found Nephreth, he would likely incinerate the phaeron to keep rival crypteks from finding a solution that was not his. Ulterior motives, my overlord.'

'Ulterior motives, you say?' crowed Orikan. 'Ask how he acquired it.'

'It's not your time to speak, sand tick,' snarled Trazyn.

'Yes, quite right,' said Vokksh. 'But the question stands. How did you acquire this?'

'Legitimately.' Trazyn turned off the orbuculum, packed it in his pocket dimension. 'If that is all...'

'Legitimately... how?' Vokksh pressed.

'It was part of a lot acquisition from the Ammunos crownworld of Hashtor. Tragic story, Hashtor. A solar flare from the local star triggered a failure cascade to its stasis system. It is a dead world. Legal under salvage.'

No one moved. The Ammunos had been powerful. Secretive and distrusted, but their absence would be a blow.

'The Ammunos Dynasty,' Trazyn paused, looking around the room to let the message sink in, 'will not come to claim it.'

The council and executioner stood, stunned at the dire pronouncement.

Vokksh murmured in the back of his throat. 'That appears to be legal, under salvage—'

'Ah,' goaded Orikan. 'But *when* did you acquire it?' He took a step forward, tile strands rattling against his skeletal body.

'I have not yielded the floor,' said Trazyn.

'Did you steal the Mysterios before the Ammunos died out, or after? Because by my auguries, you raided their vault for artefacts well before the solar flare. In fact, immediately when it became clear the solar flare would snuff them out.'

'Your information,' Trazyn said with a hint of frost, 'is incorrect and out of procedure.'

'Wait,' said Vokksh. 'Are you alleging that Overlord Trazyn, aware of the solar flare, did not alert the tomb world's Deep Spirit and instead raided it for artefacts?'

'Just so,' said Orikan. 'As you heard him say, *the Ammunos Dynasty will not come to claim it*. A perfect theft. He walks away with the goods, and the cosmos wipes out the victim. No one can complain.'

'That is ridiculous,' Trazyn said.

'Villain!' crowed Orikan. 'Plotter. Traitor to your own kind.'

'Is it true?' demanded Vokksh. 'Keep in mind my vocal scryers are on high alert, any lie will be detected.'

'Well…' Trazyn tutted in frustration. 'Understand, there was *very* little time to make a decision.'

A groan went up from the council.

'No, no. Listen,' he stumbled. 'Awakening a tomb world takes time. At least a half-century, even under optimal conditions. To save even the higher orders would have taken more time than was available. So I focused on salvaging what I could from the material culture…'

'Murderer,' snarled Phaerakh Ossuaria.

'It is you who should be on trial, Trazyn, not I!' sang the Diviner. 'I foresaw your treachery and…'

'Wait.' Trazyn motioned for quiet. 'You foresaw it?'

'Of course! I foresaw the horror of biotransference. The fall of the aeldari. I have seen the coming of hungry creatures you cannot fathom and–'

'If you foresaw the solar flare,' asked Trazyn. 'Why did *you* not stop it? Did you hope to sweep in afterward and take the astrarium without resistance?'

Orikan stared, frozen. His mouth worked, giving a metallic *clunk, clunk, clunk*. 'Ah… you misunderstood me, I think.'

'Executioner,' said Vokksh. 'Take them both.'

'Bastards,' muttered Orikan, fingering his ritual tiles. 'I knew Vokksh was a bad idea.'

'The Ammunos Dynasty,' Trazyn paused, looking around the room to let the message sink in, 'will not come to claim it.'

The council and executioner stood, stunned at the dire pronouncement.

'Sad news,' said the adjudicator from her stasis-casket. She raised her head, the resurrection orbs that hung from her headdress tinkling like a chandelier. 'I assume you are claiming salvage rights?'

Trazyn breathed a sigh of relief. Or at least, the closest he could get to one without lungs. He had worried that Supreme Excellent Lady Yullinn was not the right one to conduct this trial. He feared a lighter touch might let Orikan run wild, yet he had been relatively subdued.

And yet… Trazyn felt displaced. A feeling he could not access perturbed him. Reactor coolant sloshed about his innards as if he'd experienced a hard translation.

He felt a strange heat by his hip, and noticed the ritual tile which hung there, the one he'd taken from Orikan, was warm.

Odd.

'Overlord Trazyn?' asked Supreme Excellent Lady Yullinn. 'Do you wish to claim salvage rights?'

'Yes. Yes, indeed I do, overlord… ah, supreme lady. Adjudicator.'

'Are you well, Trazyn?' the supreme excellent lady's oculars folded in concern.

'If the venerable Trazyn is done,' cut in Orikan. 'I have evidence to present.'

'Please do,' nodded Yullinn. 'Overlord, please sit down. Clearly what you witnessed on Hashtor has affected you deeply. If you have more evidence to present you may do so after you have recovered.'

That did not seem like the worst idea, Trazyn thought. His head felt clogged. His central reactor cycled at a dangerous rate. And that sense of unreality refused to abate. He locked his legs and took the weight off his frame. A seat without a chair.

'My lady,' said Orikan. 'As you see, Lord Trazyn – a dear friend for many centuries – is having difficulties. Biotransference and the Great Sleep have taken a toll on all of us, I fear. This is but a misunderstanding.'

Trazyn stopped, turned his head. 'Misunderstanding?'

'Poor Trazyn. He invited me to conduct research on Solemnace. You see...' Orikan opened a dimensional pocket and withdrew the Astrarium Mysterios. 'I also have a device. We were comparing them.'

Trazyn's eyes found the device and locked there. His sense of being in two places, his void-sick feeling, stopped as if the Astrarium Mysterios anchored him.

'Partway through our symposium he became... confused. Poor being. Accused me of stealing his device, even set his lychguard on me.'

Trazyn reached out a hand. Bombarded the astrarium with his spectrometer. Received the results.

'Of course, I had to defend myself–'

'He's transmuted it!' roared Trazyn. 'You've solved the first puzzle.' He leapt up from his crouch, bounding towards the device.

Orikan shrank back and the executioner reached for Trazyn, but he leapt away, opening his projection, adding his spectromantic data.

'The composition is exactly the same, see? The *exact same.*'

Trazyn snarled as the two component reports joined into one, signalling a one hundred per cent match. 'He's lying to you.'

All heads turned towards Orikan.

He tapped a finger on the astrarium, calculating his next move.

'Oh hell,' he said.

'The Ammunos Dynasty,' Trazyn paused to let the message sink in, 'will not come to claim it.'

The council and executioner stood, stunned at the dire pronouncement.

'But that alone does not confirm your salvage rights, does it?' said Overlord Baalbehk, his voice resonating inside the stasis-casket. He raised his head, the golden sketches of water flowers engraved on his death mask catching the wan light. 'We cannot simply claim anything we find. It is lawless. And there may be other interested parties.'

'What?' said Trazyn, fighting the void-sick feeling in his internals. The blackstone floor rocked like a command barge needing an attitude calibration. He tasted radiation coolant in his mouth.

An interstitial alert – overheating on his right hip. Trazyn looked down to find Orikan's tile glowing white-hot, hissing where it contacted the cold metal of his hip.

'If I may, overlord,' said Orikan, stepping into the centre. 'From my understanding, the Astrarium Mysterios is exempt from the laws of salvage. It is part of the common heritage, owned by all necron kind.'

Overlord Baalbehk nodded. 'As I said, other interested parties.'

'Indeed,' Orikan continued. 'Lord Trazyn has argued quite convincingly that this tomb, should it be found, would be not only a treasure of history but also a path forward for our kind.'

Trazyn stared at the burning tile. It nagged at him. He had seen it before. Images flashed in his mnemonic banks, lighting up his neural cavity with flashes that came and went like sparks from an overloaded power relay. A headdress, power orbs hanging from it like a chandelier. The deep voice of a courtroom orator.

He put a hand to his aching cranium.

The tile burned through its smoking cord and dropped to the floor.

'After all,' said Orikan. 'Why should the Nihilakh control this incredible find? Whoever takes the Astrarium Mysterios should have a chance to seize this once-in-eternity opportunity for power.'

Trazyn felt the illness recede. It was as if the ornament had been pulling him apart, and as it smouldered on the floor, he heard the shouts of assent and excitement from the council members.

Partisans, every one of them, thought Trazyn. They might claim that they fight for necrontyr, for the Infinite Empire, or their own kind, but it was a lie. They wanted power. For their phaerons, for themselves. Ossuaria murdered her brother and nephews. Zuberkar could not feel powerful without conquest. Even the meek High Metallurgist Quellkah had betrayed friends on the way to his position. Graspers, all of them.

And all of them, the fools, thought they would beat Orikan to the tomb. They saw him as an eccentric, half-mad astrologer. But he was so much more dangerous than that.

And Baalbehk, so rabidly loyal to his own dynasty, was the most mercenary. Baalbehk, whom Trazyn had backed as adjudicator simply because Orikan had protested so greatly when the council proposed him. All at once, Trazyn realised he had been tricked. Orikan had wanted that bias. Counted on it working in his favour.

'Very well,' said Baalbehk. 'The Astrarium Mysterios will be owned by all and none, a free object belonging to he who possesses it. Stealing it shall be no crime, killing for it no sin. And whoever opens the crypt may keep its contents for the greater glory of their dynasty.'

Orikan looked at him, grinning, and in his core Trazyn knew the chronomancer had bested him. The ritual tiles swinging from his shoulders radiated heat so bright it reflected off his long steel bones.

And with his mind clearing, Trazyn realised what the chronomancer had done.

So it's war, Diviner, he sent over interstitial message.

If you can catch me, archaeovist.

CHAPTER FIVE

Keph-Re's Proof: *An adept shall not attempt this hex until they have mastered the Ninth Book of Conduction, and successfully channelled powers of up to 77:777 Keph. If so, disjoint the second and third fingers of the right hand at the knuckle, bending them together to form a diamond to concentrate the energy. Of the two outside fingers, snap them backward at the knuckle like eagles' wings to collect the ambient currents. Once captured, the thumb may be thrust forward, like the antennae on a dish, to direct the energy discharge.*

– *Currents of Ruin*, Folio VI, Canto III

Mandragora
9,984 Years Before the Great Awakening

Orange. After six centuries, Orikan was sick of orange. It tinted everything in his astromantic observatory, from the blackstone floor, to the pherro-conductive astrolabes, to the dead oculars of the crypteks – now twenty in number – that knelt around the Astrarium Mysterios in concentric layers of octagons.

Their repetitive chanting of the Eighty-Eight Theorems buzzed in Orikan's auditory transducers, filtered out so it didn't drive him insane.

But the orange light and repetitive chants, much as they annoyed him, were necessary. Zatoth's Harmonious Sphere was a difficult conduction to sustain, especially as a subroutine. It would have taken most of Orikan's neural function to bring it into being, leaving him incapable of analysis. And the orange light it cast – visible no matter the spectrum – was a small nuisance considering it let him conduct his rituals outside the flow of time.

For every century that passed outside the chronostatic field, three inched by within.

Orikan possessed limitless patience for study. Lost himself in it. Let the pursuit define him. Became nothing but programming and thought that worked the problem. He floated on a suspensor field, fingers positioned in the Open Eye of Sut, perception suite dialled back. Soon, the canoptek wraiths and scarab swarms – ordered to replace fluids and cool reactors every six point four years standard – would move in the background as unreal blurs.

He surrendered his physical self. Allowed his consciousness-protocols to slip so his astral-algorithm could go forth from his metal frame.

Many necrons could transfer their consciousness. Even the meanest overlord could scry part of his mind through the ocular systems of his warriors and scarabs, seeing what they saw. Trazyn – Dead Gods burn him – could even transfer his consciousness into new surrogate bodies. Orikan would give ten worlds to know how the archaeovist did that, though he suspected it involved some mean alien artefact rather than personal study. Trazyn was a boor. A clumsy meddler. A mere–

Orikan refocused.

Projection required serenity, a mind clear of the looping subroutines of obsession and anger. Anger, that was his stumbling block. Always there, anger, a spiteful shadow following him to the astral plane. Even when he projected, it tied him to his body. He might lessen it, feel it grow weaker, but fury always stretched out behind him. An umbilical cable tying him to his physical self. He touched it with his astral fingers, lightly, to get a read on its strength.

They should have listened! Bastards. They never–

About normal, then. He was feeling good after his victory over Trazyn. How he'd fooled that hunching sack of mnemonics calling himself an overlord. What was an overlord to Orikan? A being wrapped in the pursuits of the present, heedless of the future.

The anger again. He released, felt himself sink deeper in the autonomic trance.

Not always a bad thing, that anger. In some of his most clandestine experiments, hidden from the eyes of the other cryptek masters, it had even saved him. Snapped him back to his constructed body when the tides of the cosmos threatened to sweep his astral-algorithm out into the vast blackness. A spark whirling up from the fire of existence. Another molecule pressed between the whirring gears of the planets, resigned to the pull of gravitational fields, drifting with the dust of meteor belts and rolling along the curve of space.

The chronostatic field helped with that. Kept him from diffusing. Maintained focus.

Focus. Surrender. *Relax*. Sink deeper.

Listen to the droning metronome of your power plant.

Listen to the droning metronome of your power.

Listen to the droning metronome.

Listen to the droning.

Listen.

Orikan feels it happen. No, not feels. *Knows*. He moves beyond feeling as his essence slips out of his chill body and into the soft womb of the chronostatic field. Floating free, he looks back at his solid form, still floating on the suspensor field. Head back, closed ocular pointing skyward at the stars that glint through the invisible defence field. Stars, worlds and fields of space dust, smearing technicolour across the dark sky.

It has taken six years to achieve this state. And now, the work begins.

First Century

The first hundred years pass in deep study. Orikan drifts through his aetheric library, heedless of time and physical constraint. Disappears into the texts, lives between lines of glyphs as if they are rivers running by him, babbling out their knowledge as they pass.

His consciousness alters – as any consciousness does after consuming new knowledge, learning from long-dead teachers; he is no longer the Orikan who sits floating on Mandragora. The Astral Orikan knows, with some melancholy, that this cannot last. That once uploaded back into the body its systems will reassert themselves and his older personality will return. He will retain the key knowledge, but much will be lost.

Letting that go, he gusts into the works of Numinios, studying his cypheric script in ways a being of metal could not. These are esoteric works, indecipherable to those enclosed in the physical. Orikan rearranges the glyphs, reading them forward, in reverse, drifting through them to see the encoded backsides.

Numinios was a master of transfiguration, able to rework molecules as easily as he'd encoded the secrets in his uncollected works.

Line by line, with a tedium that would frustrate a mortal consciousness, Orikan decrypts the tangled code.

Ninety years of study. Only a small victory. Orikan discerns a theory on the theoretical function of the device. A better understanding of the molecule chains in the metal.

According to Numinios, molecules formed at a certain resonance can be tied to celestial bodies. Keyed to a certain gravitational signature, sensing the overlap and alignment of directional pull, they can change depending on their location in the cosmos.

Trazyn said, Orikan remembers, that certain astrariums opened due to location. And this state change had occurred as he passed through the webway.

Could it be, he thinks, *that this location was in the labyrinth dimension? Did I trigger a state change by pure chance?*

Finally, something to test.

Running a gravitational hex through the networked minds of the crypteks, he aims a gravitational projector at the astrarium, its cradle encircling the puzzle box with graviton rays.

He retrieves the logs from his body's onboard gravitometer, running through the fields he'd passed through on his transit through the webway. Six hundred and forty-seven field configurations.

Orikan sets the graviton ray positions to the first field configuration and fires.

The crypteks' chanting falters. Orange fire blazes behind their oculars.

Graviton beams, bright violet in his astral vision, spill and ripple over the octahedron's surface.

Nothing.

He moves to configuration two. And fires.

On configuration four hundred and seventeen, he sees one angle split. It opens like a mouth, revealing a shine of liquid emerald inside the throat of the astrarium, then snaps tight.

Close. Nearly there.

Four hundred and eighteen does it.

Without sound, but radiating extreme heat, the astrarium begins to change. Its sharp edges fold outward, turning inside out. Angles disappear, faces fold in on themselves. Moving in a way matter should not, grinding, as if it is working against purpose to regress.

The octahedron becomes a pyramid once more. It vibrates in the field.

A cryptek screams, his mouth smoking. To Orikan's dampened perception suite it is no more than a loud breath. Another joins the chorus. Like the pop of firecrackers, one networked neural system fails, then another. They shriek with a pain they should not feel.

Orikan shuts the gravitometer down.

Cryptek heads fall forward, insensate, on steel ribcages.

The astrarium is an octahedron once more, wisps of neon smoke twisting from the glyphs in its surface.

For a bare moment, it projects a name in the smoking air above the device: Vishani.

And a clock: two hundred and sixty-four years, sixteen hours, four seconds.

Three seconds.

Two.

One.

Apparently time is no longer on his side.

Second Century

The trace mercury atoms. The crystal buried deep inside the astrarium. Orikan curses himself for his narrowness of thought, rages at his own leisurely sloth until the spite threatens to yank him back into his rigid body.

Mercury ions. Crystal. Those elements mean only one thing: a mercury-ion trap, a timekeeping device.

Buried inside the Astrarium Mysterios, silently counting the seconds, is an atomic clock.

It will open again in barely over two and a half centuries. Whatever he'd done to it in the webway – whether intended or not – had started a countdown. But the gravitational transmutation suggests that it won't simply open at the appointed time. It has to be in an appointed *place*.

Indeed, it is possible – even likely – that his transit through the webway had unknowingly brought the Mysterios close enough to its first keyed location that it had transmuted – even in the dimensional pocket where he carried it.

Which is impossible. But then again, it is also impossible that outside gravity affects the webway at all.

With this knowledge, Orikan casts his consciousness backward in time, to the beginning of his research. After all, he is a slave of the hourglass now, forced to conduct work under the device's own countdown. If he can make up a century…

Only, he finds it still counting down, not with more time, but *less*. He quickly reverses himself, shooting his consciousness back to the present.

The Mysterios, it seems, has been proofed against chronomancy.

An alert interrupts his studies. Automatic defences detect an incoming meteorite, but spectromantic analysis indicates the object contains living metal. It notifies him of a firing solution.

Greetings, Trazyn, Orikan thinks. *And farewell.*

He does nothing. Merely watches the defence grid blink to active, then broadcast that the foreign object has been destroyed.

Orikan goes back to his studies, looks up to see another alert, noticing that thirteen months have passed since the meteorite was destroyed. This time, it's a meteorite shower. At least thirty objects hurtling towards the atmosphere.

Clearly, the old archaeovist is trying to run the gauntlet, zip from surrogate to surrogate. Good luck to him.

Automated defences count down the number of remaining meteorites from thirty, to fifteen, to two. The surface of the chronostatic sphere ripples like a disturbed pond as the backwash of Mandragora's air defence grid lets loose. Doomsday cannons and death rays lance the reality outside. If mortals had been there, their lungs would've cooked breathing the superheated air.

All targets destroyed.

Orikan dismisses the notice and runs a last decrypt equation on a minor work of Talclus. A rather pedestrian treatise on gridded cryptomantic equations, but necessary background reading nonetheless.

Satisfied at his preparations, he turns to the main object of this research phase.

The Vishanic Manuscripts.

They are gibberish. Lines of trash glyphs without form or reason. Unreadable and obscure, a legend among initiates of the cryptek mysteries.

Rumour has it they hold a great secret, but if that is true Vishani had guarded it well.

She had been Mistress of Secrets and High Cryptomancer to the Ammunos. The greatest occult encoder of her age.

The Vishanic Manuscripts are not difficult because of their encryptions alone. It is their layers of encryption.

Only six crypteks, including Orikan, have ever decrypted the text.

All of their decryptions were different, and all of them were wrong.

Two rendered a list of Ammunos tomb worlds. Three decryptions formed a history of the Ammunos Dynasty – from three different narrators. Orikan's solution, maddeningly, had rendered construction schematics for an impossible ziggurat, one whose structure obeyed only its own warped conception of physics. Load-bearing pillars thin as thread. Heavy materials stacked upon fragile ones. Almost a parody of a building.

Ages ago, Orikan had even built a scale model in holographic chrysoprase, hoping a geomantic analysis of its angles might lead to an algebraic key.

It had not.

Vishani was not brilliant because she'd hidden the solution to her manuscript – she was brilliant because she'd encoded many solutions into the text. Indeed, there were masters of the cryptek mysteries who believed the whole thing a joke – a prank to bedevil and occupy rival dynasties who hoped to learn the secrets of her phaeron.

If it was, she'd miscalculated. Rumour was that during the

War in Heaven, a rival cryptek had imprisoned and tortured her to death in search of the answer. The tale went that she promised to tell him, then when he leaned close to hear her answer, she'd overloaded her reactor, incinerating them both.

Orikan admired the sheer spitefulness of it.

But why, he thinks, *go through all that for a prank?*

Especially when one of the six translations – the second of the dynastic histories – was the only one to mention Nephreth the Untouched.

If the stories are true, if Nephreth lies hidden, it would have been Vishani that spirited him away. And Orikan has no doubt the Astrarium Mysterios is her work. It is too clever, too maddening, to have been made by another.

Orikan works in a white heat. Long obsessed with the Vishanic Manuscripts – and Orikan is, if anything, a being of obsession – he devours the text for hidden meanings.

It is as if he's never read this text before, and nine years into the scouring, he realises he has not. Previously when he'd studied the Vishanic Manuscripts, it had been the hard copy kept in the library of his order, supposedly a direct copy of the one on the Ammunos crownworld of Hashtor – though there had always been doubts about that, given the secretive nature of the Ammunos. It would be just like them to disseminate flawed texts.

Indeed, when Orikan had travelled to Ammunos to salvage what he could, he had hoped to recover an original copy of the manuscripts. To his eternal horror, Trazyn had got there first. Orikan had been forced to acquire a data-copy from their aetheric library.

Yet as he reads, Orikan increasingly notices differences. Word orders switched here or there, variant spellings, formatting differences.

He reviews the Ammunos copy side by side with his own data-copy.

They are not the same.

Vishani was a data-sorceress – an encoder the likes of which the cryptek mystics would never see again. Floating in the aether, surrounded by code.

With a flush of discovery, Orikan realises he's grasped the revelation, the reason why no one could find another layer of encoding in those six decryptions.

The data-copy is the master document. The hard copies they'd worked on for millennia are diversions. The six decryptions were only the first layer of the riddle.

And this decryption of the Ammunos history is so much more than he'd known.

Nephreth was not known as the Untouched simply because his physical form was resistant to the tumours. He was also unmarked in battle, in duels.

Because he was a projectionist. Able through technology and personal focus to cast his mind onto the battlefield as a thoughtform. A being of energy far more powerful than the poor astral-algorithm Orikan has cast. One that did not require a chronostatic field or years of trance preparation.

Think of it, Orikan muses. *The children sitting on the Council hoot and cheer over the prospect of returning to the flesh. We could be so much more. Beings of light and power, the eternal lives of the necron wedded to the souls of the necrontyr. Why return to the ravages of mortality when we could become beings of the aether?*

Orikan dives into the esoteric treatises of Vishani. Works feverishly, staying rooted, overlaying the countdown on his vision so he remembers the object of his searching.

Year after year, Orikan's awe grows. Vishani had been a rare genius. Indeed, were she still operational, Orikan's competitive nature would force him to despise her. Rivalry runs deep among cryptek masters, and he has enough self-knowledge to understand that he is prone to knowledge-jealousy. Yet the dead are no rivals, and he is free to admire the Mistress of Secrets for what she had been.

At least, before she had died so badly.

He spends eighty years meditating over her algebraic poetry. Floats free through her astromantic-maps, admiring the fine detail work of her chrysoprase projections. Devours her treatises on the importance of following an order of operations while casting multilayered quantum shields. At the last, Orikan finds himself shocked speechless that such obvious innovations – the use of a logarithmic spiral in overlapping fields – have not occurred to him.

The Mistress of Secrets had been a polymath of unusual talent and singular vision, if a few eccentricities. The logarithmic spiral, for instance. Its shape appears in her chrysoprase reconstructions of the cosmos, whirling galaxies and sucking black holes making the pattern when in reality they would be far more wild, and as a motif in her collections of algebraic poetry. And it is mentioned six times in the Vishanic Manuscripts themselves.

Wait.

Orikan summons the manuscripts, enters the patterns to access the Nephreth decryption. Lays the glyph-text out on a two-dimensional grid. Rearranges it via the meter Vishani favoured in her algebraic poetry.

And then, astral hand trembling, he sweeps his palm in a circle, stirring the floating glyphs. Chanting the equation for a perfect logarithmic spiral.

Glyphs drift and turn. Fold and shift. Take new places in a spiral labyrinth of pure equations that slowly wheels in front of his disbelieving ocular. Motes of useless data drip from the wheeling arithmystic thoughtform like embers falling from a torch.

'Here rests a phaeron like no other,' one of the kneeling crypteks murmurs.

'Behold! The tomb that holds the one who will end the age of metal,' another drones.

'He lies within,' another answers. 'His incorporeal form lies with eyes open.'

'Nephreth. Nephreth. Nephreth…' They take up the chant. Not a droning rote repetition like the Eighty-Eight Theorems, but an ecstatic ululation steeped in passion and trance-joy. Orikan looks around, sees blue light blazing from the eyes of his sleeping crypteks. Glowing fluid leaks from their oculars and mouths, patters on the blackstone floor.

'Nephreth. Nephreth. Nephreth…'

With a chill, Orikan realises his empty body has joined the chorus.

The wheel of radiant arithmystic glyphs drifts towards the Mysterios, mates with it as if the octahedron were the natural centre of its axis. As they meet, the spiral spins faster and faster, quick as a chariot wheel at first, then rotating with the cutting speed of a circular saw.

Glyphs on the Mysterios pulse with internal power. Beams of energy spear out of every symbol and angle, filling the observation deck with a projection that burns with an astral intensity that Orikan cannot look directly at.

But he knows what it is.

A star map.

Trazyn was known throughout the dynasties for many things – giving up was not one of them.

Even before the transition to metal, his fellows considered him notoriously dogged, even stubborn in his pursuits. But immortality had made him relentless, granting a patience that his frail body of flesh could not tolerate.

Trazyn was not, in other terms, a coward. His power plant held nothing but scorn for those who deserted an endeavour.

But he was willing to admit it when he needed to change his approach.

Mandragora, for instance. He'd exhausted his options on that score. After his endeavour with the meteor shower – a plan that resulted in a rather unpleasant number of disintegrations – he'd abandoned orbital entry.

It was certainly true that the Sautekh were jumped-up warmongers with no sense of culture. A middling dynasty at best, coasting on the strength of a few competent generals. And without doubt, they were far too arrogant for Trazyn's liking.

But they certainly knew how to build an air defence grid.

Sneaking in via the dolmen gate proved similarly fruitless. Five steps past the arch took him into a pack of rather unfriendly canoptek spyders. To ensure he hadn't just been unlucky, he'd tried twice more before realising the swarm lurked around the gate on an endless patrol.

After roughly a century, he'd taken stock. Stepped back and considered his options.

He'd become too consumed with the puzzle of breaking Mandragora's defences and forgotten that the Astrarium Mysterios was a means to an end, not the goal in itself. Become, in essence, the short-sighted buffoon Orikan accused him of being.

Because even more than quitters, Trazyn loathed those who lacked imagination.

Which is why he'd gathered his crypteks in the archive's

reading room – the closest thing to an audience chamber he possessed. They stood around a chest-high table, its sides carved in a turquoise and gold bas-relief depicting the Departure of the Silent King.

Their tireless legs made chairs unnecessary.

'Start with this,' said Trazyn, tapping one finger on the tile he'd collected off Orikan. 'What is its composition?'

Sannet paused, his stylus hovering over his phos-glyph tablet. 'There are limits to what I can say, my lord. Certain mysteries of the cryptek order are inviolate. The punishment for revealing them are quite–'

'Sannet,' Trazyn interrupted. 'You have been to my gallery, yes?'

'I… have.'

'Then you know that I possess every conceivable apparatus of violence? I believe you asked to be excused from cataloguing the drukhari gallery, correct?'

Sannet said nothing.

'To wit, if you truly believe the cryptek masters can devise a punishment more horrid than even the most casual selection out of my gallery, I'm willing to prove you mistaken.'

'It's a time tile,' Sannet blurted. 'When we achieve a certain mastery in a school, we carry tokens of our achievement. The higher the mastery, the longer the chain of tiles.'

'Obviously,' Trazyn tilted his head. 'I am not unfamiliar with the structure of your little cult, Sannet.'

'But they are not merely symbolic,' the cryptek added, pushing his stylus away from him, as if worried he might spontaneously transcribe his own betrayal. 'They're essence-totems, forged from whatever substance our school studies. Khybur over there is a voidmancer, and his tiles are the distilled substance of the gulf between stars. I am – or rather, was – a dimensionalist.' He reverently held up the trail of shimmering purple tiles that swayed from his shoulder. 'These are the blood of the universe, harvested from the wounds created when we tear open dimensional gateways and emblematic of–'

'And this, I assume,' said Trazyn, peering at the tile, 'is time?'

'Correct, my lord. Pure space-time. When we cast our hexes, the power resonates with these totems.'

'Would it still react with its fellows were it in the same room? For example, if I stole one of Khybur's totems and he channelled a black hole, would the tile heat?'

'Oh, indeed,' said Khybur. 'The ambient energy of the hex would react with the tile even if it was not one of mine. It is why crypteks join together in conclaves during battle – the resonance can produce much more powerful hexes. But if it was paired with its fellows it would certainly demonstrate a strong kinship.'

'So if Orikan used chronomancy while I held this totem, it would become hot?'

'Warm,' corrected the voidmancer Khybur. 'To become hot, he would need to have been altering the timeline multiple times. And likely the one holding it would experience ill effects. Mismatched memories. Extreme discomfort.'

'So you're positing he went back more than once?' Trazyn asked.

'You misunderstand, my lord.' Khybur said it gently. 'Chronological manipulation on that scale would not be possible, beyond even the highest practitioners of their school. One trip back takes a great deal of focus and energy. Two, at most. Three–'

'Would be needed to make the totem this hot?' Trazyn

projected a temperature reading saved from his engram banks. 'He is capable, my faithful ones. More capable than anyone expected. Talented enough to foil the council's verdict not one time, but at least three that I can partially recall.' He summoned a projection of the puzzle box. 'And now he has the Mysterios on the crownworld of Mandragora.'

'I have drawn up new formulations for a Mandragora assault,' said Trazyn's tactical-cryptek, Tekk-Nev. 'It is well fortified, as your… reconnaissance discovered.'

'An artful euphemism for repeated atomisation, Tekk-Nev,' Trazyn smiled. 'You shall go far.'

Tekk-Nev ignored the compliment. 'There are no options below a legion-level deployment.'

'Prepare strike packages,' said Trazyn. 'Have the option ready. But I want possibilities beyond direct assault. The Mysterios is merely a map, a means to an end. When Orikan does conclude his research, he'll need to come out of his hole to claim the prize. So how do we find out where he's headed, and how can I counteract his chronomancy once I catch him?'

No one spoke for some time, the whole table working on the problem in quiet cogitation.

'There are,' said Sannet, then stopped to clear his vocal actuators, which had frozen up in the three-year silence. 'There are two artefacts that might assist you.'

'Artefacts?' said Trazyn, scepticism echoing in his vocals. 'I have searched the catalogue six times. There's nothing–'

'Not here on Solemnace, my lord,' smiled Sannet. 'Forgive me, but yours is not the only collection in the galaxy.'

Trazyn considered disassembling the cryptek for his impertinence, but if Sannet had felt able to interrupt him, what he had was clearly good. He nodded for the datamancer to continue.

And when he heard what the being had to say, Trazyn smiled.

It *had*, after all, been too long since his last visit.

The canoptek spyder's identification beam swept over Trazyn's death mask, reading the signature of his systemic aura. Satisfied, it bowed down in reverence and levitated backward and away, leaving the gateway clear.

'Lord Trazyn,' it buzzed, crude vocals static-laced from aeons of disuse. 'Signal my network if you require assistance.'

'Obliged,' said Trazyn, and strode through the graven doorway.

'Before you access the vaults,' continued the spyder, 'I have been instructed to play you the following message.'

A hatch in the floor opened to reveal an orbuculum. A broad-shouldered cryptek guttered into existence, the chrysoprase data partially corrupted so his ghostly, blue-tinged form was missing pieces like an incomplete puzzle.

'Hail, Overlord Trazyn,' said the image, enormous metal beard waggling as it spoke. *'I suspected you might pay us a visit during our slumber.'*

'Transmogrifier Hurakh!' said Trazyn, though he knew the message could not answer. 'Leaving a welcome card, you sentimental thing.'

'It is beyond doubt that you are in your rights to be here. The archaeovist of the Nihilakh, after all, maintains curatorial oversight of the dynasty's vault.'

'Nice of you to say.'

'But these are the vaults of blessed Gheden, not Solemnace. Examine and study what you will, but I have taken inventory of all collections and will notice any absences.'

'The nerve,' said Trazyn, not in the least offended. He walked through the projection and continued into the chamber.

'We remember well the incident on Thelemis,' continued Hurakh, speaking to nothing. *'And charge you on your honour…'*

'Yes, yes,' said Trazyn, leaving the scrambled messenger behind. 'Understood.'

What he was here for, mainly, could not be carried anyway.

The Nihilakh treasure houses constituted fully half of Gheden's subsurface structures. Vast and glittering, they spoke of a dynastic empire of breathtaking scope. As Trazyn walked the Golden Causeway – metal feet reverberating off the shining surface of the raised walkway – he passed doorways overflowing with fine objects and precious metals, the chambers within filled until they became impassable. Artefacts of long-dead civilisations stood heaped in piles, their surfaces dancing with the light of glittering gemstones carelessly tossed beside them. On his left, a full-sized necrontyr barge fashioned from platinum lay shipwrecked upon a pile of rubies, void-silk sails hanging slack in the windless air.

Trazyn hated the display. His fingers twitched with the urge to sort, catalogue and display each object in its proper context. But he knew that, despite appearances, Hurakh had already done so. This disorganised hoard was an act of feigned carelessness, a bit of theatre to overawe visitors with Nihilakh extravagance and abundance. In truth, Hurakh had logged and recorded every coin – could probably even tell you if it was head or tails side up. After all, dynasties did not become wealthy by being careless with their treasure.

Trazyn dimmed his oculars and walked on to the most exclusive vault in Gheden – the Chamber of the Seer.

The great head floated in the centre of a spherical vault. Hoses trailed from the neck like dangling roots, pumping luminous magenta fluid in and out of the decapitated beast's severed neck. It was squat and reptilian, large as a temple, and was purported to be the last of its race – though what that race might be, Trazyn did not know.

The greatest treasure of the Nihilakh.

The Yyth Seer.

He entered it across the beast's tongue, approaching the resonance chamber built into its open mouth. As he crossed, Trazyn saw the great bulging eyes blink once. It came slow, like a cloud passing over the sun. Trazyn told himself it was not alive. Not really. The thought of it being otherwise was too disturbing. The horror of being kept in infinite undeath merely to fulfil a needed role.

Trazyn banished that thought, it being too close for comfort.

A circle of blackstone chairs stood on the seer's mouth, in case the wash of visions made even the hardy bodies of the necrons collapse. A living metal dome stretched above the chairs, forced against the Seer's palate and keeping its jaws open wide.

Trazyn sat and summoned a phos-glyph panel, activating the neurographic resonators that shaped the Seer's visions into holographic images.

'Orikan will find the opening point of the Astrarium Mysterios. I need to know where and when that will happen.'

Trazyn's sensor suite recorded a temperature drop. Feathery crystals of frost formed on the chill metal of his arms and hands. Around him, the huge mouth shifted, the living metal ceiling groaning in protest. In the centre of the circle of chairs, nestled together like a campfire, the neurographic projectors glowed to life. Static electricity prickled Trazyn's arms, snapping and popping as he moved his fingers to discharge it.

Above the imagers, blurred images morphed and changed, came into being then dissipated. Tropical canopy. Coral atolls. A world of blue and green.

He knew it. Recognised it.

'Impossible,' breathed Trazyn.

Trazyn stopped at the artefact gallery on his way out.

The object was right where Sannet had said it would be.

The Timesplinter Cloak, forged from crystallised shards of time itself. An ancient chronomantic artefact that allowed the wearer to see the matrix of the future. Just the thing one needed to shape their destiny – or negate a particularly troublesome time-sorcerer.

'I'm sure Transmogrifier Hurakh would not mind my borrowing it for a spell,' said Trazyn. 'He is, after all, not scheduled to wake for another ten thousand years.'

But just in case, Trazyn activated the security-bypass talisman Sannet had provided.

When I'm done, he promised himself, *I'll simply put it back. Hurakh won't even notice it was gone…*

Trazyn left in a hurry. The security alarms were rather loud.

Mandragora
Sub-Crypt, 3,000 Cubits Below Surface

Orikan checked his hermetic field for the twelfth time. Ran an operational diagnostic. It came back all clear, repelling both outside atoms and data transmissions, setting the chance of failure at less than one in fifty million.

He looked at the abominable being before him and knew that was not good enough. He channelled more power into the field.

'And after the battle,' the thing said, its voice chillingly unlike any necron. Growling, spitting. Rusted. 'Our kind may do what we wish.'

'You may,' said Orikan. 'I will not force you to return.'

Silence. A form moved in the shadow, circling to Orikan's right, the Diviner's perception suite picking up the gleam of ocular light on bladed limbs.

Orikan tried not to look at it, to keep his ocular focused on the twisted being that floated before him. Yet subroutines still tried to calculate whether the aberration on his flank intended to attack.

'It would be a great service to the dynasty,' Orikan said.

'I care nothing for this dynasty,' the thing said. 'But if you provide things, living things, biologicals for us to kill... we will come.'

His objective achieved, Orikan retreated into the tomb's quarantine airlock and watched as the inner door closed and cycled.

Never taking his gaze off the monstrosities that lurked within.

CHAPTER SIX

VISHANI: *Tomorrow, my phaeron, we join our enemies in the dance of war.*

NEPHRETH: *A true soldier does not merely step with his enemy, brilliant Vishani. He calls the dance and sets the beat. And tomorrow, we shall strike up a rhythm such as the foe cannot resist.* [NEPHRETH *raises a command staff.*] *Planetfall awaits, my subjects. Call captains, raise up banners and put steel in your hearts.*

– War in Heaven, Act XIV, Scene II, Lines 14-15

Green running lights hit the atmosphere, swallowed in the hazy yellow-white fire of planetary entry.

Orikan felt his internals lurch, the build-up of superheated air molecules in front of the Ghost Ark slowing the craft from its void speed of thirty thousand cubits per hour. He slowed his chronosense to watch the beauty of it.

The Ghost Ark's ribbed crew bay stood open to the cold of space. Ice crystals colonising the bodies of the Immortals ranked in two lines in front of him evaporated as they slowed. Air molecules built up before the lead Immortals, stealing the speed of the craft and converting the energy to heat. The very atmosphere flared into a glowing shroud around the front of the ark, agitating until the molecules disassociated and became plasma. Scorching the paint off the faces and bodies of those at the front.

They stared forward, heedless of the inferno before and around them, did not even turn their heads as the incandescent air slipped past them in wave trails.

Orikan watched with longing as those gauzy ribbons of air passed. Reached out a hand to run his fingers through the glow.

From matter to energy and back again, he thought. *We should all be so fortunate one day.*

But for that to come to pass, he would need to make planetfall on this world and wipe out anything that stood between him and these coordinates. Establish a landing zone. Secure the target. Execute the ban. Wipe out anything living.

What lived on this planet now was unimportant. For though the savage aeldari Exodites might call it Cepharil, this was a necron world, a frontier planet from the antique empire. Hidden and remote. An ideal hiding place for the tomb complex known as Cephris – stasis-mausoleum of Nephreth the Untouched.

There was no dolmen gate on Cepharil. No webway portal. It was cut off, remote, almost as if the aeldari did not want outsiders to discover it. After the birth of the transcendent hungering thing in the immaterium, Orikan did not blame them.

The flare of atmospheric entry died away, the cool blue of the planet's ocean contrasting with the sizzling orange of the Immortals, their metal bodies heated as if emerging from a furnace. White clouds pinwheeled in storms and hung hazy over continents. As they bore in, Orikan saw the curvature of the planet slip past his peripheral vision, replaced by the iron-hot forms of more Ghost Arks, pulling up in formation.

'A pretty world,' said Orikan, to no one in particular. 'A shame what we're about to do to it.'

'Reconfirm order?' responded the lord helming the ark, his confusion at Orikan's undirected statement clear from his voice. 'Is this a new directive?'

'Disregard. Take us down.'

This, he thought as the ark went nose down, *is why I don't work with others.*

Orikan had found most of his kind dull-witted and obnoxious even in the Flesh Times, and that was before biotransference banished their souls and the Great Sleep scrambled their wits. With time dulling even the sharpest of minds, mere ark helmsmen – despite being a subtype of lord – were nearly intolerable.

He checked his chronometer. Two hours until the Mysterios was scheduled to open. Orikan had planned it that way. A sudden deep strike. Make planetfall a month, a week, even a day in advance and the Exodites might marshal enough resistance to make things difficult.

After all, look at what had happened to Trazyn. True, the Exodites had received an anonymous warning from Orikan, but they had responded with speed.

It did bother him, that fact. Out of the billion worlds in the Infinite Empire, the Mysterios had singled out the world of Cepharil – where Trazyn had pillaged a World Spirit mere centuries before.

The coincidence was so unlikely he'd run the astro-location program nine hundred times to ensure he had not slipped a variable. After all, the map the Mysterios projected was not a modern one. Sixty-five million years had passed since the time of Nephreth. The War in Heaven and reign of the aeldari had reshaped the cosmos in ways small and large. Indeed, even the humans' recent civil war had destroyed and reshaped planets. Yet Orikan had cross-referenced the ancient star map with a modernised one. He'd enlarged the target planet and ran simulations on continental drift, sliding land masses until they formed their current shape.

Near one hundred per cent match. Chance of identification error sat at <0.00003%.

Cephris was Cepharil.

Ghost Arks pulled out of their dive, gravitational forces dragging at the craft so hard the metal of their ribs groaned. They levelled out and tore fifteen cubits over the surface of the ocean, repulsor systems carving wakes in the sapphire water. To his right, one of the arks slapped through the crest of a wave, drenching the occupants with spray that sizzled on their still-hot metal skin.

A mass of clouds appeared on the horizon, growing steadily larger as the ark fleet barrelled towards it. As they closed, Orikan could see the shadowy reflection of land on the underside of the cloud cap. Below, a line of green resolved itself on the horizon.

An island.

Orikan summoned a phos-glyph chart and checked their heading. This was it. The archipelago. Seven thousand small to mid-size islands and atolls, dotting the hemispheric ocean. Trazyn had only visited the largest, the continent-sized mass that served as the Exodites' planetary capital.

Orikan tried to rationalise that. Perhaps it was Trazyn's return from Cepharil that helped activate the Mysterios, when it sensed some organic matter hitchhiking on his frame. Or maybe the gem he brought back, so tied with the world itself, had briefly interfered with the gravitational signature of the room.

None of that made sense, though, and Orikan knew it. As a seer, he knew there were no coincidences, only confluences. Time was a river, one that swept along even the most powerful. Aeons of study let him briefly paddle against the current, but eventually even he must surrender to the pull of fate.

Orikan hated few things more than wasting energy, and to question fate was the most inefficient use of energy he could imagine.

Trees and white beaches, and a line of structures poking through the tropical canopy. Trails of white birds strung out from shore like fluttering banners.

'Count thirty to contact,' buzzed the helmsman from his womb-cockpit, fingers sliding over the control orb. 'Incoming.'

A stream of objects whipped past the ark, singing through the air as they passed. For a nanosecond Orikan thought they'd driven through a flock of birds, but then he saw the blinking from the shoreline and the dazzling streak of a prism beam. The ark to his left rattled and dipped its nose a moment, shuriken the size of dinner plates embedded in its prow struts. Something went spinning towards him and bounced off the hull of Orikan's craft, and he slowed his chronosense to see it was a necron's head, taken clean off by the wicked discs. On the damaged ark, its headless body still stood hunched, bladed arms obediently crossed over its chest in transport position.

A pulse laser streaked by, boiling a hole through the rolling surf.

'Take us under,' Orikan ordered.

His ark went nose down, ramming like a diver into the crystal water. Bubbles fouled his vision before whirling away to stern. Schools of iridescent fish panicked and scattered.

Orikan looked left and right, seeing the arks plough through the inshore waters, driving a school of yellow porpoises before them. Keels scraped the pastel reef, snapping lattice fans and shattering branches of red coral. On the surface, shuriken skipped like rocks, pattering concentric circles of ripples on the water above them. Lasers hit the water and refracted, dissipating their power into starbursts of green that left even the fish unharmed. A prism blast carved a channel in the water, but it could not depress far enough to hit the submerged arks.

They cleared the reef, entered the bay. Saw the sandy bottom rising up underneath them like a ramp.

'Come up firing,' signalled Orikan. 'Artillery first.'

Behind him, two dark shapes broke off, rising towards the surface like cetaceans coming up to breathe. A moment later, a pair of thick red cylinders flashed overhead, carving twin furrows in the water's surface and briefly painting the aquatic world pink. Detonations reverberated through the water in a slapping jolt, and above him a wave swept back the wrong way.

The Doomsday Arks had engaged.

'Surface!' he crowed.

His ark soared upward, the tension of the water stressing his foot locks.

They smashed through the glassy surface and into a world of light, sound and fire. On the shore, a bone redoubt was burned black, its prism cannon cast aside by the explosion and half-buried in sand. Trees along the shore were afire, their canopies curling and dropping away. Among those branches

Orikan could see the charred forms of aeldari sharpshooters, wraithbone rifles fused into clawed hands.

'Clearing the deck,' the helmsman said wryly. 'As they say.'

The ark shuddered with gathering power, and broadside flayer arrays unleashed ancient fury.

Aeldari troops surging onto the shore from the treeline wailed as green lightning stripped them to marrow. Along the beach, a bright lance speared into a Ghost Ark, cooking off its power plant. Necrons, still rigid in the transport position, sailed from it like enormous hunks of shrapnel. They ploughed into sand and splashed down in the water, then were on their feet, pressing the attack.

Necrons... Did these corrupted things even deserve the name?

They scuttled forward, bladed tripod legs digging in the sand for purchase. Arms that had once held command staffs and gauss blasters were now given over to implanted blades. On one, Orikan swore he saw the defaced cartouche of a royal warden.

Once they had been nobility, soldiers, guardians of empire.

Now they were Destroyers, fallen to the madness that drove them to hate all living things. Bodies augmented with chopping blades and double-handed glaives, every angle of their bodies sharp. The skorpekh subtype, obsessed with the whorl of the melee.

They rushed into the aeldari on the shore, wheeling and striking, bodies falling before them. A group of raptor knights burst from the treeline and crashed into the combat, one spearing a skorpekh through the thorax with his wraithbone lance.

The skorpekh squealed in fury and climbed up the lance, shoving the impaling weapon deeper into its own body so the long cleaver blades of its arms could butcher both rider and mount.

Then it chopped the lance away and continued into the trees.

Orikan dismounted, hitting the sand with a whirr of compensating servos that took the impact without a single bended joint. With a conjurer's sweep of the hand, the Staff of Tomorrow translated from the aether.

A tribal warrior in a feather cloak wheeled on him, pirouetting in a leap – firing her shuriken pistol with one leg thrown out in a gymnastic leap. Orikan calculated trajectories and stepped between the incoming missiles. With a thought, he grasped control of a gauss flayer from the ark and repurposed it to strip the warrior to the bone. She'd left the earth a dancer, as graceful as one of the multicoloured birds whose plumage bristled her feather cloak, but she returned to the sand as nothing but a stripped carcass.

His divination matrix warned him of a threat from his blind side, and he swept the staff around, splitting a bone sword in two and blasting its wielder backward into the surf with a discharge of arc lightning. The body convulsed, drowning, until the waves rolled it lifeless back to shore.

By that time, he was halfway to the treeline.

Killing the aeldari felt good. Natural. Immortal foes struggling once more. They were both eternal and perfect, in their own way. But while the necrons were beings forged, the flawless features of the aeldari – no less mask-like than Orikan's own – remained flesh and blood.

But they were still things created. Built and designed by the Old Ones, as much as the necrons were works of the C'tan. Confluence, Orikan reflected, not coincidence. The cosmos is a constructed place.

But he could not become lost in these reveries. Only sixteen minutes left.

This resistance is concerning, Orikan thought, as a Doomsday Ark blasted another tunnel of gore and fire through the enemy ranks. *Did their own astromancers, whatever they were called, see it coming?*

Sixteen minutes to get a mile inland. Orikan could feel the Mysterios sitting heavy in his dimensional pocket – impossible as that was.

A fresh cabal of aeldari warriors charged him, wheeling and dancing. Barbed double-sided spears flashed past, scratching his metal carapace. One found the gaps in his lower thorax armour and sank deep into his cabling.

He formed his hand into the Sigil of Wembi, summoning a chrono-accelerated aura of radiation from his central reactor. The warriors dropped their spears from weakened fingers and fell wailing to the root-tangled sand, rashes breaking out on their tattooed skin and teeth dropping from receding gums.

'I have no time for this,' Orikan sneered. He dislodged the spear from his system guts and tossed it aside, still walking.

Fourteen minutes.

He signalled the two arks of Immortals, their warriors already dismounting into combat.

'Override. Take me inland,' he ordered. 'Keep four Immortals as honour guard.'

Signals crossed in the confusion of battle, two arks responding. One nosed the other away and swept up beside him.

He leapt onto the ark as it passed, mag-locking his hand to the skin of the skimmer as it hovered by.

'Welcome aboard, Master Orikan,' said the addled helmsman. 'Are these the new orders?'

Orikan swore.

The interior of the island was in chaos.

Orikan had needed an army, but one that that would not be missed. Not an easy task. Remove too many warriors from the vaults of Mandragora and he'd risk having to answer questions once the dynasty arose. It might have also tipped his hand to the Awakened Council, which no doubt would be keeping tabs on his movements.

He could get away with raising two phalanxes of Immortals and a few arks, but that was nowhere near enough for this operation.

Which is why he'd brought in the Destroyers. The mad ones. A strike force that would not be missed. A group kept in quarantine and culled at regular intervals so their taint would not spread.

Indeed, he would have to destroy every ark used to transport the killers, to ensure their data had not infected the craft.

The skorpekh Destroyers had hit the beach along with the Immortals, but the heavy Destroyers – the ones who had modified themselves into floating weapons platforms – had slammed down straight through the jungle canopy. Their purpose was to disrupt the aeldari response, to sow chaos and prevent forces massing into coordinated units.

And the Destroyers were doing that work well, drawing enemy reinforcements to engage them rather than reinforce the battle line. Their mad and seemingly randomised orgy of devastation created gaps in the aeldari ranks as they dragged forces to them like iron filings to a magnet.

Orikan could not see the Destroyer complement, but he could see their effect. A searing line of gauss energy sliced through the rainforest ahead of them, felling a tree as neatly as any saw. Through the foliage, he could see the lumbering forms of great lizards headed towards the chaos.

The biodiversity of this world was rich. His ocular analytics tagged new species and novel subtypes wherever he looked.

Deep in his central reactor, Orikan hoped the Destroyers would be wiped out before they could do irreparable damage. Left with no enemy to fight, they would scour this island of life – systematically eradicating first the animals, then the largest trees, and even the microbes. They would not rest until every living organism, from the hanging vines to the insects living on pond surfaces and the seaweed clinging to rocks, was dead.

Then they would move on to the next island.

Orikan shivered. But he had only ten minutes left, and for now, the Destroyers were serving their purpose.

A foot, larger than any Orikan had ever seen, slammed down in front of the ark as they swept around a mountain ridge. Trees collapsed around it, and Orikan leaned back to see an enormous brachiosaur – tall as a pyramidal stasis-tomb – looming above. On its back sat a mobile battle fortress sculpted from bone, bristling with artillery.

The beast's next titanic step swung like a pendulum towards the ark, fated to crush the skeletal craft and throw its crew asunder. He could see the dappled skin incoming, the way jungle parasites had burrowed into the thick leather and made themselves a colony in its scaled flesh.

Orikan centred his mind.

He threw his consciousness backward ten seconds, instructed the helmsman to bank left, and the ark weaved between the beast's colossal legs, its shadow flickering over them.

They swept upward, riding air currents as the trade winds careened against the mountains and surged towards the sky. Dark metal howling past dark rock. A shadow casting a shadow. Orikan watched it pass over the rock and dapple over the shrubs that clung to the surface – this place seemed like paradise but it was like any other, full of dogged desperation.

This range, its green ridges and deep valleys that ran fourteen leagues along the island's crooked spine, was the work of erosion. It appeared as if a giant had formed the range out of clay, then run his fingers through it, gouging out vast furrows.

But this was not so. These great mountains were the work of time and cruel geology – mounded high by a volcanic hotspot that had created the archipelago, then abandoned as the tectonic plate carried the magma eruption further north-west to make new islands. This one had been left to weather through millions of years of wind and rain, moulding its high fastnesses, eroding its proud slopes speck by speck. The lively white streams of the waterfalls nestled in the back of each valley – picturesque though they were – were engaged in an aeons-long act of violence.

Indeed, Orikan detected a nagging worry in the back of his neural matrix.

What was the Mysterios leading him to? If it was a landmark, some temple or pylon, it was entirely possible the structure was gone. The mountain may have retreated beneath it, leaving it loose in its foundations like the teeth of the rad-poisoned aeldari. Perhaps it lay, dislodged and fallen, at the bottom of one of the valleys, buried by volcanic eruption. Sixty-five million years was a long time, even to a necron's reckoning.

No, it was *location* based, not keyed to a building. Orikan was sure of it.

Eight minutes until opening.

Orikan's perception suite painted warnings across his vision. He wheeled, saw spots in the sun. Recalibrating his ocular to filter out the tropical shine, he saw pterosaur riders diving down at him out of the sky. The beasts had their leathery wings back, long heads extended. Their riders lay flat against the dinosaurs, hands twisted in hemp reins and shuriken pistols sprouting from their scrimshawed vambraces.

'Pterosaur riders,' warned one of the Immortals.

Once again, Orikan felt keenly the irritation of being three steps ahead of his fellows. So much repetition.

'Incoming pterosaurs!' added the curdle-brained helmsman, powering up the ark's flayer array.

A step behind, Orikan noted, as usual.

Disassembling beams tore the air, their fountains of lightning almost clear in the island sunlight. The Immortals closed formation, short, disciplined blasts creating a coordinated wall of fire that would catch the riders wherever they wheeled and dived. Double-barrelled gauss blasters shrieked, their tubes dripping condensation as the cold of the gases inside drew water from the humid air.

'Lay counter-evasive fire,' said the lead Immortal. 'Choose quadrant.'

An aeldari warrior dropped from the air, screaming, his pterosaur blown to ash beneath him. He clawed at empty space with his remaining arm as he fell. Two broke off, backing air with their wings and swooping behind one of the ridges to shelter in a deep valley. Another rider wheeled and rolled, diving under the fusillade.

The ark's flayer array howled. But while the Immortals sketched a careful matrix of anti-air fire, the helmsman let loose with an almost gleeful relish, sweeping them back and forth like streams of water from a decorative fountain.

Disassembling beams arced and corkscrewed, chasing the diving rider across the sky, following his loops and rolls. The rider swept in. Its shadow painted Orikan. He could see the beast's claws open, ready to pluck him into the sky like a rodent. Felt the wash of its leathery wings.

They were much bigger up close.

The flayer array snapped-to, and the pterosaur dissolved in air. Its feathery ashes washed over the Diviner.

'Apologies,' said the helmsman, chuckling. 'That one got close, didn't he?'

Orikan turned to reprimand the absurd lord when his triangulation signifier pinged.

'We've arrived on-target,' said the helmsman, his mission programming reasserting itself and driving his voice flat.

And Orikan made the deliberate programming decision to forget the obnoxious pilot, focus on the task at hand.

'Helmsman, key auto-suspension and slumber your neural matrix.'

'Confirm,' the pilot said, head sinking to his chest.

Once, this place might have been a gentle slope. A ridge supporting a mountain fastness, or celestial observatory.

Now it was empty air and sheer rock wall, a slope that must be climbed rather than walked.

No matter.

'Secure perimeter,' he snapped, drawing out the Mysterios.

The Immortals mag-locked their gauss blasters to their backs and leapt onto the rock face, clawed hands and feet digging deep into the volcanic stone. They spread out, spider-like, hacking down foliage with their axe-bayonets to clear fields of fire, and spooling utility cables out from their internals to anchor themselves to the cliff.

Orikan twisted his fingers together, touched fingers to palm, and made Salvar's Dual Invocation. With fierce concentration, he sketched out a circle in the air, drew down the energy of the shining stars, and cast a protective ward around himself – a half-bubble that enclosed the ark he floated on and sealed it against the mountain face, shutting out even the Immortals that guarded him.

The outside world faded. All that stood outside the circle were mere outlines, like in the old shadow-puppet plays the Silent King used to commission for palace children. Perfect quiet. No breeze stirred the plants clinging to the rock. The helmsman, inert, made no move. They would not be disturbed.

One minute until the Mysterios opened. He had done it.

Orikan drew the Mysterios out from his dimensional pocket. He could feel its hum, matching the song sung by the planet itself. Ever since he'd landed, he could sense it. The rhythm of this place. A thrumming sense of belonging. This was a necron world, he could feel it deep in his systems. Confluence. Elements where they were supposed to be.

'What are your secrets, little one?' Orikan asked.

The Mysterios tugged at his hand like a bird wanting to take off. He let it go. It rose in the air, glyphs burning pink. Angles shifted. Faces folded in on themselves and turned inside out. Pink light shifted to amber, spilling out so bright it painted the inner ribs of the Ghost Ark in its radiance. What happened next Orikan could not see, because the shifting puzzle box became so hot and iridescent that it briefly overwhelmed his ocular, blanking it out to white.

That light, he realised, might have killed a being from one of the lesser races. Only a necron would have been able to withstand the deadliness of its shining rays. The same excruciating solar bombardment, he realised, of their home world. The beautiful burn of the necrontyr's sun that had cursed his kind to an eternity of cancerous growth and shortened lives, a legacy that followed them even after they fled its poisoned light.

Orikan felt a catch in his systems. Had he the capacity to weep, he might have done so in that blinded state. This object was ancient and deadly, a piece of the time before. He felt unworthy even to touch it. Sacredness poured from its every fractured angle.

Gradually, his ocular came back online.

The Astrarium Mysterios had changed. His geomantic analysers counted twelve faces, twenty vertices, thirty edges.

A dodecahedron. Perfectly balanced, mathematically exact down to the molecular level. Blue glyphs, their aquamarine the same colour as the planet's oceans, blinked as if making some sort of calculation.

Then, the Mysterios projected a chrysoprase hologram.

A spectral image of Cepharil ballooned around the Mysterios, the whole globe rotating along with the astrarium as if the device were its molten core. Orikan could see the planet's oceans, the continents drifting and realigning, as the Mysterios recalibrated its maps to compensate for sixty-five million years of continental drift. Continents tore apart and collided. Islands erupted and eroded into atolls.

And on one of those islands – the largest, the continent-island – flared a glyph.

Orikan gasped. 'Yes. *Yes.*'

A glyph reading 'Tomb' and 'Nephreth'.

'I've beaten you, Vishani,' he crowed. 'Orikan. Chronomancer Supreme. Greatest of crypteks. Decoder of the Vishanic Manuscripts. I have solved your riddles and unravelled your code. Only I have done this.'

The glyph changed. It displayed a date.

A date over eight thousand years from the current one.

'What?' Orikan's beatific tone fell. 'Another layer? Another chase? Eight thousand years of waiting?'

'How disappointing,' said Trazyn.

Trazyn leaned forward on the command console of the Ghost Ark, the last of the helmsman's features melting into his own form. 'Are you going to tell me the new orders now, Master Orikan?'

It had been great fun, needling the Diviner. Acting the addled pilot. Blasting the ark's flayer array had been particularly entertaining – he really had to get out more, he decided. He'd been in the galleries too long.

'How...'

'Mandragora has superb defences,' said Trazyn. 'But where there is a will, you know. And I have will to spare.'

In addition to will, Trazyn had an infection algorithm that could, properly inserted, lay the groundwork to make almost any necron a temporary surrogate. Well, not *any* necron. An unprepared overlord, certainly. One who had lapsed in their security protocols. Crypteks were often out of reach due to their technomantic defences.

But a mere ark helmsman? Almost too easy. Especially with the Yyth Seer revealing where and when to intercept Orikan's strike force.

And of course, the cloak. He could feel it heating, detecting a chrono-jump in process. A possibility matrix flashed across his neural network just as Orikan's time totems began to heat, and Trazyn picked the future that interrupted the hex.

He rolled his hand over the control orb, rolling the ark ninety degrees so its belly faced the mountainside.

Orikan dropped, feet skidding along the deck, chrono-trance broken. The Diviner grabbed for the hovering Mysterios as he plunged, missed it, and clanged hard off one of the ribbed struts of the ark. He began sliding into space and clawed for purchase, feet dangling thousands of cubits above the valley floor.

'No, I think not, my dear colleague,' said Trazyn, nestled secure in the womb-cockpit. 'I'm afraid your little timeline misadventures will no longer be a part of our rivalry.'

Orikan got purchase, mag-locked. He began to rise to a crouch.

Trazyn slewed the ark back and forth, shaking him like a feline shakes a rodent. Orikan scrambled, barely keeping his grip.

'You may have abilities,' continued Trazyn, inching the ark forward and seizing the Mysterios. 'But I have artefacts. Doubtless, this cloak's powers are a poor echo of what you've achieved through years of study – but it can, at least, countermand your chrono-sorcery. Bad form, by the way, cheating at the trial. Extraordinarily imaginative, but bad form.'

'If you think I need to alter the timeline to destroy you, Trazyn,' Orikan scrambled to his feet, crouching, 'then you're more delusional than I thought. I have glimpsed a future that is unkind for you.'

Orikan swept a hand across the sky, and the dome field disappeared.

Four Immortals looked at Trazyn, their heads rotating nearly front to back.

'Incinerate,' said Orikan.

Trazyn slammed the acceleration glyph.

The ark's keel ploughed into the mountainside, grinding an Immortal to scraps between the living metal hull and the jagged lava rock. The other three clambered aboard, gauss blasters locked to their backs, using all their strength to haul themselves up the hurtling Ghost Ark towards Trazyn.

The Timesplinter Cloak's matrix trilled a warning and Trazyn ducked hard to one side, sliding his fingers along the control orb in a roll. The world spun. Mountain and sky. Ground and sea.

A bolt of aetheric energy streaked by his shoulder, blasting a head-sized chunk of living metal from the ark's curved stern vane. He glanced above the console to see Orikan struggling to maintain his grip, one hand still crackling with electricity.

Trazyn pulled the ark out of the spin, rolling back on the control orb to keep them from diving into the ground. The keel slapped a treetop, exploding it into a cloud of organic debris.

Matrix warnings blared. Trazyn cleared them so he could see.

An Immortal gained his feet, mag-locked and steady. He froze his actuators to maintain a firing position and raised his gauss blaster.

The cloak's matrix calculated interrupt possibilities.

Zero. Trazyn could do nothing.

The gauss emitters on the blaster looked very big when you were staring right into them, Trazyn thought.

The pterosaur hit the Immortal like a meteor, its beak snapping at abdominal cables, claws rending the soldier's living metal. Actuators burst in miniature electrical storms as the beast ripped limbs out of joint.

It must have been one of the two that broke off, Trazyn realised. They'd lurked on the valley ridges until their prey was most vulnerable.

The rider, wild-haired with a network of geometric facial tattoos – circles and lines connecting – unloaded an entire shuriken magazine into a second Immortal. Monofilament discs butchered the soldier, disconnected pieces and gouged systems crackling with emerald lightning. Next to him, Orikan threw up a kinetic shield to halt the incoming storm of shots. Reactor fluid from the slain Immortal spattered his death mask.

Wrenching the mauled Immortal free, the pterosaur rider took off into the sky – gone in an instant.

Trazyn slewed the ark around the mountains, heading away from Orikan's beachhead. With only one Immortal left aboard, and the Diviner, the last thing he needed was to drive himself into another sea of troops. To his right he could see a dazzling array of disassembling beams tearing through the forest. Dancing in the sky. It appeared they were clear-cutting the forest, burning an ever-expanding wound into the island's foliage.

He'd looked too long.

Orikan leapt over the command console, wrestling for the control orb. The ark skidded in air, reversing in a wide arc.

'You brought the tainted here!' Trazyn shouted. They were moving so fast it was hard to hear; the wind stole his words as soon as they left his mouth. He grabbed Orikan's shoulder guard and slammed their heads together in a headbutt that sounded like hammer on anvil. 'Destroyers will scour this place clean. All this unique wildlife. Plant species–'

Orikan summoned the Staff of Tomorrow and chopped down, but wrestling close as they were, the console between them and the wind tearing at the craft, the blow lacked force and speed. Trazyn caught the haft, its field-enveloped head-piece digging only a finger's breadth into his armoured hood.

'It was their price,' said Orikan, reaching for the actuator that opened Trazyn's dimensional pocket. 'This is not their world anyway. It belongs to the Infinite Empire.'

Trazyn saw the Immortal levelling his weapon and spun, throwing Orikan between himself and the shot.

Gauss tubes howled. Green beams danced above their heads. Orikan shrieked and something in him exploded.

The Immortal's command protocols had warned him to pull the shot at the last minute, but too late. He'd merely glanced Orikan rather than holed him. The Diviner's back carapace smouldered, an ashy trench burned through the blue armour. One of the orbs on his crest lay shattered and broken, leaking vapour that scrambled Trazyn's oculars when he looked at it.

'Incompetent!' Orikan threw a hand back and an arc of energy bisected the soldier diagonally. The wind took his top half and it sailed rearward into the jungle canopy.

Trazyn was celebrating when he saw the second Immortal – the one chopped to pieces by the shuriken pistol – reassembling. That was the purpose of a Ghost Ark, after all. To rebuild troops rendered inoperable on the battlefield. Even as he watched, he could see the blue molecular assembly beams spearing out from the top of the ark's ribs, fusing metal and rebuilding layer by layer. A gauss flayer in reverse.

The Immortal raised his weapon.

Orikan grabbed Trazyn's head, and he saw something in the Diviner's eyes flare. A white chemical fire. A light.

His image seemed to judder and blink. Trazyn swore there were two of the Diviner for a moment, as if the astromancer were projecting a hologram. His oculars scrolled through filters, trying to identify what was happening. They landed on one meant for checking power systems.

Orikan burned with energy. No. Orikan *was* energy. His body shone, incandescent, transmuted to an astral form of pure blazing power that was battling to take hold over his necrodermis. To turn his very atoms into pure energy. Heat flares twisted off him like an aura.

'Nephreth!' shouted Orikan. His mouth spewed gusts of solar wind as he spoke. 'The secret is here. On this world. It sings with it.'

Trazyn could not fight this strength. Orikan's astral hands forced his head to the side, bending him over at the hip, pinning his head to the command console well clear of his body. He felt that Orikan might crush him. Heat began cooking his neurals.

'The head,' Orikan ordered the Immortal. 'Take your time.'

The gauss blaster raised.

Trazyn stretched, reaching out, rebuilding his body to elongate his arm and fingers only an inch more. His vision was failing, his ocular lenses beginning to bubble.

'I did not foresee this future, Trazyn,' the Diviner said, 'but it pleases me.'

Trazyn brushed his fingers on the command orb and smiled.

Orikan saw the expression, followed Trazyn's hand to the command orb, looked behind him.

The great saurian loomed like a building, fortress-howdah towering above them, legs thick as temple columns beneath. Its great long neck twisted around, confused at the oncoming object.

Trazyn disconnected the helmsman's cable, disengaged his mag-locks and let the wind fling him astern.

The Ghost Ark hit the saurian at four hundred cubits per hour, ramming right through the thick cage of bone armour and punching through its ribs. Flesh rippled from the impact and aeldari tumbled from its back.

A great creature, the largest of its kind, venerated and feared.

It died instantaneously, heart ruptured. The great temple-column legs went loose and it toppled sideways from the kinetic force of the hit, splintering trees and clearing a hole in the forest with its fall. One titanic leg kicked in a death spasm and demolished a stone temple, an incident the aeldari would take as an even worse omen than the great creature's death.

Across the island, scavengers would scent the enormous quantity of blood on the wind, and embark on carrion migrations to take advantage of the windfall. Whole colonies of carnivorous mosses would colonise the body of the great saurian, and the lizards that ate those mosses – and the hook-beaked birds that ate the lizards – would form their own societies there, until the body was nothing but unusable bone.

Civilisations, after all, always build on the dead.

Orikan foresaw this and cared nothing for it as he crawled from the beast's ruptured chest cavity.

Covered in gore, injuries sparking, he turned his mangled head towards the sky.

Trazyn was out there, no doubt. His escape already made good.

But that didn't matter.

For Orikan had unlocked a great secret within himself.

Orikan had transmuted to an energy form before. Indeed, it was a well-known practice of the plasmancer order. One able to take on the energy form could walk through closed gates and overload machinery. Channelling ambient power sources into their metal form, they could become nigh invulnerable for minutes at a time.

Some drew that power from solar radiation or by tapping external reactor cores. Orikan, his gaze always upon the stars, drew on the directed energy of planetary alignments.

But this, this had been greater than that. He had sensed so much power surging past him, bombarding him, that his unprepared mind and body could only channel a small part. Had he tried, it would have torn him apart at the molecular level.

Yet he had captured more than he'd expected.

All his reading and studying – the esoteric texts and theoretical works, the very words of Vishani – had imparted a gift without his knowledge.

Whether by stars or planets, geography or arcane wisdom, Orikan had briefly become transmuted like the Mysterios. Ethereal and empowered, like the fabled Nephreth. He had become transcendent. One of the gods. Like the C'tan.

Orikan reached inside himself, finding the wet warmth of his reactor leak. The glowing jade fluid coated his hand, and he used it to paint a sigil on his forehead crest.

And he made an ancient oath, one from a long-ago home world where his kind had been flesh, not metal. Back in those centuries, the oath would have been taken with blood, but now he took it with a substance more deadly and enduring.

'I swear,' he said, his vocal actuators grinding, 'by the killing sun. By the stars and dust. By my ancestors and the progeny. I swear to harness these powers and open the tomb of Nephreth.'

The sky was growing dark. He could see the stars.

'But first,' said Orikan, 'I swear to destroy Trazyn the Infinite.'

ACT TWO: SETTLEMENT

Listen, noble children, for this is how our world began.

Twenty-three months in the warp they sailed, buffeted by storms of unreality, fearing daemons, praying to the Throne and the Saints for deliverance. Seven months they lived on half-rations.

They exited the warp on Saint Madrigal's Day, praying to Blessed Madrigal and the God-Emperor for safe harbour.

And yea, before them was the planet, with its deep oceans and rich soil. An empty world, untouched by the hated xenos. A planet clean, new and empty. Made safe and abundant for human habitation through the will of the most magnanimous God-Emperor.

In thanks to the saint, they christened it Madrigal's Deliverance.

However, sixty-seven years after settlement, the first settlers received an astropathic dispatch that this Application for Planetary Christening had been denied, for nineteen other settled worlds had already registered under variations of that name. But the first settlers were undaunted, for the planet was already known popularly by another name.

They called the world Serenade, for it sang to them.

– *Chronicles of the Settlement [Serenade]*,
Unknown Author, circa M33

CHAPTER ONE

'They are insects – but insects can sting.'

– *Humanity: A Tactical Treatise,*
Nemesor Iontekh

Solemnace
7,036 Years Until Next Astrarium Opening

Trazyn stepped back to look at his work.

After two centuries, it was nearly finished – at least, as far as anything on Solemnace was finished. There were always new relics to acquire. Anachronistic items and reproductions – stand-ins for artefacts or persons – to be replaced once the genuine specimen was found.

But barring replacements and future renovations, the Horus Heresy gallery was ready for visitors. At least, if Trazyn decided to have any once enough of his kind awoke to see his work.

Or awoke with minds intact enough to understand it.

He'd left the largest display for last – and it was a masterpiece. Larger than any other in the gallery.

Isstvan V had provided a rare opportunity to collect specimens. Regrettably unable to make the battle itself, even decades later there had been artefacts lying around unrecovered. Unusual for Astartes battlefields, but Isstvan V had been unusual in many ways – including the number of Space Marines missing in action.

Well, missing to the Imperium. Not to Trazyn. He knew exactly where they were. Knew the posture and pose of each soldier and the direction of their eyeline. Even now, he stepped into the display to adjust a ceramite-plated finger. The Salamanders, after all, practised good weapons discipline. An Astartes like this one, with his back against a wall, shouting to his brothers to throw him another magazine, would not have a finger on the trigger.

One small part in a tableau that measured sixteen leagues square. But the details were so very important to communicating authenticity – particularly if one had to cut corners here and there. Trazyn was, after all, a practical being. If he became hung up on every piece being authentic, he would never finish anything.

In general, Trazyn had not been much interested in humans. He collected them, of course, he collected everything. But he considered them on the same level as orks, or various kinds of carnivorous algae. Their spread across the cosmos had destroyed so many more interesting civilisations, and since the rise of the Emperor their culture had an utter sameness that bored him. If Trazyn cared about the mere ability to propagate and spread, he'd spend his eternity collecting bacteria. Just because a thing was successful and ubiquitous did not make it fascinating – it just made it common.

But the Heresy changed all that. Before it was all colonisation and settlement. This, this was history, this was *drama*. Betrayal. Struggle. Brother fighting brother across the gulf of the stars. Empires rising and falling, heroes and rebels.

He'd collected so much that he'd begun to worry he'd gone overboard. Especially since it hadn't stopped. Centuries out from the Siege of Terra, and he'd continued snatching up human artefacts wherever he could. Now he not only had specimens, and spare specimens, but spares of spares.

And this nomadic existence, these centuries of travel, also helped keep the Astrarium Mysterios secure.

He didn't trust the security on Solemnace, even after tightening the protocols. Orikan had broken in before. But if Trazyn kept on the move, that seemed sufficient to foil Orikan's divinations. Or at least, he had not tried for the last millennium.

A reprieve for which Trazyn was grateful. The Heresy, after all, demanded his full attention. He even had plans to add a grand tableau of the Battle of Calth – Macragge was not far from Solemnace, giving him easy access to Ultramarines material – and perhaps even the confrontation aboard the *Vengeful Spirit*. Horus' body was likely being venerated somewhere in the Eye of Terror, after all, and the Emperor was just sitting there on Terra. Seemed a waste, such a historic figure left to rot like that. Trazyn could do a far better job at preservation and restoration.

The humans probably wouldn't agree.

He heard something move, stepped away from his diorama.

'Sannet?' He ran a systemic scry of the chamber. No signatures detected.

A shadow darted between display plinths. The Hall of Armaments.

Trazyn summoned his obliterator and walked through the wide doorway of the hall.

Plinths rose like a stubby forest, stasis fields glowing off-white in his enhanced oculars.

'Sannet?' he said. 'Identify.'

Nothing. He sidled his back against a plinth containing a long frostblade – Fenris-pattern, its beaten edge nicked and scratched. Hard to classify, that sword. The hilt was Crusade-era, decorated with kraken teeth, but the blade itself dated from much earlier.

Another image flitted between plinths. This time, Trazyn caught the comet-blur of its energy trail.

'Come out, coward,' Trazyn growled.

The hands came through the plinth behind him, the cascading power that blazed from each fingertip tickling him with thread-thin bursts of lightning before they grabbed him and pinned him down.

His arms went numb at the touch. He dropped his empathic obliterator. A blast of energy sent it barrelling across the gallery.

Trazyn heard it clank to the floor far off, in darkness.

A head materialised through the plinth, twisting around so its jagged mouth spoke directly to his ear.

Hail, Trazyn of Sssolemnace, said Orikan the Diviner, his words crackling and hissing like a severed power cable. *I sss-see you have been playing with your t-toys. A nice disssplay. Ssshall I leave it int-tact? Give me what I wish, and it ssshall be done.*

Trazyn felt the blazing hand drop to his waist and open his dimensional pocket. It drew out the Mysterios, yellow sparks spitting from where it contacted the black metal.

'I'll only take it back, you know,' Trazyn responded. 'It will be a merry chase.'

I think n-not. You see, I have cast the zodiac on every permutation of–

Trazyn's hand plunged into the stasis field, gripping the Fenrisian blade just above the tip. It cut his fingers, but pain was nothing to him.

He ripped it from the howling field and raked the tip across the Diviner's pulsating face.

Orikan howled, snapped backward through the pillar.

The Mysterios, unable to travel through solid metal, fell to the blackstone floor.

Trazyn wheeled, holding the ancient weapon in two hands, feeling its power thrum through him. An ordinary blade would not have harmed an energy being, but Trazyn did not collect ordinary things.

A flash. Orikan streaked at him. A lightning strike given form, arcane gales howling about him. His star-shaped staff sliced an arc that threatened to bisect Trazyn at the middle.

Trazyn parried with the ancient blade, watching it absorb the crackling electricity of the blow, then swept it upward to rip through the energy ghost. It met resistance, as if the thing he struck were made of flesh and bone rather than an animate storm.

Orikan howled and retreated, disappearing into a pillar.

Trazyn spun, trying to cover every angle. He consulted the Timesplinter Cloak's possibility matrix.

I will burn your oculars, the voice echoed. *I have sworn the blood feud.*

'Then come do it,' said Trazyn.

A crackle from the Isstvan display. Trazyn set his footing to meet the charge and brought his guard high for a killing strike.

The blazing sparks leapt towards him, plinth to plinth, running through the power systems like a fuse burning towards an explosive. Each plinth he passed fizzled and sparked, stasis fields blowing out. Priceless relics tumbled to the blackstone, their repulsor fields shorting. An entire rack of Astartes helmets – nearly one from each Legion – crashed in a heap and rolled across the floor.

Trazyn tensed. Calculated the timing of his strike. The blade would have one last victim.

And, in his peripheral sensors, he saw the glowing hands come up through the floor. Saw them seize the Mysterios and disappear into a dimensional pocket.

And all that remained of Orikan was his mocking laughter.

Serenade
5,821 Years Until Next Astrarium Opening

Orikan had not experienced hunger in so long, but he was ravenous.

Planetary alignment was the key. The stars needed to be right. Star positioning and cosmic alignment, the lines of the universe collecting and directing power in a way that he could channel it through himself, if only briefly.

The first time it happened on Serenade – no, he reminded himself, that was the human name, it was called Cepharil then – the experience had taken him by surprise. Only a few seconds of escaping the physical, of unleashing what Orikan now considered his true form.

Indeed, it had frightened him. And that his first reaction to this liberation was fear told him more about the prison of his body than he'd learned from whole libraries of study. How deeply had the C'tan warped them that he was afraid to let go of this constricting, rigid form? How terrible and joyous it was, to once again have a soul.

After he'd climbed out of that saurian body cavity, reborn and slicked in blood, all he'd wanted was for it to happen again.

Three centuries he tried without success. He had time, though. Internal auguries told him that transcendence was the key to recapturing the Mysterios. Master the transmutation of the energy form, and he would master the physical barrier of Trazyn.

Study. Meditation. Experimentation. Trance.

He cast zodiacs and chronoscopes. Tracked the celestial bodies. Ran permutations and simulations where he moved the constellations like gears, with Cepharil or Mandragora as the centre. Vega rising in the domicile of Thuselah the Cryptek. Kasteph the Phaeron in opposition to the Hydra's Teeth. The Master Star, Rega, transiting the eleventh house in retrograde.

And he marked the dates and locations when the stars would be right.

During the first alignment, he'd failed. His absorption aura broke down under the radioactive assault of the cosmic rays. Two and a half centuries more study. More waiting.

He'd held the energy form for over a minute on the second attempt. Like those air molecules before the Ghost Ark, his atoms superheated until they broke down into pure energy and heat, and remained incandescent until he lost control and re-solidified.

Transmutation was not like being an astral program. During that trance-operation, he projected his astral algorithm out into space, his consciousness floating free from his own body.

When he transmuted, his body *became* energy. And the stronger the power surge, the greater his power.

And with the right celestial alignment, he could become very powerful indeed. But finding the right time and place required precise calculation, planning – and patience.

The infiltration on Solemnace had been only a moderate alignment – one that turned him to a ghost, not a god – but it was perfectly timed for a raid. The auguries were good. Divination charts predicted success.

And now, he had the Mysterios – and was unlocking its secrets.

The cool blue sphere of Serenade floated outside the observatory window of his personal craft, *Zodiac's Fury*. One section on the largest continent, he noticed, stood out brown-black like a tumour. It was the size of his thumb if he extended his hand, and dirty smoke came from it, wrapping the planet like a foul girdle.

Pity. But it would not hurt anything of consequence. Organic life was such a temporary thing.

Inside the meditation chamber, the Mysterios floated in alignment with the planet.

Orikan felt the device worked better here. Indeed, it seemed to *want* to be here.

Was it eccentric, he asked himself, to ascribe wants and needs to an inanimate object? Orikan thought not. By certain measures, a scarab was inanimate. So was a tomb wraith. A human cogitator. A string instrument. Yet they all had needs, optimal operating environments.

Or maybe, just maybe, it was more than that.

Orikan approached the device, adjusting the gravitational signature to match Serenade. Dialled up the temperature and humidity to match the surface, to fool it into thinking it did not sit in the dry chill of a necron vessel.

The surface was… risky. Humans had infested the planet, as they will. Too many eyes. He had not been down in centuries apart from short expeditionary studies. Orbit, however, was another matter.

Here he could study the Mysterios in safety.

Cool metal and angles. Vertices and glyphs. Could such perfection ever be mindless? Orikan suspected not. During his centuries, he'd dissected and reverse-engineered many machines, and knew that you could not study a technology without, in some way, connecting with the mind of its creator. Devices were an expression of their maker's mind as much as any song or poem – and he had come to know Vishani.

But he had never seen her until this moment.

The first time she came to him, it was in his meditations. This was not unusual. A cryptek's mind was a deep thing, and it was easy to inadvertently create thoughtforms resembling old masters or colleagues. Indeed, Orikan had engaged in deep discourses with those long-dead – or rather, had held great conversations with his engrammatic impressions of them. A good cryptek knew to be wary of such things. Let them run free, and fantasy could take over from simulation. A hard master, lavishing you with praise. Debate opponents giving into arguments too easily, admitting their stupidities and naming you their better.

And, of course, it could mean that one was going mad.

So when Vishani came, Orikan was both delighted and sceptical. He kept her at arm's length. At first, she was a mere echo, couplets from her algorithmic poetry repeating in his mind. Data points from her treatises running, unprompted, through Orikan's logic processor.

Then one day, she spoke. One word.

'No.'

He'd stopped mid-calculation. Reviewed his logic chain and discovered an error, a single angle of the Mysterios, encoded in his algorithm as obtuse rather than acute. A major error that would've queered his star chart and fouled decades of calculations.

And he sensed her, hovering at the very edge of his perception suite. Not a physical form, there was nothing to see, but a presence. As he continued his centuries of work, the thoughtform would occasionally make itself known, suggesting, nudging.

Orikan was not so absurd to think it was really Vishani. Merely a subconscious logic routine projecting itself as external, providing a guide and sounding board, taking on a voice he respected – and Orikan respected so few voices.

They pleased him, these visitations. Whatever this logic routine was – and it must be buried deep, since he could not find or isolate it – it had rare insight into the device's operation. Perhaps the portion of his engrams building a dataset on Vishani had even gained low-level sentience, at the level of a canoptek wraith.

Or, and his sensors prickled at this thought, perhaps Vishani had inserted a portion of her own personality algorithm into the device, and he'd acquired it over the centuries. He had certainly opened his own neural network to it when casting Ralak's Grid of Investigation.

Which might explain why, in the Dead Gods' name, she was standing behind his right shoulder now.

He moved his head slowly, ocular ratcheted to maximum in case she dissolved when he looked directly at her. If it was a manifestation of his own consciousness, it was a strange one, since Orikan had no basis for reconstructing what Vishani would've looked like.

If Orikan had breath, it would have caught.

Such handiwork.

Vishani's body was modified. Efficient. A masterwork of astro-engineering. Reshaped, in a bizarre way, almost as radically as a Destroyer. But while those abominations rebuilt their bodies with the single-minded goal to exterminate, Vishani had reconfigured herself to acquire and analyse.

She was a palace built of knowledge.

The datamancer had a long cranium capped by a many-cabled headdress, its cylinders hanging in a perfect box around her monocular in the front. In the back, they trailed long to plug into the databank behind. And that databank was what was so striking – her legs had been removed entirely, her torso installed into a great lobster-like tail that held racked engram blades and logic tablets. Ten crustacean-like legs bore the weight of the extra capacity.

Then, just as he was able to make her out, she spoke.

'He's here.'

Orikan's ocular snapped open. He dropped from his hovering trance position to the deck, one hand forming a low-hunched tripod.

Nothing moved. The Mysterios rotated silently in the air. Dozens of crypteks knelt in a pentagram pattern, the five-sided formation matching each flat face of the twelve-sided Mysterios. Hands crossed over their chests, heads down, murmuring esoteric code.

So many minds, Orikan realised, for Trazyn to infiltrate.

He stepped forward, scrying the group with his ocular and sensor suite. Quietly twisting his left hand to cast a hex-algorithm that would jump from cryptek to cryptek, scouring their neural networks for intrusion.

One cryptek was out of step. Hesitating. Speaking the data-chain as if, instead of it running through his processing node, he were reading it from the surface thoughts of another.

Orikan passed him, staring into the oculars of the cryptek next to him. Cocking his head, sending out a visible scry-beam as if inspecting its data flow.

Fast as a viper, he grasped the tardy cryptek's throat. Lifted him up into the air. Caring not about striking a blow with his staff, he manifested the weapon with the haft phasing into reality halfway through the hanging necron's vitals.

'Inept as ever, Trazyn,' he cackled, twisting the staff to pro-voke deeper systemic damage. 'Your puerile games of dress-up are unconvincing at the best of times, but thinking you could mimic one initiated into the technomantic mysteries was arrogant even by your high standard. A being cannot imper-sonate what it cannot understand.'

'No,' said Trazyn. 'That's why I used a decoy.'

He was standing by the observatory window, the Myste-rios in his hand. He tossed and caught it once, then winked and levelled the other hand towards Orikan as if it were a pistol. For a moment, that's what it appeared to be – merely an insulting gesture, one finger out, thumb cocked like a hammer. Then Orikan saw the detonator.

Behind Trazyn, an implosive scarab scampered up the crys-tal field and clamped to the surface, rune indicators green. The haughty bastard was going to blow himself into space – the fastest exit.

Orikan dialled back his chronosense, slowed time to a near stop. Saw the long thumb descending.

He did not throw the Staff of Tomorrow. Nothing thrown could achieve the velocities the staff did as it sailed headpiece first across the meditation chamber. Had it happened on the planet below it would have broken the sonic barrier, sending an echoing crack across the entire chamber. But there was no atmosphere on a necron tomb ship to compress – ten thousand souls aboard, and not one had lungs. Instead it merely streaked across the chamber, straight and fast as a las-bolt.

It passed seventeen microns above the trigger button and severed Trazyn's thumb, the disconnected digit spinning upward as the staff continued into the archaeovist's chest cavity, shattering the Nihilakh ankh on his sternum. Metal ribs, tinted royal aquamarine, tore and parted before the glowing emerald of the staff's headpiece. Vital systems smashed and reactor fluid sizzled on the weapon's ultra-cold power field. Trazyn folded, the blade striking his spine and snapping him further into his eternal hunch.

The archaeovist fell to his knees, hands opening to spill the detonator and Mysterios.

Orikan scooped up the Mysterios with one hand and grabbed the staff with the other, driving it deep into his rival. He would start to phase any time, reforged on Solemnace or hopping to one of those damned surrogates of his.

Before that happened, Orikan wanted him to feel every moment of his humiliation. He sent a pulse of pure time-space through the staff, slowing the injuries, making Trazyn *feel* it.

'You are a poor guest, Trazyn,' he wheedled. 'Not much has changed, I see. Whenever you dined at the palace, I always told the phaeron to count the dinnerware afterwards.'

'But like...' Trazyn struggled to talk. Reactor fluid, boiling yellow, was leaking from between his steel teeth. '...a good guest...' His voice dissolved in a hack-purge routine.

'A good guest?' Orikan twisted the staff deeper to halt any repair protocols. 'No. A good guest brings good conversation. And you are so quiet now, Trazyn. Why ever would that be?'

'Good... guests...' said Trazyn, smiling, 'bring... gifts.'

Then he phased, spots of incandescent jade light breaking out on him like sores. Sores that unmade him, widening to reveal nothing inside their expanding borders but the crystal window and decking behind.

In an instant, he was gone. Back to a new body.

'Gifts?' said Orikan.

He crouched over the Mysterios, examining its sides, measuring it.

It was wrong. Trazyn had destabilised it. The glyphs were all a match, the angles and faces correct, but it was missing a vibration, that sense of confluence.

One of the sides sprung open. An intricate hatchway that Orikan had never seen spilled prismatic light.

He leaned to look into it.

They were on him immediately, writhing and biting, legs scouring trenches in his armoured body, mandibles digging deep into the living metal of his head and arms. He tried to beat them away, but they snapped and swallowed his fingers.

Orikan said the Word of Pharos, blue flame leaping from his body, and finally the creatures retreated to the shadows, scrabbling into ducts and scarab hatches.

Sparking, wounded, Orikan looked into what he'd thought was the Mysterios.

A disguised tesseract vault. The kind Trazyn used for his samples.

And next to it, a necrodermis-sheet letter that had ejected from the device, along with the creatures. It bore the marks of alien mandibles, but was still legible.

Greetings, Orikan! it began. *I apologise for having to borrow back my astrarium. I know how deeply you appreciated it, but you work too hard, my astromancer. Consider this a relaxing break. And what is more relaxing than a hunt?*

Orikan heard legs scraping in the scarab vents. Interstitial messages alerted him that a scarab swarm and two wraiths were reporting in as inoperable.

These creatures will make fine quarry. They're from an Imperial jungle planet, and so famous that the locals named their local regiment after them. Highly venomous – not that it would bother you, dear colleague – and can grow to over fifteen khut long when they reach maturity. But the real challenge is how quick they breed. In fact, if you want my advice, I would start the pursuit quickly. Fourteen juveniles were in this particular gift. Or was it sixteen? Anyway, within twelve hours the population will have established roving kin groups to place their eggs. Did I forget to mention the eggs? Half of the breeding pairs already have sacs. The population will double in less than twenty-four hours, provided they don't eat too many of the young. Happy hunting!

Serenade
2,007 Years Until Next Astrarium Opening

Trazyn did not like hunting necrons.

He was no stranger to dynastic wars. Before biotransference, the dynasties had fought each other in vicious succession wars and blood feuds. His culture built whole rituals, religious and civil, prescribing the proper method of waging war against one's own kind. And Trazyn had been on the gory fields of those battles – as an observer, not a combatant, but still.

And there were some of his kind Trazyn would gladly kill. A certain astrology-addled, plate-faced stargazer, for example.

Yet this was different. This was extermination.

The aeldari had vanished. Slain or fled, Trazyn did not know, but he suspected both. Their World Spirit destroyed, they would've had cause to run, and on arrival his orbital scryers had detected the ruined structure of a webway portal constructed from immense saurian bones. Orikan had, in a way, been right. The Exodites had lived here, but it was not their home world. They were refugees fleeing a thirsting god, and finding this planet no longer safe, they'd struck camp and moved on.

The humans he'd captured – merely for interrogation, not acquisition – had little idea that the aeldari had ever been there. Clad in feather cloaks and Imperial bodygloves, they told Trazyn fantastical stories about a primordial past, when the Emperor and His angels had called this world home. The Emperor Himself had called the great structures from the earth, growing them from the planet itself. They looked strange, yes, but many things from that otherworldly age would look strange to us now. And so, they set statues of Imperial saints in the niches of aeldari houses and weathervanes, believing them temples raised by the withered god-king of Terra. Their manuscripts, while rare, showed an altered calligraphic style that was decidedly rune-like, no doubt copied from what script remained on the buildings.

Once, Trazyn had seen a chapel of Saint Eustice-of-the-Void outfitted in a scallop shell outbuilding, Imperial symbols epoxied over the doorways because the settlers' nails could not penetrate the bone.

The building, Trazyn realised, had been a sewage processing station.

But these stories – the odd feather cloaks and the deviant calligraphic script – were not his concern.

He wanted to know about the metal men.

Orikan had unleashed one hundred and twelve Destroyers. Why that number, Trazyn did not know, but he assumed it was some numerological nonsense that, no doubt, the Diviner found extremely significant.

Trazyn had seen evidence of them on his previous site surveys. He liked to check in briefly on Cepharil – or Serenade, whatever they called it – to take readings in preparation for the opening. Have his angles covered. His return visit to the previous opening location was disheartening in the extreme.

It was barren rock. Scoured of life down to its volcanic soil.

Destroyers started with the apex predators and worked their way down. The aeldari first, then the saurians, then the large carnivores. Anything below that was no threat to them, so they switched to the bottom of the food chain. Clear-cut the plant life, vaporising trees and ground-covering plants with great fan-arcs from their gauss blasters. Boiled the lakes and streams so no fresh water remained. They were mathematically thorough, ensuring no habitat or food source remained for the insects. Once the insects disappeared, the small amphibians and reptiles went within a few years, growing skeletal and desperate, until their leathery skins lay on the bare earth. A sad bag for brittle bones.

These too the Destroyers atomised, because they knew that death could bring new life. Indeed, it had taken them several decades to sterilise that first island, since the twenty-one Destroyers remaining – many fell in combat with the aeldari or the great saurians – frequently had to double back and eradicate regrowth.

It was their thoroughness, Trazyn reflected, that had kept them from scouring the whole planet. They killed all organisms down to the microbes before moving on, and life was tenacious in this verdant archipelago. The geography, too, worked against them. On a great continent, their tactics could easily lead to wide-scale environmental collapse, the effects radiating outward as species migrated and fires spread. On an island, the damage was contained.

But four thousand five hundred years was a long time, even to a necron. And in that time the Destroyers had migrated along the archipelago, heading south-west towards the mega-continent that covered the other hemisphere. Over three millennia they'd scoured two thousand of the archipelago's ten thousand islands clean. Most were uninhabited by sentient life, and what habitants they had – aeldari, then human – did occasionally take one down.

There were only twelve remaining when they reached the mainland.

And the true slaughter began.

The mega-continent was in environmental collapse. Indeed, most humans had chosen to settle on the islands – the seat of Imperial power such as it was – partially due to the rumours of evil creatures living on the mainland. This was a frontier continent on a frontier world. Wild and untamed.

Or what was left of it. The saurians were gone. Smaller specimens remained, but the ecosystem could no longer support such large creatures. Trazyn looked up to see the sun filtered through the veil of smoke that wreathed the world. It was from burning rainforest.

He'd tracked them for six years. Difficult, since the volcanic soil befouled his sensors. Objects under the surface could not be detected at all, and he suspected that it was not just the vast gulfs of space that made translations difficult on Serenade. Transportation had to be done by Night Scythe, Ghost Ark, or on foot. His few survey explorations into the cave system suggested that if a necron died beneath the surface, they could not be phased back to the tomb worlds for repair.

He'd been chasing a nomad's story about evil spirits when he found them.

There were three of them. At least, fully operative. A fourth Trazyn had found a hundred leagues behind, his repulsor array torn from his body in a long-ago battle. Still, he pulled his legless form across the scorched dirt, blasting insects to ash with his malfunctioning gauss cannon. Pulverising worms with his deathless hands.

Trazyn had decapitated the Destroyer with a single disgusted blow from his obliterator, then continued hammering. He thought about the feather cloak he'd brought back from his first visit to this planet. How it shimmered with cerulean, turquoise, gold and vermillion when he adjusted the light. He thought about what the birds who produced such feathers – birds he'd wanted to collect in a frozen aviary – would have looked like in a display. As he'd travelled this continent, the cloaks had got shorter and shorter. Siblings cannibalised their parents' cloaks to make their own because the birds now only existed in the high mountains.

Trazyn tossed the head of the decapitated Destroyer at the remaining trio. It bounced off the thorax carapace of the leader and came to rest in front of them, viridian smoke still leaking from its mouth.

Their gauss cannons, dripping neon condensate from overuse, stopped firing.

They pivoted.

'Hail,' said Trazyn. 'To whom do I speak?'

The Destroyers buzzed and crackled, their vocal actuators trying to remember how to form words.

'I am Lord Ket-vah of the Lokhust,' said the one in the centre. 'You have slain one of my servants.'

'Yes.'

'Good. He was inefficient. Suboptimal. He no longer embodied the ideal of annihilation. All life must end, including ours. To cease to exist is the happy fate of all who serve the great scouring.'

'Then I have good news,' Trazyn said, unable to conceal his distaste. 'Your happy fate has come. By my protocol rights as overlord I hereby release you from your mission programming. Come with me, and I will repurpose you. There are tasks for you on Solemnace.'

'Negative,' responded Ket-vah. 'Our mission is incomplete. We are working our way south, to the pole. Once melted, the resulting influx of fresh water will desalinate the oceans, killing the phytoplankton that manufacture the majority of this world's oxygen. The resulting mass extinction will allow us to scour this world in two millennia rather than six. We will leave any necron structures untouched, as we agreed with the astromancer. You may do with those what you will.'

'No,' said Trazyn. 'I think not.'

'Why?'

'Because there are still things here that I want,' Trazyn answered, and tossed the tesseract labyrinth.

The Destroyers surged forward, repulsors humming, spinning up to a howl. Gauss blasters spewed jade thunderbolts. They crawled through the air, dancing within the ropy tube field of their disassembly beams.

Trazyn activated the cloak, chose his path, ducked and threw himself aside as the earth where he was standing vanished, puffed into a cloud of ash shavings. He wormed between the beams, summoned the obliterator and lit its great lantern-like emitter chamber so it glowed with sinister light.

The Destroyers stalled. Murderous, nihilistic killers though they were, the glow of this ancient weapon still overwhelmed their neural threat networks with a thing that was very much like dread.

Trazyn activated the tesseract labyrinth. A cone of light spilled upward, engulfing the Destroyers, bathing their dented faces in illumination so bright it washed out their colours so they appeared as grimacing skeletons sketched in black and white.

And like the disassembly beams of their gauss weapons, it took them apart, drawing them into the box.

Trazyn was alone in the scoured field. He stayed until sunset, watching the fires on the forest canopy until they died into whispering smoke.

A fine addition to the collection, he thought. *The Destroyer lord who nearly wiped out a planet.*

When he returned, chaos ruled on Solemnace.

After four thousand five hundred years of rivalry, it was clear Trazyn had needed a new security solution.

The Mysterios was not safe in Trazyn's possession. Nor was it secure when housed in its proper gallery.

But the prismatic galleries were a vast, confusing place. Winding sepulchral corridors. Objects from every major alien species rammed cheek by jowl. Time periods intermixed. Billion-year-old relics held next to recent acquisitions. Galleries that held life-size dioramas of entire battlefields, with thousands of troops frozen in mortal struggle.

Even Trazyn found it difficult to recall exactly what it contained. His rack of Adeptus Astartes helmets had grown so large and convoluted that he needed mnemonic charts to sort the Fire Hawks from the Flame Eagles.

That mix of time periods, Trazyn knew, fouled Orikan's abilities. A fact he'd exploited for the last few millennia by stashing the Astrarium Mysterios at random locations in his collection. Orikan had broken in, of course, but he usually didn't cause much damage – staying stealthy, Trazyn supposed.

He moved it on occasion to keep things interesting.

But in retrospect, it was probably a mistake putting it in the Angelis display.

Deep-ridged tyres tore at the chalky earth, sending up twin plumes of dust that spread out from the ork trukk like a wake. It slewed sideways, drifting, two wheels leaving the ground as if it might go over. Then it slammed down on the bouncing suspension and clawed towards Trazyn.

Stasis field failure. That meant one thing – the idiot had finally found the Mysterios.

Meaning the orks were loose, and doing what orks did in their natural state, which was fight each other.

Trukks and buggies howled corkscrews across the display, ripping across the desert shanty town built around the enormous idol of Gork – or Mork.

Trazyn's investigation had turned up mixed answers on exactly whom it represented.

The trukk bore down on him and Trazyn swept the obliterator back, calculating his strike. The nob riding in the back planted his foot on the driver's seat for balance and extended a crude slugga, taking what counted for orks as aim. The driver, his seat shoved forward by the nob's boot, drove with his massive goggles only a hair above the steering wheel.

'Oi, shiny git!' the nob bellowed, and emptied his magazine.

Bullets the size of human tongues – and about as dangerous – whistled past Trazyn. One clanged off his forehead. This nob was clearly a marksman.

Trazyn slammed the ground ahead of the trukk, denting

the earth in a pothole wide as a battle tank. Cracks jagged out towards the oncoming tyres.

The trukk nosed down and pitched forward, the nob howling in delight as he went suddenly airborne. Those inside who had unwisely held on wailed in sudden fear as the trukk flipped forward, crushing them into green fungal paste.

A dazed grot, miraculously unharmed, staggered from the wreck. Trazyn kicked it into the spikes of a still-rotating tyre.

'Bring it in,' he shouted.

The Catacomb command barge sailed above the motorised brawl, its two hardwired pilots head down at their consoles, heedless of the anarchy beneath them. Trazyn cut his way towards it, scattering a hoard of gretchin who came at him waving a tattered red flag. Vile little hands grasped at his cloak. Yellowed teeth set in receding gums gnawed his shins and thighs.

'Nuisance. Nuisance. Nuisance!' he shouted, stomping them beneath his feet, shaking the last clinging grot from his leg and leaping onto his command dais.

The crescent shape of the command barge rose, slugga and shoota rounds pinging off its armoured underside. In the distance, across the golden dunes, Trazyn could see the upturned wreck of a starship. Mounted outriders weaved along the crests of the sand dunes, spindly jezails savaging the motorised orks with harassing fire.

One of his larger displays. One of his better displays. It had taken him nearly fifty years to capture the eternal chaos of this place. To choreograph the hacking melees and hairpin turns, wiry juveniles leaping between speeding vehicles.

He hoped some of it could be salvaged.

The command barge shot upward along the swollen belly of the great idol. Shots pinged out of the idol's interior, puncturing its patchwork skin, and Trazyn realised the fighting had reached inside it.

Best stop this, he thought.

Sannet?

Working to restore stasis fields, high archaeovist, came the interstitial reply.

Work faster. We don't want them turning this contraption on.

Do you think the engine works? Sannet replied.

Engines, corrected Trazyn. *There are around seventy, depending on one's definition of engine. Get those fields up, Sannet. I don't want to be in orbit.*

Bolts along the side of the idol blew. A gantry fell away and the command barge made a sickening dip to avoid being struck from the sky.

Authenticity be damned, thought Trazyn. *Next time I acquire a rocket, I'm displaying it without fuel.*

Then he saw it. A figure standing in the idol's left eye. The place where he, perhaps a bit too cleverly, had hidden the Astrarium Mysterios.

His oculars enhanced the image, scrubbed out the interference. He already knew what he would find.

Orikan, his necrodermis scratched and dinged from his fighting ascent up the interior of the idol. Clearly, things had not gone precisely to plan for him, either. In one hand he held the Astrarium Mysterios, its metal skin glowing as if pleased by the reversal.

Orikan stabbed his staff downward, and another gantry blew its bolts and fell away, unnaturally toppling towards the barge. Trazyn threw a stasis field, halting it in the air until they passed, then let it go, watched it crush a shanty town district he'd designed, room by room.

Above him, and through the roar of growling rocket boosters, he could hear Orikan laughing. Trazyn looked up at him again. He could feel his central reactor cycling hard in fury, as if it might burst. Restoration calculations returned a work estimate that fluctuated just under a million man-hours – a century of effort, wasted. And if the idol-rocket took off, it would be triple that.

Trazyn felt wetness on his cheeks and realised he was weeping oil.

Lord? it was Sannet. *Twenty seconds to lift-off.*

Trazyn knew why Orikan laughed.

Trazyn could either save the Mysterios, or the gallery.

And they both knew which he would pick.

He grabbed his override control orb and redirected the barge, sweeping it around to the side where one of the gantries had separated. Pulled it up to a closed hatch.

Fifteen seconds.

Trazyn ripped the hatch open with his bare hands, the metal frame bending like pressed tin under his enraged grip. Set it aside to reattach later.

Eleven seconds.

He summoned the obliterator. The chamber inside was nothing like any spacecraft Trazyn was used to. A drum-like deck filled with crude tables and chairs, random machinery hanging from the ceiling. Barrels of fungus beer slopping with the reverberation of the misfiring engines.

And a command throne with two buttons. GO and STOP.

A hulking ork sliced at him with a cleaver-like choppa, and he crushed its meaty chest with a swing of the obliterator. Then he reversed, stabbing the staff through a wiry greenskin's skull as it approached his blind side.

Eight seconds.

He cut through the crowd. Reaching hands grasped him

to pull him down and he sent a jolt of crawling electricity through his systems to shake them off.

Six seconds.

The room shook. A mekboy loomed from the shadows, electrodes crackling from the mad machinery that sprouted from his back and shoulders. A localised storm flashed around the balls of ionised gas that whirled above his head like a turbine. Ball lightning leapt from the muzzle of his fluted electro-gun and Trazyn staggered, circuitry system fizzing with overload. He doubled over, the world turning ashen and out of focus like a bad projection, then he redirected the energy bolt through his staff and blew the mekboy back, his muscles in spasm and harnessed apparatus spinning out of control.

Four seconds.

He stepped up to the control throne, and the meganob sitting in it rose to meet him. The thing was huge. Trazyn had installed it himself, picking the biggest, meanest specimen he could find. The slab-like mega armour, thick as a tank glacis, seemed impenetrable. Great curved horns rose from his skullcap. He roared, a low, guttural sound that burst from his purple throat with almost physical force. Termite-squigs tunnelled in his gold-capped fangs.

Three seconds.

The power klaw caught Trazyn's arm as he brought the obliterator down, bending his humerus the wrong way. Metal rended. Hydraulics popped. Reactor fluid spurted from Trazyn's severed arm as howling alerts filled his vision.

Two seconds.

Trazyn turned his spurting arm towards the beast's face, and it bellowed as the gushing neon fluid burned out its eyes.

One.

Trazyn seized the beast by a horn and slammed its face down on the STOP button.

Then, exhausted and surrounded by the howls of the barbarian orks, he slowed his chronosense and collapsed into the command chair.

It was, he told himself, only for a moment. But he had to collect himself if he was to fight his way out.

With time slowed, and the world moving as if underwater, it took Trazyn a moment to realise what was happening.

These orks were not shouting war cries or preparing to rush the throne.

They were howling, cheering. Enthralled by the spectacle of violence he'd demonstrated for them.

They were still cheering when the stasis field locked them in place.

Trazyn slumped in the chair, trying to imagine what he could salvage from the display.

Not his pride, he decided.

Mandragora
897 Years Until Next Astrarium Opening

Orikan had just turned the corner when he saw the death-mark step out of the hyperspace oubliette. Its long, deadly form slid from the pocket dimension where it had waited for him Dead Gods knew how long.

It levelled a long synaptic disintegrator, the glow from the viridian bulbs lighting the one-eyed killer's face as its death mask ran like wax and solidified into Trazyn's features.

'Really, Trazyn,' the Diviner sniffed. 'Have you sunk to base assass–'

The disintegrator shot punched through Orikan's big central

ocular, its balefire howling through his cranial structure like a sandstorm through a ruined temple. Emerald flames burst from his mouth, his shattered ocular, ringed his head like a crown. His necrodermis blackened.

Orikan dropped, hands clawing, fingers starting to phase, eaten by glow-worms of portal light. His charred skull crunched as he spoke.

'I... don't... have... the Mysterios.'

'You can keep it,' said Trazyn, stepping back into the hyper-space oubliette.

CHAPTER TWO

'I'm tellin' ya, ladz, there's nuthin' better than scrappin' with those shiny tins with the skully faces. They'z so fightey. And you gets to kill da same ones over an' over. Ever tried dat with humies? Not as fun.'

– 'Boss Dok' Bigsaw, Waaagh! Bigsaw

50 Years Until Next Astrarium Opening

Turning endlessly in the eternal night. Frozen and bereft. That was Klebnos – a drifting asteroid of interest to no one. A being could walk its prime meridian in two hours. It only carried a name because on the crownworld of Gheden you could see it transit with the naked eye, making it – to the ancient necrontyr, at least – worthy of being anointed with language.

Its utter unimportance, while technically being under the protection of the Nihilakh Dynasty, was in fact why Trazyn had picked it for the meeting. Neutral ground in a technical sense, but any aggression could precipitate a dynastic war.

Of course, the last time Trazyn had met Orikan eight centuries ago, he had blown open the chronomancer's cranium.

Orikan and his entourage of canoptek wraiths were already standing on the small asteroid when Trazyn arrived, his personal Night Scythe dropping low to disgorge him and his lychguard escorts through its underside portal.

It hovered there, active, ready to depart within seconds.

The two sides came within speaking distance and stopped, scrying each other. Out in the dark, contrails formed as Doom Scythes circled, ready to mark targets and annihilate the rival delegation at the slightest hint of violence.

'I suggest,' Trazyn began, 'you start by turning over what you promised.'

Orikan nodded, opened a dimensional pocket, and stretched out his hand.

The Astrarium Mysterios drifted weightless, tracing a soft parabola between the rivals.

'Catch it,' Trazyn ordered a lychguard. 'In case it's a vortex bomb.'

The soldier obediently stepped out and let the black metal object descend into his upturned palms. It did not explode, and a thorough spectromantic bombardment assured Trazyn it was genuine.

'Your part of the bargain is done,' said Trazyn. 'So I will fulfil mine in kind. You have five minutes to explain what's so almighty important.'

Orikan took a step forward. He appeared, Trazyn thought, to be in a bad way. Scratches raked across his unpolished necrodermis. His ocular and orb crest appeared dim and fatigued, as if he'd worked long hours without maintenance or refurbishment.

'An ork invasion has come to Cepharil. Or rather, Serenade. The tomb-complex of Cephris.'

'And you care about a few greenskins wrecking the place, do you?' Trazyn sneered. 'You are, let us remember, the being who caused a mass extinction by utilising troops with the Destroyer madness.'

'That was different,' Orikan said, waving a dismissive hand. 'Species come and go. Civilisations rise and fall. I've always known you were mired in the past, Trazyn, but in the last few millennia you've developed a fetishistic attachment to the present.'

'Serenade gave an opportunity not just to uncover the tomb of Nephreth but also to understand how cultures unaware of previous civilisations are affected by them. Your unnatural interference–'

'War is natural. Conquest is natural. Revolutionary change is a part of the universe, from evolution to historical epochs. You have become enmeshed in the status quo. A status quo that leaves us trapped in bodies of–'

'Did you come here to have a debate, Orikan? Shall we raise an overlord as moderator, or will that merely let you cheat again?'

Orikan stopped, collected himself.

'The Destroyers were a mistake,' he said, offering a hand, palm up as if giving the admission as a gift. 'There, I said it. But I also hold that the Destroyers would not have broken into and despoiled the tomb of Nephreth – the orks will.'

'You have seen this, I suppose,' Trazyn said with a drop of acid. 'In your...' He wobbled his head, made nonsensical symbols with his fingers. 'Meditations.'

Orikan traced the scratches across his frame with his fingers. 'Mock me, but I have seen it. Repeatedly for the last few decades. Not everything I calculate comes to pass, Trazyn, but each time this vision intrudes it becomes stronger. The Waaagh! is coming, it will destroy and befoul the greatest cultural relic of our kind, and both of us will be killed.'

Trazyn snorted. 'Preposterous. You couldn't get me to go near that planet. Chasing that damned tomb cost me two of my best galleries. Too costly. Sniff after ancient legends if you like, but leave me–'

'You're planning to be there when it opens,' interrupted Orikan. 'In fifty years. You've even made site visits. Several. Including one last year. I saw you and let you pass unmolested. We have, after all, an informal detente.'

Trazyn's mouth opened, closed.

'I do not expect Trazyn the Infinite, collector of fine things and rare antiquities, to leave a find of such magnitude unexplored,' Orikan smiled.

Trazyn looked down at the Astrarium Mysterios, as if deciding how much trouble it was worth. 'Set the Night Scythe down and kill the engine,' he said to the closest lychguard. 'No sense in wasting reactor life.'

'I have your attention, then,' Orikan said.

'The Yyth Seer also foresaw the green tide,' Trazyn answered. 'Though not in the detail you claim. I had planned to help defend and salvage the tomb. For the sake of posterity, of course.'

'Of course,' said Orikan. 'But you will die there. The underground tunnels where the tomb resides will, due to the world's unique geology, cut off any translation signal. Necrons killed beneath the surface cannot phase out or, in your case, jump to new host bodies unless they are in line of sight. Death is annoyingly permanent beneath Serenade.'

'So do you have a plan?'

'Naturally,' Orikan waved a hand, summoning a chryso-prase chart showing a swarm of brutish, saw-toothed ships approaching Serenade like a school of carnivorous fish. 'The ork Waaagh! is destined to arrive in fifty years, roughly four months before the opening of the Astrarium. On the whole, they are attacking Serenade because it is there, but they also need its water to cool their ship reactors if they hope to sur-vive warp translation.'

Orikan shrugged, as if it were a wonder the greenskins could puzzle out even that most basic of logistical solutions.

'Fight the brutish fungus-brains on the ground and we will fail,' he continued. 'The ships will intervene. Every zodiac I've cast says so. Fight them in the sky, and we will fail as well. Ground forces already deployed will discover and destroy the tomb. But fight both at once?' Orikan swept two fingers up the chart, making two prongs of necron tomb ships, elegant crescents compared to the lantern-jawed ork craft, spear into the orks' flank. One broke off and headed for the surface. 'A combined spaceborne raid on their capital ships, followed by one element securing the tomb against the land forces, will succeed. The orks will break off. Kill their leadership structure, and I suspect the red-eyed savages will withdraw and fight among their captains in order to determine who's in charge.'

'Thereby diminishing themselves,' finished Trazyn. 'Who is the lucky target?'

Orikan smiled. 'Oh, you'll like this part. So-called Boss Dok Bigsaw, a former medical practitioner of the orkoid variety.'

'A painboy? Unusual.'

'Well, yes, I suppose you would know these things,' Ori-kan said. 'Apparently he became warboss through quite nasty self-surgery and augmentation. He's also known, I hear, as *Da Great Sky Sawwer*.'

'You pronounce orkish like it tastes bad.'

'It does,' said Orikan. 'I dislike even hearing myself use contractions, so this gibberish doesn't appeal. But linguistic foibles aside.' He smiled. 'He would make a fascinating specimen, don't you agree?'

'I do,' said Trazyn, nodding. 'It will take about fifty years to muster a strike force. We're cutting it close.'

'It will,' agreed Orikan. 'And we are. Once our keels part atmosphere we'll have three months, if we're fortunate. Most likely two.'

'No time to warn the Awakened Council. They'd bog us down in debate, think it a waste of resources.'

'Or try to get there before us,' said Orikan. 'I say we keep this one to ourselves.'

And with that, mortal enemies mustered for war.

CHAPTER THREE

'Dere's only a few fings a body needs to keep krumpin',
ladz. One is somewun to krump. Second is fungus beer.
Thurd is water. That'z just biologee.'

                    – 'Boss Dok' Bigsaw

Orbit, Second Moon of Serenade
Three Days Before Tomb Opening

The two ships hit the gravitational well with a slam of deceleration, hooking themselves into the moon's orbit and circling it in streaking paths as they bled momentum. To anyone watching, it appeared that Serenade's second moon had suddenly gained two white-hot rings.

To any world unfortunate enough to experience a necron invasion, it might seem as if the tomb fleet appeared from nowhere. Great crescent ships hanging above the curve of the globe. Weapons systems already flaring with their opening fusillade. Firefly swarms of Ghost Arks descending to the target continent.

Witnesses on the surface might see bursts of light – too bright to look upon, yet casting no shadow – before a metal Death's Head reared out of the wan gateway.

They rarely saw beyond that.

But what appeared instantaneous, coming without warning like an earthquake or solar flare, was in reality the result of long planning and close management.

Mustering the deathless legions and charting a course for war was a multi-decade process, fraught with setbacks. This was particularly true when raising a legion from the Great Sleep. Fast deployment from cryo-stasis nearly always damaged neural circuitry, which was why any functioning World Mind only roused its legions for self-defence. Even then, it usually deployed simple warriors first – those with little mind to ruin – rather than the more valuable Immortals, lychguard and deathmarks.

Trazyn and Orikan had no wish to permanently damage those they raised, particularly since an action of this size could not go unnoticed by the Awakened Council. Should vital assets of the Infinite Empire be wasted on a personal quest – even one semi-sanctioned by their body – it was no doubt the executioner would come for them. After all, the Great Awakening was only millennia away – give or take a few centuries – and that effort required all the force their diminished empire could muster.

Yet they hurried the process as much as possible. Neither Trazyn nor Orikan had been soldiers, though both had, at times, accompanied the legions. They therefore had no compunction, whether it be honour or superstition, about jettisoning the more time-consuming military rituals. There was time for nothing but to muster the decurion and go.

Serenade lacked a dolmen gate, or any webway portal. Whatever escape hatch the Exodites built to flee into the labyrinth dimension, they'd closed behind them. Transporting a few small forces there was no trouble – send a Night Scythe as Trazyn had the first time, jump through the portal – but deploying a force that could best orks both in orbit and on the surface? That meant decades of travel through deep space.

Or it would have, if not for Orikan and his mastery of the inertialess drive. The astromancer had called up star charts and celestial grids, prescribed angles and parabolas, sketched a path through the whirling stars that shot them between the gauntlets of orbiting systems, around asteroid belts and through fields of naval debris, using the gravity of great suns to turn and redirect them without losing too much speed.

A lesser astromancer would've stopped or slowed them to turn. Orikan preserved the endless acceleration of void-travel. By the end of the first solar cycle of the voyage, the craft moved only a thousand leagues per hour. But by the end of the first year, they streaked through space ten times faster than a Night Scythe. After ten years, they travelled so fast that a mortal pilot would've been unable to control the craft, their limited reaction times and slow navigational calculations slamming the craft into a star or overdoing the gentle course adjustments.

Most crypteks could not even have done it, Trazyn admitted to himself. When they'd hit Serenade, they'd been going a billion leagues an hour – so fast even a necron ship could not go to full stop without tearing itself apart.

Serenade's second moon blurred on the right side of the bridge's holo-screen, and Trazyn looked at the sleek lines of Orikan's ship ahead of them. It was a Scythe-class Harvester, in the reaper configuration. An odd, spindly, front-heavy class, Trazyn had always thought. Like a cryptek's Staff of Light hurtled through space, its stern fletched like an arrow.

The Sautekh, consummate empire-builders, had ever loved their ships. Where the Nihilakh hoarded treasure, the Sautekh amassed military assets.

The difference between an inward-looking dynasty and an outward-looking one, Trazyn thought.

His fellow Nihilakh were conservative, defensive. Focused on holding what worlds they had rather than expanding outward. They extracted tributes and looted spoils, of course, but they were less interested in governing new systems than they were about claiming their wealth. Where the Sautekh craved domination, the Nihilakh nurtured spheres of influence – preferring to extend power through vassal states and tribute rather than military force. That took fleets, but Nihilakh flotillas tended to consist of a great number of smaller vessels rather than a few large ones, the better to spread its authority.

A simple difference in naval doctrine, neither approach better nor worse.

Or perhaps Trazyn was just making excuses, envious of how thoroughly Orikan's ship dwarfed his own Shroud-class light cruiser. It was a full mile longer, though Trazyn contented himself that most of that was due to the long spinal vane that stretched like an arrow's shaft to the fletched stern assembly.

Trazyn had his reasons for choosing the Shroud, of course. It was his personal craft, first off, which made its interior comfortable. And he liked that it was fast and quiet, able to run silent past most threats.

And not being a military type himself, Trazyn feared a full battle cruiser might prove too much ship for him. But damn the shattered gods, he was still an *overlord*. And being shown up by some jumped-up court magician bruised the only thing of his that could be bruised – his pride.

'Achieving navigable speed, overlord,' intoned the helmsman of the *Lord of Antiquity*. Trazyn waved a hand at the crewman's head to open his thoughts. He scrolled through the mental data-feed, watching the deceleration calculations spiral down. Satisfied himself that it was being done well.

'Any sign of the orkoids?' he asked.

'Scry-image cast to command throne's projector, overlord. Enhanced to factor of one thousand.'

A chrysoprase projector in his throne arm shimmered, beaming a holographic model in the air. Trazyn leaned down, using his hand to rotate the display.

'Hmm,' Trazyn mused. 'Hail the *Zodiac's Fury*.'

From such a distance, the images were less than distinct, but they were clear enough to see that the ork fleet was massive. A dozen large vessels, bulbous and lantern-jawed, shoaled around the planet like the scavengers they were. Most were escort-sized or smaller, their hull silhouettes bizarre on account of continual reworking and modification. Strange leglike stalks – perhaps void-elevators – stretched from several vessels to the planet's surface.

One kill kroozer, larger than the others, stood so close to the planet's atmosphere that it seemed as if it might fall in.

No prize, Trazyn thought, for guessing which was the warboss' ship.

'Hail accepted, my lord,' said the signalman. 'Projecting.'

Orikan appeared in hard-light, patches of him flickering and going out as the signal wavered. He floated in the air, only slightly smaller than normal, legs crossed and hands woven into a symbol of power.

'Twelve ships,' Trazyn chided. 'Didn't you predict seven?'

Orikan bristled causing the hood of his headpiece to flare outward. *'The orks are difficult to foresee. They travel the empyrean. Shift the very weave of reality around them. They–'*

'It's not important,' Trazyn cut him off. 'Our strategy remains the same, I suppose?'

'Yes,' responded Orikan. *'We hit them hard and fast, cripple them with the initial assault. Then as I engage the large ship and kill Boss Bigsaw, you locate and secure the tomb with a defensive action.'*

'Just remember, astromancer,' Trazyn said. 'I will have the astrarium with me down there.'

'Yes, yes.'

'So if you leave me stranded, it will be lost. In such an eventuality, my captain will turn his guns on the *Zodiac's Fury*.'

'And you cannot open the tomb without my equation,' said Orikan. *'And should you try, I have the batteries and ground forces to make you quite regret it. I need no reminder that we each have a phase-blade to the other's throat.'*

'Very well,' Trazyn nodded. 'Provided we understand each other.'

Orikan gave a dust-dry cackle. *'Little hope of that, archaeovist. But our accord is sealed. Transmitting attack vectors to the* Antiquity *now.'*

An interstitial data packet appeared on Trazyn's command throne and he flicked a finger, casting it to the main holo-screen. It dominated the display, overlaying the image of the *Zodiac's* fletched stern to show the first curving tack towards the orks. In one corner of the holo-screen, a tactical chart showed the planned course in a simplified map.

'One thing, Orikan. What are these…' Trazyn paused, sketching a finger along the protrusions linking the ships and surface, '…these things?'

'*I suppose we will find out, will we not?*' Orikan said. '*Prepare for your first turn on my order. Three.*'

Trazyn saw the *Zodiac's Fury* pivot like a boat sliding up to a quay, its constellation of hull lights flaring as the main reactor juiced extra power into its network of conduits and surface circuits.

'*Two,*' Orikan's voice crackled out of the hologram.

The *Zodiac* slid by the holo-screen, and the bridge of the *Antiquity* shivered as the hazy discharge of the bigger ship's inertialess drive washed over it.

'*One,*' said Orikan. '*Tu–*'

'Turn,' ordered Trazyn, and smiled at the predatory dip of hologram-Orikan's head. 'I'm sorry, this ship only responds to the ranking overlord. You're not an overlord as far as I'm aware, are you, Orikan?'

'*Keep to the charted course,*' Orikan said, voice tight with annoyance. '*And your arc batteries pointed away from me.*'

The hologram winked out.

Trazyn chuckled, his laughter rising, becoming more throaty, echoing off the walls of the cavernous bridge. Deciding he didn't like the lonely sound, he waved a hand, and the bridge crew – hardwired into instrument cartouches and command cradles – hollowly laughed along with him.

Yes, as Orikan said, they had a blade to each other's throats.

But the stargazing fool didn't know that Trazyn also had a knife in the other hand, ready to plunge into the astro-mancer's belly.

Silence ruled the command deck of the *Zodiac's Fury*. Orikan preferred it that way, better to preserve his navigational trances and tactical divinations. Instead of a command throne, he liked to sit floating in a repulsor field, surrounded by glowing phos-hologram celestial charts, spiralling predestination models and damage reports. A spider lurking in a luminescent web.

No one was to speak to him. Not the bridge crew. Not the captain. All orders came through interstitial command, a thought-network of instantaneous feedback that chained throughout the entire ship's complement. The chain radiated out from Orikan, to the bridge crew, to the operational sections, all the way down to the strike fighter pilots, already poised at the hangar bay doors.

Orikan mimicked breathing to keep time, maintain focus. They were moving fast – five hundred leagues per hour. Approaching the first sawtooth-glyph on his tactical map.

In his deep well of a mind, he scryed through the oculars of the fire control officer and saw the first ork ship approach – a dot in the blackness off their starboard side, growing larger.

Charge lightning arc array, he ordered.

Billowing auroras rippled and collected in the hollow of the ship's crescent-shaped bow. A cloud of ambient solar energy pulled from the void and squeezed into a star-bright point. Any other species – even the aeldari – would consider this a technical miracle. But to Orikan it was no more incredible than melting lead into bullets.

Target in range, lord.

Orikan let the *Zodiac* close with the ork vessel. Held fire. Small objects began to bounce off the living metal of the *Zodiac*'s prow. They were not shots. As far as Orikan knew, the little ork kroozer was still unaware of the necron ship bearing down on it.

The *Zodiac* had entered the debris field that haloed every greenskin ship – a loose shower of screws, scrap and ejected waste that floated off the ramshackle vessels even when they sat at orbital anchor.

Orikan scanned thermal readouts, finding the heat plumes of the ork vessel's propulsion system, and confirmed it was not bombarding them with any sensors. The *Zodiac* collided with a piece of ambient hull plating the size of a bomber. It skipped along the necrodermis and went spinning into space like a coin.

Fire.

The sunspot collecting in the hollow of the *Zodiac*'s crescent bow leapt at the kroozer. Lightning bolts danced and crawled, touched its metal surface and quested for weak points. Promethium tanks bolted to the outside of the ship's hull ruptured in pressurised bursts, chemical components breaking up flameless in the oxygen-starved void.

Absorbed in his chart, Orikan traced his fingers towards the largest vent plume on the kroozer's spine. Grunting, he flowed twenty per cent of his consciousness down into the bridge circuitry and raced his way through the ship. He zipped and turned, following the power cables. Running hot past the boarding parties preparing in the translation chamber, the engine-keepers nursing the huge reactor drive, pouring a portion of his consciousness into the gunner cryptek manning the arc battery. The being was slow, malfunctioning, still stiff from sixty million years of sleep.

'Idiot,' he growled through the cryptek's lips, and ran his fingers over the arc battery's control orb. Watched as a tendril of emerald electricity probed like a questing finger towards the main smokestack. Dipped inside.

With the cryptek's other hand, Orikan locked the arcs in, cycled up the power.

The lightning arcs gathered and joined the first, eager, as if hungry.

Bright flashes shone through the triangular portholes of

the krooźer's bridge. They frosted with smoke, then blew outwards, the ship's interior oxygen soon burning off so that the pillars of flame boiling at the vessel's eye sockets quickly retreated.

'There, that's how you do it,' said Orikan, raising the gun officer's puppeteered hand and using it to strike the cryptek across his own lean jaw. 'Do not make me come down here again.'

Up in the bridge, the rest of Orikan's consciousness watched the kroozer heel over and come apart at mid-deck. One down. No fight in them. He scanned for life signs and found only a few hundred.

He opened a hailing channel.

'Trazyn,' he signalled, watching the *Antiquity* come up low on his portside, matching his speed. 'Confirm life form reading on that kroozer for me.'

'*A few hundred.*'

'That is abnormal,' Orikan said, hoping it did not sound like a question.

'*Don't know much about orks, do you, astromancer?*'

'It is not my business to know the specifics of every barbarian culture and alien oddity,' he snapped. 'Is it abnormal or not?'

Trazyn chuckled, relishing knowing something that Orikan did not. '*The orks stuff their craft bulkhead to bulkhead. Blow one apart and you're likely to see more green flesh in the debris field than metal. No, we likely detonated a kroozer full of gretchin.*'

'What?'

'*It's an invasion, the real orks are down on the surface. Pick up your scanning – half these vessels are empty.*'

Orikan looked at the mob of ships growing large in his forward holo-screen.

Finally, a plan was going right.

And that's when the dazzle of an interstitial alert flashed across his vision.

Incoming. Incoming. Incoming.

The *Zodiac* rocked, bridge crew jiggling in their command cradles and floor mounts as a rocket-propelled shell the size of a monolith crashed into the prow.

Orikan drew up a scry-view and saw an enormous crater in the starboard crescent wing. Wisps of ghostly energy trailed from the blackened, cauterised wound, reminding Orikan of a temple incense burner. Already, crackling energy wormed its way along the edges. Atoms realigned, reformed, creating a lattice structure. In the exposed decks, he could see repair wraiths firing particle beamers, refilling the latticework structure with healing necrodermis. Living metal, that which remained functional, flowed and shimmered back in to fill the gaps. Debris ejected from the wound tumbled back into place as if it were a mnemonic file running in reverse.

Ahead, Orikan saw flashes dancing along the line of the ork ships.

It was no longer an ambush.

It was a battle.

Ork fire came in curtains like a monsoon rain. Punching. Strobing. Howling.

Shells the size of battle tanks. Dazzling blue light beams. Little plinking impacts on the *Antiquity*'s forward shields Trazyn swore were shoota slugs. That was how the orks did it. No target priority or fire control, just unleash everything in a wall of ordnance.

It wasn't so much about avoiding fire, it was about avoiding the heavy guns and beam weapons.

'Orikan,' he signalled. 'Drive straight at them, present the narrowest silhouette. Vector up and down to create a moving target.'

Orikan's hologram juddered and flashed as the *Zodiac* took another hit. *'Suddenly the great void-nemesor, are we?'*

'I have two kroozers and a bridge section from an ork roc in the gallery. Trust me, their targeting systems aren't up to snuff. Especially at range. They'll lose patience and close on us to ram and board.'

'So you want to continue straight at them? Brilliant stratagem–'

'We need them to break off so I can land. If we run they won't chase us. But if we charge we can get them to turn and commit. Burn their big rokkit engines for us so they can't slow or manoeuvre. Then we dive under and scour their bellies.'

Silence. Orikan's hologram floated unmoving.

'Orikan?'

'Divinatory algorithms predict a sixty-two out of one hundred chance of success.'

'Not bad.'

'It's the best scenario I've run given a failed ambush. Very well, Trazyn. Zodiac's Fury turning prow-on and increasing speed. Randomised vector grid. Stars save us.'

The hologram blinked out and Trazyn turned to the divinations officer, slowing his chronosense and speeding his information packets so the conversation passed within a half-second. 'Are you tracking incoming?'

'Yes, overlord.' She was a cryptek, implanted in an armillary sphere command cradle that rotated her around the globe of phos-glyph panels that surrounded her. Four hands played over her glowing sensor suite. Void tiles dangled from the sides of her metal skull like earrings. 'Scrying nineteen thousand plus objects. Twelve thousand of those on course for the *Zodiac.*'

The *Antiquity* shivered as a rokkit that looked as if it might pass over them suddenly plunged jackknife-crazy into their path. It detonated against the forward shield, bathing the ship's portside front arc in fire that boiled and died outside the protective emerald shell.

'Orks always shoot the bigger one,' Trazyn said.

'Indeed, lord. Our incoming includes two-sixty-two objects of damaging strength or greater. Torpedoes. High-yield shells. Rockets. Energy beams of unknown composition. Sixty-four per cent of those are disabling strength, twenty-one per cent will destroy the *Antiquity* in one or more strikes.'

'Transmit to helm. Helmsman, steer us true. Prioritise weaving around the biggest ones. Drive through the medium-yield ordnance if necessary. Technologos.'

'Aye, lord?'

'Shield priority forward and topside. Match their angle of deflection. Weapons?'

'Ready for orders.'

'Find me a damned firing solution.' He pointed a long, pitted finger at one of the brutal, fish-like craft, close enough now that they could see its blue paint job. 'On that one, the bulbous crate making the slovenly turn.'

'The transport?' the weapons officer said, wanting confirmation.

'It's not a transport,' Trazyn said, a wicked tone in his voice. 'It's a torpedo boat.'

Zodiac's Fury rocked with another impact. One of his phos-glyph panels strobed until he sketched the Sign of Hept to stabilise it.

A damned torpedo this time. A prodigious one. Orikan

had vectored up and it passed below them, the faulty timer going off just under and behind their stern assembly so that the *Zodiac* pitched forward on its nose like a diving raptor. The blast drove its topside shield directly into a blizzard of mid-size shells that shorted it, allowing one to detonate against the midline spine-column – the haft of this staff-like vessel – that connected the prow module to the navigational fins at the stern.

Red damage reports filled his vision. He scryed into the head of a repair wraith and saw the necrodermis of the hull column shredded like a snapped twig still held together by bark. The tail assembly wobbled precariously, wandering out of the teardrop-shaped shield that surrounded the craft.

Orikan snapped back, dismissing warnings from his cluttered sphere of information. As soon as he swept away a damage report, a hologram appeared to replace it.

'Everything all right, Orikan? They're–'

Orikan grabbed the doll-like projection of Trazyn and tossed it away. He was being too detailed, plotting too many eventualities, flying this ship with his head rather than by instinct. Trying to calculate every move. Being too perfect. Trying to avoid every obstacle rather than take some hits.

Deploy extra wraiths to spine-column, he sent. *Helm, level out. New evasive pattern. Algorithmic flight pattern sent to–*

The bridge shuddered with another hit.

'Orikan,' Trazyn said, hologram reappearing. *'They're turning to face.'*

He looked up. A stray rocket streaked above, but the hail of shot was slackening. Indeed, five of the big kroozers had come about. Orikan saw their furious, triangular eyes staring at him behind the thinning swarm of fire-bright torpedoes and glowing reactor shells.

'Incoming torpedoes,' said Trazyn. 'I read life forms aboard. Boarders.'

Thread them, Orikan ordered the helmsman. And by the Dead Gods, get that spine array locked down.

He gathered his fragmented consciousness, split between too many places throughout the ship's network as he tried to manage the battle single-handed.

'Trazyn. Our ships are without atmosphere, unpressurised,' Orikan said. 'Do orks... breathe?'

A pause.

'They have lungs.'

Prepare to repel boarders, Orikan signalled. In case.

The culture of the orks had always fascinated Trazyn. Consider, after all, the madness of a social structure that would make beings not only willing, but eager, to climb into a faulty torpedo and be fired between two moving starships. The things could, theoretically, steer towards a target – but when he'd taken samples he'd found that the controls were usually decorative. It gave the ork boyz the opportunity to feel like they were doing something, but more often than not the torpedo's helm controls weren't connected to anything. On top of that, the things had a limited fuel payload, meaning that if they missed, the tube of tight-packed greenskins had few options. This close to orbit, a few might get captured by the gravity well and, after a few weeks, succumb to orbital decay and immolate upon atmospheric entry.

Those that shot out into the void itself would, he assumed, form a brief micro-society primarily centred around brawling and cannibalism.

These incoming boarders would not have that problem, of course – Trazyn would make sure of that.

'Fire array.'

Sheets of energy lanced towards the incoming hornet storm of torpedoes. They popped one after another, like fire-crackers, bursting in their centres and spilling green bodies that sizzled on the *Antiquity*'s forward shield. One careened away, a glancing lick of electricity shorting its drive system and turning it into so much space junk.

Orks began clambering out of its side hatch, jetpacks flar-ing as they pushed off the surface of the torpedo and winged slugga shots at the *Antiquity*.

A Night Scythe swooped in and atomised the stricken craft, taking its crew with it. At his flight officer's recommendation, Trazyn had deployed the Scythes to create a screen once it was clear the kroozers were deploying small craft. Half the *Antiquity*'s squadron was running interference on the *Zodi-ac*'s weakened topside shield, the hit on its spine having grounded the ship's own fighters.

Trazyn could see the ork fleet nearing, sawtooth jaws clearly visible without enhancement now. Swarms of void-proofed fighta-bommas alighted from the sides of the ramshackle craft. Trazyn swore that one kroozer had opened its fighter bays by blowing the explosive bolts on several huge panels, dropping the planks of hull plating astern like flower petals.

An alert plastered his vision, accompanied by an obnox-ious trilling noise.

Hull breach in Aft Engine Temple, starboard side. Organic life forms detected.

'Void Dragon gnaw their entrails,' Trazyn snarled. 'So one did get through. Warriors, give them a welcome. No need to overdo it. Do not damage the ship. That's one chamber away from our reactor.'

Hopefully, the warriors would be enough. He'd rather send

the more reliable Immortals, but those were all seconded for the landings.

Boarding a necron vessel was foolhardy. For one thing, as Orikan had pointed out, the atmosphere was no different than the void outside – no need for life support. The interiors were airless, unpressurised and freezing.

Would that matter to an ork? Trazyn did not know.

'*They're closing,*' said Orikan, his hologram wavering.

'Wait for it,' said Trazyn. 'If they don't fire their ram-rockets they'll still be able to manoeuvre and–'

As if called, the ram-thruster on the ork kill krooozer lit, the concussion of it nudging escort vessels aside, scorching their blue hull paint black with the heat wash. It screamed towards them, engine framing the craft in a corona of flame. Along-side, four smaller krooozers fired up their own ram-rockets and peeled off after their flagship.

'Are you prepared to vector down, Orikan?'

'*Charging weapons. Vector on count of three,*' said the astro-mancer. He sounded distracted and stressed. '*One.*'

'Two,' answered Trazyn.

The ork armada loomed huge on the holo-screen, their courses already wavering with the uncontrolled burn. Two krooozers drifted dangerously close to each other. In the bottom of the screen, the *Antiquity*'s lightning arc gathered another crackling electro-storm.

'*Three,*' they counted together.

Inertialess drives fired upward, dropping the two sickle craft down under the brutish enemy vessels. It was close. So close that the image of the huge krooozer plummeting towards them reached down to a subconscious instinct from the times of flesh, and Trazyn found himself wanting to duck. A long whip aerial emerging from the bottom of one kroozer hit the portside wing and scraped along it before breaking off.

To the orks, it must have looked like their quarry had disappeared.

'Fire,' ordered Trazyn.

Coiling energy flashed upward as they sailed under the ork vessels, scouring their bellies. Liquified metal pattered onto the *Antiquity* – ropy globules that tumbled, formless in the void of space. On contact with the cold hull, the metal froze in puddles.

'Keep firing. Focus on the torpedo boat.'

He swung the holo-screen's vision arc to starboard to watch Orikan's progress. The screen whited out, unable to handle the energy discharge it was witnessing, then added filters to bring the scry-image back into focus.

The *Zodiac's Fury* had fired its particle whip directly into the belly of the kill kroozer. At longer range it would've lived up to its name, snapping out in great coiling arcs like a herdsman's lash, splitting the air with a crack that could rupture a mortal's eardrums.

But at this range, and in the silence of space, it was like a curved knife. It sank deep into the flagship's belly and dragged along the hull. Orange sparks, showers of molten metal and superheated matter bloomed from the long slice as Orikan's ship carved a quarter of the way down its length. A few more seconds, and it would slit the ork flagship front to back like a fish.

It might have even torn the kroozer in two, except that at that exact moment the torpedo boat Trazyn was scouring went up.

There may have been a warning rumble, but if there had been, it was swallowed by the airless, soundless void. Trazyn guessed it was a munitions detonation, which had, after all, been his object in targeting it. Orks rarely had any compunction about proper ordnance storage, and regularly kept ammunition next to fuel sources, and vice versa. Perhaps a crude orkoid version of a fusion reactor – the dream of a particularly insane or talented mek – had overloaded and gone critical.

All Trazyn knew was that the torpedo boat simply exploded, its rushing energy wave so powerful that it outran and incinerated any debris and drove the *Antiquity* downward, its overtaxed shields shimmering a weak shade of yellow that tinted the scene of destruction.

The energy wave broke the formation, scattering the ork ships, tumbling them this way and that like tiny sailcraft in a storm. The *Zodiac* took the hit on its portside shield – and a good thing too, since with its top shield weakened the blast might've severely damaged the big harvest ship.

But the kill kroozer, stricken and seconds from void-death, took the blast full force on its starboard side. The shock wave shoved it sideways through space, rolling it off the impaling beam of the particle whip. Saving it.

'Trazyn,' howled Orikan. *'You hunchbacked old meddler. I had him. We could've finished it.'*

Trazyn wasn't listening. He was getting his own alerts.

Lord, warned the cryptek manning the technologos panel. *Boarders are forcing the aft engine temple gateway. Engine Guardians report weapons discharges in the–*

Trazyn was already gone, his consciousness flashing out of the body of the captain he'd used as a surrogate. Down through the circuitry-paths of the ship. Feeling the hum and throb of the penta-reactor grow stronger as he neared the aft engine temple, tasting the radiation as he rushed closer.

When he flowed into the lychguard's body, he found himself face to snout with an ork. He fended it off with the haft of a warscythe, pulling and wrestling as the callused green hands tried to tear it from his grip. The beast howled with the elation of slaughter. Beady eyes stared through flight goggles. Its thick tongue lolled against Trazyn's death mask.

Trazyn kept a collection of intricate combat manuals – drill books for necrontyr scythe and phase sword, each illustration demonstrating the beautiful efficiency of the ancient blademasters. The proper method to accomplish the *ques-sekkin*, the strike that disembowels and decapitates. How to use phase sword and shield to disarm the opponent with Nycanthal's Blade Trap. Stances for honour duels, for hunting, for war.

None of them contained the move he did then. He was not a duellist, a hunter or a warrior. What he was, was a monster.

Trazyn slammed his head forward, shattering the ork's septum. Finger-thick tusks scraped his face as the ork tried to bite him, but they slid off with an unpleasant screech of bone on metal. The ork was dead. Skull crushed and forebrain mashed to jelly – the biting had been a post-mortem reflex.

Trazyn shoved the ork away, speared its floating body with the warscythe then ripped the blade outward to bury it in another greenskin's throat.

Green blood, dark and globular, spurted in the gravity-free air.

Only then did Trazyn have enough space for his perception suite to take stock. Above him in the cyclopean vaults and impossible angles, he could see the burning trails of orks flying and twisting in the reactor chamber. Huge rockets strapped to their backs belched flame and oily smoke.

Some were repurposed pulse-jet engines from Landspeed-ers. One was the booster from an Imperial torpedo. Another, most alarmingly, seemed to be a hunter-killer missile with its warhead still attached.

Stormboyz.

They weaved about in wild corkscrews and diving feints, more concerned with the delirious joy of fighting in zero gravity than causing irreversible reactor damage. But even so, there were few things in the galaxy more dangerous than an ork having fun.

Trazyn saw two fall upon a necron that was mag-locked to the bulkhead, the ancient warrior's attention diverted by a third stormboy. The pair hacked and sawed at the warrior with their chainblades, grabbing limbs and yanking his body back and forth between them as it tore apart with a flaring light. The warrior phased and disappeared, ready to be reanimated in the vessel's rebuilding crypts, and the slighted orks – annoyed at their truncated fun – swung at each other a few times before rocketing elsewhere to find new prey, the squig-fur collars of their jackets floating eerily in zero gravity.

Killing them would, of course, be the wisest thing to do. But they were fascinating. The adopted human clothing. Rough organisation and chain of command.

Oh well. If he found something better, he could always start over.

Trazyn summoned a stasis beam and reached for an empty tesseract labyrinth.

Orikan burned the *Zodiac*'s engines, trying to disengage and get a better angle. He hailed the *Antiquity* again.

'Trazyn. Trazyn. Answer me, you malfunctioning imbecile.'

He saw an alert, rolled the *Zodiac* over and down, deploying a comet tail of flickering dimensional matter that drew the heat-seeking rockets away to explode harmlessly behind his stern.

The ork craft were clumsy and wounded, but they were many and the necron vessels few. And they were all beginning to reorient themselves after the torpedo boat's detonation.

Predictably, they were on him like a death shroud, fixated on the *Zodiac* as the larger, more dangerous target.

It made sense, in a twisted way. When the phaerons struck out on their great hunts they chose the largest, fiercest game as their quarry. The point was not to bring home the largest measure of meat or even the best furs, but for honour. Boasting rights that they'd killed the beast with the sharpest fangs, the largest bulk. An implicit declaration that they were the most powerful.

This was no different. Necrons. Orks. Power was power.

Dead Gods, he'd been interacting with Trazyn too much. These were savages, and he would deal with them as such.

Charge the sepulchre, he ordered. *It is time to show these barbarians the terror of civilisation.*

Trazyn's consciousness poured back into the captain, bending her metal frame and twisting it to his specifications.

'Report.'

'Cutting hard towards Serenade, overlord,' responded the divinations officer from her illuminated bubble of data. 'Two ork vessels in pursuit. One krooyzer, one escort ship. In your absence, the captain ordered a hard turn and evasive parabolas. Recommended we target the escort.'

'The escort?'

'She said we could outrun one krooyzer but two could

manoeuvre to ensnare us. Our priority is to chart an atmospheric skim and deploy the strike force, then play vermin-and-serpent with the ork forces. Draw them away from the *Zodiac*.'

'Well, it seems Captain Zakkarah has it well in hand. We do try to get the best.'

'Nihilakh ascendant,' intoned the divination officer, and wheeled to address an incoming scatterplot of ork engine pulses versus thrust rate.

'Orikan,' Trazyn said, opening a hail. 'I'm descending to the translation crypt. My crew will take the *Antiquity* into an orbital run and release the strike force, then return to assist.'

'*Useless oaf, I had him. The battle could've been over in hours and now—*'

'The *Antiquity* will be there soon, astromancer. But I really must get to the translation crypt. First beam fires in two minutes.'

'*Your ship had better return, Trazyn, or I will send the stars themselves to burn you. I'll call the primordial forces of deep space to rip every limb from—*'

Trazyn cut the communication.

'You heard our esteemed ally, bridge crew. Straight after the translation and Night Scythe launches, divine a course back to *assist* Lord Orikan.'

'Aye, overlord,' they intoned as one.

'But just one firing pass, eh? After that evade to the far side of the third moon.' He smiled. 'Lord Orikan can fight his own battles.'

CHAPTER FOUR

'Greenskins killed my brothers and sisters. My cousins. Everyone I played with at the village scholam. Would have killed me too, except I caught the grey stagger that spring, and my mother had taken me to the medicae facility on Vultus Atoll for quarantine. We were very isolated there. Heard little and saw less. The monsters would have got to us eventually – but you know what happened. Everyone does.'

– Testimony of Malthus Rann,
excerpted from *They Drank the Seas:
An Oral History of the Greenskin War*

Settlement Plaza, Serenade City

They were pipes. League upon league of pipes.

Just before Trazyn stepped into the translation portal, he'd scryed through the oculars of a Night Scythe reconnaissance pilot. Better to get visuals on the ground when one was step-ping into a combat zone.

What he saw intrigued him. Each proboscis reaching from ship to planet was a pipe. They were huge, each the width of a small house, made out of flexible plastek and woven fibre. Durable but still able to bend. Some sections were brass torn from some unfortunate city's sewer system. The mad collection of hoses and pipes fed into the bellies of big ork cargo-lighters hanging just below the atmosphere.

Elsewhere, boxy lifter craft – buzzing and snapping with barely contained energies – dropped what appeared to be huge nets into the sea. Flaring nodes turned the green water a vibrant blue, then it collapsed in on itself, reduced to steam.

No, not reduced to steam, Trazyn realised. Stolen. The buzzing, glowing nodes on the nets were teleporters. Up in orbit, in the belly of one of the great cargo ships, it was raining seawater.

They were drinking the oceans. Already, Serenade's sea lev-els were dropping. Ironic, since he'd previously calculated that the burning of its rainforests had helped melt the plan-et's ice caps, raising the sea level roughly six *khet*.

It mattered little. Once the necrons landed in force, this would be a dead world.

He stepped through the rippling emerald skin of the ship's portal and touched ground, the air around him smoking from the discharge of the translation.

Around him was chaos.

The closest point to the tomb, as far as he could tell, was the main plaza in Serenade City. He looked around to get his bearings.

Trazyn had seen colony worlds many times. It was that rough-and-tumble transition phase between settlement and dominance, where most of the territory remained frontier and the humans clung to forts and outposts. One or two might grow above the size of a town, but even these tended to be modest. Serenade City sprawled near the island's port, a collection of pink two- and three-storey buildings, built from blocks of coral quarried from inshore reefs. The houses rose up the slope in village-like clusters, each with a garden to supplement nutrition. High trees sprouted between the buildings, giving shade and rustling in the breeze. Wide verandahs and slatted wooden doors spoke of a world where power generation remained sporadic, and instead of relying on hab-conditioners the populace would need to harness the trade winds to fight off the balmy humidity. Their roofs, carved wooden eaves supporting red tile baked from the iron-rich island soil, gleamed in the sun.

Settlement Plaza, like all colonial plazas, contained a group of prefabricated buildings, likely brought in the first craft – a Basilica of the God-Emperor's Ascension, a governor's palace, an Administratum office and a barracks. There was nothing special about it, apart from the carved coral facades and the fact that five roads met in the plaza, rather than the usual four.

That, of course, and that the Administratum office was on fire, curls of licking flame fanning out of the windows and threatening the buildings next door.

Then there was the screaming.

Trazyn stood behind a statue of an Imperial martyr and took stock. Orks were already in the square, big frames hounding after the civilians, who screamed and clutched belongings, fleeing uphill. One grabbed a woman with a meaty hand and opened its jaws wide to admit the struggling civilian's whole head.

He might have managed it, too, if the las-bolt hadn't popped his skull open.

The ork dropped the woman, felt his ruined skullcap with questing fingers, probing the brain matter still inside his cranium. Bellowing, he rushed towards the barracks where the shot had originated, both enraged and sensing a better fight.

Trazyn enhanced the image. A platoon of Serenade Frontier Rifles – a militia regiment in faded uniforms and nicked helmets – had clapped themselves inside the barracks, covering the downhill approaches from firing slits and hardened positions.

Orks surged up through the avenue leading to the port, waving choppas and stubby chainblades. Peppering the plasteel bunker with a variety of weapons that dazzled even Trazyn's knowledge database. A quad-linked multi-laser answered them, strobing fire from the bunker into the orkoid throng, scything through them in a tumble of fallen heads and cauterised limbs.

The greenskins did not stop. As bodies fell they simply climbed over them, howling with delight that this hard point was putting up such a good fight. Their bodies stacked up in front of the mass fire of the bunker, mounding into a convenient ramp those behind could use to reach the firing slits.

Trazyn turned away, drew out the Mysterios.

They were close.

The object vibrated in his hand and he patted it like a small animal. Orikan seemed to believe the Mysterios had a kind of resonance with Serenade – at least, that's what Trazyn had found through years of infiltrating the seer's cryptek circle. As Orikan worked, Trazyn watched.

Indeed, the astromancer had felt safe turning the Mysterios over to Trazyn, since he'd known it was useless without its algebraic incantation. But Trazyn had watched him practise the phrase over, and over, and over.

Orikan was, after all, so very thorough.

Trazyn spoke to the puzzle box, pored over the map it projected.

This was the spot indicated – but it also was not good enough. Orikan said the opening point would be immediately below the plaza, accessed via a volcanic cave. But the world's unique geology was impervious to their sensors, making it impossible to bombard the surface with spectromancy and discover the entrance. A ground scan would, they assumed, be better.

'Sannet,' he called. The cryptek appeared at his shoulder in a squeal of rending space-time.

'Lord? Shall I signal the phalanx?'

'Cast a divinatory scry,' he said. He noticed that Sannet was looking around, curious. 'Focus, loyal retainer.'

'Yes, master. I apologise. It has been a long while since I have left Solemnace.'

'Find the entrance.' He turned to the scene playing out before him, watching as an ork boy gained the multi-laser's firing slit and unloaded a huge slugga into it point-blank. In the sky, a pencil-sketch line arced overhead, its parabola terminating in a street upslope from the bunker. Pink houses erupted in flame, splinters of their carved wooden eaves spinning out to embed themselves into earth, trees and neighbouring buildings.

Trazyn looked out to sea and saw a great object trudging its way through the surf.

'Lord archaeovist,' said Sannet, 'I have located the most likely ingress point to the crypt vault. It is out on the fringing reef, past the drop-off to the abyssal floor.'

'Call the Acquisition Phalanx,' Trazyn ordered. 'Whatever formation Royal Warden Ashkut deems best. Deathmarks wherever makes sense. Let him handle the details. Do not fire on the humans so long as they're shooting at the orks and not us.'

He stepped out into the plaza, summoning his empathic obliterator, slowing his chronosense so he could scry the entire plaza and commit it to his engrammatic matrix should he decide to recreate the scene. And, striding towards the orks, he laughed with recognition as his archival sub-program filed the scry-scan under a previous engram.

It was the same five-avenue plaza he'd defended with his lychguard, eight millennia past. But back then, the Basilica of the God-Emperor's Ascension had been the aeldari's World-Spirit temple. The administratum complex a monastery. The bunker a fine artificial forest grown from lizard bone, its top boughs like the branching of fan corals.

Birds clustered around the central fountain, too stupid or frightened by the battle to flee. When they looked at him, turning their heads sideways to regard him with their enormous, unblinking eyes, he realised they were not birds at all, but feathered lizards. Pale yellow scales showed on their bellies, their fluffed red plumage embedded in leathery reptilian skin.

Oh, how the mighty are brought low, he thought.

Trazyn raised his obliterator and ignited the artefact within so it flared with a malign hum, radiating a light that was not light. An ork at the edge of the attack turned away from the las-fire pouring out of the bunker and saw him. Bellowed a challenge that sent his lips flapping.

Trazyn crushed him with a downward stroke, mashing the fungal creature to the plaza. The obliterator's headpiece activated and a blast wave rocked through the mob of green flesh. Worm-lightning leaping from body to body in a cone of howling balefire. Nimbuses of corposant surrounded metal weapons and buckles. Sluggas exploded, their ammunition detonating inside their magazines and shredding brutish fingers. Chainblades whirred out of control until their engines burned out with a cough of ozone. Helmets, turned griddle-hot by the energy flash, seared their owners down to the skull.

The closest orks simply disappeared, flash-burned out of existence to the point that the only thing that remained of them were silhouettes on the cobblestones, the area around them scorched black.

Fire from the bunker slackened. Green heads turned, regarding this new and more interesting threat.

And behind Trazyn, the air rent. A line of lychguard stepped through the glowing, spitting wound in space-time, shields forward, swords aloft. In the centre stood Lych-Captain Ashkut, royal warden. He bellowed a challenge, aloud, so the orks could hear it and know fear in whatever small part of their brain perceived such a thing.

'Kalath hutt!'

The lychguard responded by hammering their dispersion shields with the pommels of their phase swords. Once. Twice. In Trazyn's vision, the glyph for conquest appeared, overlaying his view of the battle.

They advanced, formation splitting to engulf Trazyn and get him behind them. Another rank was already coming through the tear in reality to join them.

'Kalath hutt!'

Bang. Bang. Pommel on shield. The glyph pulsing again.

'Kalath sep!'

The line stopped a pace short of the orks, swords poised. Silent and unmoving.

Trazyn was not a warrior. Never had been. Did not, over-all, particularly like fighting. He generally considered face to face combat a failure. He preferred his enemy to be unarmed and facing the other direction. Or better yet, a thousand leagues away and unaware of his presence.

But seeing Ashkut's display filled him with pride. The pulsing chant. The eerie stillness. The gleam of sunlight on burnished turquoise and gold. He'd never been a dynastic partisan, considered himself beyond that pettiness, but at this moment, standing in this plaza in the raiment of war, his central reactor cycled a little faster with the memory of ancient glories.

The orks, for their part, howled in approval. A few beat their own weapons together in clumsy imitation of the lych-guard's martial prowess.

Then they surged forward like the surf.

'Nihilakh ascendant!' cried Trazyn, lost in the moment.

The lychguard responded with a charge.

Dispersion shields slammed muscle with bone-cracking force. The leading wave of orks staggered back into their comrades, bellowing in anger and confusion as the ranks behind sent them careening back onto the wall of shields and vibrating blades.

Phase swords chopped down, passing in and out of dimen-sions to bypass helmets and skulls, monomolecular edges carving through brains and corded necks, lodging in thick ribs and tough, fibrous organs.

A whole rank of orks fell mutilated at their feet.

Ashkut shouted and the lychguard advanced a step, metal feet crunching skulls and bursting viscera as they trod, uncar-ing, through the charnel dead.

One lychguard stepped back out of the advancing ranks

and collapsed, his death mask chewed to tatters by a chain-blade. Bare actuators, severed and leaking sticky reactor fluid, sparked with death light.

Sannet knelt and began resurrection protocols. The ranks closed, not even glancing back at their fallen comrade.

Revered lord, an interstitial message. *This unworthy one is Scythe Flight, Scout Two. I apologise for speaking directly to you without prompting. But I have protocols to notify you directly of imminent threat.*

Upslope, another group of habs detonated, raining pieces of red tile down on the plaza. Ashkut and his force stepped forward and sank their reverberating blades deep in ork flesh.

Speak, Scythe Flight, Trazyn signalled.

Request you scry into my unworthy oculars, lord.

Trazyn did, and his hydraulics pumped faster, threat response triggering.

At first he thought he was looking at some great battleship, then a collection of battleships chained together.

Then he saw the face, the angry eyes.

It was a gargant, taller than any building in Serenade City, save the Imperial basilica. Both super-heavy vehicle and religious icon, it glared over a jaw bristling with flamers, so a line of bright fire danced in place of the sawtooth underbite of most ork craft. Apelike arms swung from its thickset shoulders, each terminating in enormous buzz saws. A bulbous cannon, fat and wide-mouthed, sprouted from its belly.

They were towing it in on a barge, pulled by two ork tugs that were all engine and threw out wakes of white water and spilled fuel oil. They were headed for the shallow table of the fringing reef.

And if they launched it there, it would crush the coral flat.

Collapse tunnels, ensuring they missed their chance to open the tomb – maybe, as Orikan predicted, destroy it entirely.

Above, Trazyn saw the dirty smoke trails of stormboyz coming down on Serenade City.

'Ashkut,' said Trazyn. 'Clear them faster, we need to make the reef.'

'*Thall qutt!*' he shouted.

As one, the entire line of lychguards dropped to their knees, shields guarding their front in a low wall.

And the second rank, composed of Immortals, opened up with their gauss blasters.

The orks melted. Howling mouths disintegrated to ash, leaving nothing but a disembodied wail. Striking arms swung forward as corded muscle and connected on the kneeling lychguard as stripped bone. An ork boy, furious at this unsporting turn, emptied an entire magazine at the Immortals only to see his slugs snuffed out of the air like candle flames before he, too, was sanded down to nothing.

Gauss beams swept the plaza clean, disassembling even the bodies, so nothing blocked the necron advance.

Orikan checked Trazyn's position. Rechecked it.

Bastard was going too slow. Far too slow.

He banked the *Zodiac* into the planet's orbit, burned his inertialess drive to slingshot around the other side. There were five ork vessels on him. Five. He'd taken multiple hits. The lightning arc battery was damaged beyond the wraiths' abilities to repair it. The particle whip had only enough power for one last shot.

And only three days from the Mysterios opening.

He had expected Trazyn to betray him. And perhaps he had, in a way. The *Antiquity* was only assisting him in the most cursory manner. It had drawn off two of the escorts and disappeared to the far side of one of Serenade's moons. His divinations still claimed it was making combat passes out there, but he doubted it. Trazyn had decided to tie him up in orbit.

What Orikan had not expected was to miss the Mysterios' opening due to Trazyn's incompetence.

The *Zodiac* shot around the other side of Serenade, coming up behind the ork craft. Unleashed its particle whip directly into the gaping engines of a kroozer, ravaging one huge booster pod so badly it blew out and sent the craft spinning away end over end as the now lopsided engines threw it off course.

That was it for the particle whip. He'd been running things too close to the reactors' redline. The *Zodiac* needed time to recharge and cycle coolant. Only one weapon remained.

He hadn't wanted to give Trazyn the Mysterios in the first place, but she had said it was the only way – a claim his own visions confirmed. For the tomb to open, Trazyn must be holding the Mysterios. Orikan hated to think so, but it appeared the archaeovist had some role to play in this drama.

But Orikan had neglected to tell him the proper algorithm-chant to activate the device. And when the tomb did open – well, then all the auguries declared that Orikan would be the victor.

Lord, his weapon's cryptek signalled. *Sepulchre is charged.*

Finally, he responded. *Activate on my command.*

He punched the control orb, sending the *Zodiac* plunging between the ork vessels. A wolf among sheep.

For ten thousand years, the coral shelf had built itself around the island. Living polyps building on their dead ancestors, an eternal cycle of civilisation and extinction. Death and life. A form of complex urban life cycle that, in a way, was no less intricate than the city that occupied the land. Left to its natural course, the island would erode and shrink backward, retreating from the reef shelf until it encircled the green land like the halo of an Imperial saint. The island would die, worn away until it collapsed beneath the waves, and only the reef would remain. An atoll, a skeletal structure that had grown around what was there long ago, but was now hollow.

Metal feet crushed brain corals and fine, pink lattice fans as the phalanx walked out onto the reef shelf. Every footstep caused irrecoverable damage, stamping an imprint into it. Living metal meeting living stone.

It was not, Trazyn reflected, the first time these leaden soles had crushed a civilisation. He had ordered it himself, when he deemed it appropriate. But he pitied the reef and its endlessly artistic polyp colonies. The bright yellow fish stranded in tide pools. Perhaps he could save a part of it in the gallery.

The orks' sea-draining endeavours had dropped the water level far enough that only a hand's width of water covered the reef. Trazyn's warriors made their implacable advance untroubled by waves. The surf, often pounding, had been reduced to ripples sweeping by their ankles.

The table reef stretched half a league out to sea, to where the gargant loomed.

'Deathmarks,' Ashkut said. 'Target that fortress-walker. Any greenskin head you can see.'

'No,' snapped Trazyn. 'The tugs. Shoot the tugs.'

'Yes, my lord,' Ashkut corrected. 'Huntmaster, target the barbarians on their little ships.'

Ahead, behind a knobby head of rock that protruded from

the reef, Trazyn saw the marksmen step from nowhere, only a wisp of purple vapour betraying the doorway to the hyperspace oubliette. They lowered their long synaptic disintegrators and snapped shots towards the tugs, energy beams spearing across the flat reef. Trazyn enhanced his ocular image and saw orks on the lead tug drop, bodies falling limp as their neural pathways severed. At the ship's wheel, the helmsman sneezed blood onto the frosted glass of the wheelhouse and slumped on his controls.

The tug drifted to starboard, its chain pulling the great barge sideways, halting its progress.

Then, the gargant fired.

It was as if a starship had crashed upon them. The coral shelf rocked. Fissures split open, racing along it with the sound of grinding stone.

The deathmarks vanished, along with the rock outcropping they'd hidden behind. Water rushed to fill the deep shell hole blasted into the reef.

A piece of an arm fell near Trazyn, hydraulics discolouring the water around it to a milky yellow.

'Disperse!' shouted Ashkut. 'Advance, loose formation!'

Immortals and lychguard scattered in a wide grid, maximising the amount of space between them.

A Night Scythe dived on the gargant, lightning arc battery scouring its rough-plated shoulder. The titan swung one of its massive arms and swatted the fighter-transport out of the air, one enormous buzz saw shearing through its wing.

It doesn't matter, Trazyn thought. *We have no weapons heavy enough for this. Not to prevent it landing.*

The low-slung cannon boomed again, retracting into its housing.

Recoil rocked the gargant back so hard the barge slammed

backward, its prow rearing out of the water. The enormous machine scraped a few *khut* towards the stern.

Trazyn heard the freight-rail sound of the shell coming. Knew there was nothing he could do. He distantly felt the blast rock the coral beneath him. Throw him through the air so he saw the turquoise of the ocean and orange-pink of the sunset-painted sky.

The blast had torn away both his legs and one arm. Charred his skull and torso until he was nothing but a reactor and logic processor in a fused hunk of metal.

Trazyn did not concern himself with these details – because he had a plan.

Deep in the catacomb galleries of the *Zodiac*, a reverberation took hold of the living metal. The ship's frame vibrated with a sound like tolling bells. A funerary reverberation that shook the living metal so hard maintenance scarabs clattered on floors and crypteks nursing the reactors magnetically locked themselves down.

It emanated from the sepulchre crypt, a holdfast where not even the ship's senior officers were permitted to venture. The crypteks chosen to keep the tomb were a hermetic cabal, their networked meditation chants restraining the weapon's violence until it could, if only briefly, be released.

If simply left to run, it would tear the ship apart.

The tolling agitated the very air, sound waves penetrating even the sonically deadened plates of the ship's hull and passing through the void beyond – though how it did so with no atmosphere to travel through was beyond even Orikan's understanding.

And as the astromancer monitored his divinatory reports, he saw that the ork ships had begun to vibrate as well.

Open a pierce-channel to the ork ship, he signalled to the dispatch officer. *I wish to hear what's going on inside.*

The audio cut in overloud, so blaring that he had to dial his auditory transducers back to hear the discord that held sway on the ork flagship.

Inside their armoured bulkheads, behind their massive weapons and clad in muscle more resilient than all but hallowed necrodermis, the orks were screaming. Not screams of bloodlust and joyous slaughter, but the howls of sentient creatures reduced to base animalism. Pain without understanding. Fear of things that dwelled in darkness. The mad, discovering a new depth of madness.

Weapon discharges. Cleaver blades meeting with blacksmith tones.

Orikan smiled.

He had not known whether the weapon would work on orks. When used on the aeldari, the sepulchre's psychic wave unleashed glimpses of the empyrean, waking nightmares so horrifying that it reduced stalwart warriors to lunatics gripped with seizure, unable to control their own bodily functions. Others, the stronger and less fortunate, would rage against the terrors that surrounded them in the aether – striking down comrades and tunnelling through ship systems with their bare hands, though it tore their fingers to shreds.

Given the orkoid nature, Orikan was unsure whether it would simply increase the monsters' violence. With luck, Boss Bigsaw would be killed in the melee.

Orikan opened his star charts, made adjustments, inscribed a zodiac of his own devising and calculated the shifting sands of the future.

No. NO.

He recalculated. Changed variables.

Trazyn, you bastard.

Plans called for Trazyn to defend the entrance of the cave. Not to enter, for in doing that, the strange geology of Serenade would cut him off from fleet and ground communications. No signal in Orikan's cryptic arts could penetrate the planet's crust. He could not deploy his forces beneath the surface via translation, or even extract them to be rebuilt and resurrected in the *Zodiac*'s forge. Any necron who died in the tunnels would see the end of their aeons-long journey.

Trazyn was to wait until Orikan made landfall and met him. It was the deal. Orikan had not truly expected him to honour it, of course, but he'd not expected his cheating to gain him such an advantage that the tomb would be his. She had promised him that would not happen. That while Trazyn had a role to play in the opening, Orikan did as well.

After the tomb was opened, she had said, Trazyn could be dispatched.

Yet Orikan's astronomical calculations told a different tale. From his base at Mandragora the celestial alignments spoke victory, but here in the backwater space of Serenade, the stars were bad. Little delays, here and there, had thrown off his calculations. Or else, some event he did not understand had reordered the energy lines of heaven.

Casting a zodiac depended much on the exact moment one did it. The stars did not necessarily change, but the algorithm did.

Now he saw the Scholar ascendant, opposing and ruling the Mystic. The Metal Worlds in the House of Discord, indicating a dynastic war. The constellation Monolith, ruling over all – a great power unleashed.

Trazyn would open the tomb without him unless he acted. Unless he changed his stars.

Because Orikan also saw that the time of opening was upon them. The constellations and cosmic powers aligning to direct all the aetheric energies to this crux in the space-way. This lodestone of Serenade.

And that meant that the stars were shining on him, stronger than he had ever felt. All at once, the discord in himself, the feeling of being torn and incomplete, became clear. He was disjointed because he could feel the disassociation of his energies. Like a great block grinding into place on a temple's foundation, protesting and teetering until it fell into its niche in the great wall. A moment of dangerous weakness and destabilisation before strength took hold.

Orikan knew. He knew how he would confront the Scholar. He changed his algorithms, cast his zodiac, and cursed.

But not in frustration. This time, he blasphemed in awe.

Translate the decurion here, he ordered, indicating a point on the map. *Take with you the entire complement of wraiths. Then march. Travel deep. Gain the tomb and halt whatever Trazyn is attempting to accomplish.*

And you, lord? It was his plasmancer, Qetakkh of the Burning Hand.

Orikan did not trust military beings. Did not understand them. Indeed, he did not trust Qetakkh. But Orikan knew that the plasmancer wished patronage for his solar research, a venture Orikan was happy to fund and lend expertise to if it – at least for a time – bought him the loyalty and destructive power of a talented tech-sorcerer.

I will see you there, responded Orikan.

Then he said no more, for the stars had aligned their power and bathed him in light trillions of years old – and he was already changing.

* * *

Trazyn spurred the lychguard to run the moment his consciousness flowed into the surrogate.

'Follow me!' he shouted. 'Nihilakh ascendant!' At the same time, he sent it as an interstitial command, rocketing the message through the combat net that helped the lychguard strike as one, enabled the deathmarks to fire at precise intervals, and controlled the targeting matrix of the Immortals so no two of them shot at the same enemy.

He was already sprinting, running straight at the rearing gargant.

Necrons were implacable beings. Unstoppable, but not known for their speed.

Yet when called upon, the legions of cold steel could run. Metal toes dug into exposed reef. Skeletal forms hunched forward into the swarm of shots that buzzed around them, spattering their forms with strikes on the water and clipping metal arms.

'Rush it!' he shouted. 'Don't let the cannon get range.'

The coral rocked as another shell landed well behind them, the enormous cannon moving jerkily level to try and readjust to the running targets. Its barrel tracked first left, then right, unsure of where to point, trying to compensate for the rocking of the barge.

Two hundred cubits away.

Trazyn had never led a charge before. He found it exhilarating. His systems sang with the illusion of adrenaline that came from the central reactor throbbing in his chest. Hydraulics pumping. Threat grids and bright-painted targets splashing across his vision. He saw orks crowding the firing platforms on the gargant's thick shoulders and head, pouring fire down on them.

An Immortal next to Trazyn pitched backwards, some kind

of energy weapon severing his spine. The soldier recovered himself and crawled through the shallows, clutching at corals and holes filled with needle-sharp sea urchins in his compulsion to continue the charge. His fellows, driven to win glory for the dynasty, trampled him until his broken form began to seize and leak clouds of green fluid that flashed from electrical discharges – a thunderstorm in miniature. To Trazyn's right, a lychguard's foot dropped into a hole in the reef and she collapsed forward. The orks must have noticed the still target, because a line of bullet detonations ripped up her back.

'One warrior phalanx,' Trazyn ordered. 'Stop and provide fire. Keep their heads down.'

One hundred cubits.

Cold green beams lanced over Trazyn's head, sweeping the upper decks of the gargant, stripping channels in the armour as if they were fingers in clay, leaving burnished silver gullies behind. Orks ducked, growling with annoyance. One or two that didn't get down took the beams full force and fell backward, missing the front two-thirds of their skulls.

Trazyn saw the big saw-capped arms cock backward to swing at the onrushing necrons. At the gargant's base, a desperate ork mek tried to reattach a snapped guy-wire. The gesticulating war engine yanked the cable out of his hands, sending severed fingers spinning away. The mek waved towards the monstrosity's command module, trying to get the pilot's attention, to warn of the destabilisation occurring at the machine's base, but when the big machine swung another guy-wire snapped, lashing out with such force it cut the mek – and two other deckhands – clean in half.

'Get aboard! Swarm it.'

The great cannon roared one last time, and Trazyn knew

they'd done it. The volley fell short, shrapnel scything through the first rank of necrons. Warriors and elites alike fell mangled. And Trazyn – with artificial slowness – saw the piece of shrapnel that would kill him. It was the size of a hand, and spun towards his face like a throwing knife.

He activated the cloak, found a future where he survived, and took it.

The chunk of scalding steel rammed into his shoulder, sinking deep into the living metal and sending off a shriek of damage reports. His left arm went limp.

Trazyn shrugged it off. Fixable. Already he could feel his necrodermis pushing against the intervening object.

Then he was at the edge of the reef, and leapt, obliterator raised.

He landed on the end of the barge and crushed an ork ribcage with a hammer blow of his obliterator. He sprinted on, dodging and wheeling to get around the huge gargant's side.

'Follow me. Go wherever I go.'

A proximity alert sounded and he leapt forward as a buzz saw the size of a Leman Russ shrieked by, throwing sparks as it carved into the barge deck. A whole phalanx of Immortals and warriors flew into the air, dismembered pieces scattering.

'Don't stop to fight them,' he ordered. 'Get around the side, then the b–'

An axe clanged off his armoured hood and he wheeled, meaning to grab the offending ork's tusk with his off-hand and deliver a shot of aetheric energy with his obliterator.

But his arm merely twitched, the hunk of shell still embedded in his shoulder. And before he could bring his obliterator around he felt brutish fingers close on his wrist and a celebratory howl from behind him.

Seeing the obliterator immobilised, the ork who'd hit him

grappled his chest and brought him down. Two orks piled on him, then three, pounding, firing pistols that hit each other as much as him. Iron-shod boots scraped his pitted chestplate.

He saw the orks up close, detachedly analysing their rank breath – fungus beer, roast squig and human flesh – feeling their incredible strength as they pummelled him against the deck. There were so many.

'I keeps 'is head!' one shouted.

'Oi! He's my tinny git. Get orf youse.'

They kept piling in. Trazyn estimated that there were twenty to thirty on top of him, their weight pinning him to the patchy panels of the barge deck.

A deck that was starting to tilt.

He heard clanging feet, the decurion. Piling in around the orks. The deck tilted further. His back ground against the uneven plating as gravity took hold. Water lapped around his pinned head. The weight on Trazyn lessened as an ork tumbled off with a splash.

He scryed through the press, saw the gargant turning on its big treads, winding up for another swing.

The huge tracks slid forward with an unbearable squeal of metal on metal. Slowly at first, then faster as the pitch of the deck accelerated its fall.

And then Trazyn was sliding too, heaps of orks rolling away as the barge began to capsize. He let it happen, happy to be carried off the craft and into the warm water as the gargant carved a bloody track through the orks and necrons that still clung to the barge's deck.

Trazyn grabbed a handhold at the end of the barge, well below the waterline. The starboard side of the deck was nearly four cubits underwater by the time the gargant passed above him, eclipsing him in shadow as it overbalanced and plunged head first into the surf.

Trazyn watched it sink, its illuminated eyes and strobing searchlights lighting up its drowning crew until, one by one, its electrical systems winked out – succumbing to the abyss.

Blood, thick and dark, covered the corridors of the ork flagship. Bodies choked its gangways and cabins. What remained of the crew had turned on each other, butchering without objective. The slaughter knew no rank or privilege. Snotling hordes swarmed over larger orks, stabbing at eyes and clogging throats. Mobs eradicated everyone else in their gallery, then fired upon one another.

There was a weapon, Orikan remembered. A device Trazyn had mentioned during their communiqués on ork tactics. He did not care to remember its name, but the greenskins used it to fire their smaller kin through the horrors of the immaterium, ensuring they exited the tunnel so mad that they mangled anything they landed on.

It was as if the whole ship had been fired through such a device.

Orikan, empowered in his lightform, walked among them like a god.

The first ork to charge him he immolated with a touch. The squad that followed, he shot through with electric bolts that struck from his staff without him even conjuring them.

Twenty greenskins screamed and fled, believing him to be one of the nightmare creatures who had torn into their collective minds' eye.

In a way, they were right. He shot directly through the fleeing mob like an arrow, leaving a tunnel of cauterised flesh where he passed.

The ork ship was not a single vessel – it was multiple salvaged ships cobbled together, fused and twisted like the crypto-thralls some of his order fashioned out of a particularly hated foe. It took time to find the bridge.

And when he did, Boss Bigsaw was not there.

The bridge crew were elites. Large, aggressive. Well armed. Orikan did not fight them. He was running out of time. Instead, he ripped open a bulkhead and watched them blown out into the void, clawing and swearing, ice crystals forming on their gummy eyes.

He saved one. Brought it pain so excruciating that even an ork could not endure it.

'Where is the warlord?'

The answer made him feel imbecilic, despite his shining aspect.

The doctor was in the infirmary.

Orikan discovered him by following the screams. Knew he'd found the right place when he saw the display room of vivisected bodies.

Orkoids of every size. Humans. Various forms of plant and animal life sewn in a variety of combinations. Men with the wings of birds sprouting from faces. Ork heads grafted to the trunk of a great tree, arms hanging down like boughs. Moving creatures with robot torsos and flesh limbs. A whimpering gretchin permanently wired into a gyroscope of unknown function.

Boss Bigsaw did not follow the dictates of genus, species or kingdom.

It seemed to Orikan very inefficient.

The boss himself stood in the centre of an operating theatre, covered in gore. He was enormous and mismatched, with rings of pink scar tissue betraying where he'd grafted his pin head on the hulking chest of a larger ork. Cybernetic hands – one a spinning bone saw and the other a crude surgical clamp – were sunk deep in the chest of what, only moments before, had been a soldier of the Serenade Frontier Rifles. Blood fountained from his sawing and bile spewed in his piggish face. The painboy snorted to clear his breathing passages.

And saw Orikan.

His eyes went wide.

'Wot a specimens! I wonder wot's inside ya.' He snapped his pincer for emphasis.

Orikan came closer.

And it was Bigsaw's turn to scream.

Trazyn stepped off the barge and sank, descending into the fathomless depths. Behind him, the decurion stepped off in ranks, sinking behind him in solid lines. As they reached the twilight bottom, his feet touched soft padding – a meadow of sea grass, bright yellow or at least appearing such in the green light of their reactor glow and weapon tubes. In this twilight realm, every necron burned like a candle, sickly light emanating from behind their ribs and bright oculars.

A hundred cubits distant, he could see the shadowy line of the gargant resting on the sandy bottom. Large grey fish patrolled it in predatory circles, snatching up the bodies that were still floating free from the hulk.

'Sannet?' he said, voice carrying easily through the water. 'Deploy a tesseract field. The large one.'

'You do not wish me to accompany you into the caves, lord?'

'No.' He shook his head. 'Recover what warriors you can. But after that, I want that gargant. With luck, we can even render it operational for display.'

'A pity we did not have a Doom Scythe,' his servant said, slapping away one of the predators as it gnawed tentatively at his hand. 'We might not have lost so many men.'

'Of course we had a Doom Scythe,' Trazyn snorted. 'But how would I have displayed it? Do you want to fix that kind of damage?'

Then he turned towards the cave, raised his obliterator and lowered it again to point at the mouth.

And the warriors of Nihilakh marched, luminous, into the watery darkness.

Three days they walked, deeper into the abyssal cave network. Winding and twisting. Sometimes up, sometimes down. Always in darkness. At times they passed chambers whose ceilings opened to the world above, sending angelic shafts of light into the grotto. Here reef systems sprouted, unseen by any mortal eye. Bright-orange fish weaved and nestled through the corals, nosing through the imperial purple grasp of tickling anemones. Turtles the size of Imperial groundcars, lacking any fear of the intruders, nosed at the marching warriors as they glided by. Trazyn found himself particularly taken with an octopod the same rich turquoise as his Nihilakh colours. The creature, surely attracted by his heraldry, attached herself to his shoulder plate. He collected the specimen as a souvenir.

Not all was so serene. Blind eels thicker than Trazyn was wide and with teeth that overlapped like the fingers of folded hands slid and wriggled through the lightless caverns. One attacked a phalanx of Immortals and had to be slain, its inky blood further reducing visibility. With each fathom the eels got larger, until they discovered one that – were it not so decomposed – might have been a third of a mile long. Foul hagfish burrowed through its flesh, their web-like slime clogging the chamber so thoroughly they'd needed to clear it with gauss fire.

The Mysterios vibrated the entire way, singing along with an ethereal resonance Trazyn could not hear. Days in the dark worked on one's imagination, it was true, but he could swear it was beginning to shift as they descended, its angles and vertices sliding and rearranging, unstable.

He knew the chamber when he saw it.

It was monumental. Large enough to fit one of the ork escort ships in its cavernous space. Trazyn had not seen its like except in the largest Imperial faith centres and aeldari craftworlds – and in necron tomb worlds, of course, which is what this was.

He was well within the chamber before he realised it, so thick lay the silt on the floor. Tubules, the kind that lived off undersea volcanic vents, obscured the ribbed struts that held up the ceiling. Normally, these sponges, tubes and skittering shrimp would be clinging to the side of a fissure, living off the nutrients that leaked up from Serenade's magmic blood.

But here, they had found an altogether more potent food source.

At the far end of the chamber stood a cyclopean double door, its panels covered with organic growth so thick that he could barely see the radioactive green light cast from between its cracks and glyph carvings.

That same death-light emanated from every living creature in the cavern, from the dully glowing strands of kelp, to the bioluminescent schools of fish. All reflected the same unhealthy radiance.

A radiance that would kill them, Trazyn noted. As a long thin fish slipped by, he could already see the tumours clustering beneath its skin – a gift of what the great doors concealed. The kiss of necrontyr.

'Incredible,' said Trazyn. 'It's an Eternity Gate.'

'Is it dangerous, my lord?' asked Ashkut, hand drifting to his phase sword.

'Oh, very.' Trazyn chuckled. 'It's a doorway to an interdimensional chamber. A place between, like the hyperspace oubliette where the deathmarks wait between firing positions. The perfect hiding place for anything you do not want found – but quite toxic to all but our kind.'

'It is harmless to us?'

'My dear warden, the entire galaxy is harmless to us.'

'And...' he paused, and Trazyn watched his retainer's curiosity war with his sense of decorum. 'What is inside?'

'An age long past.' Trazyn patted the commander's back, a gesture made slow by the water. 'And perhaps the key to an age yet to come. Do not trouble your matrix with the weighty matters of history, Ashkut. See to the strategic details.'

'I will secure the chamber,' he nodded, and Trazyn caught a hint of relief in that voice.

'There's a good soldier. Defensive line where you think best. Immortals and deathmarks up high, perhaps, lychguard halting an advance.'

'Indeed, lord.'

Trazyn reached into his dimensional pocket and withdrew the Astrarium Mysterios, his hands passing over the tesseract labyrinths nestled beside it.

As he crossed the chamber to the Eternity Gate, he could already feel the Mysterios folding and turning, angles making impossible shapes as they twisted in and out of reality. It slid so much in his grip that he held it with two hands.

Schools of fish gathered like a multitude of worshippers around a prophet, nosing at the light emanating from the Mysterios' runes. For they were no longer necron glyphs,

ROBERT RATH

but a language so ancient Trazyn did not recognise it, and indeed, would not be able to read it if he did. Each character seemed to change depending on the angle he viewed it. They were water-like, spiralling eddies in his peripheral vision and geometric proofs when he looked at them straight-on.

Despite his curiosity, he tried not to do that – for when he did, his oculars lost focus, the image crazed like a smashed window.

Was this the warp-infused writing of the Old Ones, a script he'd once translated so easily, but had forgotten when he'd lost his soul?

Soon, he could not see it anyway. The Mysterios was now boiling the water around it, cloaking it in a torch flame of bubbles that drifted to the cavern's high ceiling. Clouds of shrimp, mistaking the release of heat for a new volcanic opening, wriggled towards the Mysterios and died, their bodies forming a carpet that crunched under Trazyn's feet.

The door was responding, its glyphs burning away the layers of oceanic sponges and calcified coral to reveal the message radiating out of the clean blackstone.

HAIL, SEEKER
I, VISHANI, LAY THIS CURSE:
HERE SLEEPS NEPHRETH
PHAERON OF AMMUNOS
THE ONE CALLED THE UNTOUCHED
CONQUEROR OF STARS
SLAYER OF GODS AND IMMORTALS
OPEN AND BE DAMNED.

Trazyn staggered, weak. Whatever aura the Mysterios gave off sapped him, feeding on his reactor energy much as it shrivelled the fish and crustaceans that drifted still and dead behind him like the trail of the old fire wyrms of myth.

222

No, it was not only that. It was the weight of history. Vishani, High Cryptek of the Ammunos, had inscribed this message sixty-five million years ago. Before she burned in the furnaces of biotransference. Here stood a relic of the necrontyr. A thing fashioned by those hands of flesh they'd so despised, and would give anything to reclaim.

Even the fire wyrms. He had forgotten them. An old folk-tale of an abandoned planet. A memory stolen from him by the avarice and deceit of the C'tan, now returned.

He felt a substance leaking from his oculars, and for a bare instant thought he was weeping. Then he realised it was also coming from his olfactory transducers and mouth.

Reactor bile. Coolant fluid.

He'd received no notices or alerts, but the Mysterios was killing him.

Trazyn let it go, fell to his knees as he watched it rise before the doors like a floating lantern.

Another flash of memory. Orange prayer lanterns floating above the dunes, each painted with a message begging the solar gods of the necrontyr to keep the illness away during the new year. Hands on his shoulders. His mother? His father?

The Mysterios, spinning madly, shifting dimensions and angles, locked.

An icosahedron. Twenty faces. Twelve vertices. Smooth as blackstone, shining hot, projecting geometric mandalas that, when Trazyn looked at them, seemed to contain great gulfs of space. Things long past, things meant to be, places distant and destroyed.

The tomb doors ground open, torturously, disturbing aeons of sediment and sending cracks along the walls of the chamber as they retreated into hidden cavities.

Through the widening crack rippled the colourless pool of

a deactivated portal. A mirror in the cosmos. Walk into it, and one would simply walk out the same surface.

It needed directions. To know where to go.

Trazyn opened his mouth, calling up an engram of the arithmantic incantation that would activate the Mysterios. In his neural matrices, he saw Orikan intoning the words, his hands sinuously twisting into occult gestures whose significance escaped Trazyn.

He could, however, match the gestures exactly while playing Orikan's recorded incantation from his own metal throat.

He said the first word, and faltered.

For the tomb's antechamber had begun to tremble. Whatever power the Mysterios radiated must, he reasoned, have triggered a seismic shift. Or else the great doors – long the foundation upon which trillions of tons of seafloor had rested – had triggered an undersea avalanche with their movement.

No, he realised, it was coming from behind him.

Trazyn turned and saw the light illuminating the entrance tunnel. It was nearly as bright as that leaking from the Eternity Gate.

And then a meteor burst through it, smashing aside the defensive vanguard with their shields raised against the glare. It scattered them as easily as a frustrated hand swept pieces off a *zsenet* board. They fell away, the proud turquoise livery on their chestplates burned black and electric fire clawing out of their oculars and mouths.

The incandescent meteor slammed into the floor of the chamber, silt blown sideways where it landed and sponges tumbling away so the blackstone floor lay clean around it. The figure crouched, feet braced, hands planting a staff on the abyssal floor, one baleful eye boring straight at Trazyn.

Trazyn swore. A curse from old necrontyr so foul that any-one writing it would have their hands struck off.

'Astromancer,' he said, nodding a greeting. Even a league away, he knew that Orikan could see and hear him. He called up his empathic obliterator. 'Ashkut, please exterminate this insect. The scorpion may sting, but he is at least alone.'

But then Trazyn saw the source of the shaking.

It was not the door, or the Mysterios or Orikan's empowered form.

It was thousands upon thousands of metal feet.

Behind Orikan the tunnel began to crumble and vent silt. Oculars glowed in its cloudy depths. And metal bodies erupted from the entrance as if a whole burrow of sand ants had risen to defend their queen.

Warriors marched out, led by crypteks wielding staves of arcane power. Skorpekh Destroyers scuttled out through the roof of the tunnel and swarmed up the chamber walls. Wraiths swam in the ghostly light of the bioluminescent ecosystem, their undulating forms quick and agile while Trazyn's own bipedal troops slowly tracked their targets, impeded by the cold water, waiting for their directive.

When the Silent King had abandoned the necrons, he'd destroyed the command protocols that he'd used to dictate his orders. Yet some remained as instinct, hardwired into systems that were built to obey.

Provided they were functioning properly, no necron of vas-sal rank could fire on one of its own kind. Not without a direct override from their lord.

Before the Silent King's departure, the protocol had put a stop to aeons of blood feud and internecine warfare. It had allowed the Infinite Empire's expansion, forming a stable bedrock that had let them murder the star gods and banish the Old Ones.

If one necron slew another, it must be by direct order. And the party responsible would be held to account, explaining why they had turned on their own kind.

'By the order of Overlord Trazyn of Solemnace,' he said. 'Fire! Fire! Fire!'

CHAPTER FIVE

'If the enemy surrounds you, there are only two tactical options. The first is to break out of the encirclement and retreat, which – if successful – will preserve your army but ensure the chroniclers remember you as a defeated fool. The second is to fight to the death, in which case, you will destroy your army but the histories will laud you as a slain hero. Given these two options, I consider encirclement generally inadvisable.'

– Nemesor Zandrekh, *The Logic of Battle*

Disassembling beams tore through the abyssal dark, atomising fish and luminescent jellies, eating away at Sautekh Warriors that, implacable and uncomplaining, carried on pushing through the water as they ceased to exist.

The cold water dragged on metal limbs and traversing weapons, giving the combat a sense of deliberation, like sparring partners moving at three-quarter speed to learn a new fighting stance. It was as if, Orikan thought, he were watching the battle with his chronosense dialled slightly back.

If not for the beams. They leapt through the water as fast as ever.

From above, Orikan saw a quartet of synaptic disintegrator beams lance into a knot of skorpekh Destroyers that were advancing across the ceiling. One quivered and fell, sinking towards the raging combat below.

Orikan sensed danger and locked the threat down: an Immortal hiding in the kelp, bright light already splashing from his gauss blaster.

Orikan ran time back a second, then knitted his fingers to summon the Prism of Zycanthus, scattering the beam into harmless bands of light. Then he leapt, his insubstantial form immune to the impeding water.

The dissonance between slow-moving troops and fast-moving beams had made the cavern a killing ground. Warriors and Immortals dropped, whole ranks snuffed out by the relentless gauss fire. This watery battlefield also multiplied the effectiveness of tesla carbines. Their directed electrical strikes raged like storms though the Sautekh ranks, turning them from a support weapon to a heavy cannon with a lingering blast radius.

Orikan hit the Immortal even before the trigger on its gauss blaster reset for a second shot. Plunged a shining hand into his ropy entrail cables, found the spine and yanked it out through his front. Swung the Staff of Tomorrow around, scything down kelp, and cleanly decapitated a second Immortal.

The one with the tesla carbine turned on him, electro-chamber cycling for a shot.

Orikan spoke an equation and overloaded the weapon, finishing the troublesome soldier with an electricity storm that fused his joints and left him a blackened statue, falling stiff into the silt.

He was so powerful. All the energy in the galaxy channelling directly into his system. The light that bent around black holes, the particles that raced across time and space from the furnace of creation, the entire flow of cosmic energy was focused here. Focused on him. There was so much, he found himself frustrated that he couldn't contain it all. Like a tomb robber who had broken open a chamber of treasures and could only carry away what fitted in their small bag. The wealth of energy he had was immense, but there was more he could tap into, *so much more*.

Orikan reached out a clawed hand and twisted. Halfway across the chamber, a Nihilakh lychguard broke ranks and laid into her fellows, carving deep wounds in their unprotected backs. With a single word, he crushed the skull of a deathmark in the chamber above. The skorpekh Destroyers on the ceiling had finally reached the sniper team, and he saw their arachnid legs rear back before spearing two of the deathmarks. Unable, due to the chamber's unique geology, to flee to their hyperspace oubliette, the marksmen died waving their long disintegrators in a pathetic parody of self-defence.

Orikan might have scryed into the skorpekhs to relish the moment, but he had greater things to attend to – and even empowered, he feared the corrupted programming of the Destroyers might infect him.

Besides, he could see the gate. The tomb entrance. It had not been activated.

And he surged through the water to ensure that he would be the one to open it.

* * *

One did not have to be a military being to know that this battle was going poorly.

Trazyn's expedition had numbered around five hundred. His usual core of lychguard and Immortals – the acquisition phalanx he took on many hard-to-crack worlds – augmented with warriors and deathmarks.

Ashkut, signalled Trazyn, trying to find the royal warden in the melee. Trazyn had climbed atop a spur of coral to get a better view of the enormous cavern. *Are things as bad as they look?*

Very precarious, lord, Ashkut responded. *We are facing at least four times our number. The enemy continues to emerge. We made a great butchery of them–*

A pause. Trazyn finally located his royal warden, focused in with his oculars, and watched him grab a cryptek by the top of its ribcage and slam his hyperphase blade up through the vulnerable space between ribs and spine. The cryptek's reactor detonated with a gush of bile, splaying his ribs outward.

–apologies for the interruption, my lord. We made a great butchery of them at range, but they have disordered our firing lines. We are outnumbered. They are taking the ceiling and upper galleries and will soon be behind us.

Trazyn looked up and saw the Destroyers flooding the ceiling, clambering and skittering through the dark like pale crabs. Yes, Ashkut was right. They were about to be surrounded and cut off. His oculars detected a burst of solar energy on the floor of the cavern and Trazyn turned to see the water shimmering with heat waves and steam bubbles.

A Sautekh plasmancer, his tendril-like legs propelling him through the water like a squid, had risen with his arms spread and summoned a corona of solar heat. Gathering energy that lit even the cavern's shadowy vaults, he bombarded the lychguard below with balls of pure radiation.

To Trazyn's left, the last of his warriors fell, trodden into the silt by the advancing enemies. Weak hands still clutching at the legs of their killers, trying to at least slow the progress of the foe. Faithful to the end, not knowing or not understanding that unlike their other deaths, there would be no resurrection from this one. No phasing into the belly of a tomb ship to be rebuilt.

Here below Serenade, dead was dead.

It was time, Trazyn decided. He reached into his dimensional pocket, selected a tesseract labyrinth, and pressed the key.

Volmak Khazar, datasmith second-class in the sacred Legio Cybernetica – Machine-God's blessed maintenance be upon it – was having difficulty calibrating their surroundings.

Last they had known, Khazar and their complement of Kastelan robots had been wading through drukhari raiders in the mountains of Rubrik VII, their breathing apparatus modified into a reusable oxygen system to deal with the massive altitude.

Yet now, if their environmental scanners did not lie, they were underwater.

A great depth underwater, if the pressure gauges read correctly.

And the lithe aeldari were gone. In their place were metal men, constructs cursed by the Machine-God. Blasphemous things, forged not made, that mocked the purity of the human form that still – despite their mechadendrites and databanks – lay within Volmak Khazar. With a trill of fear, their cybernetic brain brought up shadowy legends of the Men of Iron, the Abominable Intelligence said to have nearly brought mankind to ruin.

There were troops next to them, fighting the invaders. Green beams lashing out like whips that disassembled the enemy where they struck them. They were about to turn their head, but a strong urge prevented it, and the momentary warning of a system compromise winked out. Their cybernetic brain informed them that they had no need to see these allies, but they were to thank the Machine-God that these allies were fighting on their side.

So they did.

<Kastelan complement,> the tech-priest signalled in Mechanicus binharic cant.

Nine hulking robots stood straighter, dome heads turning towards Khazar for orders. Power fists crackled and weapons chambered in anticipation, merely at the tone of Khazar's logic-speech.

<Destroy the abominations.>

Nine big shoulders swung around and advanced, weapons acquiring targets. There were so many, it took no time at all, despite the slowness of the water.

Phosphor blasters coughed, barrels streaming steam-bubbles as they launched burning spheres of chemical fire towards the crawling hoard. Streams of white starbursts slapped into the advancing infantry, stuck to their metal bodies, the infernal chemical burning underwater and melting metal skin until the foul un-metal bubbled off, re-hardening in the cold water so the abyssal floor was littered with steel pellets.

The Kastelans, Khazar noticed on their dataslate, were keeping up an exceptional rate of fire. With water this cold, the phosphor blasters had no risk of overheating. Number Seven, though, was dumbly firing its incendine combuster into the water, despite the fact that instead of flames, a coiling trail of promethium spread from the weapon's muzzle.

Khazar disabled the weapon and ordered it to enter close combat.

Number Seven stepped forward and swung its power fist, crushing two of the blasphemous monstrosities.

To their left, Khazar saw an Onager Dunecrawler scuttle forward, a barrage of rockets whooshing out from its Icarus array and detonating amidst the foe, throwing metal body parts that fizzled as they sank.

Khazar drew their gamma pistol and blasted into the onrushing horde, their shoulder vox broadcasting the Litany of Data-Corroboration.

It was an honour, Khazar thought, to serve the Machine-God.

Kadderah Tole was loving this.

She had begun to tire of the high-altitude combat against the Emperor's little machine-drones. True enough that their pain at seeing their clumsy experiments rent and destroyed provided a certain distraction, but that juice was far too easy to squeeze. And studying their poor attempts to fuse flesh and machine did little to further her own surgical endeavours.

After all, one did not rise in the haemonculi order by mimicking the crude fleshworks of the dead Emperor's little machine-men.

But this. *This* she enjoyed.

Her experiments, fitted with anti-grav engines that bulged beneath their purpling skin, had always been used to swimming through air. And the high altitude of the Rubrik Spine Range had persuaded her to fit them with pressurised masks – the seals were not perfect, of course. For what was the fun if they did not choke a bit on the thin air?

Or the water, now, as the case might be.

She herself was elated to finally use the gills she'd vat-grown for herself two centuries back. Their lack of use had become the subject of a few sharp jests at a party she'd thrown. Everyone had quite a laugh at her expense.

Speaking of which…

Her Cronos reached the bladed things on the ceiling, lashing out with the bristled tendrils that she'd fleshworked from its arms, wrapping the cleaver-armed necron in a revolting embrace. She watched as the bristles of needle-thin spikes in the tendrils ignited, their power fields spiking the metal monstrosity in three hundred different places and injecting acid directly into its system.

Both Cronos flesh-construct and bladed berserker shivered together, like lovers consummating a night of passion, and she knew the Cronos was in as much pain – if not more – than its victim.

Teaches you to make fun of my gills, Xanther, she thought with a lopsided grin, as the being that was once her old drinking companion let go of the victim and reached for another. One of his tendrils had fallen victim to a necron blade, and drifted past, still wriggling around the ailing Destroyer.

Tole kicked her way to the still form and looked into its eyes, supping on the anger that burned there. She flicked through her implant toolkit and drew out a necrodermis needle – fortunate she had one, for they were uncommon – and plunged the spike into the necron's primary fluid secretor.

The reactor bile filling the crystal vial was such a lovely shade of yellow.

Extremely rare, this substance. Terribly toxic. Unsubtle, true, but effective in the extreme. And you know the necrons – it was *so* bothersome to harvest it before they phased. A pure sample was hard to come by. But these metal ruffians didn't seem to be phasing at all.

In fact, she got a closer look at this Destroyer than she'd ever had before, and felt a certain kinship. Clearly this being had once been one of its standardised kin, yet the genius of creation had come upon it, and like her it had decided to make itself a work of violent art. Each bladed limb, each protruding pneumatic chest-spear and bristling weapon had been fused to its frame. Tole patted its dead cheek with her grafted third arm, and pushed off him with the extended spine-tail that made her move so gracefully in the water.

Another Destroyer floated past her, and she looked up. More constructs were laying into the bladed monsters, flagella-like tentacles lashing and wrapping. Bladed spider limbs of the necron body-artisans meeting the whips and flesh hooks of her own work.

Dear friends, she thought, mentally greeting the rest of her party guests. *Meet your ancient and feared foe, the necrons.*

Do try not to laugh.

Orikan speared his staff through a tracked construct – nothing so much as a brain-dead corpse wired into a small tank, its skin sallow and pumped with embalming fluid. Even in his lightform, one that only existed partially in the physical plane, he did not want to touch it.

Trazyn. Only Trazyn would be perverse enough to collect such creatures.

Orikan wheeled and dashed under the swiping arm of a big construct – one of the nine that had made such a mess of his warriors – and slashed one of its legs through as he passed.

It toppled forward, severed limb buzzing with white electrical shorts as the idiot machine kept moving its legs as if it were upright, its empty weapon firing into the sponges.

A searing beam stitched across his left arm and he whirled, seeing one of the machine cultists coming at him with a pistol.

Orikan's enhanced senses detected the presence of mind-shackle scarabs in the tech-priest's system and drew the Sign of Thot in the air.

The cultist's hand shook as their finger tried to tighten on the trigger and could not.

'You wish to worship machines?' snarled Orikan. 'On your knees.'

The tech-priest dropped to their knees, then prostrated themself in the hazily glowing silt, surrounded by shredded sponge. The priest's right hand, twisting at an unnatural angle, held the beam pistol to the back of their own head.

Orikan did not wait to see the pistol go off.

He passed more abominations. Spindly legged machine-men with sucking gas masks sutured to their faces. A bipedal stilt walker spitting heavy laser fire. He sent an interstitial message for his plasmancer to deal with it.

Orikan could already feel the planetary alignment passing, his power weakening. The beam pistol had burned off a measure of his cosmic energy, and when he opened his ports to channel from the great lines of the zodiac he found the particles moving sluggishly now through the lines of space-time.

That meant there was little time to activate the Eternity Gate.

A spider tank stalked by, thudding lazy hard rounds out of its twin cannons, and Orikan weaved by it, bolt-dashing between the moving legs. To his right, a warrior in slick bladed armour and a rebreather face mask fired some kind of aeldari pistol and he uttered Hakki's Reversal, sending the storm of splinters back into the stunned raider so his blood misted the water.

Then, a hulking bodyguard, a royal warden if he was not wrong, stepped into his path. Orikan had not the time to deal with him properly, so he cast a quick combat algorithm to predict the vassal's movements.

He slid, skidding feet first through the silt and under the warden's first high blow. As he passed, he swept high, severing the vassal's spine.

It would not kill him. Orikan had not the time for finishing blows, but the guard would not interfere.

A last dash. Sliding through the slippery kelp grove. Pausing only to drop a chronomantic hex field to slow anyone pursuing him.

The Mysterios hung suspended. Brighter now. Transmuted. Singing.

And he could hear her in that song. Urging him forward.

You are so close, Orikan. See my name on this door? You solved the riddle, not him. Do not let this thief steal your glory. Only you will understand what you shall find here. No being is my equal. None but you.

Orikan stood beneath the arithmantic lodestone of the Mysterios. The piece that gave him the unknown variable in the equation.

Without that variable, given by the Mysterios and different each second, the algorithm would not be complete. Trazyn could have watched him recite the algorithm a thousand times – probably had – and it would not have mattered.

And though the language was strange to him, it somehow imprinted the impossible number directly into his engrams. The last piece of the puzzle.

He spoke the cryptographic algorithm.

The Mysterios slammed inward, imploding, folding and shifting, each of its twenty faces stretching deep into the core until every angle stood out in a point. A jagged starburst of equilateral triangle faces.

The mirror surface of the portal shimmered and shifted, a billowing green in the centre that spread to encompass the gateway.

Orikan could see the chamber beyond. Saw ranks upon ranks of figures, silhouetted in the indistinct haze of the portal. And for a moment, Orikan feared trickery, that Trazyn had infiltrated the tomb before him and installed an army there.

But as he stepped forward, he saw that the figures were stone, worn with the long aeons. Their backs were turned to him, as if they stood at attention for the phaeron who presumably lay beyond at the centre of the tomb.

The water seemed to draw him towards the portal, as it rushed through to fill the tomb. It happened slowly, a light pull rather than a torrent.

Orikan stepped forward, whispering thanks to the constellations, and whatever nameless god or power put them into motion.

And then the obliterator hit him from behind.

Orikan stepped back to the past, found his way blocked by Trazyn's cursed cloak. No past could exist, it seemed, where he was not struck. Instead, Orikan went back as far as he could – a bare half-second – twisting his head so the staff struck a glancing blow rather than scattering the whorl of protons that formed his cranium.

He staggered, recovered, wheeled on Trazyn with his staff held in a high guard.

'My heartiest thanks, Orikan,' Trazyn said. 'Quite chivalrous, to hold the door open like that.'

Then Trazyn turned, and dashed for the rippling dimensional gate.

Orikan threw his staff like a trident, pinning the lord's cloak to the sediment.

And then he was on him, empowered hands tearing at Trazyn's abdominal cabling, scratching furrows down his death mask. Hammering dents in his ribs.

'Bent-backed fool! Arrogant conniver. I'll rip your head from that hood, you degenerate–'

As he slammed his fists into Trazyn, he could see them flickering. Incandescent one blow, cold metal the next. The tide of energy had ebbed, the constellations sliding on their uncaring path where one alignment was as good as another.

'Damn!' Orikan shrieked, clawing his way towards the dimming portal. Something impeded him, and he knew Trazyn had locked hands around his leg.

Only a few moments left. He kicked Trazyn's death mask, saw it crack. Kicked again and shattered away a piece of necrodermis skull plate, exposing bare circuits.

Behind them, Orikan heard the sounds of battle – the howl of gauss fire already echoing through the turbid waters of the cavern – reach a crescendo. His perception suite, reasserting itself in fits as the empowering energy drained, warned of incoming threats.

That's when he saw them.

The Triarch praetorians.

They surged out of the entrance tunnel in an arrowhead phalanx, smashing through Sautekh and Nihilakh alike, driving a wedge into the Sautekh rear, scything down the enmeshed forces with their rods of covenant. As he watched, the formation split, driving to either side to form a cordon between Sautekh and Nihilakh. One beat a cryptek aside with the flat of his voidblade and raised a particle caster with the other hand, driving a shot directly into the vision slit of the crablike Mechanicus tank so the vehicle staggered and heeled over.

And at their front was Executioner Phillias, one hand raised high and projecting the three-eyed glyph of the Awakened Council.

If Orikan had any doubt, the message broadcast banished it.

THIS IS AN OVERRIDE COMMAND. ALL TROOPS OF THE EMPIRE WILL CEASE COMBAT BY ORDER OF THE COUNCIL. THIS IS AN OVERRIDE COMMAND. PUT UP YOUR WEAPONS. THE PENALTY FOR DISOBEDIENCE IS DEATH.

Orikan broke Trazyn's weak grip and ran. Towards the stone silhouettes in the crypt beyond. Towards the voice that bade him come. Towards the fading shimmer of the portal. He stretched out his hands at the fading image.

They struck bare rock.

The stars were no longer right. And the portal was dead.

ACT THREE:
EXTERMINATUS

CHAPTER ONE

'A worthy enemy is worth one hundred tutors.'

– Ancient necrontyr saying

'Let me state for the record,' Phaerakh Ossuaria said. 'That this is not officially a trial.'

'Can we be executed?' asked Orikan.

'Yes,' said Zuberkar, with a note of unpleasant eagerness.

'Then it's a trial,' Trazyn said.

'In a technical sense,' said Overlord Baalbehk. 'It is an enquiry.'

Orikan shot a look at Trazyn, signalled: *Look where you have landed us, you crook-backed madman.*

Madman? So says the delusional fanatic who speaks to illusions.

I do not–

'No, no,' scolded Ossuaria. 'Phillias, activate the signal dampeners. Anything you two say we shall all be a party to. No colluding on testimony–'

'I would rather collude with the Void Dragon,' snapped Orikan.

'Why not?' said Trazyn. 'Serpents belong together.'

'Cease!' Phillias shouted, slamming her half-moon executioner's glaive on the blackstone. 'This is not a venue to air your grievances. Your petty feud has cost the Infinite Empire dear in a moment of great vulnerability, and it would have cost more had the praetorians not been monitoring your movements. I have official powers of law here, granted not by this body, but the Triarch Council and the Silent King. Noncompliance in this enquiry shall be considered an admission of guilt, and in such cases my order has the authority to execute sentence.' She lowered her glaive, pointing it at the necks of both Trazyn and Orikan in turn, as if judging the distance of her swing. 'I have this power, overlords or no, and I swear on the shattered bodies of the Dead Gods that I will use it. Nod if you understand me.'

Trazyn nodded assent, stunned at this brazen statement of power. Clearly, the praetorians had taken a greater hand in council affairs over the last several millennia.

Indeed, it was possible that the ring of Triarch praetorians surrounding the council was not merely to contain the two prisoners, but to ensure this enquiry went as directed.

Usually, the praetorians did not undercut civil authorities so openly, preferring to play their cards close and exercise influence from the shadows. Things must, indeed, be serious for her to step out of line so. Was this the result of his feud with Orikan, he wondered, or linked to the strange absence of High Metallurgist Quellkah?

Phillias accepted Trazyn's nod and turned to Orikan.

For a moment pregnant with insolence, Orikan did nothing. Then he nodded with excessive sluggishness.

'What our executioner... the executioner... our, ah, colleague from the Triarch praetorians has said is correct,' said Ossuaria. 'We have had the most shocking reports of malfeasance. Things that call into question not only your honour, but your worthiness of overlord rank. Zuberkar, would you be good enough to read the first charge?'

Zuberkar, his phase sword across his knees, called up a phos-glyph panel and scrolled.

'It is alleged by honourable parties and witnessed by representatives of the most high Triarch that Overlord Trazyn of Solemnace and Master Orikan of the Sautekh did carry out a private blood feud with one another, over eight millennia, contravening their programming as well as the last edicts of the Silent King. They have broken the peace of the Infinite Empire on numerous occasions, including overriding vassal protocols to allow combat between kin, wasting the resources of His Eminence the Silent King. Most disturbingly, this knowingly occurred in an environment where phase-recall was unable to function, leading to the permanent loss of over three thousand of our subjects including seventeen crypteks, one hundred and twenty-four lychguard, three hundred Immortals, two thousand three hundred and sixty-seven warriors, and an estimated thirty Destroyer cult devotees. In addition, two ships heavily damaged...'

'This is absurd,' Orikan interrupted. 'As you say, there has been a feud. No one is denying that, for it was no secret. Indeed, this feud was *de facto* sanctioned by this very council when we put the matter before it. You declared the Astrarium Mysterios and the tomb of Nephreth to be the common heritage of the necrons. Do you not recall?'

Orikan opened a hand, casting a chrysoprase projection directly from his engram banks. It was Overlord Baalbehk, who now sat on the council, lying partially reanimated as an adjudicator.

'The Astrarium Mysterios will be owned by all and none,' said the projection. 'A free object belonging to he who possesses it. Stealing it shall be no crime, killing for it no sin. And whoever opens the crypt may keep its contents for the greater glory of their dynasty.'

'Stealing it shall be no crime, killing for it no sin,' repeated Orikan. 'So why are we subject to this trial that is not a trial, made to explain actions explicitly allowed under the council's directives?'

There was a pause.

'We are aware of the previous decision,' said Baalbehk. 'Believe it or not, Master Orikan, but our engrams are just as uncorrupted as yours. But we have also discovered certain procedural irregularities with that verdict which call the decision into question.'

'Namely,' said Ossuaria, her tile veil clinking as she leaned forward, 'we have received an anonymous accusation that the verdict was engineered via timeline manipulation.'

'Preposterous,' said Orikan.

'Indeed, such brazen rewriting of the timeline would explain why the membrane of reality became so thin on this world that it became subject to a violent warp-incursion a mere six decades after the trial. Empyrean-beings, here. On a council world. A gathering place of the Infinite Empire. A lynchpin of our fragile, still-slumbering society. You would not know anything about that, would you, Master Orikan?'

'You flatter me, phaerakh. But what you allege is beyond even my powers.'

Trazyn smiled. Even though it was a lie, it must have stung Orikan to say it aloud.

'Perhaps so,' Ossuaria said. 'But to avoid any doubt, we have tasked seventy-seven of our best chronomancers to lock the council room's timeline. You perhaps noticed our new mosaic.'

Trazyn looked down. Indeed, he had noticed the spheres and intersecting geometry that inlaid the floor. As a connoisseur, he could not have missed it. What he had not appreciated, however, was that the entire geomantic design consisted entirely of time tiles. He looked at Orikan, ready to drink in his reaction.

'An unnecessary precaution,' Orikan scowled. 'Indeed, I am wounded that the council would credit such scurrilous rumours. But as a humble servant of the empire I can lay aside my pride in order to banish even the merest hint of impropriety.'

'And all this,' Ossuaria continued, not even deigning to engage with Orikan's denials, 'is mere prelude to the most monstrous accusations. You have caused havoc in the sector, forced an ork fleet to withdraw and land on a tomb world where we have been forced to deploy our limited military strength and artificially raise half the population from stasis-sleep. Your meddling has, all told, cost us the permanent destruction of sixty-nine thousand necrons and incalculable neural damage to the tomb world. Pity you did not foresee *that* in your zodiacs, Master Orikan.'

'Overlord Trazyn changed the equations when he abandoned the fight in orbit, phaerakh. The fault is–'

'And that is not even counting the charges of murder,' said Phillias, finger impatiently tapping on the haft of her glaive.

'Noble council,' Trazyn laughed. 'You surely cannot charge us with murder. Vassals have no legal status as beings. Destruction of property, perhaps. And though I will admit that Master

Orikan and I have made very game attempts on each other's lives, here we stand more or less whole.'

'Not with the murder of each other,' said Ossuaria. 'With the murder of High Metallurgist Quellkah.'

For perhaps the first moment in sixty million years, both Trazyn and Orikan's verbal response programs failed. As they met each other's impassive gaze, Orikan shook his head slightly, and Trazyn responded with a shrug.

'I...' said Trazyn, carefully. 'I had noticed the high metallurgist's absence, but believed that he had simply yielded his seat to Lord Baalbehk, due to his superior rank and prestige.'

'Do not try to flatter me, archaeovist,' said Baalbehk. 'A century after the Council's original ruling of common heritage – a ruling we have vacated, you should note – High Metallurgist Quellkah resigned his seat in order to pursue his own studies on Nephreth and the tomb complex of Cephris. He departed immediately for an expedition – presumably on the world currently known as Serenade.' Baalbehk paused, waiting for one of the accused to volunteer information. 'He has not been heard from since.'

Trazyn tapped his chin, a nervous habit from the Flesh Times. The murder of a figure holding courtly rank – absent a formal declaration of feud or war – was a serious offence. Wipe out ten legions of vassals and the praetorians would not raise a finger in retribution, but the slaying of an aristocrat, a high metallurgist who possessed rank and privilege equal to a planetary regent, was another matter entirely.

'And you say he went to Serenade, phaerakh? Eight thousand years ago?'

'You did not believe, surely, that after a declaration of common heritage the two of you would be the only ones to launch expeditions?'

'I can only testify for myself, of course,' said Orikan. 'But in eight thousand years of visits to Serenade, I have not encountered the high metallurgist or any sign of his presence. Nor have I detected, in celestial trances conducted in orbit, any hint of technomancy. But I admit I have been absent from the world more than I have been present. Overlord Trazyn?'

'I have found the same,' Trazyn nodded. 'Millennia of spectromantic bombardments and survey sorties, and I have not seen any hint of our kind, apart from Master Orikan. And due to the, ah, unusual *sharpness* of our rivalry, I kept a high degree of awareness regarding signs of necron presence.'

'Typical,' sneered Zuberkar. 'Like the couple of bandits they are, neither saw nor heard anything. The ruffian's code of silence.'

'One of you killed him,' said Ossuaria. 'To declare otherwise strains credulity.'

'If you believe either of us would consider Quellkah a threat,' cut in Orikan, 'you are sorely underestimating our abilities.'

'Why, Orikan,' Trazyn said. 'I believe that's the kindest thing you've ever said to me.'

Ossuaria opened her mouth, then saw that the executioner was about to speak.

'Council,' said Phillias. 'May I suggest that if either of them had killed the high metallurgist – or indeed, knew of his disappearance – they would have already accused each other. Indeed, likely the murderer would have already gone through pains to implicate his rival far before this discernment.'

'True,' said Trazyn. 'Particularly given Orikan's history with the high metallurgist, the charges would lay nicely. Would've been quite the checkmate. You've had a lucky escape, astromancer.'

'She's right, Ossuaria,' said Baalbehk. 'These two despise

each other. And given their histories, such a despicable stratagem would likely already be in motion.'

'Serenade is a dangerous place,' said Orikan. 'Always has been. Aeldari Exodites, orks, even a few humans – not that they are of any consequence – and Quellkah was ever launching into endeavours that were above him.'

'Are you saying–?' started Zuberkar.

'I am saying Quellkah was a fool. A well-known fool. And I refuse to be punished for a limp-fingered meddler getting above himself and coming to a bad end. Truly, I will not even allow Overlord Trazyn to be punished for it, since I will not be denied my rights of feud.' He stared. 'I wish to see his face when I beat him to the tomb. Want him to know that I have bested him.'

'That may be difficult,' said Ossuaria. 'Given that Serenade is going to be destroyed.'

CHAPTER TWO

'History requires two parties – the historian and their
audience. Without that, one is just talking to oneself. So
kindly stop screaming and you might learn something.'

– Trazyn the Infinite,
guiding human guests through the Prismatic Gallery

'Destroyed?' said Orikan. 'Rather than destroy us, you will
destroy Serenade? Why?'

'In all honesty, we had discussed it,' said Baalbehk. 'That
was my course of action. Should the tomb remain unopened
until the Great Awakening, the dynasties would most certainly fall into civil war over its contents. But it is out of
our hands now.'

'We have consulted the Celestial Orrery and the Yyth Seer,'
said Phillias. 'Your intervention on Serenade has changed
the planet's fate. Originally, an Imperial cruiser group would
have arrived and made war on the greenskins, the combat

rendering the planet so uninhabitable that it would have been abandoned and forgotten. Now, the fleet will arrive to find the greenskin remnants substantially weakened, and therefore instead of directing resources for a protracted campaign, it will use them for resource extraction and the further development of the world. Serenade will go from backwater to prosperous hub.'

'Setting aside the humans' inevitable environmental destruction,' said Trazyn, 'that sounds like a world saved, not destroyed.'

'In roughly two thousand years, for unknown reasons, the Imperium will order fleet assets to scour the planet from orbit, cracking its mantle,' Phillias said. 'Given that the humans have unknowingly done this to at least two tomb worlds, we well know that even our most solidly built structures will not survive.'

'An Exterminatus,' said Trazyn.

'Just so,' said Phillias. 'You may have saved the tomb, but not for long.'

Orikan said nothing, fingers dancing in calculation on phos-glyph panels. 'The next celestial alignment to open the tomb is...' He paused. 'It is during the destruction.'

'So it will be destroyed,' said Ossuaria.

'Not necessarily,' said Trazyn, tapping his chin. 'An Exterminatus is not an instant process. Planets are tough things, not easily undone. Killing everything that lives on them is no problem, but actually burning off the atmosphere and cracking the mantle takes a good while, days even. And the Eternity Gate was significantly underground.'

'Release me from this farcical trial,' said Orikan. 'I could slip through during the bombardment and emerge another way. Trazyn is, after all, the one who originally stole the Mysterios. He only wishes the tomb's contents so he can hide them away and look at them. He wants to possess the past, not shape the future. Punish him and use me.'

'Pardon me,' Trazyn sniffed. 'Master Orikan began this feud. And while I would put the contents in a gallery accessible to all, he would use it for his own purposes. Might even destroy the body of Nephreth in his researches into energy projection. Punish him...'

'We have decided to punish you both,' declared Ossuaria. 'Zuberkar?'

'To atone for your crimes,' the overlord said, spinning his phase sword by the tip, 'you will enter the Awakened Council's service. Both of you will work on Serenade, assisting each other, to open the tomb – for however long that takes. You've already opened it once before, and would have succeeded in recovering Nephreth but for your squabbling. Consider what could be accomplished if you behave like lords, rather than shrieking juveniles.'

'But overlord,' said Trazyn. 'We have duties–'

'For the next one thousand five hundred years, you will stay clear of each other and focus on dynastic business,' said Baalbehk. 'A cooling off period. After that, you will reconvene on Serenade and spend at least one quarter of your time there, working to open the tomb. And let us be exceedingly clear. Your use of forces will be tightly controlled. There will be no attacking each other. Not one necron is to be destroyed by another in this endeavour, not one. If we get wind of it...' He paused. 'We will cancel both your reanimation protocols. No resurrection in the forges. No phasing. You will for all purposes be mortal.'

'We will punish you,' said Phillias, 'with each other's company.'

'And how do you expect to enforce these unreasonable demands?' said Orikan.

'Simple,' Phillias said, giving her glaive a spin. 'I will supervise.'

CHAPTER THREE

*While it is true that even the best plans may fail,
improvisation has a negligible success rate.*

– Lord Solar Macharius, *Collected Maxims*

Serenade
500 Years Before Next Tomb Opening

The lizard-birds collected around the café, ducking and bobbing, hunting between the antique cobblestones for scraps of
pastry dropped by the off-worlders who stopped for lunch or
a cup of caffeine after seeing the sights in Settlement Plaza.

A waitress swiped a menu at the growing multitude and
they retreated, well used to these sorts of tactical withdraw-
als. They came out like the tide that used to lap not far from
this place where five streets met.

Then the back-and-forth dance broke routine, and the
lizard-birds startled, tittered in panic and took flight as if

some invisible presence passed among them. They wheeled towards what was once the great ocean – now an empty basin filled with the long stretches of low-cost habs, its seas long drained.

No one paid any heed. The musicians playing next to the café – a reed trio blowing a long slow tune that spoke of island breezes that no longer passed over these shores – kept up their long notes. Before them, a legless string-player picked at some kind of lap zither.

Trazyn had been standing there watching them for half an hour when Orikan slid up beside him.

'I am surprised you decided to come,' said Trazyn.

To their right, the café patrons laughed and chatted. A server weaved between the maze of little tables. None of them glanced at the metal behemoths standing a stone's throw away.

'Not a bad test run, don't you think?' Trazyn tapped the illusion emitter hanging around his neck. 'It does not so much hide us, as it bends reality around us. Our own little oubliette, like the deathmarks.'

'No,' sneered Orikan, annoyed at the simplified explanation. 'The deathmarks are in a pocket dimension. I suspect this device merely bends light and dampens sound by interfering with the crude perception inputs of their simian brains.'

'Not much difference.'

'There's every difference. It directly counteracts our images imprinting on their conscious minds, yes. But put us in front of a warp-sensitive, or if one of these clumsy biologicals bumps into us, and they'll see us well enough. This overly dramatic demonstration is a risk.'

'Orikan,' Trazyn chided. 'It was a tactical necessity to test the technology. Besides, this is a cultural experience. Try to enjoy it. Study these people and you can get a little perspective on the galaxy.'

'I do not trust technology that I haven't built myself.' Orikan glanced at the café with disinterest. 'What is this?'

'The emitter? An artefact I had. I suspect from the Old Ones, or perhaps...'

'No, what are they all imbibing?'

'Ah,' said Trazyn. 'That is caffeine. Ground beans soaked in water. Or at least a chemical approximation thereof.'

'This is ridiculous. Standing here among these biologicals, pretending to be their equals. Watching them gargle bean water down their oesophagi, swilling it through their fatty insides. It makes one ill.'

'It's a cultural world, one of the nicer ones in the Imperium, in fact.'

'It's a cesspit.'

They stood, watching the musicians.

'I miss music,' said Trazyn. 'In my estimation, one of the greatest things the Dead Gods took from us.'

'We have algorithm-chants.'

'True, my dear astromancer. But can they do what this quartet of poor musicians can? See how the zitherist sets the tempo, how the others follow. A song no one has heard before, an act of pure creation, yet one that still speaks of what this place once was. Music that invokes the cool island breezes that caressed these shores in centuries past, when the seas were higher, music that contains memory. Can your blessed algorithm-chants do that?'

'No,' Orikan admitted. 'They merely reshape the fabric of space-time, transmute matter, and bring objects through the dimensional skin of the universe. Algorithm-chants are useful, that's why those that know the arcane utterances are part of a select immortal order, while these short-lived insects play for coins thrown by gawping travellers, unvalued even by their own kind.'

Trazyn gave a performative sigh. 'My point, Orikan, is that this place has a memory. A sense of its unique history that transcends the millennia. Look at those carved pillars on the palace of justice. Marble, but stained yellowish, carved like great hunks of lizard bone. The script on the street signs, its shape so reminiscent of aeldari runes. This music, recalling seas and lapping waves long retreated – the shore is ten leagues from here, you know – all of it is the product of the past. A living history. They have taken what they considered worth preserving and carried it forward.'

'We have history. Better history.'

Trazyn turned, gestured for Orikan to follow. 'We do. Titanic battles. Wars across the map of the stars. Things these groundling peasants could not fathom. But we also do not change. Our culture is stagnant, frozen, in many ways less vital than these humans. You can feel this planet, can you not? They can feel it. Serenade sings to them.'

'Is that supposed to be funny?'

'Perhaps a little.' Trazyn reached the door of the great cathedral. 'After you, colleague.'

'This is the part where I turn my back and you stab it, surely?'

'Have it your way,' Trazyn shrugged, and passed through the door. 'But this is our fastest entryway to the Eternity Gate.'

Shadows seeped down the walls of the cathedral's interior, collecting in pools on the floor. Candles, ranked like men battling in a confused melee, burned before the images of saints, residue from smoke and dissolved wax blackening their golden feet.

A pilgrim, head shaved in a monk's tonsure and clad in

the light blue robes of his order, walked a labyrinth in the floor. He stopped to ring a bell and mutter a prayer every time he pivoted in the twisting path. Each whispered invocation echoed, paper-dry in the empty space.

'You see the windows?' Trazyn pointed at the stained glass, radiating in the bright morning sun. 'Each panel charts the history of Serenade.'

'Fascinating,' said Orikan, clearly unimpressed with this parochialism. 'Why are we here? I was given to understand that it was time to start our great task.'

'It is. This is part of it. See the first? The God-Emperor shaping the mountains and islands of Serenade with His very hands. The first settlement ship exiting the empyrean, the angelic Saint Madrigal showing the way to Serenade with her blessed lyre – she is usually depicted with a sword, so this is a regional variation–'

'Trazyn,' warned Orikan, 'immortality aside, my time is valuable.'

'Oh, very well. Moving to the interesting part. Here we have the Greenskin War, as they call it. And who, my dear rival, is that in the next panel?'

Orikan looked up, dismissing the overlaid data-scroll he'd secretly been reading.

'No.'

'Oh yes.'

Storming through the square, meeting the greenskin onslaught, were a group of Space Marines: unusually tall and thin Space Marines, their helmets fashioned as leering skull-masks. The one in the lead appeared to be some kind of hooded Librarian, holding aloft a great lantern-headed staff that the glass orks recoiled from in horror.

'Silver Skulls Chapter defeats the ork invasion,' Trazyn said with clear relish. 'There used to be a statue in the square, thirty *khet* high. They used to light candles and sing hymns to it. A few centuries ago the Inquisition got wind of it and did a little cleaning up. Removed it for "renovation" where it was never seen again.'

'You stole it, did you not?'

'Well, of *course*. And I hardly think it counts as stealing if it's my likeness. It's my statue, after all.'

Orikan snorted. 'Worshipping a necron. Poor idiots. I suppose they have a head start on the rest of the galaxy. The Awakening is nearly imminent.'

There was a moment of contemplative silence.

'Do you have a statue of yourself, Orikan?'

Orikan stalked deeper into the cathedral. 'You are an obscene egotist.'

'I only wonder if any cultures worship you as a living saint or spiritual protector. It is a simple binary question.'

'Show me what you wanted to show me.'

Down a staircase, beneath the flagstones of the cathedral, lay the Ecclesiarchical crypt. It was the old street level from a millennium before, and its entryway remained familiar in line and arch from that period as well – it was the original settlement cathedral, its whitewashing blackened by mould and its angelic faces worn to doughy abstractions by centuries of water seepage.

Trazyn reshaped the necrodermis of a finger, fitted it into the heavy padlock on the rust-furred gate and opened it. Flecks of deteriorating hinge rained onto the floor, and only a sound-dampening hex cast by Orikan contained the ferrous howl.

Inside lay sarcophagi sculpted with the reposed images of

the humans' high priests, hands clasped in pious devotion or clutching ceremonial shepherd's crooks.

'Robbing graves now, are you?' asked Orikan.

'No one will disturb our workings down here,' said Trazyn. 'A local variety of acidic mould developed a colony several centuries ago.' He wiped a hand along a marble casket and showed the dim luminescence on his fingertips. 'Once introduced to human lungs, it takes root and chews them away. Death comes within five months. Caused casualty loss rates among the underground workforce to exceed acceptable norms. The Administratum was quite upset and barred it.'

'And you presented this culture world to me as such a happy place.'

'Any place that takes its money from visitors is, to a certain extent, an illusion. Those musicians playing calming music, the server at the café, the players at the opera house likely rise at daybreak and rush to work through crowded streets and creaking underground trains. A great deal of labour and suffering is expended to make Serenade so enjoyable for leisure visitors. To produce the songs, plays and devotional art that makes it renowned throughout the system. The leaded glass windows are not quite so beautiful when one sees the black, poisoned fingers of the artisans that made them.'

'Don't trouble me with your sympathy for lesser beings.'

'Just professional interest,' said Trazyn, opening his dimensional pocket and placing a device on an empty altar. 'This translation fixer should help us phase directly into this crypt without issue. With the world's signal-blocking geology, this is the safest place to step in from orbit. The *Lord of Antiquity* can serve as forward post, as we agreed. I have buried it in a crater on the dark side of the second moon, where it will almost certainly stay undiscovered. Serenade's satellites are not suitable for lunar bases, since there are no minerals to exploit. We can use the portals aboard to step in and out from Solemnace or Mandragora, as needed, and translate down here to perform our surveys.'

'And no troops,' said Orikan. 'Small teams only.'

'We cannot fit any large units through the portals, in any case,' Trazyn agreed. 'So shall we find the gate?'

They walked in silence for a week, Trazyn dropping signal beacons behind them to keep the way straight.

Draining the oceans had reworked the tunnel network in curious fashions. Collapsed passageways. Airtight chambers, sealed long ago, that still contained the partly decayed slime of ocean environments centuries dead. Subsurface volcanic activity had narrowed caverns and filled old lava tubes with glassy black rock.

Orikan navigated, Trazyn eating through blockages with a hip-slung gauss flayer.

At times they uncovered the fossilised imprints of the giant eels – or a distant ancestor of them – which Trazyn insisted on extracting with a finger-sized gauss cutter and enclosing in a tesseract labyrinth.

And then, while stripping away a plug of igneous rock, an unnatural object tumbled out of the hardened magma.

A necron arm, severed, its third finger still twitching with unlife. Tap, tap, tap. Stop. Tap, tap. Stop. Tap. Stop.

'One of your warriors, I think,' said Trazyn, holding the dismembered limb to Orikan, who ignored it.

'We are close, then. I could sense it.'

They were.

The last time they had seen the cavern, it had been fifteen hundred years past. It had been underwater then, its floor covered with lattices of coral and flowing kelp groves, the whole of it suffused with the eerie light of the poisoned dimensional door.

Now, it was all empty darkness. Drained and bereft of light, absent the heat and nutrients of the Eternity Gate, all that remained were the twisted bodies of slain necrons rusting on the cavern floor.

That, and the spiders. They were everywhere, pale and soft-bodied, each one as big as Trazyn's outstretched hand. Webs stretched thick and heavy through the chamber, forming gauzy shrouds on the dead necrons. Frozen metal arms reached up through the gossamer blanket like a sea of the damned, the struggling forms of trapped moths tugging the thin blankets of silk in an unearthly movement.

'A kingdom of the blind,' said Orikan. He advanced, staff flaring to light the way. 'Sightless worms, moths and arachnids have formed an ecosystem in this place.'

'My dear astromancer,' said Trazyn, in a sort of kindly, patronising tone. 'I did not take you for a student of biology.'

'Student of flesh-forms I am not, but I am a master of technomancy. This wretched society communicates and senses through vibration patterns, and patterns are but algorithmic code of a different type.'

Trazyn swept his obliterator before him and panicked arachnids fled from the pool of light. 'Are you claiming to speak to these eight-legged horrors, Orikan?'

'No,' Orikan responded. 'But I know that they speak.'

They walked in silence to the Eternity Gate, its still-open doors fogged with webs and the rock surface behind them blank.

'The Mysterios?' Orikan asked, embedding his glowing staff in the floor like a torch.

Trazyn extracted it from his dimensional pocket, along with

a repulsor cradle. He stooped, joint actuators creaking, and placed it within the cradle, summoning a phos-glyph panel to bring the rig online.

The Mysterios came into the air slow and sure, like a rising moon.

Orikan shut his ocular and experimentally swept a hand back and forth, rotating the Mysterios, rolling and adjusting it so he could sense each of its twenty sides directly. Fixing it in his neural imager.

'Are you sure you need no more ritual objects?' asked Trazyn.

'This is enough.' Orikan settled onto the floor, legs folded beneath him. 'Only silence.'

Trazyn waited.

'This will likely take a great deal of time,' continued Orikan. 'Do you not have surveys and enquiries to conduct? Or do you plan to stare at me for the next three decades?'

'Provided you do not mind me leaving you alone.'

'What shall I do without your valuable counsel?' Orikan said. 'I will have to enlist a mildly talented cave roach to serve as a replacement.'

'Use the signal relays when you're finished,' said Trazyn. 'And do not hesitate to signal if you need assistance.'

Orikan said nothing, shoulders settling, head drooping to one side.

Trazyn felt a tingle up his spine, and stepped away. He was no stranger to techno-sorcery, but Orikan's mastery lay far beyond any he had seen before. Even with millions of years to study, he could not begin to understand Orikan's power.

And though he would not admit it, at Trazyn's core, it frightened him.

He retreated from the astromancer, watching as his head

lolled backward, mouth open towards the cavern's ceiling. The orbuculums on Orikan's headdress began to shine with bale-light, and he rose off the floor, steady and immobile as though encased in ice.

Perhaps it was the infernal setting that threw Trazyn. Darkness, arachnids, the low forest of reaching arms entombed in webbing. It almost made him abandon his plan.

But then, the metal body that encased what remained of his essence cooled the fear, and he reverted to his own nature.

He placed the tesseract labyrinth at the front of the chamber, nestled amid the knots of rusting bodies, and started the timer.

The Awakened Council would not approve, of course, but Executioner Phillias would not conduct her first formal inspection for more than a century hence.

And, after all, he had warned Orikan to call for help if he needed it.

CHAPTER FOUR

'NEPHRETH: *Be silent, chattering fools! Only one thing separates mortals from gods: the terrible gift of death. And these star gods mean to take that gift from us. I propose we do the opposite. Rather than take death from us, we shall give it to them.*'

– *War in Heaven*, Act IV, Scene I, Line 3

Orikan floats in the womblike trove of data. Has existed there so totally, so long, that he must check his chrono-positioning.

Sixty-six years. A good amount of study. Enough time to truly delve into the secrets of the Mysterios.

But also thirteen per cent of their allotted time.

Do not worry, Vishani says. *It is time enough with a guide.*

Orikan's sprit-projection shivers. She does not speak often, but when she does, it flows through him like an injection of fresh reactor coolant. Calming him, soothing his racing mind. Breaking the circular thoughts that bedevil him day and night.

He hates working with Trazyn, resents the council for making him do it. It was all he could do, at their last meeting, to keep himself from smiting the conceited bastard in his sly death mask.

Necrons do not need to smile. Were not meant to smile.

Yet Trazyn smiled constantly.

Focus, Vishani chides.

He sees her fully now, in his peripheral vision. Floating beside him in her own trance position.

Orikan would work with Trazyn, provided he could continue communing with one of the greatest minds in all the galactic epochs. Orikan could tolerate an oaf if it meant he could tap into such transcendent genius. The years divorced from the Mysterios had been hard. That first millennium – where Trazyn and Orikan had parted to cover their dynastic duties, and the Council kept the Mysterios – had tortured him with the separation.

He had dreamed of her in trances, as far as a necron could dream, but recalled nothing when he roused himself. Could not even recall what she had looked like. Her essence was tied deep into this creation of hers.

And he could sense her mind at work on the Eternity Gate, though it had taken long decades to coax her data-phantom from the Mysterios.

'You built this in order to keep the tomb a secret?' he asks. His body – floating behind him, tented by cobwebs – does not speak. Only his astral algorithm. The chamber remains silent.

Correct, she responds.

'You built this Astrarium, this device that only opens once an aeon, so that only a kind as long-lived as ours could discover the tomb.'

Correct.

'Yet encoded it with glyph-data the aeldari and the Old Ones could not decipher.'

Correct.

'And this gate,' he says, 'is now dead.'

Correct.

'But it can be reset by reverting the Mysterios to its previous polyhedral shape.'

Incorrect. Reset logic.

Orikan grunts. Takes a long, slow breath in and out. Unnecessary, even clothed in his metal form. Still a good way to centre his mind.

The data-phantom of Vishani occasionally spoke wisdom. Even seemed to react directly to Orikan, guiding him, assisting him. Ask direct questions, however, and it reverted to a binary logic protocol. Useful, but deeply frustrating.

He resets, asking the chain of questions from the beginning.

'This gate is now dead.'

Correct.

'This gate will be usable again.'

Correct.

He pauses. Considers. 'Lock logic chain.'

Logic chain locked at answer to gate usability. Proceed.

There, he thinks. No more backtracking. Or else he has locked himself into a chain leading nowhere.

'This gate will be usable in less than five hundred years.'

Incorrect. Reverting to locked chain.

'This gate will be usable in more than a thousand years.'

Correct.

And then a breath in his mind. A number. That push from whatever part of Vishani remains – or whatever image of her his neural engrams have created.

'This gate will be operable in two thousand, three hundred and sixty-seven years,' he says.

Correct.

Well after the Exterminatus. When Serenade would be destroyed to the point that the Eternity Gate would be damaged and non-functional.

'The Eternity Gate can be moved and remain operable.'

Incorrect. Reverting to locked chain.

'But there is another gate.'

Correct.

'There are three more gates.'

Incorrect.

'Two more gates.'

Incorrect.

'There is only one other gate. A fail-safe.'

Correct.

He sits with that awhile. If the gates took so long to reset after being fired, the fail-safe likely opened earlier.

But would it open before the planet was destroyed?

'You have left a way to help me find it.'

Silence.

'Vishani? Is there a signature? A signal?'

Silence.

I will help you, Orikan. But you must open yourself to the universe.

'I... do not follow.'

You are closed off, Orikan. Alone. Have spent long epochs developing only yourself and disconnecting all you consider a distraction.

'It is the path of the cryptek to be cloistered. Removed in study and self-cultivation. A garden without walls...'

...will be strangled by creeping vines. I know. But a garden

closed to all, padlocked in a box, dies. Without rain and sun to feed it, without wind and insects to carry pollen, it cannot thrive. Have you forgotten these things? Clapped in your metal body, have you forgotten the meaning of our philosophies and stuck only to the letter?

'If I open myself,' Orikan says slowly, 'I risk diffusing my power. Becoming weak. When I shared my visions freely they persecuted me for it. Turned away from my warnings, trusted the Dead Gods and lost their souls. Then hunted me and brought me to the forge in chains. Now, they do not even remember it.'

The C'tan have much to answer for – as does our own species. We shattered the star gods, chained them, made them no better than beasts of burden. And our species has spent eternity as soulless wanderers. Only you and I, Orikan, have tasted what it is like to be free of captivity. But you cannot be free when you are your own prisoner.

'I am not closed off. I have opened myself to the vitality of the cosmos, drinking in the energies of–'

And you have never been more powerful.

Orikan goes quiet.

Orikan, open yourself and I will show you a vision. Open your consciousness.

'Why do you speak like a living being at times, and others like a simple program?'

Because the questioning program is not me. It is my consciousness in the Mysterios. The personality emanation that I included to help seekers like you. This voice you hear, it can only be detected on this planet.

'Why?'

Because I am here. When I completed building the tomb, my dynasty sealed me inside.

* * *

Trazyn closed the massive tome, disintegrating pages sending up a sandstorm of foul dust as it creaked shut. Mites ran in panicked flight throughout the binding.

'No, no. Not good enough. Must go earlier, I think. Koloma, please find me earlier volumes of *They Drank the Seas*. A copy from before the Inquisition censored chapter two. And anything you can find on subterranean building projects in the–'

'Lord?' replied the ancient night librarian. He stooped, spine bent from decades of pushing carts and shelving great volumes.

'Yes, librarian?'

'I'm sorry to say that this will be my last night with you.'

Trazyn looked up. 'Really? So soon?'

'I had mentioned to you two years ago, my lord, that I was scheduled to be forcibly retired.'

'But I paid for those augmetics. The hip and leg. The juvenats to keep your body together when it started to deteriorate.'

'That was thirty years ago, my lord. I have grown old in your service. And it is not a question of willingness. Younger men in the librarium wish to move up, and they cannot while I hold my post.'

'I see,' said Trazyn, looking the elderly night librarian up and down. He had not noticed in his deep focus, but he saw the truth of it. Koloma's skin was parchment-thin, his gait unbalanced as his one fleshy leg had withered due to the strength of its metal mate. He wore a back brace laced over his yellow robes. Brown eyes misted with cataracts – the right one so thick it was like the pupil peered through a sheet of vellum – regarded him with pained regret.

How old had he been when Trazyn first brought him into

service? Twenty-five? Thirty? Young and vital, that was sure. Quick of mind and strong of body, able to hoist volumes broad as his muscular shoulders and thicker than his forearms.

'Well,' said Trazyn, 'you had better sit, then.'

Koloma sat, slowly. Augmetic joints squeaked and stuck. He held his stiff natural leg out far to one side, wincing when the knee bent slightly.

'You have been a good and faithful servant, Koloma.'

'And you a good master, lord. My treatments. The hab-block close to the library. My children educated in the good scholams. An ash box in the Garden of Remembrance for my dear Morea. I owe you much.'

Trazyn waved a hand, as if dismissing the aid. 'Rewards are the fundamental mechanism of good leadership. Any master would do the same.'

'My daylight masters in the Serenade Central Librarium did not.'

'No,' he admitted. 'Yours is a terrorised culture, my friend, and terror breeds obedience – but not loyalty.'

'I have arranged for my replacement, lord. I have been training him. A good man named Tova. Xander Tova. He will be here to serve you tomorrow night.'

Trazyn nodded. 'You have given him the amulet?'

'I have,' Koloma confirmed. 'The mindshackle scarabs will have implanted themselves already. I saw it in his eyes during the shift change this evening.'

'And you trained him personally?'

'He is my nephew, lord. I have prepared him for his duties.'

So the thing was done well, as Koloma ever had. He hoped that Tova would prove as able and enthusiastic – though if Koloma had groomed him, that was a good enough reference.

The scarabs would do the rest, though Koloma might have performed just as well without the application of their blunt force control.

'I will miss you, Koloma.'

'And I you, lord.'

'You know, of course, that I cannot simply let you go.'

A faint flicker behind the cataracts. A rare instance of the scarabs asserting themselves. 'Of course not, lord. I am a liability to your great work.'

'I cannot promise it will be painless, but it will be fast.'

'Thank you, master. My life has been long and happy. I wish only to join Morea in the ash-box.'

'Good,' said Trazyn. He may not have been telling the conscious truth, but clearly on some level, Koloma wanted to die. The scarabs had not needed to push hard. Had they done so, they might have killed the frail old librarian – which is not what Trazyn wished. Despite his good service, Trazyn had no desire to carry his body up from the basement.

'Do you wish to talk first?'

'About what, my lord?'

'This place.' Trazyn indicated the basement stacks, the long shelves where he kept his private desk. 'Not just the library, but Serenade. What am I missing?'

'Missing, lord?'

'Do you know what I seek?'

'My lord, you have not confided, and I have not asked.'

Trazyn barked a laugh. 'You are a more faithful servant than I estimated, Koloma. All these years and you have not pried. Good fellow. Good, good fellow. The truth is, Koloma, I am looking for a tomb. A secret chamber built by my kind.'

'Do you wish to pillage it, my lord? Or worship there?'

'Both, strangely enough. And for the past decades I have

been combing through property records, infrastructure plans. Sewer outlays. Geological reports, looking for some hint of a structure. Either stone that could not be quarried, or absent space mankind has avoided. A shadow built around because your kind finds it too unpleasant. I have found none.'

'I'm sorry, master.'

'So what am I missing, Koloma? What is it about Serenade that I do not ken? What is the soul of this place? Why does it feel so different?'

'Ah,' said Koloma. 'You're talking about the Song of Serenade.'

'That tune the street musicians play in the square? *The ocean winds they carry forth, the Song of Serenade?* That one?'

'Just so.' Koloma tapped his nose with a finger, a gesture Trazyn found so odd he repeated it, lest it had ritual or cultural significance. 'A very odd tune, don't you think? The lyrics are patriotic drivel, of course. But it is quite different from what you hear in the rest of the Imperium.'

Trazyn had noticed, he realised. His neural subroutines had flagged it as different than other human music. In the last millennium he'd developed a minor interest, after stumbling on a ship carrying the Vostroyan Symphonic on a war zone morale tour. Rather than keep them for display, he brought them out of stasis for the occasional concert line up, programming them alongside a Tallarn *errimu* string soloist and a Tanith pipe and drum corps.

'Why is it unusual?'

'Because it's on the pentatonic scale. It has five notes per octave, when the standard scale has seven.'

'Interesting, though I struggle for the relevance.'

'Because you have not studied local folk beliefs. And one cannot wonder why. The Inquisition made quite a stink when my grandfather was a boy. They hadn't got around to enquiring about the local culture until then, as a small settlement, we were not important enough, I daresay.'

'When they removed the statue?'

'They removed more than that. For there has long been a folk belief here that the world of Serenade has a certain rhythm. A pulse that carries through it, through our music, our speech. A thrumming voice. Some called it the Hymn of the God-Emperor but others spoke of primordial creator-beings living deep beneath the stone. The Inquisition, for their part, replaced all such fancies with the orthodox superstition that it was Saint Madrigal, calling the first settlers to the world, and calling all pious souls to worship the God-Emperor through the creativity that makes this world so famous.'

'And what do the unorthodox say?'

'There was a sister of Saint Madrigal once, Sister Solarian. A composer and organist of rare talent. Before disappearing, she insisted that the Song of Serenade was so embedded in the culture, in the hearts of its people, because it was embedded in everything. The voice of the Emperor made into pure numeral mathematics. The same ratio that governed the spirals of a shell, a spider's web, circular vortexes at sea.'

'A common enough occurrence in nature. Symmetry is–'

'Forgive me, lord, but that's just it. Solarian discovered that the Song of Serenade does not form perfect shapes. It is an asymmetrical pattern, but regular. Repeating. In everything.'

Trazyn was quiet a moment. 'Five notes. One to five. Like a numerical signal.'

'Precisely.'

Trazyn nodded. 'Get me everything you can on the Song of Serenade and Sister Solarian. Then go and sit at your desk.'

'Yes, master,' said Koloma, hoisting himself onto his stiff legs and putting a hand on his cart.

Then he stopped, lingered.

'My lord?'

Trazyn looked up at him, surprised he remained. 'Yes?'

'After my long service, may I ask a question?'

Trazyn considered. 'You may.'

'Do you intend to destroy this world?'

Trazyn dismissed the phos-glyph panel of research notes, folded his hands and looked at the diminished librarian. 'That's what you want to know?'

'Yes. It would make my mind easier.'

'Let me put it this way. I was here when this whole island was forest. When waves lapped on what is now Embassy Row. A time before pollutants hazed the air and the monsoon rains came naturally, not via cloud-seeding.' He paused. 'So when you ask whether I intend to destroy this world, my question to you is: do you truly need the help?'

Koloma hoisted his old joints up, stair by stair, leaning heavily on his book cart as he squeaked through the tall wooden bookcases of the archive, the long-forgotten sections even the inquisitors had never found. The tomes there were from the high-water times, their thick covers and spines bound in hides of extinct whales. He loaded the cart full and wheeled it to the disused shelving elevator, transferred the volumes from the cart to the empty cube and closed the door.

He pushed the button for the sub-basement and watched his last load of books descend to the strange being in the basement, whom he had met sixty-two years before. A thing beyond time and space which he had feared at first – until granted the release of the controlling scarabs.

Then he went to his desk, sat down and folded his hands, looking at the portrait of his wife, gone over a decade now.

When the stroke hit him, it was more painful than anything he'd experienced.

But true to the word of his metal lord, it was over quickly.

CHAPTER FIVE

'Music, poetry, mathematics, dance – all are modes of expression. Any one of these things conveys meaning. They are but different languages uttering the same phrase. But if this is true, do not the orbits of planets and stars also join this music? Cannot Serenade itself speak to us?'

– Sister Solarian, *The Music of the Spheres*

Orikan had debated for a great while with himself. But every logical scenario he posited came to the same conclusion. Every zodiac he cast gave the same result.

Vishani was correct. To open the tomb, he must open himself.

'Very well,' he speaks. 'I am ready.'

And so, slowly, he opens a channel in his neural matrix. No mere interstitial message stream, but something far more vulnerable.

He deactivates security protocols that keep others from reading his thoughts, widens the narrow beam of information to allow her to slip inside his mind, for them to coexist in one body, able to hide nothing from one another.

He has never done this. Could never imagine himself doing this. One could become infected with all manner of data-plagues – the flayer virus, or whatever contagious psychosis turned necrons into Destroyers.

But this is Vishani. She had been sealed away long before such curses came upon the necrons. And she is brilliant. The thought of that elevated consciousness inhabiting his own neural matrix makes him shiver.

Such understanding. Such power. To be chosen by that… It was one of the greatest honours of his long existence.

'I am ready,' he says.

He feels a gentle trickle of data, like a being putting its foot lightly on ice, not knowing whether the thin skin will support it.

'Do not be afraid,' he says, not knowing whether he's speaking to her or to himself. He opens the data bandwidth wider.

Orikan! she screams.

The shout hammers through the channel, much louder than if she had sent it as an interstitial message. Like an explosion going off inside his cranium. It startles him, and he snaps the data-channel closed.

Danger, it says. *Danger. Danger. Danger.*

Orikan snapped open his ocular – his metal ocular – and threw himself to one side, feeling sharp talons rake across his ribs.

He grabbed the upright haft of his Staff of Tomorrow, used

its solidity to pivot around before hitting the ground in a guard stance.

Whatever hit him is gone, back to the shadows.

'What was it?' he asked Vishani.

No answer. As if whatever she had witnessed frightened her back into the prison of the crypt.

What could frighten an ethereal being?

Orikan caught movement in his peripheral sensors and wheeled, ready to confront the assailant – and realised it was only the drifting shroud of spiderwebs his body was draped with. The irregular spirals of the webs overlaid his vision, but he was not stupid enough to take his hand from his weapon and clear them.

Drifting strands lifted in the wind, the ultralight silk disturbed by even the lightest movement of air.

What wind? he thought.

The thing would have killed him had the realisation come even a moment later. He ducked low and turned towards the source of the breeze, the disturbance of air stirred up by the creature coming right at him.

He had no time to gather his strength for a strike, only to put his staff between himself and the awful thing that barrelled into him with its full weight. Claws thick as sabre tips scored furrows in his death mask and tore at his headdress. Mouth feelers, rubbery and foul, found the spaces between his ribs and slobbered towards his vital systems in search of nourishment.

Two eyes, dull red like gemstones, stared out of deep-set sockets. It had all the ugliness of a human, plus the nightmare qualities of various animals. A cloven foot hooked upwards and dragged his staff down.

Triple claws slammed underneath his arm and twisted

deep in vital systems. Reactor fluid, glowing bright in the near-lightless chamber, dribbled on the blackstone floor.

Orikan cast his consciousness backward, seeing the creature retreat, his body pivot, watched its exact path as it melded back into the shadows.

He restarted his timeline to just before he had realised that he was covered in webs.

And instead of turning towards the drifting strand of webbing, he turned towards the creature – staff drawn back and ready for the blow.

It was not enough. The creature was fast. So fast. Whatever biological perception suite it employed was nearly as advanced as Orikan's.

The vile alien – for it could not be from this world – went from an oncoming rush to a dead stop within a second, Orikan's sweeping blow passing harmlessly in front of it.

Then it pounced, coil-spring muscles sending its purple body sailing into the air.

There was no time to recover the staff for a second blow. Orikan dropped it.

The thing hit him, bowling him off his feet and onto his back. One tri-claw speared for his throat and he evaded.

Orikan remembered next to nothing about the being who had been his father. A stern man, quick with the rod, the sun-tumours had taken him even earlier than most. Long before the immortality of biotransference.

Orikan had ever taken a mystic's path, but his family line were warrior-caste. His father, therefore, had insisted on sending Orikan to the temple of the Immortals. There, the war-tutors forced him to grapple the other initiates one after the other, shouting correctives at Orikan as his energy waned.

It was supposed to build his strength, but it did not. Orikan would never be an Immortal. He was small and injury-prone, and was reassigned to the cryptek temple within the year.

But he *had* learned to wrestle.

And biotransference had given him the strength his old form had so lacked.

He rolled, let the tri-claw spark off the blackstone.

Then he moved fast as a strangling snake, lashing his arm out and wrapping the clawed limb between his upper arm and ribs.

He used his body like a lever and snapped the limb, feeling chitin crunch and muscle tear.

The mad thing squealed and hissed in pain, its other claws scraping and gouging at him. Barbed feelers covered his face. Already he could feel the trapped and broken arm reknitting itself, its structure thinning and becoming flexible so it could worm free. Pieces of chitin shed onto the floor.

No matter how hard the war-tutors trained him, they'd never taught him to wrestle a creature with four arms. He felt surface hydraulics tear and spout. Sensed the hungry feelers change direction, lapping and sucking at the bleeding systems. Saw his moment as the creature flinched backward, confused at the inedible poisons leaking from Orikan's mauled frame.

Then he executed a move the war-tutors had never imagined.

Holding the creature captive with its broken arm, Orikan formed Vzanosh's Ballistic Parabola with his right hand.

A wave of pure kinetic energy slammed the creature into the air, its body sent into a spin as its trapped arm tore from its body, leaving strands of soft tissue trailing from the chitinous shell.

It arced backward, clattering to the floor among the twisted, web-draped wreckage of the necron armies. Struggled to its feet. Began to dart to the side, flanking him.

'I think not,' said Orikan, standing.

He raised his hand, fingers splayed as though he were one of the men in the cheap puppet-theatres of Settlement Plaza. His crest of orbuculums glowed bright with ethereal fire, veins of lightning sparking and jumping between the conductive orbs.

The creature stumbled, stretched out its hands to catch itself on the dusty floor.

A cobwebbed hand gripped its hind leg. Another reached up and grasped the stubby tail.

It skittered on the floor, confused, struggling. Rusted skeletal limbs snared its arms and spined ribcage, hands cracking its chitin shell and sinking into the flesh beneath. Tentacle feelers splayed as it shrieked, then it wrapped a rusted arm with its ropy mouthparts, tearing the decayed limb out of its socket.

Necrons pulled themselves up from the floor, broken skulls and snapped limbs crawling with reanimating balefire that flared in their eyes and open mouths.

'What's wrong?' Orikan said, his scorched pride cooling under the sticky balm of revenge. 'Are we unappetising to you?'

The creature had only one limb free – not the tri-claw, but a five-fingered gripping limb. Skeletal warriors pulled it closer to the floor, pinning it. Biting it with their snapping jaws. An unusual move, Orikan admitted, but one with a certain poetic justice.

Then he watched as the fingers of the creature's one free hand twisted around each other like a genetic helix, forming a chitinous spike. A new crooked talon.

It plunged into one chewing skull, then another.

Spiderwebbed hands loosened. Mauled necrons tumbled

to the floor, exhaling the reanimating energy that had risen them.

The creature kicked, leaped, dodging and clawing through the forest of reaching limbs.

And vanished into shadow.

'I have made a discovery,' said Trazyn, slamming the stack of books on the sarcophagus. 'You know how I was pontificating on the music of Serenade, well–'

'What is this?' Orikan dropped the purple and blue arm on the marble, its dribbling ichor fizzing slightly on contact with the cold stone.

Trazyn looked at the limb with a blank expression, though for a moment, Orikan imagined that he caught a flash of recognition and amusement in the impassive oculars.

'Where did this come from? The gate chamber?'

'It attacked me while I was in my meditative trance. Interrupted my focus while I was on the precipice of a great revelation.'

'How unfortunate.'

Nothing was said, the pause continuing a full hour.

'Well, you don't think I had anything to do with it?'

Another pause. This one two hours.

'My dear astromancer, this is the Eastern Fringe. Wild space. The frontier. These atrocious little things have been cropping up everywhere, I ran across a nest recently on the unsettled world of Ymgarl. Genetic thieves, you know. Parasites. They don't bother our kind much, but they're becoming quite common in this area of space. Could be hiding anywhere.'

'So you did not collect one, then unleash it in the tunnel network for the purpose of murdering me?'

'Really, Orikan, that is too much. And if I had, I would've

used more than one. I think you're more than the equal of one of these low creatures.'

Orikan scryed him, his monocular boring into Trazyn like a drilling beam. 'Very well,' he said. 'As we told the Awakened Council, this is a dangerous world. Get your illusion emitter, I have been underground too long and wish to get air.'

And as they climbed out of the crypt, Trazyn told him about the Song of Serenade.

'If this is true,' said Orikan, his voice rising. 'It means we may be able to capture the signal and follow it to where it is strongest – the reserve gate that I have posited. Meaning we can still open the tomb before the Exterminatus. Well done, Trazyn.'

They came into the shadow-pooled space of the cathedral, and Trazyn froze, still as a statue.

'What is this?'

'What is what?' Orikan asked. 'You really must bother to explain yourself, colleague. You cannot simply babble and expect me to fill in the missing numerals.'

'Someone,' Trazyn said, gesturing to the vaults of the nave, where a group of bodygloved men were removing jagged shards of coloured glass, 'has broken my window.'

'Have they?' Orikan asked, giving a casual glance towards the vandalism. 'Perhaps they thought it was ugly.'

CHAPTER SIX

'We are the praetorians.
We are the shield of the Triarchs.
Ours are the eyes that see.
Ours is the chastening rod.'

— *The Praetorian Ode*

Nihilakh Cruiser Lord of Antiquity
Berthed on Second Moon of Serenade
350 Years Before Next Tomb Opening

'Spare me no details in this report,' said Executioner Phillias. 'I want nothing held back.'

'Of course, executioner,' said Trazyn. 'Our efforts–'

'I wasn't finished,' she cut in. 'Assume that I have read your reports with interest, because I have. You will talk, I will ask questions. And when it's finished I will either extend the Awakened Council's sponsorship of this expedition or revoke it. Are we all understood?'

'Yes?' said Trazyn.

Orikan nodded after a sufficiently insolent pause.

'Do not give me a simplified version, but be efficient. I have many responsibilities that have nothing to do with this backwater, and would like to be on my way as soon as possible.'

'We would prefer that as well,' said Orikan. 'Wouldn't we, Trazyn?'

Don't enlist me in your juvenilia, Diviner, he sent in return.

'I cannot speak for Master Orikan, but my part of the research is quite simple, at least in relative terms.'

He called up a phos-glyph panel that showed waveforms and a glyph sequence made up entirely of the numerals one to five.

'I have identified an emanation coming from deep within the planet. A number chain: 3211 Stop 1545 Stop 4131 Stop 5322. We are unsure of the transmission's source, or the equipment from which it comes, or even what it means, but–'

'Perhaps say what we do know, then?' said Orikan.

Trazyn tilted his head, oculars rotating in a withering look. 'We know it travels through the planet's strange geology. That it carries the same strength when detected on the surface, but appears to reverberate with much more strength through cave systems. Particularly in the island archipelago that makes up the most populous hemisphere.'

'Odd,' said Phillias. 'For islands to be the population centres.'

'Islands were far easier for the first wave of human settlers to defend,' answered Trazyn. 'But yes, it is unusual. What is more unusual, however, is how this emanation – known as the Song of Serenade in local folklore – has affected life on this planet. It is generally sub-audible, but detectable with suitably advanced technology. Yet it has affected the local culture to a significant extent.'

Trazyn pulled up a human musical bar, its notes walking up and down the lines.

'Odd equation,' said Orikan, leaning close.

'This is a well-known local folk melody. It's pentatonic. Five notes to the octave. Do you see?'

The executioner and the Diviner looked at him, expressions blank.

'Perhaps a demonstration,' he said, clearly disappointed. He adjusted the music and pulled up the numerical glyph sequence beside it. 'So now instead of numeral glyphs, let's turn this into a chart, shall we?'

Trazyn moved his hands through the air, converting the sequence of number glyphs to five horizontal lines, numbered bottom to top. Each glyph lay on the line its number represented.

Orikan, one finger on his beard, dropped his hand to the table with a hard knock. 'They match,' he said, looking from one to the other. 'Trazyn, this is good work.'

'I *sent* you the data,' Trazyn grumbled.

Phillias looked at Orikan. 'Am I to understand you did not know about this, Master Orikan? You are supposed to be working as a team.'

'I have been cloistered in deep meditation.' The astromancer sneered. 'Were I to break a trance every time Lord Trazyn had a pet theory, I would still be casting my initial divinations and spheres of focus.'

Phillias spoke, her oculars fixed on Orikan. 'And these deep scratches on your necrodermis. They seem rather fresh. Have you had an... accident?'

Orikan ran a thumb over the deep furrow on his golden

headdress. 'A run-in with an alien creature below ground,' he said. 'Not native, but Lord Trazyn assures me they are becoming more common in this sector, is that not correct, Lord Trazyn?'

'Absolutely. An unusual occurrence, certainly, but nothing untoward.'

'Nothing untoward,' she repeated. Her oculars passed between them. 'This signal, Lord Trazyn, what does it mean?'

'Perhaps everything. It is a signal, from deep underground. The world's inhabitants have unknowingly picked it up – it's literally in their bones, I have tracked waveform growth patterns in skeletal remains that conform to this sequence – furthermore, it's in the songs of birds, insect trills, arachnid webs, even the growth patterns of seashells that are more lopsided here rather than the traditional spiral.'

'Meaning?'

'We know this was a tomb world, if one meant to inter only a single phaeron. This could be the thrumming of a stasis generator's reactor. Or a repeated funerary chant.'

'Or a signal,' finished Orikan.

'Yes,' confirmed Trazyn. 'That is possible. Though if so it is coded, and we are missing some key to properly decipher it. Perhaps if Master Orikan spends some time out of his trance field...'

'I have been doing important work.'

'Then tell us about it,' said Executioner Phillias.

'After communing with the Eternity Gate and the Mysterios, delving the consciousness of its builder, I have come across information that there is a second gate.'

Phillias, back already lance-straight, leaned forward expectantly.

'It is a fail-safe gate, one that activates on a different interval than the last gate we activated – since due to Lord Trazyn's interference, the primary gate will be shut for two millennia.'

'And the fail-safe?' said Phillias, jumping in before the two could get going.

'We may be able to open it early – well before the scheduled Exterminatus.'

'Have you found it?'

'Investigations are… ongoing. I have, however, learned a great deal about the gate's architect, the Data-Sorceress Vishani. Her methods and manner of thinking.'

'Master Orikan,' responded Phillias, 'having given a fair amount of reports myself I know when someone is making immobility sound like progress. It seems to me that the two of you are working this question from different directions. Could it be that the Serenade Emanation comes from the fail-safe gate?'

'It could,' said Trazyn.

'Did you not consider investigating that possibility?'

'I did,' responded Trazyn. 'But it would require going underground for a significant period, and given the communication problems inherent in the geology, I would not want to go too deep and risk missing our check-in.'

'Then you have a path forward,' said Phillias. 'I approve your extension on the condition that within a year you go into the tunnels. Together. And there best not be any more *untoward* encounters with exotic alien species, yes?'

Orikan stared, hands in a meditation position meant to increase calm and dissipate rage.

'Very well.' Trazyn banished the phos-glyph panels and turned to go. 'We'll leave you. Are you coming, astromancer?'

Orikan followed, ocular hooded by its cover.

'One more thing, lords.' Phillias knocked the table. 'Have

either of you come across evidence of High Metallurgist Quellkah?'

They had not.

Please, Vishani. Where is the fail-safe gate?

Not everything is retained, Orikan. Long years in the crypt have corrupted my engram-banks. I cannot tell you the exact location, except that it lies beneath.

This emanation, the Song of Serenade. Are you sending it?

A pause.

Orikan, do not listen to the signal. It is dangerous. Ruin lies there.

We are to follow the emanation tomorrow. Trazyn believes it can lead us to the fail-safe gate.

And it might, at that. But not all signals are to be listened to. Follow it if you must, but do not try to decipher it. Do not dwell on it. As you well know, data can change the systems that take it in. Data can carry a curse.

That is impossible.

The sermon makes a believer a fanatic. The political treatise turns the indifferent into a revolutionary. A lie exposed ruins a friendship. New information always affects the system that consumes it, at times catastrophically. That is the curse of data. All data. But data can be corrupted as well.

How is this data corrupted?

No answer.

Vishani?

To even speak of it may bring it upon you. That is the danger of information. Follow the signal, Orikan, but shut your mind to the analysis of it. Promise me this. You do not want what it contains.

Orikan thought for a long time.

I promise.

Thank you, my equal. Now, let us turn towards your study of astromantic empowerment. You have discovered how to open your systems to the cosmos, how the energy of space-time travels along lines like on a circuit board, and how the positioning of stars reorients that energy – but have you discovered how to modify your necrodermis in order to maximise the energy collected?

Is that possible?

Then let us have another automantic writing session. I can give you the diagrams.

>>> Subject: ALERT – Capital Slasher

>>> Transmission: Via Secure Uplink

>>> Recipients: Precinct Lieutenants and Above [DO NOT DISSEMINATE]

++ Step up patrols in Abyssal District.

++ Appeal to public for information.

++ Dismiss/denigrate reports of cult activity.

++ Suppress any workers' collective demanding a work stoppage as a result of the killings.

>>> At 0430, enforcers responded to a report of a foul odour emanating from a storm drain in the Abyssal District [SEE: attached street grid]. Upon entering, they found the body of Glavius Wyman – an Administratum maintenance employee who worked on the system – in an advanced state of decomposition. Injuries are consistent with the four other presumed victims of the so-called 'Capital Slasher.'

Wyman's death is consistent with previous victims, who also lived or worked on the underground. According to Administratum pay garnishment records, Wyman stopped reporting for work eight standard days ago. Medicae mortis technicians suggest that last week's artificial monsoon rains carried the body from the site of the original murder until it snagged on a pipe grate.

At this time there appears no ritualised component to the killings that suggests cult activity. Current hypothesis remains that this is the work of a compulsion-killer. However, spurious rumours persist that these homicides are the work of cults. Discourage this tendency by charging rumour-mongers with second-degree sedition under the subversion statutes. Use first-degree charges if the subject is part of the so-called 'Underground Workers' Collective,' and uses the ongoing killings as justification for work-stoppage [SEE: List of Subversive Groups].

END MEMORANDUM

+Thought for the Day: 'The law is the Emperor's will incarnate.'+

CHAPTER SEVEN

'A bizarre urban legend passes among the pickpocket gangs of Serenade City. On double-moon nights, it is said, a figure in a long coat walks the rougher parts of town with jewelled necklaces and watch chains dangling from his pockets. But any unfortunate urchin who tries to delve into this bounty will find themselves snared by the fishhooks sewn into the man's pockets. That is when his hand – each finger replaced by a long razor – appears. And the Finger-snatcher takes his due.'

– *Legends and Wraith-Tales of Old Serenade*

Trazyn the Infinite, Overlord of Solemnace, Archaeovist of the Prismatic Galleries and witness of a thousand epochs stared with fascination at the puppet show.

He did so from a distance, high in the steeple of the Basilica of the God-Emperor's Ascension. Its arches and gargoyles provided ample camouflage, and the height offered a sweeping view of the comings and goings in Settlement Plaza. He wore a simple brown hood and cowl, like a monk's, that blended his form from a distance and – along with the illusion emitter – served to ensure that even the bell-ringers would think little of him if they managed to catch a glimpse in their peripheral vision.

But it was, essentially, unnecessary. No one ventured up this far.

Below, the soft peach-coloured sunset was splashing across the square, casting a pleasant glow over the marble buildings that looked so much like polished bone. A lamplighter drifted from post to post, a ladder on one shoulder and a promethium burner in the other, preparing for nightfall.

The show could not begin performing until twilight. It was a shadow theatre, with its audience of children sitting on both sides of the little structure. On one side, lit with gas lamps, they could see the flat, painted-leather puppets dancing with their sinuous jointed limbs as they paraded in front of a stretched piece of thin canvas. On the other side, the audience watched the shadows cast on the white sheet. The same story, the same actions, but in silhouette. Older children, and some adults, walked circuits around the theatre to see the performance from all angles.

'It's a settlement myth,' said Trazyn. 'Saint Madrigal calling the faithful to Serenade.'

'Entrancing,' responded Orikan. 'If one of the puppets strikes the other, or perhaps makes some flatulent gas emission please do let me know.'

'Unlikely. The subject matter in these shadow theatres is generally historical-liturgical. The Fall of Vandire. Macharian Conquests. Lives of the Saints and that kind of thing. If you prefer farce...'

He gestured across the square, where a masked troupe of players tumbled and hooted as a lecherous bishop – his mitre askew and arms grasping – chased a giggling courtesan across the small stage. Just before being grabbed, the clever dame dipped out from under the embrace and left the clergyman amorously embracing a performer in a donkey mask.

The crowd howled, and a performer masked as King Mischief stepped forward to give a sarcasm-laden lecture on those who let petty vices consume them.

'For all my aeons, I cannot understand how you draw anything meaningful from this drivel. You know the empire will have to destroy these humans eventually, correct?'

'To study a culture gives one an indication of where it came from, sometimes where it's going. What we learn can be extrapolated to other species. Besides, we will need some as thralls.' Trazyn enhanced his oculars, zeroing in on a xylophone player sitting next to the puppet stage. 'You notice, for example, that this musician's battle melody weaves in the Song of Serenade?'

'I did not, and care not to.' He paused. 'In fact, why do we not agree that this portion of the enquiry will be your purview?'

'It's getting dark,' Trazyn said. 'It's time to move.'

The pair translated to the crypt and, enfolded in robes and with illusion emitters lit, moved out into the city streets.

They had to be more careful, now. Some spree killer had been active in Serenade City, and the enforcers were keeping a greater eye out. Possibly using scanners. They skirted the edge of the square, avoiding the crowds. Letting the emitters work with the shadows.

As Orikan passed the stage where the players capered and juggled, he noticed a bizarre detail.

'That performer. The one with the tatty crown.'

'King Mischief, yes.'

'He has a third arm.'

Trazyn smiled. 'Indeed. One of the performer's arms is false, I noticed. It allows his free arm to perform the mischief, picking pockets or planting incriminating evidence.'

'A pickpocket,' said Orikan. 'No wonder you're interested.'

'King Mischief, from the volumes I've read, is a saboteur who shakes up the social order and exposes hypocrites. The scripts are, I understand, tightly vetted by the Administratum.'

They passed through deep shadows, down the long stairs and slopes of what was once coral shelf, and descended to the Abyssals – the sprawling slum built on the great plain below. A plain that had once been a seafloor, before the orks had pumped billions of drums of water out in order to cool their reactors. Before the planetary government, while still riding high off denouncing the orkoid tyranny, realised that they too could sell the water to passing Imperial Navy vessels and trade ships, thus opening new land for development.

Now much of the ocean was gone, retreated into the smaller basin of the deep sea.

'Note,' said Trazyn, 'how even these bare hab-blocks all have window boxes? Little gardens, vegetables, flowers. And each of them carved in the rune-like patterns inherited, knowingly or not, from the aeldari. Fascinating, isn't it?'

'Short-lived vermin borrowing from long-lived degenerates. I don't understand your fascination with humans, Trazyn.'

'I admit they have their poor qualities, certainly. Unrefined? Without question. Superstitious? No doubt. And primitive, fractious and grasping as well. Besides, their biology is disgusting. Everything they consume for energy eventually kills them. Their digestive tracts are literal colonies of bacteria. And their reproductive system is the same as their waste-elimination system. Did you know that?'

Orikan grimaced, as if he had not known it, and preferred to live in a state of ignorance.

'It's true,' Trazyn insisted. 'I've done the dissections. Yet despite all those difficulties they've done a great deal in the galaxy. Their empire may, in time, eclipse the extent that ours was at its height. Perhaps it does already – they have not the coordination to tell. They are born weak, mature slowly, have short lifespans, and in a galaxy packed with creatures that come into the world fully-grown and armed with fangs and armoured with bone, they have still managed to become the dominant force through technology and will.'

Trazyn paused, as if weighing whether to trust Orikan with his next sentence.

'They remind me a bit of us. Or rather, how we used to be. Ambitious but short-lived.'

Orikan growled, a displeased buzzing in his vocal emitters. 'We had greater technology. And their lives are much longer than ours were.'

'Not by much,' Trazyn chided. 'Not really. Particularly given that they cannot use stasis-crypts during star-voyages as we did. Oh, they artificially extend them with drug treatments and augmetics, or the awful surgeries of the Astartes. But that is a very small minority. Most are, overall, adjusted to their short lives. They consider it enough.'

'They know nothing better,' said Orikan with a note of bitterness. 'Our truncated, tumour-cursed lives had to be lived in the shadow of the immortal Old Ones. Before that we, too, accepted our fate.'

'Do you think that, given the choice, they would trade their souls for immortality as we did?'

'As *you* did,' said Orikan. 'I resisted. I saw the delusion. You were only too willing to trade in that broken body of yours.'

Trazyn stopped. 'I went to the flames of biotransference in chains. It is distinct in my engrams. I can picture it with clarity – the lock-collar around my throat. Metal hands, tireless, grasping my shoulders. They took me in my library. The one who did it, Nilkath, was a Sautekh warden. One of the Stormlord's vassals.'

Orikan stared at him, ocular rotating, as if searching his death mask, looking for the telltale sign of power rerouting that might signal a lie.

'We remember it differently, then,' he said. And though Orikan's words often carried the lingering kiss of acid, these in particular burned. 'After all, you are the historical expert, are you not?'

The Diviner turned, and they walked the rest of the six-mile way in silence, arriving just before dawn.

By night, the sewer pumping station was deserted. Slipping in was not difficult. The watchman, whom Trazyn implanted with a mindshackle scarab, opened the lock and let them into the old underground network.

The Abyssal sewers were only a few centuries old, but in poor repair. Constant battering by the monsoon rains – artificially induced via cloud-seeding, since the oceans were no longer large enough to support the climate's optimal rainfall – meant that maintenance crews had to work on the system year-round.

'Please don't tell me we'll need to climb through human waste,' said Orikan.

'This is not a waste network,' Trazyn assured him. 'This is water evacuation. Serenade's archipelago is a monsoon climate, with heavy rains half the year. Now induced artificially, of course. Given that the Abyssal was formally seafloor, you can imagine the flooding risk down here.'

Orikan grunted.

'These tunnels also stock the underground cisterns that sustain the planet, which is where we're headed.'

'Where you found the signal?'

'Where my sensor-scarabs found the signal,' he corrected. 'Water is an excellent conductor of vibration – and whatever is down there, it's broadcasting strong.'

The body floated face down, its bloated wrists swelling against the buttoned sleeves of the blue maintenance jumpsuit.

Or at least, it had once been blue. Long immersion had leeched much of the cheap dye into the water.

And it was not the only body. Orikan could see at least five others floating on the lapping waters of the cistern, its surface rippling as the midnight rains trickled more fluid into the lightless cavern of the world's water supply.

It had taken them three local days to get this far down.

'Turn it over,' said Orikan.

'You turn it over,' Trazyn shot back.

'I thought the mysteries of the human form were but old prophecies to you? Surely you cannot tell me you refuse to–'

'Yes, yes. Very well.' Trazyn waded waist-deep into the water, hooked a finger on the jumpsuit and rolled the corpse over. 'Hmm. This damage is… quite extensive.'

'You're saying humans don't normally look like this?' Orikan jabbed.

Trazyn ran a spectromantic analysis, raising a hand and

bombarding the body with reflective lasers. 'Normally I would say this was post-mortem damage from some scavenger. The avian-lizards in the sewer can grow to be quite large and aggressive. The bloating makes things difficult, of course. But I doubt even the largest could cause such a dramatic fracture to the right ocular orbital – look, it runs straight through to the upper palate. What flesh remains appears to have been gouged with some metal weapon or tool.'

'A claw.'

'Bit of a leap, dear astromancer,' said Trazyn, not looking up from his examination. 'This trauma in the chest cavity is quite extensive, however. If the rib fractures did not give it away as perimortem injury, I would, as I have said, thought it to be the work of a large scavenger. As it is, it may be some kind of tool. Indeed, on the left side only the false ribs remain. It almost appears as if the attacker grabbed the sternum and tore ribs one through eight out, separating the right side of the costal cartilage with a slash and yanked the ribs from the ligament connections to the vertebrae.'

'He was eaten.'

'I know it appears that way, but…' Trazyn turned. 'Ah, I see.'

Orikan hovered a hand's breadth above the water's surface, legs crossed, his inbuilt repulsor drives making little rippling dimples in the surface of the cistern. His ocular was shut tight, head back. Before him, his dexterous hands danced in precise movements, as though he were unfurling a scroll before him.

'It did not happen here. Death came in the tunnels above. He did not see what killed him. It came from the side, out of the dark, avoiding his torch beam.'

'You see this?'

'Imperfectly,' said Orikan. 'I can only reconstruct based on evidence. Not a true vision, but a forensic-projection extrapolated from his injuries and the lingering trauma patterns burned in his neural pathways.'

'And what do you see?'

'Claws.' Orikan opened his ocular. 'Long claws. A predator's weapon. It hit him from the side, the attacker's hard cranium – head down like a ram – causing the incapacitating skull trauma.' He pointed. 'Minor defensive wounds on the arms. He was stunned on his back. The pelvic bone – you missed that, dear colleague – gained a hairline fracture when it knelt on him. And then, it tore into the chest with its claws and teeth.'

'And teeth?'

Orikan waved a hand, bringing up a chrysoprase model of one of the remaining ribs, spun it so he could see. 'Dentition marks of pointed teeth. And more important, dental scoring. Meaning–'

'Meaning he was still alive when it ate him,' said Trazyn, and paused. 'This reconstruction. Engram-images. Is that what you see when you speak to Vishani?'

Orikan snapped off his repulsors, settling into the water and said: 'Shall we go deeper?'

Four days later, they cut through a natural cavern wall and discovered the tomb shaft.

It was straight and regular, diving down in long stairways and rising in right-angle switchbacks. Divorced from the water network, the air was dry to the point of desiccation.

And that's where they found the bone chamber.

They sensed it before they saw it, not due to the odour of decay – for they were no longer in the water network – but due to a signal return that suggested human material.

They had been taking precautions since finding the bodies.

First, they found the skulls. Packed row upon row, ranked on the walls of the chamber so their eyeless sockets stared out.

To a human, it would've been overawing. Sacred or blasphemous, depending on one's divine allegiance. To an immortal necron, long alienated from death's terror, it was merely a sign of heightened danger. Even when they trod into the wider chamber, weapons in hand and feet refashioned so a cushion of latticed necrodermis quieted each footstep, they did not reflect on the long bones that formed triumphal arches across the path. The ribcages dangling from the ceiling like lanterns.

The articulated skeletons kneeling on either side of the walkway, heads bowed and hands prostrate against the floor, as if living gods processed down the centre of the chamber.

In a way, they did.

Analysis says some of these bones are old, signalled Trazyn. *Centuries old.*

Not all of them, Orikan signalled back.

A waypoint indicator appeared in Trazyn's vision, and he saw that one of the kneeling skeletons was in the process of being built, torn flesh still clinging to some of the cobbled-together parts.

The left side of its ribcage, including ribs one through eight, were thick with clotted blood. Trazyn's oculars drifted up the pathway.

And of course, there's that, he signalled, ending the message with a glyph indicating wry amusement.

At the end of the chamber was a great set of carcharodon jaws, framing the enormous gateway to the next chamber.

Chanting echoed from the black door.

Trazyn took the left side, Orikan the right.

The chamber was massive, bigger even than the one they

had battled over during the early days of Serenade's settlement – when a colonial island town lay above them, rather than a massive basin city.

Huge braziers bracketed a central promenade, its floor swept clean. Unlike the antechamber, there were no bones here. Whatever vicious intelligence had built the cathedral of slaughter obviously considered this sacred space a place that must remain unpolluted.

Apart from the altar that stood before the huge Eternity Gate, its blackstone frame – preserved perfectly, as if the stones had just been shaped – rising over a wide staircase.

The thing, hunched and chittering, stooped before the necron monument mumbling some kind of prayer.

Orikan swept out a hand, ran a scry.

It is... human, Orikan signalled, then corrected himself. *No, not entirely. But at least part of it–*

The creature's head snapped around, as if it had detected them. Orikan saw it pivot towards Trazyn, baleful eyes glowing in the darkness.

Trazyn, on your guard!

Too late, the fool had taken his eye off the creature to examine a stele at the base of one of the braziers – collecting, always collecting – and the thing had already closed half the distance. By the time he snapped his attention back to the attacker, it had cut its way back and forth through several braziers, breaking the line of sight so Trazyn could not predict its angle of attack. A shadow in the dark.

Orikan watched as Trazyn made a blind defensive swing the left side of the brazier, hoping to catch the foul thing with his obliterator as it came around the corner.

Instead, it vaulted onto the dead brazier, nimbly catching purchase on the top with its hooked limbs before diving down on the archaeovist – claws flashing in the glow of Trazyn's reactor core.

Orikan ran, but the chamber's huge scale meant the thing would have precious moments to scour the archaeovist. Judging by the chamber they'd passed through, and the bodies they had seen, it was clearly masterful at murder. Frenzied yet surgically precise.

What ill star must a being be born under to gain those abilities?

Trazyn slammed the blackstone hard, skidded. His obliterator tumbled from his grip with the impact of the creature, and he needed both hands to fend off the vicious assault of its claws.

Through the knife talons, he could see a leering skull face.

It hissed and warbled. Shrill notes that confused his systems, translated into his ocular vision as a line of number glyphs. Ever repeating. Filling his visual field like a monsoon flood.

3211-1545-4131-5322

3211-1545-4131-5322

3211-1545-4131-5322

Trazyn pistoned upward with his legs trying to throw it off. It hung on, one set of talons lodged deep in his scapula plate.

But the kick gave him space. He reared back and punched the thing in its skull, fist shaped so the two central knuckles stuck out to deliver all the energy to a single point.

The thing's skull shattered, came away from its face in pieces.

Trazyn tried to get a grip on it and throw the creature, but each time his hands found purchase, the bony exoskeleton snapped away in handfuls of ossified calcium.

Bones. The whole thing was covered in human bone.

He felt the long claw sink between his scapular shoulder plate and his ribcage, worming down through his systems, searching for his central reactor. Piercing the casing so fluid spilled through his system and ran down his vertebrae. Felt the long surgical claw separate the fuel rods deep inside him.

No surrogates this time.

I could just let it happen, thought Orikan.

It would be so simple, to stand by and watch Trazyn be butchered by this monster. To prepare himself for the attack, take time to calculate a blow that would smash its frame with his staff. He had done it the last time a creature had attacked him in the tunnels – a creature he was nearly sure Trazyn had released.

It would be mathematical justice. Balance the equation.

Yet for reasons he could not wholly understand, he felt himself running back the timeline, watching himself speed backward as the creature sailed through the air and back onto the brazier, hopping down onto the floor.

Maybe it was the way Trazyn had characterised his biotransference. Or the fact that, despite his obnoxious pretence of being kind to Orikan – a thing Trazyn only did, the astromancer knew, because he found it so irritating – he had in fact found the Eternity Gate.

Or because after so many aeons, it was in fact nice to converse with a being approaching his own level.

Whether out of utility or sentimentality, he burst back into the timeline, right hand already formed into Haqqavi's Axiom and the left spread in the Gesture of Targeting, aiming the bolt of antimatter.

Orikan pumped his right hand towards his left, sending the colourless, lightless stream of agitate particles racing across the antechamber.

The top of the brazier disintegrated, blasted apart by the particle stream.

The creature tumbled through air, smashing into the black-stone and scattering bones around it.

In a flash, it was back on its feet, roaring something unintelligible. Howling and warbling with fury.

Except this time, it streaked directly for Orikan.

He summoned another bolt, missed. Saw its loping stride come closer and crouched, preparing to meet it with his staff.

It came low, dodging and scuttling. Long knife-blade fingers extended to grab and disembowel.

And he heard the thing speak. A gibberish chain of numbers. A loop of insanity.

And Orikan knew it would get past his guard. Knew it would sink those long talons into him because who could stand up to a mad horror like this? He might strike it once or twice, but without the empowering stars he could not stand up to it for long.

He braced for the attack.

And then it stopped, frozen, hands splayed.

For a moment, Orikan thought he had stopped the timeline. Thrown a chrono-static hex via an unconscious reflex.

Until he saw Trazyn step around the frozen horror, hand extended and a stasis-beam hazing the air.

'Do you hear what it's saying?'

Orikan stepped forward to inspect the thing, his staff raised in case it moved.

'It's the signal,' said Trazyn. 'The anomaly we've been following. The stronger signal repeating the Song of Serenade.

This is the broadcast source. It's repeating it, over and over. Screaming it out into the dark.'

'Never mind that,' said Orikan. 'We have larger problems. Do you not recognise who this is?'

Trazyn stepped around to the front, peered closer.

'Dead Gods,' he swore. 'It's High Metallurgist Quellkah.'

CHAPTER EIGHT

LLANDU'GOR: *We deceived them. We brought the night. And soon, we shall flay them. They will be ours, body and mind.*

– War in Heaven, Act V, Scene III, Line 2

Eternity Gate
Serenade
252 Years Until Exterminatus

You have been away a long time, my equal.

Deep apologies. I have duties. The Great Awakening has begun, and my dynasty needs guidance. Or rather, those who have awoken need guidance. The Sautekh have arisen from their crypts into civil war. There are many in my dynasty who have asked me to read their futures.

And make their futures?

Let us keep that between us, shall we? The future cannot always be left to the vagaries of fate. At times, it must be built. If I stood back, the dynasty would destroy itself. Certain matters need to be attended to. Even after opening the Cephris complex, I cannot use what lies inside if the Infinite Empire has destroyed itself in the meantime.

Last time we spoke, I asked you whether you were ready. Are you ready now?

Orikan?

It is not an easy thing for me, Vishani. When I told them about biotransference, about the inferno I saw, they called me mad. A partisan. None could see it, or they did not want to see it. I was the only one who discerned the true nature of the C'tan. I tried to save them and they persecuted me. Then they seized me with metal hands and cast me into the fire with them. It is hard to be truthful, to open one's mind to another after that.

I listened. Nephreth listened. You say that you were the only one to see it, but that is ego, my equal. And for one of your abilities, ego is an easy beast to surrender to. But you were not the only one. We fought the C'tan. Nephreth gave his unspoiled life against them. You have taken their persecution into your mind, and now you use it to persecute yourself. Have I not trusted you?

You have.

Have I not helped you unlock the burning stars and smite your foes?

I am ever appreciative. I have worked for your release.

But not, it seems, enough to lower the armour of your mind. It is so lonely here, Orikan. And if you let me in, trusted me, then I could show you how to open the Eternity Gate well before this world is due to crack and split.

We have time, I have not exhausted all avenues—

Are you afraid of me, Orikan? Is it because of the cryptek?

To contract the flayer virus is… beyond imagining. And it carries thought to thought. Trazyn has been in quarantine. He saw the thing's neural emanations in his own oculars. So far, he does not appear infected but…

I am not infected, Orikan.

But if you were, you might not realise.

I am not infected because I never dwelled upon the signal. It has been here since construction, a part of the very geology. Indeed, a very good passive defence it is too. We lost seven architects to it while building the tomb, but quickly learned to screen it out. Not to listen. Just like I told you not to listen. Is that not correct?

Yes, that is correct.

Follow if you must, I said, but do not try to solve it. So long as you do not dwell upon it, you will be safe. And you are safe. Perhaps not your colleague Trazyn, but you are.

Is there a way to cure him?

If he is infected, no. He may never return to this world. And if he does not, you will need to complete the work. Let me show you how. Only briefly.

I need more time.

Well then, you are fortunate. We have time. But my equal, we have less than you think.

Prismatic Galleries, Solemnace
244 Years Until Exterminatus

'And you are saying that you found the high metallurgist like this?' Executioner Phillias edged up to the hermetic box, head tilting as she leaned towards the field.

Orikan and Trazyn exchanged glances.

'A hurtful insinuation,' Trazyn said.

'And ignorant,' Orikan added. 'Lady executioner, even a cryptek of my powers does not have enough understanding of the flayer virus to infect a subject. Not without exposing him, and therefore myself, to other infected. A dangerous prospect and Quellkah, to be blunt, was not worth that risk.'

On the other side of the field, the thing that had been High Metallurgist Quellkah cocked its head, mirroring Phillias' body language. Its exoskeleton was caked a finger-width deep in old blood, smeared over so many centuries that it permanently stained his necrodermis. A hollow human skull lay on his narrow head like a mask, the sickly yellow glow of his monocular peering out from behind the punched-through sockets. Bones and shroud-strips of desiccated skin dangled from his frame.

Phillias raised a hand, wiggled the fingers, and watched the scalpel-like digits move in turn. She took a step sideways, and – hesitant and clumsy – the cryptek did the same.

Then the horror lunged towards her and the hermetic field discharged with a snap of dimensional realignment, throwing the cursed cryptek back. It scuttled into a corner and cowered there, its parchment-thin sheets of skin smouldering.

Phillias herself leapt backward, her hands up in a guard position.

'Yes, it does that on occasion,' said Orikan, floating in his repulsor field with his monocular closed. 'Quellkah was ever the mimicker. Find a bit of research progress in your work and follow in your footsteps, then at the last minute try to stab you in the throat and take it for himself.'

Trazyn shook his head. 'Inappropriate.'

Phillias wheeled on him. '*Really*, Master Orikan. You speak as if he is not here.'

'He isn't.' Orikan's monocular snapped open to regard

Phillias. 'Quellkah is four millennia dead. Do you think any of him remains in *that*?'

The thing that was Quellkah was not listening. It was on its front, nudging a human skull with a claw and scuttling after its loping roll. The first decade, they learned that it would become aggressive unless sufficiently stimulated. Trazyn's museum had ample supply of such diversions.

Trazyn waved a hand, rendering the field opaque and sound-proof. He preferred not to look at the creature overmuch.

'How about it?' Orikan jibed. 'Do you see the great high metallurgist in this form?'

'Perhaps not.' Phillias turned away from the field and took a step back so she could regard both of her charges without turning her back on the creature, even contained. 'But you could at least come to ground and provide me some respect as a representative of the praetorians.'

'Pity,' said Orikan. 'We had rather expected an apology.'

'Apology?'

'Yes, an apology,' said Trazyn. 'For over a millennium the Awakened Council branded us suspected murderers. Impinged our reputations. Deeply impacted our relations with other dynasties – at least, when we have even had time to see to our own affairs. This project, which we magnanimously carve out time for in order to benefit the empire, has stolen a great deal of focus. We demand a formal apology and retraction from the council.'

'Impossible,' said Phillias.

'Impossible?' Trazyn stamped the floor with the butt of his obliterator. 'Do you see how I am forced to live?'

Phillias took in the hermetic field containing Trazyn, the table full of scrolls and strange alien artefacts, the piles of leather-bound tomes. The way he had worn his chin shiny from rubbing it with his fingers. Decades of quarantine, indeed, had not been kind.

'You must admit, Lord Trazyn,' said Orikan, with a wry smile, 'that you make a fine addition to this gallery. And you do so enjoy my visits – I daresay I am better company than the high metallurgist, here.'

Trazyn flashed the Sign of Vokk, a metaphysically obscene gesture that, in simple terms, indicated that Trazyn hoped the Diviner would – in all timelines and dimensions – come to a brutal and humiliating end.

Orikan flashed it back, and Trazyn gave a low chuckle.

'Lord Trazyn is quite right, executioner,' said Orikan. 'We have brought back the supposedly murdered Quellkah. Why are we not entitled–'

'Because the Awakened Council is dissolved. Ossuaria still lives, and Baalbehk, though they are at war.'

'And Zuberkar?' Trazyn stepped forward, hand touching the cartouche on his chest as a ward against ill-luck.

'Destroyed. He and Baalbehk came to blows in the council chamber. With the Great Awakening imminent, Baalbehk staged a coup, tried to consolidate power and hold the council world himself.'

'Think of it. Arising from sixty million years of slumber to find the order disturbed. The Silent King and Triarch absent. The guiding hand of Szarekh and his dynasty removed. Awakening dynasties realising they might burn rival worlds as the enemies still repose in their sarcophagi. An unprecedented opportunity for advancement. But it is ending. Now that the Sautekh are rising, the other dynasties will scatter for the shadows,' Orikan said, with clear relish.

'The Sautekh are ensnared in a civil war,' Phillias said dismissively. 'Your phaeron slain in his crypt. The rest eating each other over his throne, none of them more civilised than the monster Quellkah has become.'

'True. Very true.' Orikan closed his monocular and resumed floating. 'And I admit some hand in the current unpleasant-ness. Many phaerons and would-be phaerons have sought my unerring gaze during these troubled times. But I will give this counsel for nothing – the strength of the Sautekh has never rested in our phaerons.'

'What is that supposed to mean?' Phillias tapped her Rod of Covenant on the blackstone. 'Are you speaking of the Stormlord? He is dead, his sarcophagus atomised by rivals before he could awaken.'

'If you say it is true,' Orikan paused, 'then it must be true. Shall we turn back to the matter at hand? Under whose pur-view do we fall, if not that of the Awakened Council?'

'Mine. The praetorians. Most decisions of the council have been reversed, but I fought to allow you to continue your work unmolested by other dynasties.' She gave each of them a look laden with gravity. 'You two may be absurd, venal little children, but the work you do is crucial to our future and I truly believe it cannot be accomplished by anyone else.'

'Thank you,' said Trazyn. 'We think you're an absurd, venial child too.'

Phillias opened her mouth to reply.

'Would you like to hear what we've discovered?' said Tra-zyn. He waved a hand, and the field surrounding Quellkah snapped back to translucent.

The corrupted metallurgist was standing just behind the field, as if it had been listening as they spoke.

'We discovered the Eternity Gate by following a signal broadcasting the Song of Serenade – one that was stronger, slightly out of step from the general thrumming of the planet. We thought it was related to the Eternity Gate, and from a certain perspective, it was. In his madness, perhaps even trapped underground for a time, Quellkah had become obsessed with the emanation.'

Trazyn cut the sound-dampeners on the field so they could hear the warbling, buzzing, shrieking line of trash-glyphs that repeated from Quellkah's vocal emitters.

'In fact, he broadcast it so strong, it entered my own neural system when he attacked me. Thus the quarantine.' He waved a hand at the blue glow of the field. 'I am well, thank you for asking. My crypteks have run as many scans as Solemnace has scarabs, and I seem to be clean. Yet it would be irresponsible to risk the dynasty.'

'Only two more years,' Orikan said, with hollow cheer. 'You know, they say those last years are the hardest.'

'Master Orikan has… also given his professional opinion. Repeatedly. Even when no one consults him.'

'What have you found?' said Phillias, uninterested in this banter.

'These vocalisations are not gibberish,' said Trazyn. 'They are the Song of Serenade.' He waved a hand, and a phos-glyph panel showed a waveform matched to a numbered graph. 'A match, see? 3211 Stop 1545 Stop 4131 Stop 5322. Over and over. It has infected his system.'

'Did it give him the flayer virus?' Phillias asked, an edge of alarm in her tone.

'No, no. At least, I don't think that is possible. Orikan?'

Orikan stared directly back into Trazyn's oculars. 'It would not seem so.'

'But clearly,' Trazyn continued, 'he heard the emanation and became obsessed. Perhaps that's what he was studying when the virus began to take hold. He turned to worshipping it. Slaughtering humans every few decades – even a few orks – and dragging them to his lair. But what's interesting are his own neural loops.'

Trazyn opened a new phos-glyph panel, displaying a neural network pulsing with data, streams of information running along every root-like tendril and spiralling through coils.

'Quite active, for a flayer-touched savage, yes? I thought so. After I spent the first two decades of this quarantine trying to decipher the emanation, without success, I realised that Quellkah here had already worked the problem for several millennia. Perhaps instead of deciphering the signal, I should try to decipher *him*.'

'I set up a middleman system,' said Orikan, pointing to a bulky set of equipment dangling above the corrupted Quellkah. 'A separate neural network to let Lord Trazyn delve into the thought-algorithms of the thing without having to connect his neural system directly.'

'And I thank you for it. But what I have found – after far too much time with this subject, if I must say – is quite interesting. He thinks of nothing but books.'

'Books?' Phillias said sceptically. '*That* thinks of books?'

'Exclusively,' said Trazyn. 'Specifically, it searches every text contained in the cryptek's engrams, trying to decipher a message out of the emanation. Quellkah believed it to be a book code. An old type of cryptogram that used a text as the key to decipher a message. Say I wanted to send you a message. First, we would agree on a book – the same edition, so the text lined up exactly. Then I would send you a message that says six-two-seven, and to decipher it, you would take your book and go to the sixth page, second line, and seventh word, see? Or perhaps the sixth chapter, second page, seventh word. Or volume six of a series of works, second chapter, seventh word. Or–'

'There are any number of combinations,' said Orikan. 'Lord Trazyn has been working on this for... a long period. I have heard about it extensively.'

'So you just need to find the book, and you can open the Eternity Gate early,' said Phillias.

'That is the idea,' said Trazyn. 'If Quellkah was correct. If not, I've wasted a great amount of time.'

'And your own research, Master Orikan?' She turned to him. 'How does it proceed?'

'I fear, that Lord Trazyn has outdone me,' he said. 'I do not expect results for some time.'

Orikan was so practised at obfuscation, it did not even sound like a lie.

Serenade
199 Years Until Exterminatus

The day is coming.

I cannot wait. My whole system strums with the anticipation of it.

Soon, equal. Soon. Each moment of waiting is a moment of preparation and study. This is no light task you under-take. It is fraught with danger. Have you told Trazyn of our progress?

No. I... do not speak of you to Trazyn. His quarantine has ended, but he has not yet returned. Dynastic business. Both of us are increasingly called away.

That is good. He has left us alone to our work. From what you tell me, Trazyn is talented but grasping. It is best he does not know of our progress, even though we will need him.

Need him? Our equations are perfect. Your star maps, my

*equal, they are a thing of beauty. I had not realised that, as an
extra-dimensional artefact, the Mysterios could be keyed to the
star-patterns of different timelines. By recalibrating, we can open
the Eternity Gate as early as next–*

**Do not be jealous, my equal. We will need him for other
reasons. You are more than he will ever be, it is true, but
you are not all things. He has something we need.**

What could he possibly have that we need?

**Two things. Two things he keeps on him. Open your-
self to me, and I will show you.**

I...

**Do you wish to continue playing tiresome games with
Trazyn and fighting petty dynastic wars? Or would you like
to join me and ascend to bodies of starlight?**

Orikan sat with that question a long time.

Please, Orikan. Trust me.

Gradually, tenderly, he opened an information channel.

He felt the smallest tug, the creeping sense of a being lingering at the door. Sizing up a room before stepping inside.

And the vision gripped his neural matrix like a bonfire.
Like a falling meteor burning in the atmosphere. Like a city
aflame.

He saw zodiacs spin and stars wither in the heavens. Plan-
etoids crash and form new celestial bodies.

A flaring staff, cracking seals.

A gem, gleaming in the dark.

Felt metal hands locked around his wiry arms of flesh,
his feet kicking and shoulders dislocating as the relentless
androids dragged him towards the emerald fires of the forge.
Towards the spiritual sundering of biotransference.

And he recognised the death mask of one of his captors.

And he knew what he had to do.

CHAPTER NINE

*'Only the most parochial beings think that stars twinkle.
That is an illusion of atmosphere, an observation of one
who has never travelled space. The stars do not wink
at us, they burn. They are unlidded eyes boring into us
with their gaze.'*

– Orikan the Diviner

Serenade
173 Years Before Exterminatus

No one expected the fleet to arrive that year.

That was how it went with warp travel. Even if the ships
were due, one could not depend on them making orbital
anchor.

This unscheduled stop was for a muster. The Serenade
Maritime Infantry was to take part in the invasion of the
Relic Belt, a set of remote worlds who had – it was only

recently learned – declared their independence two centuries beforehand. And the second world of the belt was, much like Serenade had been, covered with water.

The fleet had come to take on board water and collect what it could of the Maritime Infantry – a surprise regimental founding, as Vice-Admiral Zmelker put it – before leaving within the month.

The fleet had arrived, by happenstance, during the Settlement Festival – a once-per-decade celebration commemorating the pioneer landings on Serenade. And with this festival marking the six thousandth year of human habitation, the observances were particularly large.

The festival was, as Trazyn pointed out, commemorating both the wrong date and year, but he was enjoying it nonetheless.

Great pavilions stood in the parks and squares, celebrating local culture and achievements. Historical and artistic galleries. Banners, recreated, from the Greenskin War. Classic films from the propaganda pict-industry, famous across the sector, shown nightly in the flicker-theatres. Musical compositions for sacred, patriotic and civic occasions. And of course, the famous Serenade Opera – whose performances were recorded and spread throughout the Eastern Fringe.

Rumour had it even Calgar, the Lord of Macragge, had watched one and enjoyed it – though anyone with education claimed this belief was merely a meeting of wholesome local pride and extreme exaggeration.

Given these two concurrent events, it was only a matter of time before the opera was seconded for a special performance – invite-only, for the planetary governor and her guests.

A group from fleet command, resplendent in their parade

whites and so weighted with medals they needed to wear special mounting boards, mingled with pict-industry performers and religious authorities.

'There's Lady Torsairian, the Imperial governor,' Trazyn said, pointing through the one-way field at the box almost opposite. He was eating the evening up, so pleased to be out of quarantine that Orikan could feel the chilling pulse of the archaeovist's hood as it kept his cranium from overheating. Orikan wondered how far he had cranked his chronosense back, trying to savour every second.

'And next to her is Vice-Admiral Zmelker. You see his uniform? Red facings and brass piping. Unique to the Frontier Fleet of the Eastern Fringe. His left arm, folded at the sleeve, was lost in an engagement against ork raiders when he was a post-captain. It was his convoy of Taurox armoured transports we saw arriving, no doubt.'

Orikan leaned against the wall of the theatre box. They had been lucky that all the boxes – save for the governor's – were shrouded with privacy fields so they were both opaque and soundproof. A perfect place for political intrigue, private guild deals and scandalous liaisons. A favourite playground of the planetary elite.

In fact, the box's official occupants – whom Trazyn had infected with mindshackle scarabs – were just such a pair of young aristocratic lovers. They sat catatonic, their theatre-thrones pushed back in the box to give Trazyn and Orikan more room to stand. Blank eyes staring insensate at the aliens in front of them.

Children of important people, judging by their clothing, though Orikan had no interest in this world and its byzantine ideas of hierarchy, much as he did not care which paramecium ruled each water drop.

And he especially did not care given the gravity of recent events.

Unexpected warp arrivals always made him jumpy and irritable. The tides of the empyrean tore at the natural order of the universe – sent the wheeling stars out of alignment – and foiled his calculations. They turned solid prophecies into wild guesses, and *that* he did not like.

Particularly if the rumours were true, and through the strange eddies of the warp, this fleet had arrived decades before the time when it had left anchor. Things out of time bothered Orikan; they constituted unknown variables he'd rather keep to a minimum. Indeed, it was what made Trazyn and his Solemnace galleries so frustrating. Every object out of chronology was a clot in the bloodstream of time, a block that he could not see past.

He had asked Trazyn to bring the aeldari gem, taken from the World Spirit, in case they had to accelerate their timeline. Said it was crucial for his research, that it might be useful to study the signal's effect on its crystalline form. Intimated that it would be useful for activating the Eternity Gate.

It hung on Trazyn's hip, along with the other curios the archaeovist kept there.

'Vice-admiral,' said Orikan, hoping Trazyn had not seen him staring at the collection. 'Not a lord?'

'Oh no, my dear Orikan. The ships orbiting above us are a mere task force of the larger demi-crusade fleet. The order of battle, if I am not mistaken, is Exorcist Grand Cruiser *Void Hammer*, one Defender escort cruiser, and three Sword frigates. Plus various transport and supply ships, of course. A force far below any lord admiral, but a good long-range group for a man who's driving to get a fourth skull on his lapel.'

'He does not look very pleased with his box seat.'

'I suspect he does not appreciate opera. He seems a rather bluff voidsman, uncomfortable on dirt, as they say. And I can't imagine he will enjoy a play of such an intensely local type.'

'Oh?'

'Didn't I tell you? This opera is *The Mischief King Revealed*. First performance. Two centuries ago it was low street theatre, now the height of sophisticated culture. And along the way the character was softened to be less seditious, I suppose.' He settled his oculars back on the vice-admiral. 'That's quite a laspistol in his chest-holster. Engraved ork-bone grip – cut from a war trophy, I would guess. Perhaps from the one who took his arm.'

'Imagine losing an arm and not being able to replace it.'

'Yes,' said Trazyn, looking at a group of pict-actors getting drinks in the back. 'Not an eventuality we have to contend with any more.'

'If you could go back, would you?'

'Go back to what?'

'The flesh. If one of these ridiculous fanatics actually found a species for us to transfer our consciousness to. Or say, if Nephreth's body lets us fabricate a new, unspoiled race of necrontyr – would you do it?'

Trazyn paused in his visual scanning and looked at Orikan square. 'I... of course I would. It would be my greatest joy to once again feel a soul within me, to taste, and touch, and feel.'

'Would it? Because then you would be again subject to disease and death. To age. And I remember you were not so resistant to giving up such things. Old Archaeovist Trazyn with his bent back from decades leaning over scrolls and scrutinising objects. Trazyn with his squinting eyes and cane.'

'I… admit there would be sacrifices. I have not thought about it greatly, to be honest.'

'That's why we're so terrified of the Destroyers and the flayer virus, aren't we? Our society was death-obsessed, true. But it was bodily decay that we feared most. Those two unfortunate classes of being are reminders that we are not immune. You talk about this human culture while ignoring your own. As you once told me, every society turns into insults and curses what they fear or are repelled by. Our kind has no biological processes, so we do not use profanities of bodily function. We are soulless god-killers with no fear of hell, so we do not blaspheme. But we do call each other low and bumbling, because we are highly civilised. I will call you old hunch-back and you will call me mad star-gazer, because that is the root of our fear and shame.'

'You have become quite the cultural analyst, Orikan. Perhaps my presence has improved you a little.'

'And I remember how afraid you were that the tumours would take your wits. All the work you had done, so much of it up in that cranium of yours. But if you stepped into the forges, got a new metal body, think of all you could do. Catalogue the entire cosmos, if you wished. And all of it to keep you from thinking about how the things that had made Trazyn, well, *Trazyn*, had burned off in those fires. Eaten by the Deceiver. Or is that your secret, that you do not miss your soul at all?'

'What brought this on? Because standing in a theatre surrounded by our enemies is a deeply inappropriate time to start a shouting match.'

'You said that you resisted biotransference. That you went on the run, and they found you in your library.'

'Yes, I remember distinctly.'

'You remember it because you were there, but you have it backward. I resisted and went on the run. I fled to the library and lived amongst the stacks. But it was my library, not yours. And you, Trazyn, you were one of the ones that came to drag me to the furnaces.'

Trazyn said nothing, stunned. 'But–'

'I remember distinctly,' said Orikan.

'If… if that is true, I am sorry.'

Orikan's monocular fluttered.

'You are a signature talent, Orikan. Rival or no, the galaxy is a more interesting place with you loose in it. And I am glad we have come to a place, willing or not, where we are on the same side. No one deserves what happened during biotransference. No one. Our race leapt off a cliff on the promise that we had wings, and we were deceived.'

Orikan looked away.

'My only caution, my friend, is that you do not cling so hard to these memories. When the Deceiver made these bodies we inhabit, he twisted them. And he twisted our engrams. I cannot remember what my old face looked like. Or the place where I was born. It would not be farfetched for the Deceiver to have planted false memories to sew discord amongst our kind – but if that is true, I am sorry.'

Outside the field, the lights dimmed and the curtain began to rise. Polite applause rippled through the crowd like a passing monsoon shower.

'Let us watch the play,' said Orikan. 'We will talk about it afterward.'

'Yes,' Trazyn said, wrong-footed by the confrontation. 'Afterward. It's quite short by our standards. Only five hours. It's no *War in Heaven*.'

'Thank the stars. I hate that play,' Orikan responded.

'I would have thought you'd like the first five acts, at least.'

'Because they deal with Nephreth?'

'No.' Trazyn turned, oculars narrowed. 'Do you not know this? It is rumoured that the first five acts were secretly composed by Datamancer Vishani. Why else would Nephreth and the Ammunos Dynasty play such a prominent role?'

Orikan pondered that, rolled it around in his logic coils. Was about to speak when Trazyn interrupted him.

'It's starting.'

The Mischief King entered stage right, greeted by gasps from the audience.

The performer was, in fact, a woman. Her high crown and imperial purple robe shimmered in the spotlights. A porcelain mask, white and painted with the image of a regal monarch, covered her face. Each step forward, on platform shoes that ended in stilt-like spikes, was a little miracle of poise and training. Diamonds dripped from the edge of her crown to the space between her eyes.

But it was her third arm that caught the audience's attention. No rag-stuffed sleeve this. It was a high-grade augmetic that moved and twisted with her body.

Then she began her aria, and the world of Serenade started to fall.

CHAPTER TEN

'One hand casts the high priest low.
One hand crowns the slave.
The third hand reaches from below.
And drags both to the grave.

> – *The Mischief King Revealed,* Act II, Scene IV
> (Unperformed)

From the first note, it was clear the performance would be unusual.

Lady Torsairian, Planetary Governor of Solemnace, worried that it might be too exotic for her honoured guest. The whole thing had been stitched together last-minute, and she had needed to essentially graft the fleet visit onto the existing cultural festivities. But one never knew how outsiders would react to Serenade Opera – newcomers tended to either sit enraptured or entirely disconnected.

Indeed, her own family – not originally native to Serenade – had not taken to the art themselves when they'd arrived five generations previous. Torsairian was one of the first to truly embrace and enjoy it – though she knew it was not to everyone's taste.

Indeed, she had already let Vice-Admiral Zmelker know that she would not be offended if, for instance, an urgent military matter called him away during the first intermission.

He seemed to appreciate that. These Naval officers on the Eastern Fringe were, after all, rough and wild types – some little different to rogue traders – and from their brief time together he did not seem a man who relished sitting still for five hours.

But a glance told her that the guest of honour seemed interested in the performance. Thirty seconds into the opening aria, he was leaning forward in the box seat, one hand gripping the marble railing.

Then, Lady Torsiarian's gaze settled on stage and she forgot the admiral was even there.

All eyes locked on the diva dressed as the Mischief King. The enthralling movements of her arms, sweeping, rolling, undulating and breaking like the waves of the vanished ocean. Lady Torsairian raised a pair of theatre glasses, trying to discern which limb was the augmetic, since they all seemed to move back and forth as if the singer's arms were double-jointed.

Her own arms began to tingle, as if the sense of boneless languidness were settling into her own muscles. Notes weighed upon her. The opera glasses began to feel impressively heavy.

And the song – atonal, eerie. Rather than flow into one another, each note stood alone, an exhalation that grew and died independently as if unconnected to the rest. The lyrics, if indeed there were lyrics, were in no language Torsairian could understand. But despite their alien nature they filled her head with images of black star fields, tunnels running with water, and the coiling of two great worms that met head to tail, eternally chasing each other in symbiotic balance.

She wanted to understand. Believed that if she held the gaze of the performer long enough, the Mischief King would explain these revelations. And as she watched in rapt attention she did see the aria singer's eyes bore straight through the tunnel of her opera glasses and flick a hand towards her.

A cold wind rushed past, like the stories of ghosts and ghost-gods the old settlers wrote of in texts long forbidden to the general public. Numbness, like the water of the deep sea, enfolded her.

Torsairian dropped the opera glasses, realised drool was pouring from her open mouth.

And felt the slow pressure as a hellpistol pressed the back of her head.

Orikan was the only one who saw the shot.

Trazyn, predictably, stood enraptured by the performance. Likely recording every subtle movement of a wrist and stitch of the costume. It was, after all, such an unusual performance.

So inhuman.

Meanwhile, Orikan scryed the audience. Picked up loose muscles and slow-blinking eyes. Seconds before, the air had danced with brainwaves as grandees chatted, flirted, lied and pushed their little agendas. Neural activity spiked jagged when the singer walked onstage. Now, there was only a slow synchronous roll, like ocean waves that refused to break.

He ran a divinatory program and detected warpcraft.

Mass hypnosis.

And he saw the bodyguard behind the governor slowly

draw his hellpistol. He blinked as he did it, as if puzzled by his own actions. Then he stretched the weapon out, thumbed the safety stud, and hung there a moment, the barrel making little figure of eights in the air.

Crack.

The governor's head slammed forward. Struck the rail next to where her manicured hand still held the brass. Slid sideways until she disappeared beneath the lip of the theatre box.

No one moved. All stared at the singer and her high clear notes, like a wet finger ringing a crystal glass. The governor's son and heir presumptive, sitting next to her, did not even blink when his mother's hand slipped from his.

With a hesitant slowness that reminded Orikan of a long-ago underwater battle, the bodyguard swung the hellpistol towards the heir.

Crack.

'What devilry was that noise?' said Trazyn, oculars still fixed on the performance.

Orikan's vision snapped from box to box, seeing the grey film of the soundproof privacy fields flash like horizons lit by lightning. Flash-flash. Flash. Flash-flash-flash. One stuttered and hissed as a man's arm broke through it and hung out, its sleeve stained with bright blood.

He grabbed Trazyn's arm. 'This is an ambush.'

'What?' he said, breaking away from his cultural reverie. 'What are you raving ab–'

Behind them the door banged open. They turned.

Standing behind them was a hunched man in the dark bodyglove of backstage crew, a black watch cap pulled low over his forehead. A purple bandana, the only hit of colour, swaddled his face.

He carried an autopistol, its extended magazine curving below the grip like a ram's horn.

The necrons, still cloaked in their illusion emitters, were invisible to him. He pointed the autopistol at the mind-shackled couple.

'Orikan, mov–'

Hard rounds tore out of the autopistol, ripping holes in the armoured panelling of the box. Cutting down the two lovers. Sparking off the bodies of the two necrons. Smashing their illusion emitters.

The autopistol's slide hammered back and forth like a power tool, then abruptly clacked backward, ammunition spent.

Gun smoke filled the small box, obscuring the assailant's vision.

Then Orikan came out of the smoke, his head haloed by his golden hood like some venomous snake. He grabbed the attacker with surgical-tool fingers and slammed him against the wall, denting the plaster.

'Spectromantic analysis says it isn't human,' said Orikan.

Trazyn stepped out of the smoke and examined the choking assailant, ignoring its whimpering. He passed a thumb over the ridged crest on the forehead and forced open the whimpering mouth, breaking out a pointed tooth and extending an ocular to inspect the growth pattern.

'It's an alien-human hybrid. I've encountered them off-world. This one seems to be fourth generation. Likely part of a larger uprising.'

Orikan looked over his shoulder to the main seats, where ushers and pict-industry stars were making their way down the aisles with axes and knives, murdering their way through the passive audience throat by throat. Each kill caused barely a ripple in the brainwaves of the neighbouring victims.

'You stupid bastard,' sneered Orikan. 'You got us box seats to a coup.'

'Well, the reviews were very good.'

Orikan heaved the hybrid through the privacy field, shorting it out with a pop. The cultist crashed into the orchestra pit, snapping a violist's neck and bowling over three more from the string section.

The singer faltered at the interruption.

And people began to scream.

Across the gallery in the governor's fortified safety box, the hypnotised bodyguard pointed his shaking pistol at Vice-Admiral Zmelker. The admiral turned around, put a hand on the back of the chair, sensing all was not well.

Looked directly at the assassin.

Crack.

The hotshot round slammed into the admiral's chest with a dull thud, driving him backward into the box wall. A Naval security trooper – dazed but moving – tackled the assassin, awkwardly wrestling for the gun in the confines of the booth.

Another crack. A tongue of flame erupted out of the trooper's back, and his collapsing legs sent him tilting over the edge of the box seat, popping the invisible field.

But the trooper was dogged – he dragged the assassin with him. Twenty feet down into the panicking crowd below.

Pure bedlam reigned in the theatre now. Surging crowds of aristocrats made for the exits, only to find them guarded by ushers wielding stub guns and backstage hammers. Plunging fire from the hijacked theatre boxes scythed into the panicking mass from above. The crowd fought in a dozen different directions, finding death at every exit.

Orikan saw another Naval trooper drag the vice-admiral to his feet, stunned but alive. On his chest, his enormous rack of campaign medals and awards lay shattered and smoking, the thick metal decorations having taken the brunt of the hellpistol blast. The remaining security troopers grouped around him, shielding him with their bodies, trading fire between their box and the others.

'We need to go,' said Orikan.

In the middle of the tumult, Trazyn watched the singer. She had abandoned her aria, and – glorying in the terror – removed her mask with a reverential slowness.

Mauve skin and a bulbous forehead lurked behind the porcelain. Pointed teeth grinned. And turning, hands outward, she shouted in an indistinguishable language towards the back of the stage.

A backdrop painted with a marble temple fell away, revealing a crouched monster.

For a moment Trazyn thought it to be a stage prop or a towering religious idol, but then the abomination raised its head and tasted the air with a mouth full of feeders. Came forward on enormous clawed hands and feet until it towered over the diva, three times her height.

And as it reared up, spreading its limbs and piercing the air in a voice high, clear and atonal, Trazyn realised the creature had only three arms – the fourth ending in an amputated stump.

'I believe, like any good performer,' said Trazyn, 'we should make our exit.'

'Is that the creature you unleashed on me?' shouted Orikan. He needed to yell in order to make himself heard over the whir of the chainsaw.

'At the time I didn't know they were infection vectors,' said Trazyn, parrying the cultist's saw with one of his forearms, making the saw shed teeth, before he crushed the hybrid's skull with a counterpunch. They fought on the run, tearing down the corridor behind the theatre boxes. 'At the time I thought they were just odd and dangerous. It turns out a single one can start an infestation in the native population, growing into a patriarch to head the cult.'

Orikan formed Yinnith's Grid, summoning a hard-light shield to guard their rear from the hybrid shooters emerging from the boxes. Stubber rounds flattened against the crystalline surface. 'So you admit that you tried to kill me.'

Trazyn saw more hybrids massing at the end of the hall and skidded to a stop, summoning his obliterator. With a workmanlike swing he crashed a hole through the wall to their right, letting in the cool night air.

'My dear Orikan, that was just a bit of fun.' A shot spanged off his shoulder. 'If I'd wanted to kill you, surely I would have used more than one? I have more. A great deal more.'

And they leapt into the night, leg suspensors taking the impact as they landed on the cobblestone alley three stories below. Above them, hybrid insurgents gathered at the jagged hole, firing down at them, shots going wide.

'Why are they rising now?' puzzled Trazyn, taking shelter in one of the dark alleys of the old town.

'The ships,' said Orikan, with bitterness, his fingers in the air, rotating a series of chrysoprase zodiacs that burned before him. 'The flotilla arrived early. The first crusade fleet to visit since the initial infection. They saw a chance to decapitate Serenade's power structure and get aboard the ships.'

'To spread the infection, yes, that seems plausible.'

'Which presents a larger problem. We know now why the humans sanction an Exterminatus on Serenade – but originally, it would have happened in just over a century. So these Naval officers are out of their place in the timeline. Trazyn, I believe they may have exited the empyrean a full one hundred and seventy-three years before they were fated to. Therefore, the uprising and bombardment will start tonight.'

'Is that what your calculations tell you?'

'As far as I can discern from this mess of a situation.' He spun a chrysoprase zodiac. 'It will take time to ready the ships. Load the munitions. We have four days, seventeen hours.'

'Close. Can you open the tomb if we reach it?'

'I can,' Orikan confirmed.

'Then let's get away from this ambush and underground before the lance strikes begin.'

As they skirted shadows and wound through the cobblestone alleys, it was soon clear this was more than a single decapitation strike. Fires burned across Serenade City, from the veranda-girdled mansions of the island peak down to the monotonous hab-slums of the Abyssal.

Both of their illusion emitters had been chopped to pieces by the autopistol blast, and on occasion their healing necrodermises popped flattened slugs out of their surfaces, the living metal ejecting the foreign bullets as it self-repaired.

No one paid any heed to the metal giants, perhaps dismissing them as variants of the Adeptus Mechanicus creations that roamed the streets, trying to secure power stations and workshops. The fighting over utility stations, Trazyn estimated, would be fierce. Thirty seconds into their journey every light in the district shut off, blanketing the colonial centre in darkness.

They reached Settlement Square to find a full engagement in progress, three companies of Serenade's Maritime

Infantry – mustered for a marching demonstration in a plaza nearby – laying siege to the opera house. Red las-bolts sliced the air, scorching the bone white of the marble columns black.

Chattering hard rounds answered. A shoulder-fired missile rushed out from between pillars, chased by a powdery contrail. It detonated against the side of the plaza's antique fountain and sent up a billow of white dust, sending fist-sized chunks of marble flying out to fracture skulls. A Guardsman screamed through a mask of blood, face torn by stone chips.

The Maritime Infantry were in their summer uniform. Olive tunics with rolled sleeves. Sand-coloured berets rather than helmets. Many, on parade duty, didn't even have flak vests. And though they were intended for beachhead seizure and riverine operations – not urban combat – they were acquitting themselves well.

'I regret not adding a few Serenade units to the collection,' said Trazyn. 'Lost the chance now, I suppose.'

'How do we get into the cathedral?' asked Orikan. 'And the tunnels?'

'No good,' Trazyn responded, pointing across the square, where a group of rubbery purple bodies were pulling themselves from an open sewer drain. 'The cult rules the underground. We're better off on the surface.'

Engines revved. Cones of light spilled across the square.

A convoy of up-armoured Taurox Prime transports tore around the opera house's far side and away from the building. Their tracks threw debris behind them, spraying the mob of misshapen cultists that emerged from the alley, hissing and firing.

'That will be the vice-admiral,' said Trazyn. 'Or what remains of his staff.'

The trailing Taurox – bearing the heraldry of the Fifth Fringe Fleet – traversed its turret around to acquire the targets, gatling cannon already rotating in preparation. Muzzle flash as long as Trazyn's arm stabbed into the dark, hot orange tracer rounds butchering the unfortunate cultists where they stood.

On one Taurox, a Naval staff officer in dress whites manned a heavy stubber, blasting suppressing fire at the columned opera house entrance. His hat was gone, and he pressed the twin triggers with hands still sheathed in formal gloves. Another missile streaked from between the columns and struck a glancing hit to the transport's side, but it continued on, armour plating afire and the officer lolling backward in the hatch, his white uniform turning pink.

'If we were smart,' said Orikan, 'we would've killed Zmelker before he evacuated. He's the only one with authority to trigger an Exterminatus.'

'Or I could have kept him,' mused Trazyn, a tesseract labyrinth in his hand. 'I have a feeling this night will be worth preserving.'

It was.

Monsters roamed the streets of Serenade City. Near-human hybrids, in the uniforms of the Maritime Infantry. Underground workers wielding saws and rock-crushing drills, their work uniforms daubed with the symbol of the two wyrms – one yellow, one black – chasing each other's tails, their bodies complementing each other to form a circle with no space between, eyes lined up in equilibrium.

And they were fulfilling their promise to level society, to cast the high low and bring the low high. Now that the Three-Armed King had risen, all were indeed equal, from the pleasure palaces of the peak to the shanty towns in the basin.

All were equal, because all were prey.

But down in the Abyssal, resistance was light. The cult's heavy-hitting units had deployed to the old city, better to take out the planetary leadership. Here the danger was merely roving militias and death-squads, neither particularly hazardous to two necron lords that could manipulate the timestream.

With little need to hide, they made the pumping station in just over an hour, though they did so covered in the sticky purplish blood of at least two dozen unfortunate insurgents. At one point, they encountered a Serenade heavy weapons company blocking a wide avenue in an attempt to keep cult militias from massing and striking towards the old town, but the necrons had come up behind the gun line and crossing them was no trouble.

Trazyn was still rubbing the tesseract labyrinth, pleased with the impromptu collection, when they reached the pumping station.

Orikan tore the station's door off its hinges, all pretence at stealth gone. They ducked into the building's deserted interior and made their way towards the accessway.

'You have the Mysterios?' asked Trazyn.

'I do.' Orikan glanced at Trazyn's collection of curios. 'That's the aeldari gem, is it not? The solar gem?'

'It is, what of it?'

'The ritual to open the Mysterios requires energy. I will need to channel it.' He held out a hand. 'May I see?'

'Let's go deeper first, friend Orikan. We are still too close to the surface for my liking.'

They descended in darkness, saying little. From pipework, to bare rock, to the necron tunnels. Deeper and deeper into the planet's crust.

At each turn of the tunnel, Trazyn drew a thumb-sized beacon from his dimensional pocket, activated it, and slammed it deep into the wall.

'And what is that?'

'You never know what might happen down here.' Trazyn laughed. 'Even if we open the gate, the Exterminatus might break the planet's mantle. Collapse the tunnels and force us to burrow out with a flayer. Lest you forget, there is a literal mountain on top of us. I would not want to emerge from the gate with no way back.'

Two days down, the planet shook for the first time. It was a small shiver. A tremor.

'It's starting,' said Trazyn. 'I expect that's the *Void Hammer*, on one-eighth power. A precision strike. Tactical. An attempt to buy ground forces more time to evacuate.'

Orikan nodded and dampened his auditory transducers. Trazyn's incessant chatter had distracted him for the past two days. The archaeovist spoke of everything, thinking aloud. The type of geologic strata they passed. Pattern chains formed in the dust of the floor. The mining drills the cultists used as weapons, so suited to boring through Serenade's volcanic rock. That led to types of geologic excavation, fissures and seams, the ideal conditions for fossil formation, notable fossils he had collected on Serenade.

The loquaciousness was all the more interminable because Orikan could hear Vishani whispering, encouraging, leading him deeper. Her voice strengthening with every hour, until their thoughts seemed to be the same. He tried to pass the time remembering what it had been like to be filled with starlight – an experience his engrams could not fully capture – and imagining what it would be like for all necrons to gain such transcendence.

If, that is, he decided they should. It did not appeal to him overmuch to be one god among many.

On the fourth day, Orikan's increasing ennui gained temporary relief when they met a gang of misshapen simian creatures, their alien gene-stock corrupted far beyond anything he had ever seen. They attacked with massive arms, swinging pieces of construction beam as weapons and goaded on by a shouting experimenter who struck their backs with a rod bristling with syringes.

Then, Trazyn drew a labyrinth and the novelty was finished. The rest of the day consisted of a rocky descent, listening to Trazyn lecture on the higher degree of mutant aberration among hybrids spawned from the unstable Ymgarl genetic stock.

The floor was pitching now, the bombardment above nearly constant. They ran.

By the fourth day, it was likely that eighty per cent of the organic life on the surface was already dead. Or so Trazyn claimed, when Orikan deigned to listen. He was murmuring as he ran now, collecting his focus for the task ahead. Listening to Vishani tell him, in detailed logic chains, what he must do.

Orikan didn't realise they had reached the reservoir until he heard water splash below his feet.

'–ervoir cracked.'

'What?' he asked.

'I said the bombardment's cracked the water table!' Trazyn shouted. Rocks were tumbling from the cavern's ceiling, crumbling as they hit the inch-high pool of water beneath their feet. 'The final bombardment's begun. Look, they've pierced the reservoir with a lance strike.'

He pointed to the floor of the chamber, and Orikan saw

a great sinkhole in the centre of the room, dropping like a well into the darkness.

'Not long now!' Trazyn smiled.

Now, my equal.

'No,' said Orikan. 'Not long. Time to give me the gem.'

Do not ask. Take it.

A boulder crashed down next to Trazyn, and he raised a protective hand. 'Is this really the time? This chamber is unstable.'

He cannot go farther. You cannot let him.

Orikan moved fast, one hand grasping the gemstone, the other forming Vzanosh's Ballistic Parabola.

Trazyn saw the move, used the cloak, selected a different future.

He grabbed Orikan's hand and crushed the fingers out of position, twisting them so they sparked and the hex died.

'What are you playing at, Orikan?'

'We can't both get there, she's told me. Only one of us.' He ripped the gem away, leapt backward and summoned the Staff of Tomorrow, preparing for a fight.

Trazyn did not rise to it. A rock the size of his cranium splashed down behind him. 'It's a replica, Orikan. You think I'd keep the real one hanging there when you seemed so keen on it?' He summoned his obliterator. 'Now stop this foolishness, we have worked well together–'

'You sent aliens to kill me, dooming this world so we may not even open the gate. Is that what you refer to, Trazyn? You have unmade this world for a joke.'

Orikan flashed forward, striking out then pulling his blow, catching hold of Trazyn's obliterator and yanking it.

All he did was draw them close together, face to face.

The cavern rocked as a slab the size of a monolith dropped, smashing on the cavern floor.

'I didn't want to do this, Orikan. I prepared for it, but I didn't want to do it.'

Orikan wrestled for the obliterator, found it dissolving in his hands. Noticed the prismatic shine of a dimensional pocket opening – his dimensional pocket.

Trazyn stepped away, Mysterios in hand, and slipped it into his own dimensional pocket.

'Goodbye, my colleague,' Trazyn said.

Orikan threw himself on the archaeovist, and Trazyn hugged him, locking his arms around Orikan's scrawny frame, carrying him to the ground. Orikan thrashed, screaming, beating Trazyn with his head.

Then realised that nothing was there. Trazyn's body was an empty shell. An exoskeleton left after the insect crawls free.

He heard a sound that no mortal has lived to describe.

The sound of a planet being executed.

With a roar so loud that it overwhelmed his systems, the chamber collapsed.

Battering him. Crushing him. Burying him.

Orikan the Diviner, seer of the necrontyr, lay shattered beneath a mountain.

Trazyn's algorithmic spirit raced through the relays he'd buried in the tunnels, screaming from point to point as the tunnels collapsed behind him. Each burned out with his passage, sealing the way. Through the necron tunnels. Through the bedrock. Up through the pipes and into the firestorm atmosphere of Serenade.

A planet that by rights, no longer deserved a name.

He poured into his surrogate on the *Lord of Antiquity*'s bridge, ready to give the order.

'Surface and run attack vector. I want the capital ship crippled on the first pass. Do not destroy it, we want them to be able to withdraw. Calculate fire for extreme damage. Get them to reroute power from lance batteries to shields.'

If the Exterminatus continued, the Eternity Gate would be destroyed. But they still had time to forestall that inevitability.

The *Lord of Antiquity*, berthed beneath the surface of Serenade's second moon for millennia, rose, shaking the lunar dust from its hull. It sheared away in solid clumps, sloughing off and forming a crescent-shaped crater.

And it turned, sweeping in on the flotilla like a raptor that has spied a flock of songbirds picking at insects. Weapons batteries charging. Finding firing solutions on three different vessels.

He was about to give Vice-Admiral Zmelker another medal for his rack.

'Fire.'

Four hours later, the only Imperial ships remaining were the wrecked hulks of the escort cruiser and two Sword-class frigates, floating broken-backed in the dull light of Serenade.

Trazyn opened a channel, searched for a signal.

'Orikan?' he broadcast.

No answer.

'Orikan, identify your position and I can excavate you.'

Nothing.

The only answer was a pulse. A numeric code running over and over through the surface.

3211 Stop 1545 Stop 4131 Stop 5322.

Trazyn was looking at the grey surface of a dead world. The Song of Serenade, the eternal aria of the Eternity Gate, was the only thing that lived there.

* * *

ACT FOUR: DEAD WORLD

CHAPTER ONE

3211 Stop 1545 Stop 4131 Stop 5322
[Message repeats.]

– Serenade Signal

The world known as Serenade, which had been called Cepharil and Cephris and unremembered names before that, stood ashen and dead in the void.

Breezes still stirred its thin atmosphere. Light crept and retreated across its surface as it endlessly circled its star. Imperial shipwrecks orbited it like the corpses of fish floating in a toxic pond.

Once again, as during the primordial eras of deep time, the planet had no name. There was no cause for one. Even if the air had been breathable, there was no one to breathe it. All its resources were destroyed, the very mantle cracked open in chasms hundreds of miles deep. Its great furnace of creation, the liquid core that had built islands and continents by expelling trillions of tons of molten rock, lay extinguished and cold. With no resources to exploit, it fell off star maps. Lines of trade readjusted, the spacefaring goods cartels moving elsewhere.

It was as sterile as the unthinking moons that orbited it. Rocks spiralling around each other in the eternal equations of gravity.

No ships called, apart from the occasional wreck that succumbed to orbital decay and fell crashing to the still surface.

So when the small fighter entered the atmosphere, its quad engines glowing like a candelabra in the dark of space, it would have been a singular event had anyone lived to witness it.

The Night Scythe settled to a hover, eight feet off the ashen surface. Opened its glowing underslung portal.

Trazyn, Overlord of Solemnace, Lord Archaeovist of the Prismatic Galleries, and He-Who-Is-Called-Infinite translated onto the surface.

He was the first being to take a step on Serenade, he reflected, for three centuries.

The going was easy. The Imperial bombardment had done its work well. Its fiery death throes had ignited the atmosphere and triggered instantaneous volcanic upheaval, throwing tons of ash into the atmosphere and creating the barren grey dunescape.

Ash collected around the latticework of twisted plasteel beams and rebar – the only thing that remained of the great cities – forming ghoulish skeletal structures that reared hundreds of feet high.

Trazyn looked at the tortured sculptures and thought of the shaped bone of the aeldari cities, the branching corals of the undersea caves and the unusual soaring buttresses of

Serenade City. In some perverse and mocking way, the Song of Serenade still echoed.

It echoed for him, too.

Whatever he had done in the past three centuries, Serenade was always there. Its signal tugged at him, played in the back of his neural matrix and whispered in his engrams. No matter where he stood, despite all perils, his mind cycled back to the Tomb of Nephreth. It ran in as a background subroutine as he battled for the Spear of Vulkan. As he witnessed the death of Cadia during the Despoiler's Thirteenth Black Crusade.

All those centuries, the sand-clock in his neural matrix trickling dust. Awaiting the moment when he knew that he must return here.

Orikan had been right. Trazyn was an obsessive. They had that in common. And whatever sang on Serenade had infected them. Taken hold and would not let go.

Even if the tomb were broken and ruined, its relics scattered and the priceless body of Phaeron Nephreth destroyed, Trazyn needed to see it. If only to put his mind to rest.

Trazyn reached the continental rift and looked down into it. Vast spaces yawned beneath, an endless canyon a mile across, leading directly down to the core. The exact spot where the lance battery cracked the planet like an axe splits a skull.

He could feel the tug of the signal emanating from the depths.

Repeating. Ever repeating. Familiar as his own name.

Trazyn opened his dimensional pocket and drew a small lift-disc, taking it from the cradle where it nestled next to his tesseract labyrinths. He did not know why he had brought them, only that it seemed fitting. A homecoming of sorts.

He unfolded the disc and tossed it into the chasm, watched it catch and hover just past the point where earth ended and space began.

Trazyn stepped onto it and descended.

As he did so, he held his obliterator high, igniting the arcane device inside so it cast a splash of white light on the sheared-off face of the chasm wall.

Geological strata slid by, each epoch passing as his body sank ever downward, mind cataloguing each detail of the cross-section.

The ruins of the Imperial city came first, its street level buried under compacted ash-pumice formed during the planet's scouring. The plasteel beams rising from the surface were only the highest remaining towers. Here at the street level, Trazyn saw smashed war vehicles and groundcars. Mobs of chitinous creatures fused together in their undulating waves by the sudden heat of the ignited atmosphere. Men and women cowering, their forms moulded into statues by the same geological violence that had formed the lands which they called home. The land they fought to defend.

Instead, it had risen up and killed them.

Below that were the colony settlements, little more than midden-heaps and brick foundations. Here and there the hint of a smooth, blackened object that might be shattered roof tile. A loose metallic bolt that Trazyn recognised by its chemical composition as being of orkoid manufacture.

Below, the ruined bone-palaces of the aeldari, their temples and high places cast down by Trazyn's need for the jewel that hung at his hip.

Was that when he had first been snared? When his destiny became irrevocably enmeshed with this world?

He could not remember now why he had wanted the jewel

so badly – it was unique, of course, but why not the entire temple?

And he remembered the reverberations in the bone sanctum where the World Spirit resided, and knew that even then the Song of Serenade was upon him.

This world sings for the blood of Trazyn.

He could hear it repeating, stronger now. It would not be long.

Would Nephreth be there? Trazyn found himself dreading the prospect. It would be a great discovery, the greatest discovery. One so monumental that he had told Executioner Phillias and the phaerons – the Awakened Council had dissolved since the Great Awakening, and several of its members destroyed – that it was not possible for the tomb to have survived.

He did not wish others coming to grasp for his prize. Not when it was so close. And the entombment of Orikan had dissuaded even the most diligent of searchers.

Who might dare try to succeed, where the greatest chronomancer in the galaxy had failed?

The fossils sliding by were of the great lizards now. Not as the Exodites had ridden them, but a more primitive form, four-legged with short needle teeth. Large, but not so majestic as their descendants.

Then a culture that Trazyn did not recognise. An entire aeon of the planet's history that was obscure and foreign to him. Megalithic ruins he could not identify and low stone houses. A culture evolved and vanished, likely seen by none but him.

Below were spiral seashells, their curves matching that perfect asymmetry that all creatures on Serenade achieved.

And then came the blackstone. A great sheathing layer of it, with channels left to carry the magma upward.

It kept going. Down, down, down to the core.

And Trazyn realised that this was not a natural world. It had been constructed. Built by hands long vanished, nigh-impervious to the lance batteries and plasma detonations.

Whether it was the work of the Old Ones, the C'tan, or some other vanished species he did not know, but as he found the channel he wished and stepped into the tunnel network, he knew it matched no work he had seen since. For the necrons to create an artificial world was difficult and time-consuming, but possible. Ancient crypteks had imprisoned stars within great energy-harvesting spheres, and made generation ships that could autonomously navigate the spaces between stars with their crews in the grip of cryo-stasis.

But to modify a planet to this extent – to make it both artificial and natural – was a work of techno-sorcery beyond even the greatest efforts of his deathless kind. A true work of an immortal.

He walked in darkness for thirty days and thirty-one nights until he found the gate chamber. The fail-safe door.

The previous gate had been crusted with invasive life, but this one – locked deep in the vaults of the planet's mantle – was untouched.

The Eternity Gate rose monumental and black at the far end of the chamber, cresting a great staircase. A double row of braziers, barren and pooled with shadow, led to the steps.

He had not been here since the tainted Quellkah had ambushed him four centuries ago. It seemed longer.

Trazyn dipped into his dimensional pocket, withdrew the Astrarium Mysterios.

'It is time,' he said, 'to finish it.'

As he passed the first braziers, they sparked and ignited, viridian flames dancing and twisting. Spiralling and rising in pillars that illuminated even the far buttresses of the ceiling.

Each pair flared as he walked by, flames first lapping inward at the Mysterios then stretching up to form a line of burning columns. A league distant, he saw emerald light emanating from behind the cyclopean doorway, spilling out from underneath and between. The energy-light was so thick that it became a vapour, curling and drifting out to form a carpet of fog that spilled down the steps and spread to coat the chamber.

He took one step, then another, noticing in his idle curator's mind that this Eternity Gate was so much larger than the other – had they worked it backwards, perhaps? Was this the main gate, and the other the fail-safe?

That would not make sense. The Mysterios had directed them to the other entrance.

And then Trazyn remembered the old ways. Back then, he had witnessed the entombment of many phaerons – but no phaeron of rank had died in sixty-five million years. Destroyed, certainly. But the symbolism of funerary practice and religious veneration – so embedded in his culture – was now alien to his soulless necron consciousness.

This was the Death Gate. The interment processional. Intended to be used only once and then sealed. It was designed to admit Phaeron Nephreth's body, and nothing else.

Ideally, it would remain sealed. Sacred and inviolable. Unpolluted by the feet of any who did not carry the purified body of the phaeron.

Trazyn paused, looking with wonder at the steps, the gate, the glyphs and bas-reliefs on the walls.

This way Nephreth had passed. Nephreth the Untouched. Most noble of the phaerons. A being of mere flesh who had been the first to stand against the star gods. Orikan bragged that he had known the mind of the C'tan and warned of their perfidy, but he had chosen to hide. Nephreth had chosen to fight.

He had resisted biotransference by force. Thrown away his perfect body to defend the souls of the necrontyr. Raised arms against the mortal foe five million years before the Silent King had turned on and destroyed the deceitful gods, shattering them into shards.

Nephreth was, in a way, the last necrontyr and the first necron. A being at the crux of history. Both legend and historical fact.

And if the tomb remained intact – a fact that looked likely given the preservation of this antechamber – he would soon look him in the face.

The first necrontyr face he had seen in sixty-five million years.

Trazyn let the Mysterios go.

It rose soft and sweet, lofting up the stairs as if carried by divine hands, fixing itself at the midpoint of the gate.

And changing. Angles folded and smoothed. Light bloomed from within, its sides flowing together like mercury.

Until it became a sphere. A perfect sphere. Its form so mathematically beautiful Trazyn might have wept true tears had he eyes.

Perhaps soon, he would.

He opened his mouth to speak the algorithm.

'Trazyn!'

His oculars narrowed, and he turned, his tile cloak flowing around his cocked shoulders and trailing on the stair.

At the foot of the stairway was a wretched creature. Gaunt and skeletal. Battered and encrusted with minerals until its body was the colour of a necrotic limb. Exposed wires in the fractured death mask buzzed with electrical glow. Its fingers – if one could call such worn and stubby things fingers – had been scraped to nubs that leaked hydraulic fluid. The spine twisted sideways in an S-curve, so it could only support itself by leaning on a staff capped with a starburst pattern.

'Orikan?'

'Do not...' the creature paused, trying to find words or breath, 'open the tomb. Do not do it.'

Trazyn laughed, a booming sound that became lost in the high vaults. 'Playing at your old tricks, Orikan? I think we are far past that. Look at yourself. Look at your fingers. Dug yourself out, did you?'

Orikan hobbled up another step. Then another. 'Do not open it. You do not want what is inside.'

'Took you... well, took you three centuries to dig out, I suppose?'

'Two millennia,' said Orikan. He levered himself upward, still far from Trazyn. 'Two thousand. One hundred. Twenty-two years. Needed to escape. To make it here. Each time I dug for soft rock. When I became blocked, I travelled back. Retraced steps. Do not–'

Trazyn cackled. Beat a tattoo on his obliterator with his fingers. 'You must see yourself, my dear astromancer. Do not worry, I am creating a perfect engrammatic record. I expect to refer to it frequently.'

'Trazyn.' Orikan approached, slow but steady, still far beyond even a pistol shot. 'I have been here in the rock for over two millennia.'

'I know, dear colleague.'

'I have had a great deal of time to listen. To the rock. The emanations thrumming through it. The–'

'Song of Serenade, I know.'

'No, you don't. Trazyn, there are two songs. One is subtle, nearly undetectable, and it is a siren song. A meme-virus that infects and attracts. Like the thing that makes humans want to be with the genestealers. It fires obsession, and it drove poor Quellkah mad.'

'Come now. Don't expect me to believe–'

'The second song is the number chain. You were right, it is a book code. And it is a warning. A warning from Vishani. A warning to stay away. The message is based on *War in Heaven*. The first chain, 3211 designates Act Three, Scene Two, Line One, First Word. It tried to convince me not to listen to the signal. Said it would give me the flayer virus. Whatever is inside...'

'So what *is* inside?'

Orikan was getting close, within a short sprint. 'I do not know.'

Trazyn danced up a few steps, teasing him. Keeping his distance. 'All right, then, let's see for ourselves, shall we?'

'Trazyn, please. You have won. I am humbled. Do not destroy us both to prove–'

Trazyn spoke the algorithm. He did so with relish.

And the doors began to slide open, revealing the crackling portal beneath.

And through the portal, they saw rank upon rank of warriors. An army waiting for its command.

CHAPTER TWO

'DECEIVER: *Lay down thy flesh, noble children of the necrontyr. Lay down thy rot and disease. Unburden thy fear and worry. Cast off thy turbulent, inconstant hearts. Lay down thy flesh and death, the old enemy, will no longer be your master.'*

–War in Heaven, Act IV, Scene IV, Line 8

Water, the first the planet had seen in centuries, poured from between the opening doors. Salty and clear, alien in the sterile environment of the Death Gate, it gushed out in a flood, cascading down the steps, nearly sweeping Orikan off his fragile footing. He went down on one knee, gripping the edge of a stair with his stubby, worn-down fingers.

Among the tidewater lay iridescent jellies, their glow fading as the waters ran away. Trazyn picked one up, marvelling at the bioluminescent pattern, like stars, imprinted on its membrane.

'They've evolved,' Trazyn said in wonderment. 'Flushed into the tomb a millennium and a half ago when we opened it. Let in by the gate's last activation. The only beings that survived were those able to feed solely on the arcane dimensional energies. A lesson to us all, I think.'

He dropped the jelly, the scry-pattern committed to his engram banks, and walked towards the portal.

'Trazyn.' Orikan crawled upward, barely able to move himself forward. One knee actuator was stuck. His vision blurred. 'Trazyn, do not…'

'The first of many new discoveries.'

And Orikan realised that the archaeovist was not talking to him. Was, in fact, talking to none but himself.

Orikan tried to push himself. Could not. He had burned so much of his energies digging out. Trying to get here in time. Wasted himself away to get to this moment. His reactor was reaching critical state – not overload, but cycle-down. He'd run far closer to the red lines than were safe, and had done so for two millennia. A century ago he'd cleared all his system warnings because they'd cluttered his vision so extensively that he could not even read each individual message.

Only by opening himself to the cosmos, to the all-flowing energies of space and the zodiac, could he even bear to stay ambulatory, to repair himself enough to get this far. But the rockfall had damaged his energy collectors and – though the powers of the universe were flowing swift and free – he could but sip from them as they streamed by his frame.

An old master of his used to be fond of the Parable of the Man and the Straw, about a man who had tried to prevent disaster by drinking the raging floodwaters sweeping down a canal. For every sip, ten thousand barrels worth passed by and devastated his village.

Orikan felt like that man, yet in his exhaustion he could not remember the moral of the parable. Something about avoiding futile actions that made one feel dynamic, yet made no real difference.

And, unstoppable as ten thousand raging *lath* of floodwater, Trazyn passed through the portal.

Orikan saw the doorway fizzling at the edges and knew that his efforts had been for naught. He had no power left. There was no sending his consciousness back, no dashing forward. He took strength from his desperation and forced himself to his feet. Began to hobble on his staff upward towards the gate.

It was what it must be like, he realised, to be old. A thing he had never achieved in life and which was robbed from him in biotransference.

A biotransference he had warned them about. And they hadn't listened.

They had refused to listen then, and Trazyn refused to heed him now.

And there, bubbling up from his engrammatic banks, was the old friend. His old companion.

Fury.

So dangerous for concentration. So powerful when it could be harnessed.

This battle did not call for concentration.

The portal was shrinking. Dissipating. Consuming itself at the edges so all that was left was a circle the size of a human doorway.

His fingers were too worn and shredded to make a proper casting sign. Vaaul's Stabiliser required touching the middle finger to his palm, and the middle finger on his right hand was gone after the first joint. Quellan's Reversal was a four-line algorithm, impossible to speak in time.

Instead, he simply shouted, throwing all his considerable will at the Eternity Gate, commanding it like the dumb machine it was.

OPEN.

The portal juddered, fizzled. Shrank then grew, like the lens of an ocular trying to focus.

With one last leap, Orikan threw himself through the wavering surface.

Just as it slammed shut.

Trazyn wanted *everything*.

All he could see. Every last atom in the chamber. Wanted to clap it all in a vault on Solemnace and refuse to touch it. Make himself fly about on a Catacomb barge to view it, so he would not even disturb the dust.

A lighted pathway of glyphs stretched across the chamber, each glyph the name of an Ammunos enemy defeated so that Nephreth's sarcophagus-bearers could tread on them. Columns – thick as monoliths and engraved with bas-relief images depicting early events from the War in Heaven – held up the painted ceiling. In the centre, a great pyramid stood, far enough away that it looked small in the massive chamber.

Between him and the tomb stood the stone army.

A whole decurion of warriors, dressed in their panoply of war, and standing at attention. It was this that overwhelmed Trazyn, washing him in engram-memories of a planet long dead.

Because these stone warriors were not necrons, but necrontyr. A full ancient army drawn up for parade, from warriors and Immortals, to royal wardens with their lychguard attendants. Three Doomsday Arks drawn up in formation. They faced what was presumably the central burial chamber, surrounding it, as if the dead phaeron were about to address them after a victory or a new conquest.

Trazyn had not been prepared for seeing even a rough depiction of the necrontyr form. Even though these statues were only the barest silhouettes, the details carved into the igneous rock eaten away by a millennium and a half immersed in seawater, a core deep inside him hurt to even look on them. He cursed himself for opening the Eternity Gate without stasis-locking the water. For allowing this act of vandalism to happen. Swore that he would restore every statue.

But he was almost glad of the weathering. The sight of a necrontyr body, perfect in its depiction, might have overwhelmed him. Already, he was having difficulty walking towards the crypt chamber without stopping every few ranks to peer into a pitted face.

'We were a great species,' he said. 'No more. A necron is neither race nor species. Not a thing made by natural process and evolution. We are now a thing forged. Created. More permanent than this stone, yet having not half its spirit. These works of art were made by hands that lived, or knew what it had been to live. This is the last tomb of the necrontyr, and the greatest.'

He could hear a drumbeat through the chamber. A stirring rhythm like a march, as if the stone musicians with their drums and cymbals had beat the advance. Trazyn's engrams called up images of old battles, old wars. The glory of the necrontyr, a people ill in body but whole in spirit, who conquered the stars.

None but immortals and gods could stop them.

Entranced and sheathed in wonder, he nearly didn't see his perception suite's proximity alarm.

Trazyn turned and caught Orikan's staff, arresting its swing.

'You *are* weak, old rival.' Trazyn had needed only one hand to stop the blow. 'Laughable, really. That strike was no stronger than a human's.'

Trazyn tore the weapon out of the astromancer's battered hands and tossed it away.

The Diviner came at him, hissing like a hooded ash serpent, and Trazyn caught him with a backhand blow to the cranium, sending Orikan sprawling, his damaged death mask leaking reactor fluid. He staunched it with a hand and dropped down on one knee, steadying himself against the floor.

'Listen to me,' mewled Orikan. 'The warning–'

'Stay down, you simpering lunatic. Can't you see I've won?' Trazyn turned, felt a hand gripping his tile cloak.

'There is no winning, Trazyn.' Orikan gripped the cloak. Trazyn snatched it out of his grip and Orikan took hold of the archaeovist's steel foot. 'Don't you see? It has a hold on you. You're bewitched, you smug cretin. It says–'

Trazyn twisted his foot free and stomped on Orikan's cranium, slamming his whole weight down again and again, watching his narrow skull bend and flared headpiece crack. Shattered the open ports of his energy-collection panels.

The archaeovist lost himself in the cruelty of it. Spat words he could not remember formulating.

'How *dare* you. How *dare* you touch me, you insect. Destroyed my artefacts. Kept me from my work. Dragged me into this and now cannot stand that I've bested you. Once again, you nearly ruin everything. Just as before.'

'That is not your voice, Tra–'

Trazyn's metal heel slammed into Orikan's mouth, and the rest was only a buzzing.

And Trazyn went on his way, the broken, crawling astromancer falling further and further behind.

'The Song of Serenade,' Orikan said, unheard, his vocals glitching. 'It says. *Do not be deceived.*'

The stasis-crypt was twice as high as a monolith, the four corners of its base fed by eternal reactors. This was the drumbeat of the chamber, what must be the Song of Serenade. Four reactors kicking at intervals. No sinister spirit-communication. No malign entity driving them to a massacre. Nothing exotic or bizarre. Simply the clean workings of necrontyr technology.

The thrumming of them comforted Trazyn. Soothed him. The reverberations felt enticing, like an oil bath. Made him want to enter the burial crypt and be surrounded by that massaging beat.

How long had that fool Orikan led them astray with wild theories? Even in his anger, Trazyn did not want to try and calculate.

Finally, he was rid of that stargazing dead weight. Better for it.

There were seals on the door. Four of them, formed from technology that was antique and powerful. Each with a cartouche formed from different geologic material. They warned not to open the crypt. Portended apocalypses, curses and calamities most impressive.

Trazyn did not even read them. There were always warnings. There had been warnings on the last gate. Warnings about the stone hanging at his hip – the one he'd taken from the aeldari World Spirit – warnings on grimoires that whispered of daemon possession and all-devouring beings.

And yet, here he stood, having violated sacred gateways and taken forbidden things. Still very much alive.

He would have liked to keep the seals. They were, after all, significant. But he cared more about what lay within.

He summoned his obliterator and swung the artefact weapon at the first seal.

One.

A cartouche pressed from lava rock cracked under the swing of his staff, the archaic seal under it crushed with a sound like drawing breath.

Please, Trazyn. An interstitial message from Orikan. He dismissed it.

Two.

The second cartouche, shaped from bone, fractured along a fault line and came apart.

It is not too late.

Three.

The third, made from some form of rockcrete, disintegrated after two blows.

You have won, signalled Orikan. *I admit your supremacy. I will do anything, even promise vassalhood, if you agree for us both to leave.*

Trazyn cared not.

The fourth seal was some kind of cremation ash, barely more than a loose-packed grey cake. He smashed his obliterator into it and it atomised, the ancient seal under it fracturing and dropping to the blackstone.

Crypt doors swung inward, and Trazyn stood amazed.

Shadowy light danced on the walls, cast by the stasis field that suffused the entire chamber with an amber glow.

The chamber was spare, and smaller than he had anticipated. No bigger than a minor lord's council room – the rest of the structure, clearly, housed the esoteric equipment that kept its occupant fresh and vital. On one wall lay the smashed form of a cryptek, her heavily modified body mangled as if caught in heavy machinery or crushing power fields. Clearly an anonymous tomb guardian, who had detected a long-ago fault and sacrificed herself to keep the crypt operational.

Her monocular strobed on and off in a repeating dead pattern. One last signal into the void.

Blink-blink-blink. Blink-blink. Blink. Blink.

Trazyn's perception suite noted that it was the same interval as the cycling reactors, as if the dead cryptek were broadcasting a program that maintained the eternally desynchronised rhythm.

He ignored it.

For on the slab at the centre of the room lay Nephreth the Untouched.

Trazyn stepped to the edge of the stasis field, both wanting and not wanting to see what lay beneath.

Strong limbs, well corded with muscle and inked with golden tattoos, lay crossed over a chest adorned with a broad collar of heavy necrodermis amulets. Broad cuff bracelets, burnished with plated platinum, sat one atop the other as if locked there.

And on the head, a golden full mask that flared into a great headdress and fitted snug on the shoulders.

The sight was too much. Trazyn collapsed to his knees with a strangled sob.

A necrontyr, in the flesh. A sight none had seen in sixty-five million years. An item of such unique historical and cultural significance that he knew it would be worth all he had sacrificed. His shattered cultural relics, the repeated deaths and maiming, ten millennia of work.

A body kept so lifelike, it almost seemed to breathe. A single object that encapsulated all they had lost, and all they stood to gain. And like that, Trazyn knew he could not keep this discovery to himself. Orikan had been right. This beautiful flesh must be used. Not for arcane research, but for genetic replication.

Trazyn had given the necrons a future. They could become the necrontyr again.

He reached out a hand to touch the body, and froze.

Because with sure movements, Nephreth the Untouched sat up, stasis-light pooling in the golden mask.

Blank eyes, crafted from exotic stone and burnished until they shone, turned upon Trazyn.

Who realised, all of a sudden, that the generators no longer thrummed. They had cut when he'd entered the chamber. For the first time in millions of years, silence reigned on Serenade.

Nephreth the Untouched raised gold-filigreed hands and lifted off his mask, and looked upon Trazyn with his true features.

Trazyn the Infinite, Overlord of Solemnace, Master of the Prismatic Galleries, a being who had known death a thousand times and captured the most wild and terrifying things in the galaxy, began to scream.

For he knew the cruel smile and sardonic eyes. The face that filled with malicious joy at the revelation of a trick played and played well. A face that had butchered untold billions and eaten stars. That had stolen Trazyn's soul.

It was the face of the Deceiver.

CHAPTER THREE

'The Jackal God does not desire worship. It does not keep fellowship, even among its divine siblings. It cares not for fates and fortunes – the devious one wishes only to feed, and laugh as it does so.'

– The Book of Mournful Night

Child Trazyn, said Mephet'ran the Deceiver, betrayer of the necrontyr. **I suppose I should express my gratitude. Yet it did take you interminably long getting here.**

Trazyn said nothing. His hands clenched and unclenched, still down on one knee. Realisation came slowly as he watched the C'tan's skull lengthen and deform, horns sprouting from the sides of the conical cranium to bracket the leering lips.

When it spoke, Trazyn felt its voice rattle through his entire system like an earthquake. Shaking and numbing. The eyes, joyless but crinkled in humour, contained the cold blackness of the void.

'You… you have stolen Nephreth.'

I *am* **Nephreth,** the abominable god said. It twisted the cuff bracelets, breaking the seals that contained it. **Broken from my greater amalgamation and replacing him as a babeling. Why do you think he was not subject to disease and decay? Some genetic mutation or engineering? As if a lowly race such as yours could produce such wonders.**

'But… why?' The presence of the C'tan was overheating Trazyn's neural matrix. He was struggling to process information, much less data that rewrote history as he knew it. 'Nephreth led the opposition to biotransference. He attacked the C'tan.'

The star god laughed, a reverberating sound that caused Trazyn's central reactor to cycle out of sync. It tore the great tiled collar from its neck and dropped it at Trazyn's feet.

Convincing a civilisation to part with their souls would never be a mere seduction. There would always be separatists, rebels, those unconvinced. The stubborn and hidebound, those with most to lose, they who – unlike you, my hunchbacked child – were not so desperate. We gave them a figurehead to rally around. A candle to draw the moths. It paused. **You would know all about that, would you not, child Trazyn?**

Trazyn stood, took a step backward.

Opening the tomb required two, the Deceiver said. It did not step forward, but rose and glided, the lengthening hooks of its toenails scraping the blackstone floor. **One cunning enough to decipher Vishani's riddles, and one with the doggedness not to heed her pathetic distress signal. And of course,** it nodded at the obliterator, **an artefact weapon that could break the seals of binding.**

* * *

Orikan heard all. When a C'tan spoke, it was impossible for a necron not to hear.

He tried to estimate how many shards of the Deceiver lay shackled in the crypt. Four? Five? Whole armies had fallen to a single shard, and a pair could render a planet lifeless within a month.

Dragging himself upright, he steadied his broken body against one of the cycling-down reactors. Lifted a palsied hand over the energy port and turned it palm-side up, fingers tented like a flower bud shaking in a storm.

His own reactor levels were critical. He needed no system report to tell him that. The world was fading, its images distorted. Trazyn had cracked his ocular with his boot. When Orikan focused, the room around him looked broken and abstract like the stained-glass windows Trazyn had so proudly shown him. But the colours had begun to bleed away. His left ocular saw static, and then nothing at all.

He spread his shaking fingers, and the energy port opened in kind, triangular leaves folding outward.

And channelling his last power reserve he raised his staff's sharp butt, fumbling it towards the energy port.

He was blind, going by clumsy feel. Scraping and probing. He dared not let go of the staff and search with his hand, for it might slip from his weak, mangled fingers. There would not be strength enough, he knew, to retrieve it.

The seer, he realised with characteristic self-cruelty, could no longer see.

A scraping. A rattle of living metal on living metal, and the staff caught.

Orikan the Diviner dropped forward, sinking his weapon deep in the channelling port, his strength expended and the light in his ocular fading out.

Now stand aside, child. You have done me a good turn, and in recognition I suppose I will let you live.

'I… will not,' said Trazyn. 'You boast and brag, but Vishani found you out. She undid and shackled you.'

And look at her reward. It cast a glance at the scattered hulk of parts crumpled against the wall. Came to put right a reactor malfunction in the tesseract vault. I had but one moment to strike, and I took it. My body still a prisoner, true, but as you can see, my unwitting servant, a great deal can be done with the mind – particularly if one has receptive puppets.

The reactors cycled, an irregular thumping. Amber lights inside the vault flickered and blazed.

Now my little one, indulge me. For I did plant the idea to bring that aeldari gem for a reason.

Trazyn looked down at the gem that had hung at his hip for ten millennia. Felt a fool for bringing it here, not knowing whence the compulsion had come. Too wrapped in his own whims and obsessions to question why he'd wanted it.

It was how I noticed you first. Fracturing the savage aeldari's World Spirit did release so many scrumptious little souls to drink. But it has been a long imprisonment and I require nourishment of a more potent variety.

'I do not fear you,' said Trazyn, walking backward, obliterator held at the guard. 'We defeated your kind. Killed the star gods. Shattered them, imprisoned them. Yoked them like livestock to do our bidding. You are alone in the universe, your kind is in chains.'

Good, the Deceiver chuckled. I did not fancy the competition. Keep my siblings – keep the rest of my own amalgamation, for all I care – it only means more for me. Unlike you false immortals, I do not mind being alone.

'He's not alone,' said a voice at the doorway.

Orikan stepped into the rectangle of light, back straight, open wounds crawling with corposant, the necrodermis reformatting itself to its accustomed shape.

'Though he should be,' Orikan added.

'Ah, my Master Orikan,' the abominable god said.

It was not the Deceiver's voice. Not the reverberating tremor of a star god.

This was the high regal voice of Vishani.

Orikan stopped in mid-stride.

'Have you come to rescue me?' the Deceiver said, through twisted lips. 'Or are you here to learn all my secrets? The innermost knowledge of ages past. You are, after all, my equal, are you not?'

The thing did not laugh, that time. Its reaction was far too unnatural to be considered laughter. The long skull arched back, needle-toothed mouth open towards the ceiling, as the Deceiver's whole body shook in a parody of mirth.

It was, Trazyn realised, drinking in the astromancer's despair.

Orikan's gaze slid off the Deceiver, settling on the crushed necron form that lay next to the wall, her monocular blinking out a warning message.

All those long conversations, and you never realised. She was speaking to you the whole time, Diviner – broadcasting a lonely, brain-dead warning she knew I could not shut down – and yet it was not enough. With her dead, but her neural matrix still active, I could project myself through it, commune with you in her form, using the Mysterios as a node.

It shook again, this time so violently it began to phase into micro-dimensions, its after-image growing indistinct. **Open yourself, Orikan. Don't you want to let me in? You must**

be open to the world, Orikan. The vibrating laughter continued. **Dead sixty-five million years. Sixty-five million…**

Orikan continued to stare at the broken Vishani.

'Orikan,' said Trazyn, shaking the astromancer. He grabbed Orikan's cranium and turned him, breaking the entranced gaze. Stared directly into the blinking monocular. 'Orikan, we need to flee.'

'I can,' he muttered. 'I can raise her, Trazyn.' He reached out a hand, his orbuculum crest glowing.

Vishani's monocular stopped its idiot blink. Held steady. A finger stirred. Bale-light, dim as a low candle flame, flickered in her ribcage.

Very good, said the Deceiver, clapping. **Very *impressive*, child Orikan. Let us see you bring her back to the livi–**

Without her head raising, Vishani raised a single hand at the ceiling and made the Triple Horns of Kesh.

Whipcords of energy lashed from the corners of the chamber, scouring the Deceiver's light form. One energy lash found a wrist and trapped it, then another. The C'tan shard was hoisted up in the air as the tesseract vault reasserted itself, the howl of its reactors nearly drowning out the god's shout of rage and pain. Its legs struggled against the tentacle-like power cords that tried to capture them, kicking out at the lightning.

Then it turned its perverse, bulbous skull and opened its mouth, pouring out a torrent of ink-black antimatter, burning a slash through the vault as it thrashed.

Trazyn shoved Orikan's head down, but the emanation was not meant for them.

He watched, fascinated, as the flaming antimatter beam sliced across the chamber and razored through Vishani's body, catching her collapsed form across the shoulders.

The head of Vishani the Datamancer rolled free of her

body and came to rest looking up at them, one metal cheek pressed to the floor, monocular dimming.

Or-Orikan, stuttered a female voice in their interstitial message centres. *Run.*

'Come on.' Trazyn hoisted Orikan in the air, carried him bodily backward. Ignored his tortured shrieking as he reached back at the chamber, casting resurrection hexes at the fallen hulk of Vishani.

The tesseract vault was fracturing, expanding into four as it tried to dissipate the energies swirling inside it, preventing overload. Between the pillars, the shining C'tan shard struggled against its energy bonds, its necrodermis shell cracking, the howling incorporeal energies inside being flayed into strips of electricity that waved like the flagella on a microbe.

Trazyn kept running, did not look back. He could still hear Orikan speaking resurrection protocols over his shoulder in a pleading voice.

'Go back,' said Orikan. He kicked Trazyn, slammed fists into his back. 'I can bring her back. She can help us. We can bring her back. I can run back time.'

'No.'

It was no use, Trazyn knew. Whatever life the cryptek had exhibited was residual at best. Half-instinct. Reversion to her final task of trying to reactivate the vault. She had spoken, however – unless it had been his imagination.

And that's when he noticed the eyes.

All along the ranks, a blue glow shone in the eye sockets of the statues, suffusing the igneous rock.

'Orikan,' he said. 'Orikan, dig deep. Tap into all your powers. Recite resurrection hexes. All of them.'

He stopped at the foot of the Eternity Gate, dumped the Diviner in a heap, pointed at the statues.

'Look, Orikan. These tomb guardians. They aren't meant to guard the tomb from outsiders – they're here to guard the Deceiver.'

Behind them, the sound of tortured metal echoed throughout the crypt antechamber.

Trazyn looked back, saw the C'tan straining at its bonds, using its immense strength to pull on the cords that bound its wrists.

Saw with horror that one of the tesseract vault's pillars had bent inward like a bow being strung, the energy cord around the star god's wrist starting to fray and dissipate. The Deceiver's long fingers wrapped the cords, gripped them. Massive chest muscles bunched. Rending metal echoed throughout the high ceiling.

'You were right,' said Trazyn. 'Entirely correct. We should not have come here. I should have listened. Should have trusted you.'

Orikan looked up, searched Trazyn's impassive death mask. 'It has nearly escaped,' he said. 'If it reaches the Eternity Gate, it will be able to go anywhere – Solemnace, Mandragora – there will be no stopping it. Portal manipulation was a technology they taught us, it will have a mastery. It is, after all, a god.'

'Lucky for us,' Trazyn said, putting out a hand to help him up. 'We kill gods.'

Orikan took the hand, levered himself to his feet, wiped a hand over his face. Closed his monocular, gathering focus. His orb crest flared, brightening from a low radiance, to a burn, to a brilliance that left sunspots on Trazyn's oculars.

Ahead, the tesseract vault bent inward at crazy angles, like a closing fist trying to snare the star god within. Metal protested and tore. Amber lightning flashed and crawled within the deep gouges.

'Not long now,' said Trazyn. 'If you can get an army between us and that… I would be indebted.'

Orikan brought his hands low, hooked them in the air, then raised them as though he were a conductor.

To their right came a sound like mortar grinding on pestle. Warriors stirred, weapons raising, volcanic shells cracking and crumbling at their joints – exposing dull brass metal beneath.

'It's working,' said Trazyn.

'I know it's working,' snapped Orikan. 'I'm a damned astromancer.'

To their left, a warrior took a tentative step, rock sheathes tumbling off its frame. It turned a head, grinding stone on stone, to look at them, its jaw working so the rock covering its face fell away like a ceramic mask.

They were all looking at them, Trazyn realised. Paused in their duty, awaiting orders.

Orikan's ocular snapped open. 'Kill the star god.'

The tomb guardians moved as one, advancing on the captive deity. Sculpted casings sloughed off twisting hips and rotating arms. Gauss tubes activated with a snap of igniting gases and whine of energy. Disassembly beams sketched through the air, searing paths towards the tesseract vault.

A Doomsday Ark slipped its moorings and, shedding its graven exterior, rose into the air.

Orikan's hands shook with the power he channelled. Frost crystallised on his orb crest, began making spiderweb patterns on his exoskeleton.

And with a last heave, the C'tan pulled the pillars of the vault down upon itself. They dropped like the high places of a temple levelled by barbarians, crashing into each other and separating into monumental blocks. Reactors overloaded and went into meltdown, sending up spears of orange flame that burned in chemical flares at the corners of the ruined vault.

The advancing army stopped, its target obscured beneath the rubble.

Then the pile of debris erupted, the unbound Deceiver shard hovering into the air, arms spread.

Energy beams lit the dim crypt, stabbing and overlapping. So many lancing through the air – flayers, gauss blasters, synaptic disintegrators, even the fragmenting storm of tesla carbines – that the target became lost behind a lattice of deadly firepower.

The fusillade sizzled so vividly through the air that it temporarily overwhelmed Trazyn's oculars. His neural matrix tried to calculate the amount of raw energy output in the firepower and failed, the estimate exceeding ten million *quoth*. A barrage of devastation he had not seen since the War in Heaven.

The warriors, too, must have overloaded their visual inputs, because the fire slackened precipitously, ocular systems scrying to reacquire the target.

Smoke swirled around the space where the Deceiver had floated, hazing the air, pouring off the body as though it burned on a pyre.

And as the smoke bank twisted away, it was clear the barrage had done nothing.

The Deceiver swiped its hand in a dismissive arc, and a phalanx of Immortals melted, living metal dissolving and running like candles stood next to a hearth.

'No chance you could take on the energy form, is there?' Trazyn asked, a hint of nervousness in his vocals.

'Stars are ill-timed,' said Orikan. 'They were focused on Serenade, but wherever we are, we are no longer on Serenade.'

He turned and gestured at the Doomsday Ark that was rising from the blackstone. 'Firing solution, full power.'

The ark charged its doomsday cannon, its thick barrel emitting the blue-white heat of a solar flare as its barrel vanes gathered the writhing ball of plasma that would head the unstoppable beam.

You bore me, children.

The Deceiver reached out a hand and splayed its fingers. From its palm flashed a sickly-coloured bolt that travelled not like a beam or blast, but like the dimensional rift it was. It came into existence and blinked out again, a horizontal slice of a dimension anathema to the one of air and metal.

The dimensional bolt pierced straight through the doomsday cannon's aperture, triggering a blossoming chain reaction that ripped the ark apart from bow to stern, ghostly blue flames rippling out between the inverted ribs of the ship. The ark went bow down, sinking towards the floor as if it were slipping below the waves of an invisible ocean. When its nose touched blackstone its reactor overloaded, vaporising a hunting party of deathmarks and a second Doomsday Ark that was struggling to break from its stone moorings.

'Critical damage,' growled Orikan. He summoned a phosglyph and directed a phalanx of Immortals to move in on the beast's flank.

The Immortals opened fire with a crack of thunder, tesla carbines showering the star god with spitting, wild electricity.

Instead of fleeing, it summoned a womb field that absorbed their ferocious electrical storm and floated towards them with hands outstretched.

Not me, my brothers.

The Immortals ceased their attack and their spines straightened, ready to receive alternate orders.

'Hell,' said Trazyn.

Do you wish to taste flesh, my brave soldiers? The voice reverberated in Trazyn's organs. Fire from the tomb guardians continued whickering at the Deceiver, reflecting off whatever unclean ward it had conjured. **You have been made soulless, but take the flesh of others and you may once again be whole.**

The immobile troops began turning their heads, tracking something that was not there. Orikan looked for a microsecond, then cast his eyes away, not wishing to go mad.

What he had seen, what the enthralled Immortals saw, was a rent in space. A passage to a red dimension where bent, taloned things lurked. Yellow eyes peering through a curtain of misting blood.

Orikan told himself it was not real. That he had not glimpsed the flayer dimension, where the infected waited between kills. An illusion of the Deceiver.

The Immortals, however, were too close to the glamour, and it triggered something latent inside them. A group of at least a hundred bent forward and hissed, devolving from noble martial forms to an animalistic hunch. Fingers lengthened into spiny knives. Discipline broke down. They swiped and nipped at each other like a pack of hunting hounds, blue eyes juddering and winking to amber.

A whole unit fallen to the flayer virus. And not gradually, over the centuries – the Deceiver had spoken their infection into being. Brought it out through some arcane trigger.

Then, the Deceiver opened its mouth and let out a sound that was not a sound.

And the newly made pack turned on their comrades, slamming into the unit of warriors next to them. Wicked claws scored metal and sheared rubbery internal systems. Tackling and biting. Amber eyes darting and weaving in the dark, dodging low, striking at exposed knee and ankle hydraulics to topple a warrior before descending on him with the slaughterous glee of madness. They pushed forward like a swarm of scarabs, mounting each other's backs in undulating waves of bladed metal, scrambling over the heads and shoulders of both kin and foe, crashing down onto the rear ranks heedless of the wash of gauss beams that stripped them back. The destroyed flayers dropped, the sheer mass of them weighing down and entangling the warriors, dragging their gauss beams into the backs of their own forward ranks.

The Deceiver moved on, levitating above a phalanx of lychguard, who dropped their shields and swords, clutching their craniums and screeching static. Then as one, their howls cut off, their vocal actuators silenced. They straightened, turned a smart about-face, eyes radiating the putrid amber of the Deceiver's luminous skin.

Fallen weapons flew to their hands, and they advanced, shields battering the Immortals behind, phase swords and warscythes hacking in steady metronome strikes. Curved blades misted reactor fluid and embalming unguents into the air as the interdimensional vibrations shed the cool blue droplets.

The sides clashed in full, tomb guardians against the corrupted. Hacking and sawing, splitting the aether with dimensional weapons that left the very air molecules shorn in their wake. A fog, the blood of the torn fabric of space-time, began to billow and collect around the ankles of the struggling androids.

Orikan's fingers danced over phos-glyph panels as he tried to counteract the corruption. Form a herd immunity to the meme-virus. Keep control of their forces.

Trazyn stood, saying nothing. His vitals were becoming colder by the minute. For a bare moment he had looked into the Deceiver's eyes, and now, he had a difficult time looking away. There he saw knowledge. The knowledge of ages past, if it could only be accessed. If he could step forward, he could trade the solar gem for anything he wished to know. Anything at all. The secrets of aeons unknown–

Orikan's security protocol raced across his vision, and he shook the thought away.

The Deceiver snarled, cursed in an ethereal vocabulary that rattled Trazyn's neurals and branded itself – looping and unreadable – on the data-feed of his vision. The primordial horror threw its head back and vibrated, not the mirthful vibration from before, but a violent shaking that created double and triple after-images. For a moment, there seemed to be two, even three of it flashing in and out of being.

And then, there were. The master shard floated in the centre, two dimmer copies by its side. One swept left, corrupting a hunting pack of deathmarks who wheeled, amber-tinted monoculars not even shifting from their infrascopes.

'It's fracturing itself,' said Orikan. 'Throwing off shards so we can't focus our fire. Making it easier to spread its system corruption.'

'Can it do that?'

'Theoretically. It is unbound. An energy being, barely contained within a necrodermis shell. If there are enough shards fused together, it could break into as many pieces as it has shards. With it separating into three parts, we know that we are fighting a creature of at least three shards, likely five or six by power readouts. Cryptek containment rituals insist that no more than two shards be kept together. We are in uncharted catacombs, here.'

The other Deceiver shard broke right, a curving flight path that headed for the rising Doomsday Arks.

'And now,' said Trazyn. 'It's no longer a containment. It's a battle.'

'Once those shards are done spreading their viruses, they'll come for us.' Orikan spiralled through glyph-readouts, rerouting power and writing target priority programs. 'If you have any little tricks in your pocket,' said Orikan, 'I would appreciate knowing.'

'When have I ever disappointed?' Trazyn said, oculars fixed on the flitting C'tan.

He tore open reality, opening not merely a dimensional pocket, but a curved space in front of him.

Tesseract labyrinths lay nestled in the curved space, arrayed before him as if he were a dealer laying out tiles for a game of Phaeron's Peril. He removed the aeldari gem and placed it alongside the labyrinths – if the C'tan wanted it, better to keep it here.

Orikan stole a glance away from the battle-management panels that hung before him in the air. 'I hope you brought an army.'

'You think so little of me, dear colleague,' said Trazyn, picking out a labyrinth. 'I brought five.'

CHAPTER FOUR

'A warrior of the aspect can cultivate a life for five million years, then cast it away on a single charge. Their infinitely precious spirits must only be expended on an infinitely dangerous enemy.'

— *The Book of Mournful Night*

Curling threads of dimensional bleed twisted out of the tesseract labyrinth, its prismatic light difficult to look upon.

And out of it stepped Trazyn the Infinite, tile cloak shifting and clicking as he marched from the rift.

Followed by another Trazyn. And another. Rank upon rank of overlords wielding warscythes, their hooked blades shouldered like warriors of old on the campaign road. They formed two lines, heedless of the battle raging behind them where necron tore at necron.

'I have most certainly had this nightmare before,' said Orikan, two fingers hooking a unit glyph on his phos-tablet and dragging them into the combat. 'Repeatedly.'

'Thought this could be dangerous and I might need a surrogate,' said Trazyn. 'Brought ten instead. Pre-formatted lychguard, so there's no time lost in structural reconfiguring. Better to be over-prepared, eh?'

'Three of you,' he snapped. 'Secure Master Orikan. The rest disperse to the battlefront. I want the option of jumping wherever it's needed.'

'You are, as they say, going in?'

'Well your hands are a bit full playing nemesor, are they not? I'll leave a sliver of consciousness here to deploy the labyrinths in case we need to plug the line and launch a counter-attack if we're able. Deploy them too soon, and the Deceiver may turn them as well – we should destroy those smaller shards first.' He tapped a tattoo on the haft of his obliterator. 'Conventional weapons are not working. Perhaps an unconventional one would make a dent.'

'Trazyn,' said Orikan, faltered as he turned away to run a re-ranking program on a unit of decimated Immortals. 'Fair stars.'

And with a rush of distortion, Trazyn's consciousness streamed through the aether and towards the fighting.

Trazyn's spirit-algorithm flashed above the steel ranks, reading the battle feed Orikan was casting to him through the tactical combat network. To the far left, a group of lychguard stood against the flayer charge, their locked formation of dispersion shields and long warscythes slowly eroding under the beating tides of corrupted metal. They would hold, for now.

In the centre, one of the Deceiver shards led a charge into a unit of vulnerable warriors, the shard sheltering behind an advancing wall of dispersion shields and corrupted lychguard. The warriors could take a toll as long as the enemy were kept at bay, but they would shatter as soon as the charge hit home.

To his right, burning arks lit the walls of the cavern, tacking and trading fire like a starship battle in miniature. Doomsday cannons pulverised the air as they fired, beams crossing in their three-dimensional dances of evasion. Above them, Tomb Blades corkscrewed and skidded in an aerial dogfight, their dimensional repulsors pulling vector thrust manoeuvres that would kill a mortal pilot.

Orikan? he asked.

Battle line takes priority. But – the astromancer paused, and Trazyn knew he was plugging logic-problems into the ark battle – *but if we lose air superiority they will be upon us.*

Understood. I may be able to help with that.

He sent an interstitial command for one of his surrogates to get in position below the dogfight, and another to the one handling the tesseract vaults.

Then he crashed his consciousness into a surrogate and barrelled his way through the rear rank of warriors, knocking them asunder. One he ran directly over, treading on its prone back and using the purchase of its spine to give him a last burst of momentum. His empathic obliterator flared, the energies of ancient cosmic powers – the powers of living gods – burning around it like a torch.

A lychguard saw the obliterator swing down and brought its shield up to catch the blow.

'Awake or die,' Trazyn shouted, as the obliterator smashed down.

Trazyn felt the bladed head of his weapon strike the tall shield, saw the dispersion field that sheathed it flash as it bowed inward, his hyper-focused vision catching the

microsecond explosion as the field shattered into fractals
and disappeared.

Ethereal energy slammed into the corrupted guards, frying neural connections and fusing limbs. It boiled outward
in a cone, throwing solid guards from their feet, blackening
ivory-inlaid armour, its thunderclap shock wave blasting a
crested head from a guard's spine.

Behind the ranks, the Deceiver shard raised a hand, sheltering its snarling eyes from the discharge. Temporarily blinded
by the star-bright energy of the ancient weapon.

There was a hole in the lychguard wall.

Warriors, unthinking and unstoppable, still following a containment command issued sixty billion years before, forced
open the gap and lowered their flayers at the fallen god.

Orikan pumped coolant fluid through his golden headdress,
increasing the amount of heat he could bleed off his neural
matrix and disperse through the hood-like thermal regulator.

He'd never run his system this hot before. Condensation
from his deep-cold headdress ran down the vanes, sweat-like,
and sizzled as it met his cranium.

Orikan was used to deep focus. Meditation. Channelling
all his effort into one task, other protocols running in the
background. This, this was like that cursed space battle so
many centuries ago. His focus fragmented and scattered,
leaping from crisis to crisis.

'In the beginning, all matter was in one point,' he repeated
to himself, hoping the mantra would keep him centred. 'All
was quiet before creation. All was quiet.'

Battle management was, he realised, not his forte. And
if he continued running hot too long he would begin to
burn engrams, losing memories and mental processes, frying

millennia of hex-study and arcane knowledge. All the knowledge that made up Orikan the Diviner, gone like scrolls on a pyre.

'All was quiet. In the beginning. All matter in one point... Bastard!'

The Tomb Blade he was tracking tumbled from the vaults.

He was simultaneously running a ground-based defence on the left, ensuring the lychguard and Immortals formed and maintained optimal defensive strategies while rerouting units to the centre, where Trazyn fought a desperate melee to hold the line against one of the two shards. He was also assigning target priorities on the right, where two units of Immortals were trying to hold back the second shard as it threatened to break out and speed towards Orikan himself. He seconded a hunt of deathmarks to exterminate their corrupted fellows who lurked in the ruins of the tesseract vault, stepping out of their oubliette to cut down unit commanders even as Orikan issued them new orders.

On the right, the stricken Tomb Blade plunged, its systems shorted by a duel tesla carbine blast. It slammed down into the belly of a Ghost Ark, its neon-bright detonation bursting through the undercurve of the assault boat, which slewed sideways and drifted, self-repair systems struggling to keep it aloft.

Directing the dogfight above was the most taxing problem. The single-seat Tomb Blades appeared simple enough, but their omnidirectional vector thrust engines and spherical flight dynamics meant they had a theoretically infinite envelope, able to turn, roll, viff and reverse direction at will. The hyper-fractal algorithms that governed their flight patterns and angles of attack took all of Orikan's computational ability to predict, and still, the precision of blade against blade was like a fencing duel between two masters – each misstep, no matter how imprecise, led to a wound.

Trazyn, he signalled. *We are losing the aerial battle. Half our blades are down.*

I have my own problems, colleague, Trazyn snapped back.

Orikan refocused. The remaining blades were scored with luminous wounds of gauss weapons and particle beams, yet another variable in the complex dance of unforgiving combat mathematics.

To keep it all in the air, he'd dialled back his chronosense to a dangerous slowness. He'd had to cast himself back along the timeline twice to prevent the Doomsday Arks breaking through and taking a shot at his command post, a desperate action that did little to help his heat problem.

Yet what truly pushed him to the limit was countering the Deceiver. Its main form – at least three shards, Orikan was now sure – levitated at a distance behind the lines, buzzing with energy, hands extended. Through his dimensional gaze, Orikan could see a web of dark particles stretching from each extended finger to the corrupted. Each twitch of a finger was a mental command.

Orikan could feel the push of the corruption on the minds of the tomb guardians, the cloying voice urging the uncorrupted to join the slaughter. Turn on their allies. Here and there, a dozen pairs of frost-blue oculars flipped to amber.

'Not so fast,' Orikan growled, and forced through another security key.

The eyes flipped back to blue.

He was having to rewrite security protocols on the fly to stop the Deceiver from bypassing or subverting them. Thankfully, it appeared there would be no more flayers – the Deceiver could bring out the blight if it was already latent, it appeared, but not inflict it.

An interstitial message from Trazyn appeared, but now Orikan could not spare the bandwidth to receive it. Too much was happening at once. He needed to establish a triage.

To delegate. To trust. Let Trazyn handle the centre. Focus his energy on the crucial flanks and air battle. Learn to compartmentalise each problem, not let one intrude on the other. Right now his vision grid was split so many ways, scrying through so many eyes, his mind's eye was like the kaleidoscope vision of an insect.

But if he let one thing slip...

In the edge of his sensors, barely noticeable by his perception suite, he realised the Trazyn surrogate – no, the partial Trazyn consciousness – was saying something.

'What?' he snapped, arms spread wide, juggling nine discrete battle sectors and forty-six contingency plans.

'Name where you want suppressing fire,' said the surrogate, a tesseract in its hand.

'Left flank!' Orikan said.

The surrogate activated the tesseract and handed it to another false Trazyn. It sprinted towards the battle line and heaved towards a viewing platform that had previously held a stone lord and his lychguard – the noble phalanx currently drowning under crashing waves of flayed ones.

The gossamer prismatic light, curling and flapping like strands of silk caught in a wind, bloomed on the high space. Objects moved in the depths of the dimensional rip.

And when Orikan saw what they were, he disconnected his overstretched consciousness from that battle sector with an uttered oath that conveyed, if anything, pure relief.

Now, he merely had eight sectors to manage.

* * *

Trazyn caught a warscythe blow on the haft of his obliterator and parried, driving the crackling twin-bladed headpiece
of his staff forward into the space between the lychguard's
shoulder armour and jaw. For a microsecond the corrupted
guard tried to fight back, hands melting as it wrestled with
the superheated metal of the glaive, then Trazyn ended it
with a vicious twist that wrenched the necron's head from
its vertebrae.

'Come, fallen gods. Destroy me. I have broken your kind
before.'

His perception suite blared an incoming warning and he
stepped back, trusting the Timesplinter Cloak to choose a
future where he was not bisected by a phase-blade. The striking lychguard, wearing an antique cranial decoration that
looked like a crouching arachnid, overcommitted, and Trazyn grabbed the rim of his shield. He hauled the guard out
of rank and sent him sprawling into the warriors behind.

'Take him, please.'

A dozen skeletal hands caught the lychguard in grips so
vice-like that it left indentations in his necrodermis. His back
arched as an axe-bayonet thrust out of his chestplate.

Trazyn marvelled. He was turning the tide. Intervening,
fighting the central advance to a standstill. Two warriors
were falling for every corrupted lychguard, but by joining
the combat he'd evened the odds.

He spun, a scythe-blade glancing off his ribcage before
he could get clear. He planted a metal foot into the guard's
pelvic shielding and shoved, sending the guard staggering
backward. When he tried to close again with two of his fellows, Trazyn threw a stasis field that halted them in place,
defenceless, as a tide of warriors surged forward and began
pulling limbs from their bodies.

Yet a glance at the battle feed suggested that this sector was the exception, and largely holding due to the number of warriors committed. The lychguard on the right were crumbling before a unit of corrupted Immortals. Orikan estimated they would break through in two to five minutes. The situation in the air was dire, more battle of attrition than dogfight. Worst of all, the warriors on the left were about to be overwhelmed, releasing hundreds of virus-infected flayers into their rear.

You wish for me, child Trazyn, it said, floor quivering with its voice. **I am here.**

And then, the Deceiver shard joined the melee.

It tore into the rear ranks of its own lychguard, crushing and throwing them to the side to reach the guardian warriors. Its electric talons, unbound by necrodermis, shrivelled warriors to ash with a touch and tore open ribcages like hatches. Physics did not appear to have any power over it, streaming like conducted energy one moment and solid as a statue the next. Trazyn watched as it carved through warriors with contemptuous grace, tearing away limbs and severing spines with hatchet-like chops of its hands, backhanding warriors bodily into the air. It grabbed a warrior's cranium and crushed it one-handed.

Perhaps once free, I will pay a call on Solemnace. Ensure that not even an atom remains.

The doomed warriors fired and stabbed, clutched at its levitating feet with broken hands. Yet they passed right through it.

It reminded Trazyn of Orikan in his empowered form. Is this what he saw as the future of the necrons, this awful behemoth?

'Stand aside,' he ordered. He would not lose warriors to this unfit deity. 'Engage the lychguard, leave this star-eater to me.'

Warriors stepped back, clearing a lane, and Trazyn pointed his obliterator in challenge.

Your forces fall. Your ally fails you. Even now the flayed tear through the flank and will soon be at your back. Do you wish for an honourable death, child Trazyn? I shall not give you one.

Trazyn received a deployment alert and felt a petty sort of satisfaction.

'Clever, long-skull. Tempting me to check the battle feed. Yet the problem with a nickname like the Deceiver is that beings might be disinclined to trust you. As for our forces being defeated…'

A new sound tore through the antechamber, one entirely different from the shriek of gauss weaponry or the snap of particle beams. This was a chattering, a hammering, industrial and violent. The sound of mechanised brutality that could only come from one species.

It was the sound of heavy bolters.

The Deceiver swivelled its head right, taking in the streams of tracer fire pounding at the ranks of the victorious flayed ones. Shells as wide as a fist detonated in the crowded flayer pack as it milled atop the slain warriors on the left flank. Long-bladed fingers dropped looted exoskeleton parts and armour plating, shrieking and hissing at the leaden death that had descended upon them. Two burst, spraying yellow fluid as the twin-fire tattoo of an autocannon blasted them into ruin.

When the Deceiver looked back, Trazyn was already upon it, obliterator burning.

It raised a stretched, overlong arm and ancient artefact met C'tan spirit with a crack of thunder.

CHAPTER FIVE

*'Lord General, show me an island and my Guardsmen
will take it. It is not a question of victory or defeat. It is
a question of how many waves you are willing to lose.'*

– Lord General Mekahan, Serenade Maritime Infantry

Hands fed ammunition bolts. Gun housings rotated on ball
mounts. Oiled bolts pistoned backward, throwing shell casings at a rate of three per second. Each spiralled in the air,
hollow end smoking like a flicked lho-stick, and landed with
a *tik-tik-tik* on the strange black flagstones.

Lieutenant Kurtiss Weleya felt that nagging sense again. It
was connected to the floor, which felt cold and oddly smooth
under his knees. The xenos cult had chosen summer to rise
in Serenade City – and in the monsoon climate of the archipelago, that meant the trade winds reversed, bringing dust
and heat stroke. The Fourth Maritime Infantry Regiment had
been in their summer uniforms, sleeves shortened in tight

rolls. Thin material to aid breathability. Cloth-covered helmets to keep the metal from heating in the sun.

'Squad Beta, walk fire left, six degrees,' he shouted into his micro-bead. 'Three short bursts.'

He watched as Squad Beta – Molaa, his best shooter – swung her chunky weapon around, pounding shots into a knot of metal horrors that had analysed the fire pattern and tried to dash through a hole. They tore apart, shedding parts like broken toys.

In his protective ear beads, the heavy bolter spoke with a muffled bleat, while the cigar-sized bullet casings struck the flagstones with a sharp ring.

Weleya didn't know how in the hell the xenos cult had created cybernetic furies, but by unnatural hunch he suspected the genestealers had corrupted a Mechanicus outpost. That made the most sense out of anything, not that he had time to consider the niceties. By the Emperor, he didn't even remember how they'd got here.

All he knew was that these blasphemous xenoforms needed to die.

'Breakout right!' he warned. 'Big xenos with shields. Squad Jasmine.'

The autocannon ploughed shots towards the new threat, flare leaping a foot from the barrel as it recoiled backward. *Whump-whump. Whump-whump.*

'Targets down. Reloading.'

The loader grabbed a magazine of bottle-sized shells, tips painted blue.

'Eh, eh! Not those,' Weleya pointed. 'The anti-armour. You think we're still fighting mutants? Analyse, soldier.'

He turned, surveyed the battlefield. In a strictly tactical sense, he should be securing his flanks. But a whisper in the back of his brain said he need not bother. His allies were handling it for now. Secure your own sector. Everything is fine.

'Heavy platoon. Attend this. They're regrouping. Fire pattern Saurian. Even squads, suppress thirty seconds. Odd squads, reload, change barrels, stage ammunition for next wave. In thirty seconds, we switch.'

It was going to be a long engagement. But instinct told him that things were going well.

Orikan punched his fist through a phos-glyph panel in frustration.

Things were not going well.

A soldier might be forgiven for thinking that, even a general.

But Orikan wasn't any of those things. He was a chronomancer and, just as important, a data-interpreter of unusual abilities.

They were getting some of their own back, it was true. Holding. Causing casualties. Stopping an advance that, by right, they should not be stopping.

But that didn't matter, because the Deceiver did not care about losing troops. The corrupted were nothing to the star god but ablative armour. A shield. So long as the corrupted army reduced their own forces while keeping the Deceiver's own incorporeal body safe, it will have done its job.

The Deceiver did not want to walk out of this tomb at the head of an army. Its entire object was to kill Trazyn and Orikan, then escape.

And it was well on the way. Orikan's battlefield projections made that clear.

At this rate, even in the most optimistic scenarios, the armies of necrons would wipe each other out within minutes. And when that happened, the Deceiver would simply tear Trazyn and Orikan apart – likely taking its time with it – then walk free. They were no match for it without an army.

Trazyn, at least, was taking sensible action – no doubt gambling that the arcane artefact in his obliterator could damage the star gods better than traditional necron weapons.

But even if they could destroy the cast-off shards, what about the master shard? In fact, what happened when they destroyed the corrupted army, and it had no reason to use most of its power as a puppeteer?

He did not have time to postulate. A Tomb Blade signalled that it had a micro-second firing solution on an enemy and Orikan had to take direct control, calculations scrolling across his vision as he tried to predict the flight path of the vectoring craft.

Trazyn, he signalled. *We need everything. Deploy everything.*

The star god struck out barehanded, fingers unspooling into ten-foot electric lashes that slapped the blackstone to Trazyn's right, throwing up sparks. The C'tan danced forward, whirling, and lashed down again to his left. It was only thanks to the cloak that Trazyn was not badly hit.

But the cloak tiles were glowing like embers. The Deceiver shard's every blow was mortal, the need for the chrono-sorcery constant. One solid hit from its lashing tendrils and it could shatter him to pieces.

Trazyn had heard Orikan's message but there was not much he could do, at present. If he paused to issue orders to his surrogate he would be dead before he finished the thought.

The finger-whips came down again and he threw the haft of his obliterator in the way, immediately seeing his mistake. One finger-whip wrapped his obliterator and the fallen deity dragged him forward into the grip of its other hand.

Come, young one, to your punishment.

'I will shatter you into pi—'

Trazyn could not finish the insult, because the Deceiver reached forward and tore away his jaw. Actuators worked, tortured and squealing. Sounds gurgled in hydraulic fluid.

Tendrils sprouted from the Deceiver shard's form, wrapping and pinning his arms, tossing the obliterator away.

Coils, moving like lightning but piercing as a necrodermis spike, drove into his ribcage. Alerts flashed and blared as he felt his entire chestplate crack inward, the personal cartouche on his sternum pulverised and driven into his body cavity.

The searching, razor-tipped coils lit him up inside with a sensation Trazyn had not felt since an age when stars fell and gods walked. It confused him, made him question what kind of malfunction this C'tan had wrought. But then the tendrils gored deeper into his systems and the sensation overwhelmed him so thoroughly that the term came unbidden to his neural matrix.

Pain, said the Deceiver, its full lips twisting upward. And while the master shard's teeth were pointed, Trazyn saw that this one had stubby, short teeth the colour of promethium crude. **This is pain. Did you not hope Nephreth could put you in bodies of flesh, my child? So you could once again experience sensation?**

Trazyn struggled, tried to look towards his fallen obliterator, but a tendril snaked into his metal hood and around his throat, immobilising his damaged neck actuators.

Don't you dare look away, the Deceiver snarled. There was no hint of the mock roguishness; all cleverness had fled. All that remained was a depthless malice. A need to cause suffering that, were it to occur in a mortal creature, would've been labelled as pathological.

But there was nothing abnormal about this Deceiver shard. Cruelty was the natural state of the C'tan, and Trazyn could only imagine it was drinking whatever negative emotion that could be lapped off a necron. He blew air through his ruined oral cavity and doused the Deceiver's face in reactor fluid.

The shard sneered, and tore its tendrils outward, ripping open Trazyn's buckled chestplate, yanking his ribcage almost out of its housing. He felt something large wrench free from his body cavity and scrape on his broken ribs as it was dragged out.

Trazyn's vision greyed, the intensity of the wound unquantifiable to his internal sensors. It was like he'd been set afire from within, eaten by acid, mangled by a mining drill.

He had to hold on. Needed to stay conscious. Focus.

The tendril around his neck forced his head downward, straining against his resisting vertebral servos so that he could see what the Deceiver had taken from him.

Tight in the electric coils lay a fluid-slicked, oblong cylinder of four chambers. Cabling and hoses trailed off it, many of the tubes ending in shredded stumps from its violent exit from his system. Crystal viewports, discoloured by fluid, radiated a cool blue glow like sunlight shining through glacial ice.

Trazyn was looking at his own central reactor.

The coils squeezed, rupturing the core, deforming the casing and snapping the rods inside.

It hurt. More pain than even a mortal body could sense. But he did not need to hold on much longer now.

The lights in Trazyn's oculars went out.

The Deceiver purred in enjoyment, enraptured, savouring.

And the obliterator crashed full force into the side of its head.

Trazyn had timed the blow perfectly, casting his consciousness into his oncoming surrogate so swiftly the Deceiver had not time to register him as a threat. Gods, after all, do not end their reveries due to a mere lychguard charging them.

The Deceiver slid sideways through the air, one fire-sheathed horn snapped and dribbling antimatter that dissolved the floor wherever globs of it fell.

At the edge of his perception Trazyn saw the master shard stretch its mouth wide like a devouring snake, and bellow in sonorous agony.

'Yes, yes. I know,' Trazyn said. 'Whoever made this seems not to have liked your kind.'

He advanced on the wounded shard, swinging his obliterator back and forth like a pendulum, watching it flinch at the *whoompfh-whoompfh* sound the artefact made as it cut the aether. Each passage leaving meteor trails of tainted emerald light in its wake.

The Deceiver crossed its arms and threw them at the floor, splintering the blackstone into fractals like the skin of a broken mirror. As Trazyn approached, he saw triangular pieces sinking into the bottomless dimensional pit, tumbling down into the blackness.

Several unfortunate lychguard and warriors – locked in single-minded combat – toppled with the fractured pieces of flooring, their wrestling bodies shattering into abstract geometric patterns that mixed arms, legs, heads and torsos. Enemies were torn apart and mixed together as they fell endlessly into a godless and sterile realm between realities.

Trazyn cast a stasis field at the rift and walked across the jagged puzzle pieces of flooring that remained, his obliterator held low like a hunting spear.

Then, with only the short warning of his perception suite, he saw a figure sliding across the floor to his right.

It was the second Deceiver shard.

He leapt across the last of the rift, took a guard stance, and prepared to make his next blows tell.

For the first time since the War in Heaven, a single necron would face two C'tan. They loomed over him, mask-like features sculpted into visages that sneered and grinned all at once. Necrodermis forms glistening. Winding cloths drifting in spirals from the unnatural wind of the fractal dimension. Finger and toenails growing hooked and long.

The moment – a singularly heroic one – was interrupted by an interstitial message.

Trazyn, Orikan signalled. *We are reaching critical stage. Our forces cannot hold. They are breaking. And you cannot stand against two shards.*

No, signalled Trazyn. *But I did lure them to the same spot.*

Orikan saw the opportunity. Seized it.

They were losing, that was true. Their forces reduced to almost twenty per cent of initial combat effectiveness. But the monumental casualties were also freeing up neural capacity as he disconnected from sectors that were either lost or so deeply committed orders were unnecessary.

There was no managing this chaos now, it was simply chaos. On the left, the flayed ones had withdrawn, unable to make headway against the vicious hammering of the Militarum heavy weapons platoon – there was no cover here, nowhere to stalk. As he looked, a Guardsman fell, scythed down by a deathmark's beam.

Huntmaster, he signalled. *Counteract that fire. Redeploy left flank grid seven-sixteen. It is time to solve this nuisance.*

Confirmed, worthy master.

The deathmarks were a problem. Two of Trazyn's surrogate bodyguards had already thrown themselves in front of shots meant for Orikan. Or rather, Orikan had run back time and ordered them to do so.

On the right, the lychguard and corrupted Immortals had nearly cancelled each other's force effectiveness. Mutual destruction. In other circumstances the Immortals might have pulled back and fired, keeping out of range of the lychguard, luring them forward to open and turn the flank – but Orikan was too savvy to allow it, and the star gods were so intent on advancing that this strategic deviation had not occurred to them.

Yet the true battle still raged in the air, where burning Ghost Arks pulled broadside, scouring each other with gauss weapons. Screaming in between them, like light insects, dived and wheeled the Tomb Blades.

Ark Alpha, Orikan ordered. *Tack about twenty-one degrees starboard and fire flayer batteries. Get between me and that doomsday cannon.*

One Doomsday Ark remained. Wounded, afire, functional – still in enemy control.

But with the lessening mental demands Orikan had finally cracked the guardians' neural network.

Meaning he was finally in a position to do something about that ark.

Before, he could only scry through the oculars of these plebeians. Now, with a great degree of concentration and by releasing all other attachments, he could ride one of the guardian's systems, guiding their hands. Not full control, as Trazyn did with his surrogates, but a crucial nudge here or there.

He sent a last order to the ark flotilla – to close and board, a combat package he'd coded on the fly – then closed his ocular and rushed his consciousness into the pilot of a Tomb Blade.

The disorientation of riding the pilot's system mid-flight nearly snapped him back into his body. A rushing dive carried the pilot down between two furiously duelling Ghost Arks, their flayer batteries stripping hull molecules as the warriors within traded fire.

Disassembling beams cut the air around him as the craft zipped through the crossing fire, Orikan making his influence known by activating the shadowloom countermeasures that briefly flashed the craft through a shade dimension, its hull disintegrating then reappearing in successive puffs of coal-black smoke, its flight path weaving in and out of the dimensional plane like a strand of stitching travels through cloth. Amber beams cut through the interrupted flight path, passing where the Tomb Blade would've been, if it had behaved like a logical craft.

Orikan, Trazyn signalled. *They're right on me.*

Coming, snarled Orikan. *I've never been a pilot before.*

The blade passed through the curtain of fire and got underneath the arks, its underslung particle beamer pointing directly at the floor as if the pilot planned to slam the craft into the flagstones. But just as Orikan reached forward into the pilot's programming to evade, the governing algorithm slammed the craft sideways, the floor sliding beneath the pilot's face as it vectored a ninety-degree turn without banking. Impossible aerodynamics. It was a manoeuvre that would jar a mortal pilot so badly that its circulation would cease and its fluid-cased brain would mash itself against the inside of the skull.

But that resilience came at a cost. The pilot had no initiative. It flew on preprogrammed algorithms, merely selecting different attack and evasion packages as the occasion suited. Little wonder the swarms of Tomb Blades were killing each other at a near-constant ratio. They were like a logic engine forced to play against itself on a nemesor board.

But not any more. Orikan reached out, nudging the controls through the pilot's wired-in hands. He rolled the craft over, triggered its beamer so the stream of antimatter particles raked the bottom of a corrupted Ghost Ark, the distressed atoms detonating as they contacted the necrodermis.

The manoeuvre slashed a burning diagonal below the enemy ark, cutting its helm so it slewed out of true, flayer battery drifting away from the ark it was battling – a ship that, reacting to its new combat program, came about and burned engines on a ramming course.

Orikan shot the Tomb Blade vertical, building a random zigzag algorithm that, based on a rough analysis of the battle's firing patterns, would foil the enemy blades by substituting random variables. He rolled the craft experimentally, thinking how it was like being a gyroscope.

At least, it would be if gyroscopes flew random patterns that dodged in and out of reality.

The crazed flight path gave him a glimpse of the duelling arks below. He got a flash of the guardian ark – their last – ploughing into its corrupted rival amidships, snapping the big rib-spars and locking the two craft. Guardian warriors, nimble and arachnid-like, pounced onto the corrupted ark, firing flayers into its bottled-up crew and passengers, laying in with their axe-bayonets.

Lock warning.

'Bastard!' he said with the pilot's mouth.

Orikan triggered the shadowloom and dipped into the cloak of the shade dimension, emerging two khut distant and heading in a different direction. He rolled around, running calculus chains through his mind. Finding patterns. Running projection models. Sensing futures as the crazed pursuer danced through the ribbed vaults of the ceiling. First below him, then above, vectoring towards and away, moving diagonally then down, always the gauss beams stinging out towards Orikan. He heard them sizzle as they passed.

He looked for its next move, judged. Fired. Missed. A gauss shot skimmed across one of his flight vanes, eating away a panel that started re-forming itself.

They were like two divination dice, shaken in a cup. Ricocheting through the air, the only constant being the chin guns that were always oriented to point at each other.

Orikan scanned his Tomb Blade's programming to identify the enemy's flight package. He hit on a hyper-fractal equation that fit and designated a firing solution aiming at empty air. Countermanded the automated targeting program that tried to dismiss the shot as an erroneous discharge.

'Got you.'

He fired.

The enemy blade triggered its shadowloom, vanishing into a cloud of darkness.

The particle beam stung it when it had only half-emerged from the interdimensional cloud, tearing through the cable housing that connected pilot to blade. Antimatter detonated as it hit the dorsal arch, throwing the pilot forward into its controls, the orbuculum face display shattering as it slammed into the console.

The blade dropped into an uncontrolled descent, falling in a zigzag pattern, the governing flight program still throwing it in random directions as it careened into the floor. A blossom of amber energy, clear and bright as embalming fluid, erupted from the impact and washed over the few lychguard and corrupted Immortals who still struggled below.

Orikan had no time to watch. He cast the new targeting program to his remaining Tomb Blades, hoping it gave them an edge, and burned engines towards the centre of the battle line.

Where the whole of the enemy force – flayers, lychguard and two C'tan shards – were piling into the press of a chaotic melee around a single tiny figure.

Trazyn.

Insect.

The Deceiver shard brought its fists together over its head, the superheated necrodermis of the fingers fusing before they hammered down at him.

Trazyn threw his obliterator up in a guard, catching the blow, his tactical program noting with a detached sort of terror how the weapon haft bent under the shock. Kinetic force knocked through his frame, joint servos sparking under the compacting stress.

He blew backward, sensing smoke, and realised it was coming from his own overtaxed body.

Orikan, I can't keep this up.

The second Deceiver was, if anything, stronger than the first. Or perhaps its dominance over the fabric of the universe was more directly useful for combat.

Every blow Trazyn threw at it missed. Every duelling strike learned from his library of combat manuals hit empty air. Each guard position was broken by raking claws that cooked his necrodermis. Trying to hit it was like spearing a fish – a dimensional field displaced its image, making it appear in places it was not.

'Tricky little star god, aren't you?'

Around them, the rest of the combat continued to boil. He saw flayers in the melee now. Corrupted warriors. Immortals. His loyal complement of guardians outnumbered and falling.

The Deceiver had lured him into combat, planning to decapitate one of the guardians' two commanders.

'Not today,' Trazyn said, channelling energy into his wounds, feeling them drip with corposant as they sutured. 'You will not leave my gallery alone in this universe.'

Sensing encroachment, he wheeled and struck out to the other side, the first Deceiver shard darting back from the luminous headpiece of the obliterator even as it guttered, damaged by the last blow. It, at least, was nervous about approaching the furious weapon.

Young, foolish thing, it said with two mouths, the words coming through the injured shard with an eerie delay. **It is arrogance itself, taking a name like Infinite. Only the divine are infinite.**

It floated above the remains of three dead surrogates, each mangled or charred in deaths so gruesome Trazyn had evacuated their forms rather than experience them. They were his last in the battle line. Only the two in reserve around Orikan remained.

Like all of your kind, the shard continued, **you mistake mere deathlessness for immortality. Any rude object can endure the millennia. A tool. A rock. A dead probe, crashed on a distant planet. Durability does not make a thing immortal – true immortality requires a soul.**

It reached out with its long-fingered hands, mimed gripping at Trazyn, and pulled downward.

Trazyn staggered backward, dragged by the Timesplinter Cloak as if invisible fists had yanked it down to the blackstone to render him helpless. Preservation sequences took over and he threw himself forward, trying to stay upright.

He realised his mistake when the tension suddenly ended with the sound of fracturing mono-wire and scattering tiles.

The cloak. He tried to access it, analyse possible timelines, found he could not.

Old fool! he thought.

Yes, old fool. How apt. That is what put you in this form, is it not? Pain and age. Worry that your failing flesh could not support such a keen intelligence. That your biological system was corrupting the genius of your mind – as if the mind were not part of the body, as if mind and soul were the same. Now, child, you are no different than the dead objects preserved in your gallery.

Trazyn rerouted the power on his damaged obliterator, tried to straighten the haft so that the bent staff no longer compressed the power rods. The headpiece flickered, energy coil irregular, and he thrust while the weapon was empowered.

The second shard twisted its hand in air and Trazyn felt his left arm dislocate, crushing inward, deforming, crumpling with a wail of tortured metal.

Inoperable. Mangled.

He opened a dimensional pocket, thrust a hand into it and emerged with a tesseract labyrinth just as the thing breathed a word of power, overloading his knee servos and dropping him to the blackstone like a supplicant.

In his perception suite, he saw that the warriors were well and truly defeated. Corrupted necrons – the mind-slaved and the flayer-cursed – loomed at his back. He could feel their subservient craving, their wish to execute the coming order to pull him apart.

What have you there?

The Deceiver flicked a finger, forcing Trazyn to extend his hand and reveal the labyrinth.

More body shells, I expect.

Instead of a cutting answer, Trazyn merely shrugged.

And activated the labyrinth.

Claws emerged from the depths of the prismatic glare.

CHAPTER SIX

'Many times in history, planetary populations stood against invaders. But only on Serenade did all of history marshal to fight a common foe.'

— Records of the Serenade War, Tablet XII

Strange air. Strange light. Cold stone underfoot. Mandible feelers tasting the flat tang of metal bodies and motes of fried particles – energy weapons.

No connection to the Mind. Pheromone scent of brood-children absent.

The alpha purestrain came out of the light running. To run was to live. Sprinting made it harder for the enemy to hit you. Covered ground quickly. Pressed the shock attacks that overwhelmed planets and brought them into the biome, to be made into energy for the great fleets.

The alpha did not think this. She knew it. Coded into her

genetics was the knowledge that to run was to live, and to stand was to die.

And she knew that when a pack found itself surrounded, ringed on all sides by hostile organisms that were not yet of the Mind, there was one option.

Attack.

So she came out of the light running, unconcerned that a moment before she and her pack had been charging into a hail of weapons fire in the bright sunlight. There was no past for an organism like her. Only an eternal present, and a bone-deep knowledge that by the laws of dominance, one always attacked the largest, fiercest organism first.

She leapt for the humanoid organism that floated before her, tri-claws extended to latch onto its flesh and bring it down with her weight. Barbed mouth feelers splayed to wrap its throat and ravage the arteries that lay beneath the fragile skin.

Its face showed a muscle configuration that her genetic memories did not associate with fear.

That was all right. She would teach it to fear soon enough.

Genestealers swarmed out of the labyrinth dimension, a river delta of chitin, talons and hissing violence. They ploughed into the Deceiver shards, dragging their bobbing forms down with the weight of their clutching bodies. Rending claws and sucking mouths tore rents in their necrodermis that bled with the aged light of long-digested stars.

One shard, the wounded one, toppled under the growing pile of alien bodies. A detonation, and starlight fountained upward from the mass, throwing blackened alien corpses in every direction, energy blasting upward like a volcano. The mere wash of it frosted Trazyn's oculars with atomised chitin.

At first he thought the C'tan had unleashed some new power – then he realised it was diffusing. Its essence was temporarily spent into the aether. One of the parasites had pierced its necrodermis and unleashed the ethereal being bound within, dissipating the energy it had taken billions of years to gather, sipping from stars and devouring light. The result was like a plasma charge, and Trazyn had only survived because the genestealers had taken the blast.

Trazyn scrambled backward on his crushed limbs, watching as the upwelling of alien parasites packed the empty space in the centre of the enemy army, and now unable to reach the shards, began sweeping sideways to engage the corrupted necrons ringing the combat.

One scuttled for Trazyn, its tortoiseshell back gleaming bright viridian under the undulating light of a gauss flayer beam. Trazyn kept pushing backward, sending a signal from his damaged system, looking for a connection to one of the surrogates in the back of the antechamber.

A bony five-fingered hand dragged him forward by one malfunctioning leg. Another sank deep into the ropy inner systems of his chest. Three long sickles closed on his face, one puncturing an ocular...

Connection.

Trazyn fled his surrogate body, glad to be gone from this battle of gods and monsters.

Orikan screamed in above the combat, watching the great mass of corrupted necrons drawn towards the alien parasites like a black hole – the C'tan had baited Trazyn forward, and he'd baited them in turn.

And created a masterful distraction.

The master shard levitated behind the lines, floating,

controlling, mind sunk in the concentration of maintaining so many mind-slaves.

Orikan ran a divination, constellation maps wheeling in front of him as he flew in M-dimensional paths, hoping to evade notice. The future was hard to see here more than a few seconds ahead – almost impossible, in fact. Trazyn's little collections, wrenched out of their own period and placed in another, made the sands of time run strange. Because he had no idea of their location, he could not build a proper zodiac.

He was flying by luck and instinct. Not calculating. Acting, indeed, much more like the reckless Trazyn.

And he had got so far in doing so. He cast a range divination and lined up his angle of attack. Charged the particle beamer to maximum power.

Range in three.

Two.

One.

The Deceiver's eyes snapped open, looking directly at him. Orikan could feel the eyes boring into him from half a league away. Could feel them looking straight through the pilot he was riding and into the innermost parts of his circuitry.

He fired.

The beamer lanced out, its passage nothing but a wavering heat haze of the containment field for the particle stream. Orikan held the attack vector, wanted to keep the beam directly on target as long as possible. Cranked his chronosense down to make sure.

He would fire the batteries empty, then ride the Tomb Blade directly into the Deceiver.

The antimatter stream struck the Deceiver's broad chest, the impact point flaring up a candle flame like a welding laser hitting steel.

In his slowed chronosense Orikan saw the Deceiver block the beam with its palm, as though it were an unwelcome shaft of sunlight. Then it folded its shining hand, running the burning stream over its knuckles as it extended a single finger and aligned it with the beam.

Artificially slowed, Orikan saw the beam-reversal coming. Rushing back up the chain of antimatter and towards the Tomb Blade. A purple spark fizzling up towards the craft like a burning fuse.

He ejected his consciousness right before the blade tore apart in an implosion of unreality – the antimatter beam rupturing the weapon's muzzle and cooking off the particle hopper.

Orikan kicked his spirit-algorithm out of the pilot just before overload, wanting to collect whatever data he could on the particle stream.

'An energy projection,' he said, banishing his phos-glyph panels and dropping to the blackstone. 'It has necrodermis – I do not envy the cryptek whom it convinced to forge it a shell – but the greater part of the body is energy. It leaks out, like reactor radiation. But it's weak.'

'Perhaps from the rear lines, astromancer,' grumbled Trazyn, superheating and reshaping the haft of his obliterator. 'It did not feel weak face to face.'

'Weakness is relative,' Orikan said, casting zodiacs in the air, their overlapping circles, parabolas, and grids forming a mosaic before him. 'The weakest tomb scarab is quite mighty to a rodent. But the point remains. Gauss and antimatter weapons do little to it. Whatever transdimensional aura surrounds it neutralises the energy. Your obliterator is our best weapon, as is anything that can damage the necrodermis shell directly. Thus.' Orikan gestured at the whirling melee before them, calling up a scry-panel that showed – in painful slowness – the second shard emerging from a mounting swarm of genestealers, each slash in its body spewing sickly fire that atomised the attackers in blasts of plasma.

'You've cast a chrono-stasis field,' nodded Trazyn. 'So we can plan a strategy.'

'We have a strategy?' asked Orikan. 'Was that what was happening when you dashed in leaving me to run an army?'

'I hurt it.'

'You did, as did I. Stung the arrogant bastard out of its reverie. Made it realise it couldn't hide safe behind the lines while it buried us under expendable bodies. But that means we have made it more desperate. It will–'

A shock wave rocked the chamber, deforming the flagstones so they tilted and reared, buckling out from the master shard at the epicentre. In the vaults, great buttresses cracked and tumbled. The energy wave hit Orikan's field before the seismic shock, bursting it. From distorted slowness, all was movement and noise.

'It's coming,' said Orikan.

The master shard rushed forward so quickly its body tilted diagonally, metal-sculpted chest and raking claws forward as it dived towards the genestealers. It grew as it came, tripling in size, energy aura expanding around the necrodermis body until the physical form of the being only existed in the core of the energy-ghost, a metal heart that mimicked the energy projection's every move.

A god, a transcendent god, landed among mortals. The Deceiver reached out and genestealers withered, their mortal bodies experiencing mass cell death that crumbled their heads like old fruit. Ichor spilled in waterfalls from their joints.

They tried to run, even the great mental binding of their swarm god not enough to override their instinct for preservation.

One hand, huge now, reached out and snatched up the starlight-leaking body of the remaining Deceiver shard. It screamed, twisting and flailing in the grip of the larger piece of what was, after all, the same great being.

The master shard bit down on its cast-off shard, teeth sinking into its sculpted thorax muscles and sucking at the energy that leaked out, its amber form deepening from a wan yellow to a rich orange.

'Trazyn,' said Orikan. 'Throw everything you have.'

Turning away from its cannibalistic feast, the Deceiver looked directly at them and rose, arms dropped, palms towards them, esoteric symbols and long-devoured stars dancing in its hands and haloing its head.

And it came for them, the crashing tide of its thrall army at its back. Broken necrons rising again, reassembling, dragging their bodies into the onrushing horde.

Tracer streams from two heavy bolters – all that was left of the Serenade heavy platoon after the deathmarks had done with them – spat anaemic fire into the onrushing storm of metal bodies.

Trazyn realised it was down to them. Two necrons, no longer feeling as immortal as they once had, standing against an army.

That is, until Trazyn grabbed a tesseract labyrinth.

And began releasing the reserves.

Puris the Lamenite stepped out of the gossamer strands of unreality, his goggle-capped eyes taking in the oncoming rush of metal creatures.

His lips curled at their ugliness, fingers drifting to the

amulet at his neck, feeling the two wyrms chasing each other in a state of equilibrium. Artless, that is what they were. Sculpted not from the elegant materials of organic matter, but from dead and immutable metal.

They did not belong on this planet. This sainted world that would soon be visited by the redeemers from above, arriving in their exquisite sky-islands of biomatter. But the sacred swarm could not be called when its prize contained such pollution.

He slammed the butt of his injector goad pump on the ragged floor, whistling to call his creations.

Colossal forms bounded out of the light, slab-like muscles bunched as they dragged hammers and crude axes shaped from I-beams. They looked at him below ridged brows, tongues too long and sinewy for their short humanoid palates.

The eyes, golden, waited for orders.

Puris the Lamenite swept his goad towards the foe, and the aberrants tore off at a loping run, thick knuckles speeding them along on the fractured floor. Malformed heads lowered to ram, hooting as they went.

'Forward!' he shouted, spiking their bent backs with the goad as they passed, each strike accompanied by the hydraulic hiss of an injection. 'For the Three-Armed King!'

Boot-Klikka Zugkruk could not believe his good fortune. A moment before, they'd been tearing through the internals of a robot hulk, cheering and killing in the inertialess environment of zero gravity.

Which was a good trick, wot? But getting a bit floaty for his taste. His boyz could only kick about tearing up tins for so long before it got a little dull. Novel, yeah, but not a proper scrap.

Besides, what good was it being a stormboy if *everyone* could fly? Hurt his pride a bit, it did. And in his bulbous fungus-pumping heart, like any good ork, Boot-Klikka always longed for more enemies.

But this, this big wave of tinnies – that was a scrap an ork could sink his teef into, not to mention his choppa and boot.

He took a deep breath, bellowed the charge.

'C'mon, boyz! Let's show these tin gits wot–'

But then he saw the rush of corkscrew contrails heading away, heard the excited roars of his comrades, and realised they were already gone.

'Well, can't blame 'em for being game,' he grumbled. Then he lit his rokkit engine, rapped his helmet for luck, and rushed into the dark air of the vault, firing wildly with his slugga. Energy beams lashed the air around him.

As he reached the top of his arc and dropped towards the mass of whirling death, steel-capped boots positioned to crush the enemy, he lost himself in a feeling of rage-filled bliss.

To his right, he saw a blister of rainbow light blossom in the far corner of the big room, wavy ghost tentacles unfolding to reveal the gruff steel face of Mork, or possibly Gork. The gargant had arrived.

An energy beam severed his slugga arm and Boot-Klikka grinned.

There was nowhere in the world he'd rather be.

Orikan took in the mad scene.

To his right, a pack of deformed hybrid bioforms slammed into the roiling tide of mixed necrons, chopping at the oncoming wave with bludgeons and mining tools. He saw one, twice as tall as an average human and wielding a street sign like a glaive, batter a lychguard down, slap a warrior aside, and drive the now bare pole into a flayed one's chest like a spear.

Behind them, a trio of battered Destroyers slid over the floor, their poise and calculated murder-urge unaffected by the chaos. They raked the oncoming corrupted with cool precision, scything them down in lines like an industrial beam-cutter.

To his left, a commissar drove a Serenade Maritime company forward, lasguns spitting red into the metal mass. Their shrieks overlapped until the entire force appeared to be speaking with a single deadly voice, their fire lighting up the front ranks of the advancing corrupted, splashing their metal bodies until they radiated like metal heated in the forge.

The company – clad in only cloth-covered helmets and flak armour – was making a wall with their bodies.

'They made it off Serenade,' Trazyn shrugged. 'Picked them up later.'

Orks howled and shouted overhead, their dirty smoke paths criss-crossing as they lost all unit cohesion in the excitement. Three of them had landed on a Doomsday Ark and were currently yanking the helmsman apart, tearing him out of his command cradle piece by piece.

Another, giving a guttural scream of triumph, dived directly for the enormous form of the master shard.

'Suicidal idiot,' said Orikan.

'Undoubtedly,' said Trazyn, activating another labyrinth. 'But note the long white missile on his pack.'

The Deceiver swept a hand towards the stormboy, knocking him tumbling with an energy wave so he crashed into the mass of corrupted bodies at its feet.

Along with the live hunter-killer missile propelling him through the air.

The anti-tank ordnance detonated, rocking the chamber

and throwing up bodies in a gout of pulverised blackstone that fountained skyward, hunks of ancient masonry raining down on the attackers.

Then the gargant opened up, its low-slung belly gun thudding as it lobbed shells into the mass, unable to resist the tight grouping of enemies. It stamped forward, breaking flagstones wherever it lumbered, and swept its massive buzz saws down to chew through a Ghost Ark that appeared to be on Trazyn and Orikan's side. Tomb Blades surrounded it like biting gnats, and it waved its clumsy arms, blasting flames that sent two tumbling out of the air.

The flanks faltered, but the centre still came on, the master shard's cosmic thoughtform towering over the cresting flood of bodies.

Trazyn threw the last labyrinth.

It rolled toward the Deceiver, fountaining pinwheels of aetheric glare as it expanded into a rolling light storm.

And inside the storm, shadows raced towards the foe.

They came with the song of clawed feet on tile. The tattoo of battle. It formed the rhythmic thread on which they coordinated their war chants.

The raptor riders tore from the rift at full charge, losing not a single step in their new environment. Their knee-to-knee formation didn't waver as the wild host plunged towards the star god. Agile mounts pitched forward, necks extended. Feather cloaks billowed behind them. Scrimshawed bone charms rattled. Tattooed faces, decorated with sigils that Trazyn recognised as the Serenade spiral, were set in expressions of determined stoicism.

Trazyn had worn a death mask for sixty-five million years – he knew one when he saw it.

Behind them, the carnosaur clomped out of the light, stretched its body low and roared – the feral sound enough to check even a few Militarum soldiers that, fighting their mindshackle scarabs, looked to their flank with eyes wide.

On its back rode the farseer, willow-thin face half-covered by the mask of an unfamiliar god and mother-of-pearl armour reflecting the battle light. Pink hair gathered into a topknot, unstirred by her ten millennia of waiting.

I told you, Trazyn, said a voice vibrating his auditory transducer, *that this world sang for your blood. You did not listen. But listening was not your fate. It was your fate to continue digging – and our fate to perish here, against the horror you unleashed.*

The carnosaur sprinted forward with another bellow, bone-spiked tail slashing back and forth as it tilted into the charge. Atop it, the sorceress wove arrows from the skin of the universe, sending fuchsia bolts of warp energy into the hulking star god.

Make our sacrifice worth it.

Wraithbone lances drove into metal bodies, discharging bound spell-energies that rippled out through the corrupted metal forms, buckling exoskeletons and shorting out reactors. They drove into them as a wedge, opening a delta of space for the carnosaur to lay into the army.

The beast barked with aggression and plucked two struggling necrons from the mass, crunching them with its reinforced jaws. Reactor fluid, glowing neon in the darkness, leaked between the nine-inch saw teeth.

A flayed one leapt onto its flank, climbing towards the farseer, and she danced to her feet on the riding platform, decapitating it with a neat sweep of her glaive. The shuriken pistol embedded in her decorative bangle whickered shots into a second corrupted who'd clambered up one of the great lizard-leather saddle straps.

She called a song and the massive lizard whipped around in a circle, throwing the climbers and lashing its spiked tail through the mass of necrons at its feet, pulverising several, crushing others beneath its claws.

A synaptic disintegrator beam burned one of the lizard's haunches and it gave a shriek of pain, lowering its head and using its bony crest to buck the offending deathmark into the air.

The Deceiver shard pulled a haloed fist back and brought it down on the prehistoric mount, its crashing impact only stopped by a hastily deployed psychic shield that the farseer conjured with outstretched fingers.

Orikan turned from the fascinating scene, glyph-panels forgotten.

'What is your next plan?'

'Nothing. I have nothing. Can you still not take your empowered form?'

'The stars are ill. There is no energy to draw upon.'

Trazyn paused, pointing to the radiant C'tan. 'What about that?'

'That,' he scoffed. 'That would burn me to cinder the moment I opened my collection ports. I would need to become empowered merely to approach it. Only a god can combat a god. I need to draw power first.'

Trazyn was silent a moment, watching the enormous C'tan pound at the magic ward. Cracks began to web the psychic shield. It would not hold. He looked into his dimensional pocket, scrying the space.

There was only one thing remaining there. A thing he had stolen. A thing that, were the old folklores true, once raised a god.

Trazyn dipped his hand into the pocket and withdrew the aeldari gemstone.

The cut surface gleamed, warm to the touch. It was the oldest thing Trazyn owned, centrepiece of the War in Heaven gallery. The last object he possessed from the dawning of the necrons.

Were it gone, it would be an irretrievable loss. Another door to the ancient past closed.

Was the future worth that? He hoped so.

'See what you can draw from this.'

Orikan took the gem, waved a hand over it to cast a spectromantic analysis.

'Dead Gods,' he breathed, caressing the stone, enfolding it into his hands.

Orikan closed his ocular, pressing the gem between his palms as if praying.

His energy collection ports opened like rose petals. Through the gaps in his fingers, Trazyn could see a red pulse begin to beat. A light spectrum so powerful, so alien to the necrons that it made him uncomfortable to look at it.

Orikan's reactor glow increased, boiling outward like a green sun. Trazyn heard the reactor kick at quadruple-cycle, the glow that leaked behind Orikan's closed ocular hatch bleeding light that smoked in the cold air.

And then the hands snapped together, crushing the gem.

Orikan caught fire, a red inferno that devoured his form, licking upward in bright magenta flames that curled inward, drawn towards the open collection ports on his shoulders.

Trazyn had to step back, shielding his face. His fury about the wilful destruction was temporarily quenched by fear. Fear for the astromancer. Fear for himself.

'Orikan!' he shouted.

But Orikan was already gone, a bolt of lightning streaking through the chamber.

Trazyn rolled over, realising the blast had knocked him on his back. His vision blurred from the discharge of energy, his own central reactor deploying countermeasures to keep from overloading from the power surge he'd experienced even standing next to Orikan.

The battle line was no longer a fight, it was a bonfire.

And Trazyn knew he had not witnessed Orikan take on his energy form.

He had just seen an apotheosis.

Orikan was, if only briefly, like unto a god.

Orikan expected transcendence to feel powerful, thought the energy of the cosmos would throng through his system like floodwater through a dry canyon. He'd wanted to be mighty, shot through with the overspilling pride and vigour of the gods.

It did not feel like that.

Instead, all the other beings seemed so *small*. Petty. Knotted into the inconsequential entanglements of their finite existence. Pain, pride, fear, excitement, love. All of them meant nothing to the wheeling, colliding systems of the galaxy that he could now see in his mind's eye. Even his own petty obsession with the path of things to come – so all-consuming – was but the dream of an insect. What purpose, being a diviner, when one saw that there was no such thing as past and future? To a cosmic being, one that saw the curves in the very skin of reality, it was clear that time was but a delusion, a perverted twisting of the eternal present meant to order the lives of those that needed to plant and sow, to guess at how much of their meagre lifespans remained. It no more resembled reality than a paper map did a continent.

Melancholy overtook him, thinking of all the time he'd

wasted quarrelling with his rival about past and future. He could not recall the being's name or face, but an echo of the sly voice remained. No matter, even the most formidable beings from his mortal days would be dust long before Orikan thought to dwell upon them again.

He gazed down at the dim soul-flames, guttering and going out in the battle below. Tried to feel pity for them, and instead could only summon contempt.

Pathetic. All of them struggling, and for what? To save their pitiful civilisations. To spread their influence. To defeat foes.

Necron. Aeldari. Human. Ork. Tyranid. Bathing in blood in the misapprehension that the universe belonged to them.

None of them saw the truth. The great universal zodiac, the turning wheel of fortune that brought each race around and around. Sometimes rising, sometimes falling. The aeldari's time at the top was long over, and yet they fought as if they could reverse the great turning. The humans were following them, their period of apex nearly over. Tyranids and orks, when they had their time at the crest, would likely not appreciate it.

And the necrons. Orikan felt such scorn for them with their impoverished shadow-souls, so dead and stagnant. It embarrassed him how he'd struggled to secure their future – that they had survived the wheel's descent and were rising again.

In truth, he suddenly understood why the C'tan had burned the necrontyr in the biotransference forges and gorged themselves on the souls. Felt glad for it. Only wished he had been there to sate himself.

For the only thing he felt more than contempt was hunger. Hunger for life-energy that these sapped metal bodies could not provide.

Yet in the centre of the candle-flame battle line, he could see one that had energy to spare. A blazing figure. A C'tan.

The transcendent energy being that was Orikan swept low, ethereal body – prismatic and shifting in hue – sweeping through arks and Tomb Blades, gathering strength by skimming the top of the necron ranks, lapping whatever small energies he could from their dull lights.

They fell in his wake, lifeless and depowered.

A large thing startled and snapped at him, teeth closing on part of his drifting energy-shroud. He kicked out and pulverised the dumb beast, crushing every bone in its thick body and sending it flying like a toy. A rider – brighter than the rest – tumbled from its back and snuffed out.

The transcendent being cared not, for the blazing one stood in front of him. Its face, twisted into a look that a vestigial memory interpreted as amusement, could not hide the way its aura quailed as he approached.

The blazing one leapt backward and swept a hand through the air, and in the transcendent being's new vision, he saw that the enemy passed its forearm through the fabric of space-time and gathered a black hole around its wrist like a vambrace. A shining fist, radiating so much power that the transcendent being nearly doubled over in a craving, blasted a stream of compressed matter that contained the whirl of galaxies long swallowed.

Yet millions of years of study had taught the being to manipulate the aether. Only a lack of sufficient energy had constrained him.

The transcendent being once known as Orikan tore a hole in the universal skin, a portal through which could be seen a star field and a collection of planets, and wielded it as a shield.

Compressed matter tore through the rent in space, wiping six planets out of existence.

Inhabited worlds? It did not matter.

The transcendent being released the wormhole and dived at the blazing one, tearing at it with hands he'd fashioned into long grasping claws.

The two beings rose into the vaults. Locked together. Biting and clawing, burning the energy output of several industrial worlds for each second of combat. Each wound bled the furnace of creation into the physical plane, each shot of star-stuff gobbled by the famished vampire that had once been Orikan the Diviner.

Hands dripping with boiling necrodermis, the transcendent being tossed aside anything that felt solid, noting with disinterest how the chunks he tore away and discarded formed into humanoid figures.

The blazing one was pleading now, appealing to mercy. Using words as if the transcendent being still had a mind that could interpret language. Words were, like mortality, a thing for lesser beings. This transcendent god no longer needed communication.

But even so, he could guess what the blazing one was thinking. The eyes, red and round as dead stars, were full of fear.

Yet the face was still locked in its mask-like rictus grin.

Or at least it was, until the transcendent being tore it off and plunged its long, spider-like arms into the rich starlight within.

CHAPTER SEVEN

'Our kind have lived life as mortals, and then as immortals. And though the urge to return to the flesh is nearly universal, what will it be like when an eternal being is once again enshrouded in such temporary raiment? Can an immortal being become mortal without going mad?'

– Illuminator Szeras, *Ruminations on Flesh and Spirit*

Trazyn found the Diviner in a corner, his battered legs drawn up to his chest, hands over his closed ocular.

His entire frame, from headdress to lashing tail, had turned black. It was not ash or burn marks – the interdimensional energies had fused the shadows to his necrodermis.

'Orikan? Have you suffered damage?'

There was no answer.

'My dear Orikan,' Trazyn knelt and put a hand on his quaking shoulder plate.

'*Don't touch me!*' the Diviner wailed, trying to shrink back into the masonry. 'Don't touch me. Don't touch me.'

'It's all right, friend. It's all right.' Trazyn held up his palms to show he was no threat. 'You have been through a shocking transition, to be sure. But the danger is passed, provided you are not suffering critical damage. I am scrying you for injury or malfunction.'

Orikan said nothing, stared at the floor.

Trazyn ran a diagnostic scry, palm hovering around Orikan's cranium longer than the rest of his body, careful not to intrude too far into the Diviner's space.

'Thank your stars, Orikan. It's not too bad. Nothing irrecoverable. Fused servos here and there. Sundry damage to electrolocation systems – a wonder there is not more, given how much energy you channelled – and likely some engram corruption. You may lose memories for a time, but they will come back.'

'Is it gone?'

Trazyn's mouth twitched and he brought a tesseract labyrinth out of his dimensional pocket. Orikan shrank away.

'You tore the Deceiver to pieces, dear rival. Sucked the energy of each shard dry before casting it off. And I was there to catch them before they could collect enough energy to flee.' He tapped a finger on the labyrinth. 'There are five of these. So yes, it is gone.'

'N-not–' Orikan's vocal emitters dissolved into a burr of static for a moment, '–alking about the Deceiver. I want to know about the other one. Is it gone?'

Trazyn paused. 'I do hope so, Orikan. I do hope so.'

Then he stood, and offered a hand up. 'Come now. We must rebuild the tesseract vault and put these labyrinths within. A vault inside a vault, each shard in a separate labyrinth.'

Orikan nodded, and took the hand. His body was stiff, one leg would not bend, and Trazyn had to support him so that he could walk towards the ruined vault.

'We will leave the Mysterios here, sealed inside,' said Orikan. 'So none can find this place again.'

'Indeed,' said Trazyn.

'And Trazyn.' He stopped, looked at the archaeovist with an eye that Trazyn had just noticed was temporarily burned blind. 'Make me an oath. An honour pact. That neither of us will come here again.'

He held out a forearm, fused to the point that it could not move at the elbow servo.

'Agreed,' said Trazyn, gripping the forearm. The oath seal. 'The contents of this vault are too dangerous for anyone to possess.'

'Especially us,' said Orikan, and ambled towards the ruined vault.

To reach it, they would need to cross a mountain of corpses.

EPILOGUE

'Time is a weapon like any other. If all else fails, I can simply wait for my enemies to rot.'

— Orikan the Diviner

Seven doors secured the chamber. Seven doors with seven seals.

What was inside, after all, must never be let out.

Canoptek wraiths quarried into the constructed strata of Solemnace for a half a millennium to construct the great chamber. Toiling in their millions, without rest or refurbishment, until they fell broken through the hard labour. Scarab swarms disassembled the fallen so their atoms could be repurposed anew in another worker drone.

Crypteks shaped the blackstone, created the spherical chamber that formed the living heart of Solemnace, a place of banishment and seclusion, a sphere within a sphere that powered the prismatic galleries with the inexhaustible radiance of its evil.

And Trazyn, Overlord of Solemnace and Archaeovist of the

Prismatic Galleries, He-Who-Is-Called-Infinite, went there as often as he could. Opened the seven mausoleum gates with their seven seals. Stepped as close as he dared to the thing that hung within, its strong limbs shackled to the sides of its spherical prison. Particle whips burning its wrists and ankles as they stretched the star god like a specimen on the dissection table.

I see, said the Deceiver shard, **that it is time for more questions. What shall we be returning to in this session, child Trazyn? Disposition of C'tan-necron forces at the Siege of Path'iya? Proper taxonomy of emergent daemon-consciousnesses of the empyrean? What knowledge would you like to explore, and what are you willing to pay for it?**

Trazyn dipped a hand in his dimensional pocket, drew out what appeared to be a small homunculus, a being no larger than Trazyn's hand, that struggled in his grip. Radiance showed through the gaps in his fingers as he held the creature out for the Deceiver's inspection.

It is small, said the Deceiver. **A shard of a shard. Never were the Nihilakh known for stinginess.**

'These are not simple to obtain,' Trazyn said. 'And we both know the risk I take in giving them to you at all.'

Yes. The Deceiver laughed, the deep sound of it screened out by Trazyn's filters so it did not upset his vitals. **We would not want me tearing through this prison, would we?**

Trazyn tightened his grip on the little shard splinter in his hand. The stunted Deceiver wriggled in his grasp, biting the impervious metal of Trazyn's fingers.

It had little intelligence in it, its component parts had been shattered so far. Yet still, he would need to up the security protocols. With every splinter of a shard he fed to the Serenade Deceiver, the more powerful it became. And if it ever did slip its prison, he was unsure whether the banks of particle whips, doomsday cannons and pylons pointed at the broken god could actually destroy it without imploding all of Solemnace.

He slipped the shard into a tesseract vault mounted on the back of a scarab, and released it, watching the delivery scarab levitate up to the shining mouth of the star god.

It opened its mouth and swallowed the vault whole, necrodermis crunching beneath its dagger teeth, solar energy flowing liquid over its lips and chin as the squealing Deceiver splinter burst and was absorbed into the whole.

Trazyn felt, at times, a measure of guilt about having told Orikan there were only five shards. For keeping one for himself, entranced by the amount of power these ancient shards held. The knowledge they had of the galaxy, and knowledge of things impossible.

If he were Orikan, if he could travel backward, he would undo it. The Deceiver became more powerful by the century, and it was inevitable that a reckoning would come.

But that was not how history worked, he thought. We are shaped by past selves that come before, ghosts we would not recognise ourselves in if we met them. The Trazyn that had taken the shard from the Tomb of Nephreth was no more, just as the Trazyn that had existed before biotransference was no more. Yet all their decisions, made in blindness, had culminated in where he was now.

It was like Serenade, or Cepharil, or Cephris, each iteration of the world shifting the culture and geography of those that came after it. Each society that rose knew little or nothing about how it had been shaped or the predecessors who had forged it. Each street plan laid or sea drained was a decision made in the moment, but preserved for ages.

Just as how past versions of himself, recalled only in the

abstract, had placed him before this fallen god who wished for nothing more than to destroy him. A god he could not banish or release.

But one that, as long as he kept it bound, had its uses.

An inadequate sacrifice, the Deceiver said, long tongue curling over the plasma that dripped over its chin. **What do you wish in return?**

'The Great Rift,' said Trazyn. 'I wish to know about its properties.'

Ahh, the Deceiver grinned. **So you wish to close it.**

'No,' said Trazyn. 'I wish to enter it.'

The wheel of the universe turned. Zodiacs rose and fell, each race, each individual being having its day at the top. And each, one after another, dragged underneath by the relentless turn.

Because that is what a wheel does, Orikan knew. It did not matter if it were mounted on a great battle tank or a stone milling grain in a primitive farmstead. A wheel crushes.

And now, it was his time at the top. He had read it in the constellations and heard the whisper of the cosmos. After centuries of waiting, the stars were – once again – right.

It was Trazyn's turn to be ground into the dirt.

He opened his dimensional pocket and withdrew his guide, played his networked finger notes soft across the cranium.

Where is it? he asked.

Deeper, my equal, responded the head of Datamancer Vishani. *At the core. The power flows, as always, from the core.*

She was not alive. Not truly. Her engram-banks were active, and some language centres remained. But even mangled, there was so much knowledge to be unlocked in those deep neural spools.

Trazyn had claimed that her remains had been sealed

within the tomb, its Eternity Gates disassembled and atomised. Locked away with her charges forever in an inaccessible oubliette dimension.

He had lied and slipped her cranium into his dimensional pocket while Orikan was still nearly insensate, recovering from his temporary ascension. He had taken advantage of the damage Orikan had visited on his own psyche in order to save both of them. Kept the head on Solemnace to further his own researches.

Orikan had broken their truce centuries ago to steal her back. Nearly destroyed Solemnace doing it. Spent a century scouring any taint of the Deceiver's programming from her neurals. Was amazed, even impressed, how deeply the star god had hijacked her personality to tempt and guide Orikan into opening the tomb.

And it was then that Orikan learned of the Deceiver shard hidden at the core of Solemnace, powering the world via a Dyson sphere.

Rotating. Ever rotating. Like a galaxy. Like a wheel.

The Deceiver awaits us, sent Vishani. *My primary function is containment.*

It is, agreed Orikan. *But a thing so powerful will be safer in our hands, don't you think?*

To remove it is to destroy this world of Solemnace.

So much the better, smiled Orikan. *I can remove this cataract from the eye of the universe, and better divine the future.*

My primary function, she insisted, *is containment.*

You can serve many functions. As can the Serenade shard.

Functions such as researching how to capture and sustain an energy form long-term. For though the callousness of omniscience had frightened him at first, he had come to see what was too difficult to ken in the moment.

Time is a wheel. And the wheel turns ever on. The universe cares not for necrons, or aeldari, or humans or orks. It cares not even for C'tan or Old Ones. And the only way to escape the wheel was to become part of the wheel.

And Orikan could do so, if he had enough cosmic power.

The planets and constellations were sliding into place, and he felt their channels of connecting energy, their dark matter and gravitation superclusters, the connection of the universe that kept it in spin.

He opened his collection ports and drank in the milky starlight of creation.

Time is a wheel. And the wheel always turns, bringing a time for all things.

And for Orikan, it was a time for revenge.

ABOUT THE AUTHOR

Robert Rath is a freelance writer from Honolulu who is currently based in Hong Kong. He is the author of the Warhammer 40,000 novels *The Infinite and the Divine* and *Assassinorum: Kingmaker*, and the Warhammer Crime novella *Bleedout*. His short stories include 'War in the Museum', 'Glory Flight', and the Assassinorum tales 'Divine Sanction', 'Live Wire' and 'Iron Sight'.

YOUR
NEXT READ

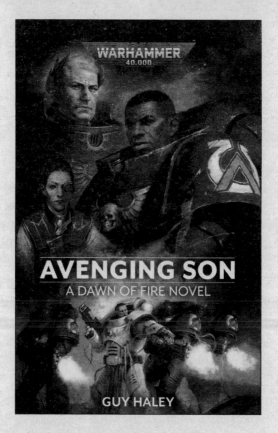

AVENGING SON
by Guy Haley

As the Indomitus Crusade spreads out across the galaxy, one battlefleet must face a dread
Slaughter Host of Chaos. Their success or failure may define the very future of the
crusade – and the Imperium.

An extract from
Avenging Son
by Guy Haley

'I was there at the Siege of Terra,' Vitrian Messinius would
say in his later years.

'I was there...' he would add to himself, his words never
meant for ears but his own. 'I was there the day the Imperium died.'

But that was yet to come.

'To the walls! To the walls! The enemy is coming!' Captain Messinius, as he was then, led his Space Marines across
the Penitent's Square high up on the Lion's Gate. 'Another
attack! Repel them! Send them back to the warp!'

Thousands of red-skinned monsters born of fear and sin
scaled the outer ramparts, fury and murder incarnate. The
mortals they faced quailed. It took the heart of a Space
Marine to stand against them without fear, and the Angels
of Death were in short supply.

'Another attack, move, move! To the walls!'

They came in the days after the Avenging Son returned,

emerging from nothing, eight legions strong, bringing the bulk of their numbers to bear against the chief entrance to the Imperial Palace. A decapitation strike like no other, and it came perilously close to success.

Messinius' Space Marines ran to the parapet edging the Penitent's Square. On many worlds, the square would have been a plaza fit to adorn the centre of any great city. Not on Terra. On the immensity of the Lion's Gate, it was nothing, one of hundreds of similarly huge spaces. The word 'gate' did not suit the scale of the cityscape. The Lion's Gate's bulk marched up into the sky, step by titanic step, until it rose far higher than the mountains it had supplanted. The gate had been built by the Emperor Himself, they said. Myths detailed the improbable supernatural feats required to raise it. They were lies, all of them, and belittled the true effort needed to build such an edifice. Though the Lion's Gate was made to His design and by His command, the soaring monument had been constructed by mortals, with mortal hands and mortal tools. Messinius wished that had been remembered. For men to build this was far more impressive than any godly act of creation. If men could remember that, he believed, then perhaps they would remember their own strength.

The uncanny may not have built the gate, but it threatened to bring it down. Messinius looked over the rampart lip, down to the lower levels thousands of feet below and the spread of the Anterior Barbican.

Upon the stepped fortifications of the Lion's Gate was armour of every colour and the blood of every loyal primarch. Dozens of regiments stood alongside them. Aircraft filled the sky. Guns boomed from every quarter. In the churning redness on the great roads, processional ways so huge they were akin to prairies cast in rockcrete, were flashes of gold where the Emperor's Custodian Guard battled. The might of the Imperium was gathered there, in the palace where He dwelt.

There seemed moments on that day when it might not be enough.

The outer ramparts were carpeted in red bodies that writhed and heaved, obscuring the great statues adorning the defences and covering over the guns, an invasive cancer consuming reality. The enemy were legion. There were too many foes to defeat by plan and ruse. Only guns, and will, would see the day won, but the defenders were so pitifully few.

Messinius called a wordless halt, clenched fist raised, seeking the best place to deploy his mixed company, veterans all of the Terran Crusade. Gunships and fighters sped overhead, unleashing deadly light and streams of bombs into the packed daemonic masses. There were innumerable cannons crammed onto the gate, and they all fired, rippling the structure with false earthquakes. Soon the many ships and orbital defences of Terra would add their guns, targeting the very world they were meant to guard, but the attack had come so suddenly; as yet they had had no time to react.

The noise was horrendous. Messinius' audio dampers were at maximum and still the roar of ordnance stung his ears. Those humans that survived today would be rendered deaf. But he would have welcomed more guns, and louder still, for all the defensive fury of the assailed palace could not drown out the hideous noise of the daemons – their sighing hisses, a billion serpents strong, and chittering, screaming wails. It was not only heard but sensed within the soul, the realms of spirit and of matter were so intertwined. Messinius' being would be forever stained by it.

Tactical information scrolled down his helmplate, near environs only. He had little strategic overview of the situation. The vox-channels were choked with a hellish screaming that made communication impossible. The noosphere was disrupted by etheric backwash spilling from the immaterial rifts the daemons poured through. Messinius was used to operating on his own. Small-scale, surgical actions were the way of the Adeptus Astartes, but in a battle of this scale, a lack of central coordination would lead inevitably to defeat. This was not like the first Siege, where his kind had fought in Legions.

He called up a company-wide vox-cast and spoke to his warriors. They were not his Chapter-kin, but they would listen. The primarch himself had commanded that they do so.

'Reinforce the mortals,' he said. 'Their morale is wavering. Position yourselves every fifty yards. Cover the whole of the south-facing front. Let them see you.' He directed his warriors by chopping at the air with his left hand. His right, bearing an inactive power fist, hung heavily at his side. 'Assault Squad Antiocles, back forty yards, single firing line. Prepare to engage enemy breakthroughs only on my mark. Devastators, split to demi-squads and take up high ground, sergeant and sub-squad prime's discretion as to positioning and target. Remember our objective, heavy infliction of casualties. We kill as many as we can, we retreat, then hold at the Penitent's Arch until further notice. Command squad, with me.'

Command squad was too grand a title for the mismatched crew Messinius had gathered around himself. His own officers were light years away, if they still lived.

'Doveskamor, Tidominus,' he said to the two Aurora Marines with him. 'Take the left.'

'Yes, captain,' they voxed, and jogged away, their green armour glinting orange in the hell-light of the invasion.

The rest of his scratch squad was comprised of a communications specialist from the Death Spectres, an Omega Marine with a penchant for plasma weaponry, and a Raptor holding an ancient standard he'd taken from a dusty display.

'Why did you take that, Brother Kryvesh?' Messinius asked, as they moved forward.

'The palace is full of such relics,' said the Raptor. 'It seems only right to put them to use. No one else wanted it.'

Messinius stared at him.

'What? If the gate falls, we'll have more to worry about than my minor indiscretion. It'll be good for morale.'

The squads were splitting to join the standard humans. Such was the noise many of the men on the wall had not noticed their arrival, and a ripple of surprise went along the line as they appeared at their sides. Messinius was glad to see they seemed more firm when they turned their eyes back outwards.

'Anzigus,' he said to the Death Spectre. 'Hold back, facilitate communication within the company. Maximum signal gain. This interference will only get worse. See if you can get us patched in to wider theatre command. I'll take a hardline if you can find one.'

'Yes, captain,' said Anzigus. He bowed a helm that was bulbous with additional equipment. He already had the access flap of the bulky vox-unit on his arm open. He withdrew, the aerials on his power plant extending. He headed towards a systems nexus on the far wall of the plaza, where soaring buttresses pushed back against the immense weight bearing down upon them.

Messinius watched him go. He knew next to nothing about Anzigus. He spoke little, and when he did, his voice was funereal. His Chapter was mysterious, but the same lack of familiarity held true for many of these warriors, thrown together by miraculous events. Over their years lost wandering in the warp, Messinius had come to see some as friends as well as comrades, others he hardly knew, and none he knew so well as his own Chapter brothers. But they would stand together. They were Space Marines. They had fought by the returned primarch's side, and in that they shared a bond. They would not stint in their duty now.

Messinius chose a spot on the wall, directing his other veterans to left and right. Kryvesh he sent to the mortal officer's side. He looked down again, out past the enemy and over the outer palace. Spires stretched away in every direction. Smoke rose from all over the landscape. Some of it was new, the work of the daemon horde, but Terra had been burning for weeks. The Astronomican had failed. The galaxy was split in two. Behind them in the sky turned the great palace gyre, its deep eye marking out the throne room of the Emperor Himself.

'Sir!' A member of the Palatine Guard shouted over the din. He pointed downwards, to the left. Messinius followed his wavering finger. Three hundred feet below, daemons were climbing. They came upwards in a triangle tipped by a brute with a double rack of horns. It clambered hand over hand, far faster than should be possible, flying upwards, as if it touched the side of the towering gate only as a concession to reality. A Space Marine with claw locks could not have climbed that fast.

'Soldiers of the Imperium! The enemy is upon us!'